J. BARTON MITCHELL

TOR

A Tom Doherty Associates Book

NEW YORK

THE RAZOR

Copyright © 2018 by J. Barton Mitchell

A Tor Book
Published by Tom Doherty Associates
175 Fifth Avenue
New York, NY 10010

www.tor-forge.com

Tor® is a registered trademark of Macmillan Publishing Group, LLC.

The Library of Congress Cataloging-in-Publication Data is available
upon request.

ISBN 978-0-7653-8792-9 (hardcover)
ISBN 978-0-7653-8794-3 (ebook)

Our books may be purchased in bulk for promotional, educational, or business use.
Please contact your local bookseller or the Macmillan Corporate and Premium
Sales Department at 1-800-221-7945, extension 5442, or by email at
MacmillanSpecialMarkets@macmillan.com.

First Edition: November 2018

Printed in the United States of America

0 9 8 7 6 5 4 3 2 1

For my mother, Jackie.
Thank you for being my personal Gable (in all the good ways).

PART I

CHARON

ONE

RAZORFALL

Every time he closed his eyes, he was drowning. Water poured into the car, flooding the leather interior as it sank into Elliott Bay. He remembered looking to the passenger seat and the shock that washed over him. The wound in her head. The spray pattern on the window. How her hair floated up with the rising water, copper strands shining in the city lights outside the shattered glass. He watched her vanishing in the cold, and realized two things.

He didn't know who she was.

And he was holding a pulse pistol . . .

The world shook and jarred Flynn awake. He was staring through the shuttle's tiny window again.

The starfield from before had been replaced with something more distinct now. Inspiring and frightening all at once. He recognized it instantly. A planet. 11-H37. Unique in all the galaxy. Utter darkness on one side, raging heat on the other. He could just make out the slim streak of green that split the two massive halves. It looked tiny, nestled precariously between its giant siblings. It looked like it was being crushed.

It was called the Razor.

In spite of everything, Flynn felt excitement looking at it. Everything that had made him what he once was came from this world. Then again, it had also made him who he was now.

The image of the planet, fire and ice split in half, lasted a moment longer, then the shuttle hit the atmosphere and the windows were full of red streaks and Flynn remembered where he was and why and for how long and reality came crashing back. Excitement faded. Fear returned.

He sat back in the hard, cracked seat and breathed deep as everything around him shook again. Before the heat shields slid down over the windows, he saw the ship's energy field flare to life with a bluish, crackling sheen. He wondered how many shuttles actually made it through the planet's ionosphere to the surface. The numbers probably weren't even published. After all, the ship was remote-piloted, and as for the occupants . . . well, no one really cared about *them*, did they?

The shuttle shook again. He jarred upward before the restraints on his ankles yanked him back down, biting into his skin. A strange static hum built in the air; he could hear it even over the engines. He felt the tingling on his skin, felt his ears begin to itch. It wouldn't be long now.

There were thirty seats inside, screwed into each wall, forcing the occupants to stare at one another. A woman with worn-out skin, a big scar over her left cheek, and wiry, muscular arms sat in front of him. She was breathing heavily, the pace increasing each time the ship contorted. To her left was a kid with more tattoos than Flynn had ever seen—swastikas and hash tags, skulls and dragons—his head shaved clean, no older than twenty. The tats and the head made him look tough, but Flynn could hear him whimpering, trying not to lose it. The pattern repeated everywhere he looked, in the eyes of every person who was shackled to the shuttle. He'd never met any of them, but he could guess who they were. Killers. Thieves. Gunrunners. Tweakers. Smugglers. Hackers.

No matter how shrewd or scary they had once been, they were all frightened now. All of them. Because everyone knew where they were going.

The shuttle vibrated. The static hum grew louder. The edges of Flynn's vision were beginning to whiten and flare out.

Next to the kid with the tats sat another man. He didn't seem absorbed in his own anxiety as much as everyone else. Average height, in good shape, and his hair was wavy, probably even stylish a few weeks ago, before whatever happened to get him on this shuttle. There was a sense of order about him too, the way he corrected his posture each time the craft rocked, the equal lengths of his shoelaces. He had a different look. It felt like he didn't belong here as much as everyone else.

Flynn could relate.

For a moment, the man looked up and the two stared directly at each other.

Then the shuttle contorted violently and they both closed their eyes, waiting for what was to come.

The static hum became a whine, and then there was a scary groaning from the window behind his head as the fuselage began to stretch and bend. Flynn felt the gravity press him into his seat, but sensation in his feet and hands was gone now. The white in his periphery grew. Nausea blossomed in his stomach. The static whine filled his ears, threatening to burst them as the shuttle rocked and shook.

Flynn passed out. There was nothing but darkness.

Until pain lanced through his body, jarring him back awake.

Electricity. It burned and froze, contracted all his muscles at once. He would have yelled, but his body was locked down.

He heard people moan, recognized the sounds of vomit hitting the metal floor, could barely make out blurry shapes moving through the shuttle. They all looked the same: shades of gray and black, with a single glowing spot of color on their arms. One of them stood above Flynn, a gargoyle with horrible elongated arms and glowing blue eyes and a sword that crackled lightning.

"Wake your ass up," the thing spoke to him harshly, a frightening, staticky mess of sound. The sword arched down. More pain, lancing through him, hot and cold.

Flynn tried not to vomit at the streaking pain and the leftover nausea from the entry. He wanted to curl up in a ball, but he was still shackled to the seat.

The pain refocused his senses. He looked back up and saw that it wasn't a gargoyle at all. It was a man. Wearing a gray and black armored uniform like the half dozen others now inside the ship. A yellow, holographic patch glowed on his arm, flashing and morphing between a logo of a spinning circle and the word *Admissions*. The glowing eyes were the reflected light from the HUD in the helmet he wore, and the sword was just some kind of electrified baton that sparked and fizzled.

"*Wake up!*" the figure barked, his voice emitted electronically from the helmet.

Flynn's face stung in pain as the man backhanded him, hard. He tasted blood.

Another armored man moved to the woman on his left. His club sparked as it struck her. Flynn could see her body contort. The pattern repeated everywhere in the shuttle, which was no longer moving. They'd landed. They were being woken up from the unconsciousness that came from passing through the Razor's charged ionosphere. Not gently, either.

Moments later, rapid-fire metallic clicking echoed up and down the interior as the shackles on the passengers' legs and arms disengaged. Half the people inside fell to the floor, still dizzy and sick. Flynn managed to stay in place, but just barely.

A man stepped inside from the rear air lock, and as he did the guards all stood straight. The silence that followed let the sounds of vomiting and whimpering fill the cabin.

The man wore the same gray and black body armor, the same yellow holographic patch, but unlike his men he had no helmet. He was tall, older than the others, with a gray buzz cut and a tightly trimmed white beard. The way he stood—perfect posture, feet shoulder-width apart, hands clasped behind his back—he looked exactly like what he probably was: former UEG military. He swept a stern, unsympathetic look across the passengers.

"Ladies and gentlemen," he said, his voice carrying easily in the cramped confines of the shuttle, "let me be the first to welcome you home. The last home any of you will ever know. But most definitely . . . the one you deserve."

One by one, the whimpering and the complaining stopped. Every person inside the shuttle, down the line of seats and restraints, looked up at the guard captain; his armored suit, his shined boots, his short hair, flanked by his men. It was all very real now.

"Get them up," the captain said, then stepped back into the air lock without looking back.

The back of Flynn's head stung as a fist knocked him forward. He barely managed to stand through the dizziness and disorientation. Ahead, he could just make out a hallway beyond the air lock, made of drab, faded cement. Words had been stenciled there in a nondescript yellow print.

11-H37. HARD LABOR COLONY. LIFETIME INCARCERATION.

A line had been drawn through the *11-H37*, and another word was scrawled hastily in its place. *Razor.*

The paint was fading and old, and something about that, the fact that something so obviously against protocol had been allowed to remain for so long, implied many unsettling things.

A boot kicked Flynn forward with the others, marching them in a line toward the air lock, and every step he took toward the faded words gave him a feeling of finality. It was all really happening . . .

TWO

MADDOX

Maddox had been here before, but it was still all new.

He could see Personnel Entry through the glass partition where the new prisoners were being herded. He'd left through that port two months ago. Now he was returning through Prisoner Intake. Definition of irony.

Yellow lights flashed above the mechanical doors that began to seal off the shuttle they'd arrived on, and when they shut, it was with a heavy, metallic thud that jarred through everyone in the concrete room.

He and the other prisoners, probably forty, had been marched into the intake area by the guards and assembled into rows of three. He knew there were three automated processors. He'd watched them do their thing before, often with a detached fascination, marveling at the efficiency with which human beings became prisoners, and prisoners, in turn, became numbers.

Glancing at the line next to him, he saw the same man who had been sitting across from him on the shuttle. Thin, with wiry fingers and soft hands, and a presence that had an odd depth to it. His stance lacked the ruggedness of the other prisoners'. Everything that had made him who he was, was internal, Maddox could tell. People like that, the Razor tended to grind up first.

Still, he'd managed to keep it together during Razorfall. He hadn't cried out when the guards struck him. But Maddox had seen this place change its fair share of people. There was no way to know who the man would be after year three or four, if he survived that long, but it was certain he wouldn't resemble the person he was now.

Of course, Maddox could say the same thing about himself, couldn't he? Year three or four . . .

Jesus.

The line advanced. Person after person. Until Maddox and the other man were next.

A guard waited there, brandishing his club, the processor line beyond him. Like most, he wore the armored helmet, the HUD behind the viewscreen making the "eyes" glow blue. If there was recognition on the guard's part when Maddox reached him, Maddox couldn't detect it.

If not now, he thought, *soon*.

"Strip," crackled the guard's disturbingly amplified voice.

Maddox unbuttoned the hyperstatic suit everyone had to wear on the shuttle for landing. When he was naked, the guard motioned him forward toward the processor.

The transporter was metallic, shaped like a sled, with sections branching off from the center for the arms and legs. Maddox stepped in and winced at the cold metal on his skin. It wasn't meant to be comfortable, but nothing on the planet was. The guard strapped him to the transporter, then slapped on the head restraint. All he could do was breathe and blink, and even doing that was uncomfortable.

"Enjoy the ride," the guard said through his helmet, then struck him across the face. Maddox tasted blood as the conveyor system locked on and shuttled him forward.

Everything went dark. Strange lights flashed in his peripheral vision. He could hear screams in the distance. Curses. Weeping. The high-pitched rattling of the guards' electrified batons.

Maddox's heart pounded. He knew what was coming.

A computer monitor appeared above him, following along, lowering just inches away, until the only thing he could see was the dim reflection of his face in the dark glass.

The monitor flashed. Words scrolled.

Prisoner Intake Process, v.12.4.5
Identity confirmation scan . . .

From the dark, a metallic arm descended. Attached to it was a small reticle that drifted down toward his right eye.

Stare into the reticle, do not blink

Red light burned into his eye. On impulse Maddox looked away—and then jolted in pain. The sled was electrified. It stung bad.

COMPLIANCE REQUIRED
Stare into the reticle, do not blink

Maddox swallowed, did as the monitor instructed.
The red light flared again. It lasted a second, then the laser shut off.

Inmate Identified
NAME: Maddox, James
ID Number: 28444
Conviction Date: 8/21/2174
Infraction: First-Degree Homicide, Conspiracy and Embezzlement,
    Human Trafficking
Blood Type: O Rh D Negative
Medical Concerns: None
Biotech: None
Tattoos: None
Gang Affiliation: None

First-degree homicide.
The other charges were bullshit, of course, tacked-on infractions to
cover the asses of the ones who were still alive. But the homicide . . . that
one he owned. That one was legit.

Basic Sterilization Protocol . . .

A hiss of sound, like the buzzing of bees, materialized ahead of him as
the gurney moved into the dark. His body passed through a thick mist of
freezing liquid. It burned like acid.
Maddox couldn't help it. He screamed.
His cries ripped the dark like those of all the others around him, as
whatever microbes he'd brought along were burned away.
The monitor reappeared, descending down. It flashed on again.
Maddox's breath came in short bursts. He knew what was next.

ID Implant Protocol . . .

He tensed as he read the words. A new arm hummed down toward him, a mix of sharp, wicked-looking contraptions dripping with anti-septic.

The restraints around his neck tightened, locking his skull in place. The strap on his chin cranked down, forcing his mouth open. Maddox choked, gagged, barely able to breathe.

He could just make out the tiny polymer drill at the end of the arm shriek to life as it descended.

Instinctively, Maddox tried to twist out of the way. His eyes shut tight. The drill pushed into his mouth.

A sound like saw blades on metal filled his head. Pain, a mix of ice and electricity, lanced through his jaw as the drill plunged efficiently through bone and cartilage and nerve.

He screamed with the contraption inside his mouth, struggled, tried to turn, but there was nowhere to go. Pain just kept pouring into his head, filling him up with white heat. He started to black out.

Then the arm pulled out of his mouth, and Maddox gagged again.

He'd just been implanted with the same microchip all prisoners on the Razor received. If he ever wanted to get it out, he'd have to remove his entire jaw.

The monitor flashed above one more time.

> Intake Process Complete
> Prisoner ID Number: 28444
> Prisoner Group Designation Color: White
> Thank you for your cooperation
> Cooperation means reward
> Resistance means punishment

The monitor went dark, but it didn't lift away. The transporter ground to a halt. Maddox was still a hundred yards from the end of processing. His eyes narrowed.

Then the figures appeared above him, two on each side.

They weren't dressed like guards. No helmets. Lighter, camouflaged armor. Much more physically fit. One of them leaned in, smiling unpleasantly. A muscular, balding fellow with a handlebar mustache.

Maddox knew him well.

Reed. He'd been in Maddox's unit before. In fact, all four of the men above him had. They'd been like family once.

"Hey, sunshine," Reed said. "Ain't you a sight?"

Maddox flinched as the big man took his chin between his two calloused fingers. It still hurt bad from the implant. "How's the jaw? Always figured that had to smart like a bitch."

Maddox said nothing. Even now, he was still detached, still felt blank. He wondered, though, how long that would last. At what point did not having anything to lose no longer count for something?

"Nothing to say?" Reed asked, still sporting the smile. "Well, that's okay. Not a whole lot to talk about anyway. But we do have *one* thing to get to."

One of the other men moved closer. Maddox remembered his name too. Jericho. He raised something up. Something Maddox wasn't surprised to see. A metallic shape at the end of a crude pole. Another man lit a blowtorch and held it close until the shape on the end began to glow orange and hot in the dark.

It was the same shape the guards all wore on their arms: two circles, a larger one with a thinner one inside it. The symbol of the Razor.

"Went out of our way for you, Maddox," Reed's voice told him. "Don't want you feeling lonely. Made sure there'd be old friends where you're going."

Jericho brought the superheated iron closer and closer. Maddox gritted his teeth. In the dark, the two circles burned into his vision.

Reed leaned in so he could look Maddox in the eyes. "You had it all once, boy. Sometimes I wonder if you even knew. But you threw it away. And for what? I mean, you gotta *wonder* what the point of it was. Right?"

Maddox stared at him, breathing hard. He could feel the heat of the iron near his neck now, could see it glowing hot in the corner of his eye.

"The only thing I wonder about," Maddox answered, his voice hoarse and raw, "is what the fuck took me so long."

Reed nodded, seemed to accept the answer. "Fair enough." The only thing Maddox could see was a faint orange glow from the branding iron.

"Welcome home, Maddox."

Maddox screamed as the brand sizzled into his neck, searing his skin into flakes.

It lasted only a few seconds. That was a plus.

The beatings, though, they lasted longer. All four of them worked him hard.

As the blackness began, in that moment he had anticipated for so long, Maddox saw exactly what he expected.

He saw the woman, dark black skin, dreadlocks, eyes like coals. Saw her in that storage container with all the others when the air lock sealed it tight.

Everything he'd done after that had been because of her, but it had all been too late. And now he was here. Where he belonged.

Maddox passed out as the blows rained down.

THREE

VALUE

The only time Flynn had ever tried to kill a man was with his father's gun.

Jeremiah was on the ground with a knife to his throat, and Flynn grabbed his pistol from the dirt and aimed it at the man holding the blade.

That was a long time ago, back during the Outlier Revolution, when smugglers were raking in credits supplying colony "revolutionists." The rebels were still being backed by the Autonomy then, which meant their credit was good, and that's all that mattered to gunrunners like Jeremiah, Flynn's old man.

The rebels tried to dupe Jeremiah when he landed, tried to take their merch without paying. Complications ensued.

Flynn had never held a gun before. His fingers barely reached the trigger, his arm shook as he tried to keep the barrel up. He could only faintly hear Jeremiah snarling for him to fire.

The man on top of his father, the one with the knife, he'd locked eyes with Flynn then. And the man froze.

Flynn always wondered what prompted someone who could overpower his father (not an easy task) to freeze at the sight of a small boy holding a gun. The reality of just how low his life had managed to spiral? Or the fact that he was looking at a kid he was either about to make an orphan or a killer?

Either way, it was the distraction Jeremiah needed. The man's throat got slit, and the other rebels ran. The fight had been beaten out of them long ago.

When it was done, Flynn's father struck him across the face so hard it rocked his head around.

"If you draw," Jeremiah said, a thin line of blood where the blade had rested under his chin, "you *pull*."

Flynn opened his mouth, but his father hit him again. "If you draw, you *pull*. Say it."

All Flynn could do was nod; he was too scared.

His face stung again, another hit. "*Say* it."

"If you draw, you pull," Flynn said in a quivering voice, tears starting to form. Jeremiah stared down at him, the contempt clear in his eyes, then shoved him back toward the ship.

He'd never gone on another run with his father again. Two years later, Flynn booked passage on a freighter to Earth, paid for his ticket by modifying the ship's engines to an efficiency rating that equaled something like a two-generation upgrade. Flynn was fifteen. Even then, his talents were starting to become apparent.

And now, as he marched with the other prisoners, it occurred to Flynn that he was right back where he'd come from. His father's world. And he wasn't in any better a position to survive it.

Through the buildings of the starport, Flynn could see the sun half buried on the horizon. Hours from now, it would still be there. There was no day or night cycle here because the planet's orbit was such that one side always faced the system's red giant star. That side was called the Cindersphere, the one permanently drenched in fire, with temperatures of almost a thousand degrees. The other side, the Shadowsphere, was just the opposite. Locked in ice and utter darkness, it was an environment hundreds of degrees below zero. Two halves, completely opposite, and both deadly.

But right in the middle was a thin, fragile sliver of atmosphere where everything precariously and perfectly aligned, just enough to sustain life. Where Flynn was now. The Razor. And it was where the people who put him here intended he spend the rest of his days.

He moved his feet, shackled to the men in front of him. The inmates had been marched down a long tunnel, past automated gun turrets and into the permanent dusk outside Intake. Dozens of large-form tracks crisscrossed the ground here, headed in every direction, and massive trains sat waiting on them, the vent stacks on their roofs churning out plumes of black smoke.

The ionosphere above the Razor was highly charged, which not only made landing here incredibly risky but also made operating aircraft impossible. As a result, ground transport was the only option for moving people and supplies, and a massive rail network had been built for that purpose.

Flynn would board one of the trains and be hauled away. All he knew was that he'd been assigned to a Surface Mining Vehicle, or SMV, massive, land-based crafts nicknamed "Crawlers."

It was ironic.

One of his first assignments at Maas-Dorian had been on the design team for the Series 7 SMVs, larger than a space freighter, three hundred feet tall and thousands long. Lance had wandered through a few of them after hours, when the assembly bots were off-line. Even ventured into the unfinished prison level and stood in one of the future cells. The clear plexisteel walls and security fields hadn't been installed yet, but even then it was clear just how small a space it was to live in.

Flynn and the others were herded toward a train, various cars stretching down the line. Fuel runners, supply haulers, water tankers, crew cars for guards coming on and off tours, and, of course, inmate transports. Just big steel boxes designed to move prisoners. It all showed how much effort went into keeping the planet running. But that was to be expected. In many ways, the Razor was the most important planet in the galaxy.

Flynn tripped as a guard shoved him inside the train car, and he fell face-first onto the dirty, metallic floor. Because the prisoners were all tied together, he pulled down the men in front and behind him in a heap. Knees and elbows dug into his back.

"Goddamn scrub," he heard a voice say. A knee slammed into his ribs. He felt a fist grab his hair and shove his face hard into the dirty floor. He couldn't breathe, and with the shackles, he couldn't move either.

Then the crackling of electricity. Yells from above.

Voltage coursed through him again. He screamed.

"Move," an angry, electrified voice ordered. "It's *all* you idiots have to do."

Hands yanked Flynn to his feet, shoved him forward into the car. Guards yanked his arms over his head and they were clicked magnetically into place on a railing near the ceiling.

"Legs forward." A boot kicked his knees. The shackles on his ankles locked into place too.

He was rigged to a rack inside the train, just like everyone else, like slabs of meat in an ice locker. The horrible realization occurred to him that he could be stuck in this position a long time, hanging from his arms, unable to move, unable to sleep, unable to do anything but bear the pain. The Razor was small compared to the rest of the planet, but it circumnavigated the entire globe, a ninety-eight hundred mile stretch populated with supply depots, mining facilities, garrisons, and other prison infastructure. It could take weeks for the train to get where it was going.

"This will not be my life," Flynn said.

The car's large steel door slammed shut and everything went dark inside. The shackles bit into the flesh of his wrists as the train started moving and the gravity pulled him tight against them. Without the door open, the air inside quickly turned hot and stale, and sweat soaked through Flynn's clothes.

"Think it," a voice said next to him. Forceful, but not harsh. It felt like an admonishment.

Flynn looked. It took a moment to recognize the man hanging there. His face was swollen and red, bloodstained, one eye black and sealed shut. It was the same man who had sat across from him on the shuttle.

The man sagged in his arm restraints. He didn't look back at Flynn. He didn't seem to have the strength. Flynn winced. He had no idea what had happened to the man back at Intake, but he'd come out on the worse side of it.

"*Think* it," the man said again, his voice hoarse and torn. "Never *say* it. Anyone hears that, it's the end of you here. Shows weakness. Shows you're unsure. Shows you could be dominated."

The statement was troubling. *Dominated* . . .

"You've been here before?" Flynn asked.

"Yeah," the man said with bitterness. "Just not on *this* train."

Flynn was confused. He'd never heard of repeat offenders on the Razor. Incarceration here was for life.

"Maddox," the man said by way of introduction.

"Flynn."

"Shake your hand, but . . ." Maddox rattled his wrists, magnetically attached to the railing, just like Flynn's.

Flynn smiled a little. "Do you know where we're going, Maddox?"

Maddox's chains shook again as he nodded. "The *Charon*. Her supply depot's a couple hundred miles south. Captain's named Braga. More corrupt than most, not as much as some. Solid mining numbers, means he pushes his prisoners."

Flynn studied the man. "How do you know all that?"

"Someone told me I was going to meet an old friend. That means the *Charon*."

Flynn had no idea what any of that meant, but whoever he was, Maddox knew a lot about this world and how it worked.

"Talking too much," Maddox said. "I do that. Who'd you used to be?"

Used to be . . . Flynn swallowed. "I was an engineer. With M-D."

That got a reaction. Maddox tried to turn to look at him, but tensed as he did, wincing. "Good. That's real good. You can use that."

"For what?"

"For not dying. Let the captain know. Tell a guard. Not a sergeant or guard-captain, just a grunt. Less likely to be making deals of their own on the floor. Lower-end guys will run it up the chain for a reward. Do it quick, though. Sooner you get under the captain's protection, the better. You won't survive long in GenPop."

Flynn stared at Maddox. "Let the captain . . . know *what*?"

Maddox exhaled slowly. "Everything on this rock runs on M-D tech. If you can work with it, you're valuable."

"They have mechanics here, people who can fix—"

"Not talking about *fixing* things, least not that way."

Flynn was still confused.

"Look, this whole planet is rotten. Everyone who works here is out for themselves. If you have a way of profiting them, you're valuable. You'll be protected. Just remember, when you meet with the captain, whatever deal you offer, you only get to offer once. Make it worth his while. Show *value*."

Flynn thought about what Maddox was saying. *Value . . .* How, though, he still had to figure out.

"And make sure," Maddox went on in his hoarse voice, "you never fully deliver. Once you stop being valuable, you're through. Stay valuable."

"Why are you telling me this?" Flynn asked. It was a fair question, given where they were. After all, he and Maddox had only just met.

Maddox's head turned slightly. "I don't know. Maybe because I had the chance to help someone once . . . and I didn't. Anyway, it's just advice. Advice isn't worth a whole hell of a lot."

Flynn studied Maddox's shadow. "I didn't do what they say I did. I'm not supposed to be here."

"'Supposed to be' doesn't count for much on the Razor."

Neither of them talked after that. They just hung in their chains while the train car buckled and shook rhythmically around them.

This will not be my life, Flynn thought to himself this time, but the idea was starting to feel hollow.

He closed his eyes and managed to fall asleep.

FOUR

KEY

They were just tattoos, the wings. Red, blue, yellow, angel-like, stretching from her neck to the curve of her lower back. A small act of vengeance. She got them the same night Mace beat her for the first time. Her skin was caramel brown, with a sheen that somehow always made it look wet, the only gift from her Hispanic mother she ever got, and Mace demanded she keep it bare.

They itched right before the second beating, the skin red from eight or so hours of needlework, and ever since, they'd flared up when something bad was coming. Probably just intuition, but it was never wrong, and they were itching real bad when she woke up.

Key's eyes snapped open.

Above her, the same view. The bottom of Nia's mattress, tarnished in odd, brownish shapes. The stains were like clouds. She'd spent months deciding whether they looked like faces or ships or letters, when they'd first gotten to the *Charon*. Now it had lost its allure.

Nia stirred above her as the intercom blared through blown speakers outside their cell. Three short blasts. Followed by the staticky voice of whichever asshole was on morning shift today.

"Rise and shine, lords and ladies. Getting more worms for you to play with. Supply dock line up in five."

There was a groan from Nia, above, and the shifting of her weight as she rolled over. Outside, the sounds of stirring began to fill the cell block: harsh laughter, curses, the occasional sound of someone puking. Nia's naked legs swung down from the bunk and dangled next to Key's head.

Key rubbed her back on her less-than-soft sheets, scratching the wings on her back.

"Worst hangover." Nia's voice was still crusty with sleep.

"You were there," Key answered, stretching her arms out as much as she could in the cramped bed. "After we scrapped that mining probe in the Kublai Cluster."

"Yeah." Nia's voice was disappointed. "That was mine too."

It was a game they played—or rather, a game Nia played. She racked her brain for experiences equally as bad as their current one. Rarely did anything measure up. But it made Nia feel better, so Key played along.

Nia hopped off her bunk, onto the floor. She was naked except for her underwear, and the scars up and down her body stood out. Knife cuts, gunshot wounds, teeth marks. An impressive collection for someone so young. Just eighteen, barely legal. And locked up here for the rest of her life.

And whose fault is that? Key asked herself bitterly.

Nia stretched, catlike, ran her fingers roughly through her spiky, multicolored hair—shades of pink and purple—then moved for her locker.

Key's was next to it. Other than that, the toilet and the bunks made up the whole of their accommodations. The walls were carved with the scrawlings of hundreds of former inmates. Names, dates, boastings, insane ramblings. The walls were metal; to read them you had to get at just the right angle to catch the light.

That had lost its allure too.

Two jarring blasts from the intercom. Two minutes to go.

Key moved for her locker, scratching her scalp with her fingers. Her hair had progressed beyond the stubbly, sharp phase and was actually starting to get soft. It was time to shave it again, but the hair maintenance bot had been down ever since the brawl between Bloodclan and Grimm two weeks ago.

What was a girl to do? Bargain for a fucking razor?

Key yanked open her locker, stared at the same contents she saw every morning. Clean red jumpsuit, freshly vacuum sealed. Shined boots, black, with yellow laces. Thermal socks. Standard issue synthetic cotton underwear, the scratchy kind, also vacuum sealed. All of it newly cleaned, smelling of detergent. The lockers were automated. Stick in your gear at night, it got whisked away to Laundry. Cleaned versions appeared when you woke up. That was one plus to hard labor incarceration. Key hated doing laundry.

"You ever wonder if we get the same clothes every time?" Nia pondered, pulling her jumpsuit from the bag. "Or am I swapping with all the other size ones?"

"Since we're the only reds, the only size one you're swapping with is me."

Nia smirked. "You're not a size one."

When gang members or ship crews hit Intake, they were all assigned to the same Crawler. Not only that, they wore the same color, probably to help the dipshit guards know who was who. She guessed the logic was that gangs and crews were already used to working together, which added up to increased productivity. And productivity was all the people who ran the Razor were really interested in.

Key slipped the clothes on. The suit was more than just a covering; it had electrical clips and hose inserts for connecting to a variety of other suits, much more cumbersome. Heat suits for mining, rad-suits for working the Crawler's reactor, pressure suits for atmosphere generator duty. Key zipped hers up, slipped the sleeves around the mag-bracelets on her wrists.

Then she heard something drip.

Key looked at Nia. The girl was staring down at the floor, at a small pool of blood. It was dripping from her nose.

Nia looked dazed, wiped her nose with her wrist, smearing blood all over her face. "Well. Shit."

The girl's knees buckled and she fell to the floor, blood everywhere. Key grabbed her before she hit.

God damn it, Key thought, *not now*.

When the seizures hit, Nia got nosebleeds. It looked worse than it was. So far, they'd managed to avoid her losing it on duty, but it was just a matter of time.

The final buzzer sounded over the intercom. One minute to be at the front of their cells before the beatings started. No way they were making that.

Nia moaned in her arms. She'd been their crew's most recent hire. Mace picked her up at Eros station. Another stray, it looked like to Key, but the girl had proven herself tenacious. She was like a rattlesnake bred with an arc welder, had dropped Fleer with a kick to the balls on the second day, after he tried to pull her into his room. Key liked her, immediately felt protective of her. After all, being a teenage girl on a ship full of horny ice pirates was tough.

Key knew. She'd been that girl once.

A loud buzzing ripped down the cell block. She could hear the pinging of locks snapping free, then the rattling of clear polysteel doors sliding open. Groggy voices, boots scraping the metallic floor, shock-sticks sparking.

Nia moaned in Key's hands. She could smell the urine where the girl had pissed herself.

Key swallowed. "Nia. Gotta wake up. Gotta get off your ass now."

Getting beat wasn't a problem; Key was used to that. What she was worried about was that they might learn what Nia really had.

Lucord's disease, also called Xytrilium poisoning, common among X miners. Big shock that something powerful enough to run every reactor, biocomputer, and electromagnetic hub in the galaxy was dangerous to handle. Get exposed to enough X, it started breaking down your body. All the little pieces that held it together. Nia had caught it here, a few months ago, and it was a death sentence on a prison Crawler. Dozens of inmates came down with Lucord's every year. And every one of them went missing shortly after.

"Nia . . ." Key shook the girl, blood everywhere. It was coming out of her mouth now too. "Gotta wake up. Gotta—"

"The *fuck* is this?"

Key didn't need for the guard to have his helmet off to know it was Drake, a short little prick that had tried twice to have his way with her. Both times he'd left with scars.

Key spun around. Drake and another guard, both in gray armor, blue spinning holograms on their arms, stared down at her and Nia. "Drake, listen—"

Drake's baton rammed into her stomach, doubled her over. A second hit slammed her to the floor. Nia fell to the side.

Drake grabbed Key by the hair. Sharp pain as she was dragged across the floor.

"Contraband search," Drake said above her. "*This* one."

"What about the other?" a second guard asked, baton sparking, moving toward Nia. "Looks like Lucord's."

"Let you know," Drake replied, dragging Key into the hall. "Depends on how well we get along."

Laughs echoed from the other inmates in the F4 as Key was dragged into view. Different colors of jumpsuits, different colors of skin, lined up and down the hall. Key felt hot anger. She bit, she clawed, she went for balls—the usual. Another strike with the baton made everything go blurry.

The door to the interrogation room slid open and Drake threw her inside.

The room was just a metallic square, with a table in the center and some cameras along the ceiling. No clear polysteel walls here. What went down in this room wasn't for general consumption.

Key scrambled back against the far wall, trying to shake off the haze. She felt blood on her forehead.

Drake tapped some buttons on his wrist controls. The lights on the cameras all faded out.

Key tensed. "Anything goes in my mouth, you *lose*."

Drake just laughed. In a strange, calm way she didn't like. "I don't guess it's gonna come to that."

He tossed something onto the table. A small metallic box, about the size of a cigar case.

"Two minutes before they start wondering what's up," Drake said.

Key stared at him in complete confusion. The tension from before seemed to vanish from the room. Key wiped the blood from her scalp. "Two minutes for *what*?"

Drake moved back toward the door outside, sealing it shut. "Hurry the fuck up. You get busted, I get busted."

Key cautiously looked at the box on the table. It seemed innocuous. It also didn't look like anything she'd seen on the *Charon* before. Shiny, perfectly proportioned. New.

Slowly, she moved toward it. There was one latch, keeping it sealed. Key flicked it open with her thumb.

The lid raised up automatically. Inside was a digital screen . . . and a single syringe. A hypo. Filled with a pale blue liquid, ready to inject.

What the hell . . .

The screen inside flashed to life. The image of a man appeared. Sixty or so years old. Thin, pale, bald; small black wireframe glasses. A gray suit, gray tie, all nondescript. He would have blended in, in any colony or Earth city. You never would have looked twice. Key had a feeling that was the point.

"I will refrain from using your name, in the event this message is intercepted," the Suit said. He stared at Key with an unsettling detachment. Like this video was one of dozens of things he had to do. "You have been identified as a candidate capable of carrying out a task my employers require completed. You have been identified as someone with the proper . . .

motivation. You will have noticed the syringe. The injectable inside is Doxypaxoline-190."

Key felt the world swirl away and vanish. She stared down at the syringe with a new, sharp focus.

"You are most likely aware of this medication's high success rate for achieving remission of Lucord's disease.

Key's eyes were locked on the syringe.

"My employers are willing to guarantee delivery of nine individual doses of this medication, enough to remission your cellmate's condition. There is no need to describe the general unavailability of Doxypaxoline-190 on the Razor. As such, I'm sure you will appreciate the value of our offer."

Xytrilium poisoning, what Nia had, required a special medication, Doxy-190, the thing the Suit claimed was in the hypo. Doxy-190 contained *processed* Xytrilium, the only thing that would counteract the raw stuff running through Nia's veins.

Maybe that was because the two didn't get along well.

In larger quantities, when processed X met raw X, they tended to *explode*. In a way that disassembled whatever particles were nearby. So any form of processed X was strictly forbidden here. Not even the Bloodclan could get Doxy-190 through the supply depots. Key knew this because she'd asked, and Whistler had laughed in her face. Which made what was happening set off all kinds of alarm bells.

"Skepticism, on your part, would be natural," the Suit continued, as if reading her thoughts. "I suggest you administer this dose to your cellmate and observe its effects. When you are convinced of its legitimacy, you can proceed with our proposed arrangement."

Key looked back at the screen. The Suit was staring at the camera exactly as before. It was a recording of course, but it felt like he was looking right at her. Calm. Detached. Something about how confident he was bothered Key.

"There is a new inmate joining your SMV this afternoon. We would very much like it if he were to . . . not survive his incarceration."

Key smirked. So that was it. They wanted her to off someone.

The Suit's image on the screen was replaced with a still frame image of a very different person than Key expected. Thin, unassuming, with curly hair, blue eyes, and totally bereft of the hard edge you generally saw on the Razor.

For lack of a better word, the guy looked . . . normal.

The Suit's image reappeared on the screen. "Once we have confirmation of the inmate's termination, the remainder of the medication will be provided at monthly intervals. Rest assured, my employers are the kind who find that failing to honor agreements is . . . unprofitable. And profit, one might say, is the reason anyone does anything . . . which is why you will accept. That, and the fact that you are very close to having nothing left to lose. Aren't you?"

The Suit paused, let the words have their impact.

Whoever he was, he clearly knew more about Key than was comfortable.

"The guard will escort you back to your position," he said, finality in his tone. "He will ensure nothing happens to either you or your cellmate while you evaluate our proposal. We look forward to completing this arrangement, to the satisfaction of all parties."

The screen went dark. Just like that, he was gone. Key was left with the box and the hypo. She stared down at it, still unsure.

"Put it in your pocket, princess," Drake said. "Hide it under a mattress. You won't have to worry about cell inspections; it's been taken care of."

Key felt icy fingers on her spine. If this was all legit—hell, if half of it were fucking legit—whoever was pulling the strings here was beyond powerful. And they had played the right angle. Because it was true, what choice did Key have? She was about to lose Nia. She was about to lose *all* of them. And that was a weight she couldn't bear.

The hypo was cool in her hands, heavier than she expected. Drake moved forward and picked up the metallic box, then looked at her through his helmet, cocked his head to one side. "Supposed to have interrogated you. Maybe you need a few bruises to make it look convincing."

Key stared back. "You want it to look convincing, asshole, *you* should be the one with the bruises."

Drake scowled and yanked her out of the interrogation room. As he did, Key thought of the picture of the man that the Suit had shown her. The one she was going to kill. She thought of his features and face, committed them to memory. And his name.

Flynn. Marcus Flynn.

FIVE

SURVIVAL

Flynn jarred awake.

His wrists hurt from where they dug into the ceiling shackles of the train car. So did his mouth, searing pain from his jaw all the way to his ear where the intake machines had drilled into his teeth.

The train was stopped now. The prisoner car's giant steel door had been slid open and prisoners were being disconnected and marched outside, one at a time. A guard appeared next to him, staring at Maddox, who was hanging limply. When the guard saw the back of Maddox's neck, he smiled.

"Well, look at this." The guard slammed his baton into Maddox's lower back. Maddox sagged, but he didn't cry out. "Got us a Fink." The baton lashed out again. Maddox groaned. "Welcome to the *Charon*."

With the light from the door, Flynn could see the back of Maddox's neck in more detail, and it looked like something had been *burned* there. A crude brand. The same symbol the guards wore on their shoulders. Two circles, one inside the other. The symbol of the Razor.

Fink, the guard had called him. Flynn didn't know what it meant, but it clearly wasn't a title you wanted to be labeled with.

Maddox fell to the floor like a bag of bricks when the guard unhooked him. Flynn's shackles came off next.

"Get him moving," the electrified voice ordered Flynn, "or it's *your* ass."

Flynn knelt down, started pulling the man up.

"Don't . . ." Maddox said weakly. "Not . . . good . . ."

"Just shut up," Flynn whispered harshly, hands under Maddox's shoulders. Up close, Flynn could see all his injuries. How was this guy even conscious?

The two moved forward together, other prisoners in lines on either side of them. They stepped off the train, into the muddy light of the Razor's permanent dusk.

Guards were taking the locks on the ankle shackles of each prisoner and snapping them into place on a large metallic rail that arced its way across the muddy ground.

The rail, Flynn could see, split ahead and moved in different directions. Those directions split farther, branching out like a spiderweb. Once you were attached to it, the rail determined exactly where you could go, and judging by the bearings and gas compression lines Flynn could see inside it, it would pull you back and forth as needed.

He felt a sense of dread when a guard finally locked his own shackles onto it.

With a jolt, Flynn, Maddox, and all the other condemned jerked forward. They had no choice but to walk or be dragged, and it was leading them toward a giant facility ahead.

Flynn could guess what it was. A mining Crawler supply depot.

Crawlers themselves were enormous. It only followed that a facility that resupplied them would be equally so.

Flynn had never worked on the depot designs at Maas-Dorian, but he was familiar with them. Five stories tall to match the height of the mining SMVs they serviced, with two massive docking berths at angles from each other. These depots were dotted all around the Razor, supplying the Crawlers operating around the planet.

Flynn could see the giant circular tracks that ran around the circumference. When it was time, the entire depot rotated in place, so that the docked Crawlers faced the opposite direction from which they had entered. A necessary design, because Crawlers couldn't move backward. Adding a secondary transmission on a vehicle that big would have been cost prohibitive. So someone had solved a problem on one platform by implementing a solution on another.

It had been his favorite part of being an engineer. Problem solving. He'd been good at it. It was probably the *only* thing he was good at.

Problem, he thought in his head. *Surviving in a world of violence, when violence isn't your thing.*

The advice given to him by Maddox echoed in his head.

Solution: prove yourself valuable to those in power.

Easier said than done, of course.

The rail led right to the building's main door, where the prisoners were already being led inside. It would be Flynn's turn soon, and his pulse raced.

The reason the Razor was the most dreaded prison sentence in the galaxy wasn't because it was hard labor. Most prison colonies were. The reason was because it had something the others didn't.

Xytrilium.

X.

More than a fuel source, more than a compacting agonist for biocircuitry, in the centuries since its discovery, Xytrilium had quickly come to power the galaxy. It was near impossible to find a system or generator or capacitor that didn't run on X. There were no alternative power sources, because there was nothing more powerful than Xytrilium.

But X had its drawbacks. For one, it only occurred naturally on planets that met a variety of qualifications, mainly a specific distance from the unique radiation of red giant stars. And because of the Razor's unique orbit, one side constantly being bathed in that unique radiation, the Xytrilium here was the purest and most potent ever found.

The purer the Xytrilium, the more powerful the machinery or computer that could be powered. Which meant whoever controlled the mining rights to the Razor could produce machinery and computers far more powerful than those of their competitors.

Maas-Dorian, Flynn's former employer, had made sure they owned those rights for the last several decades. And they had become the most powerful corporation in the galaxy as a result.

Maddox was just ahead of Flynn, moving under his own power, but barely. He hobbled forward, pulled by the rail with everyone else.

Flynn wondered if he would ever see Maddox again. Crawlers, depending on the model, could hold five hundred inmates each. He and Maddox could be assigned to completely different cell blocks, given completely different assignments. But it was what it was, Flynn told himself. He had to look out for himself now.

When it was Flynn's turn, he passed through the depot's main door, the rail pulling him along.

The supply depots were modular. They came down from orbit in pieces, then assembled themselves in satellite-designated landing zones. The later-version depots could do it in six hours, and wherever he looked he could see the evidence. Beams of composite steel, cut to size. Paneled walls. Everything square and interlocking. In the ceiling, far above, the blades of huge vent fans spun slowly, slicing the auburn-colored light beams that filtered through from the sky. The floor was protocarbon—super strong, super light—and the footsteps of prisoners walking in unison were ominously muted.

The room was small. Guards lined the floor, watching, batons ready. Laser sights streamed down from above. More guards on the railing near the ceiling, pulse rifles ready, waiting for an excuse.

In the center of the room, something was painted on the protocarbon floor.

Cooperation means reward. Resistance means punishment.

The track led right to the stenciled words, making every new prisoner who came through stare down at them as they moved.

One inmate, a large, muscled girl, clearly with hormone implants, spit on the words as she moved. The reaction was swift.

Her shackles unlocked from the rail. Three sets of gauntleted hands yanked her down. The batons sparked. Flynn winced at the blows, could see the girl's legs twitching on the floor.

"Keep moving," another electrified voice growled.

No one argued. The sound of groans and thick thuds of batons hitting flesh echoed nearby.

In front of Flynn, Maddox eventually reached the rail's terminus, where it branched off in different directions. Standing there was a guard, face covered by a helmet. After the guard asked a few quick questions, Maddox was transferred to a new rail. It pulled him toward the right.

"Gang affiliation?"

It took a moment for Flynn to figure out the guard was speaking to him now. "What?"

"*Gang* affiliation," the guard repeated impatiently.

"No." Flynn managed. "No . . . gang."

His shackles were unhooked, then clicked back in, and Flynn was pulled after Maddox. At the end of the new railing stood about fifteen prisoners, and Flynn noticed different rails led to different groups, each group given a different color of jumpsuit. When Flynn reached the end of his track, a guard handed him his own jumpsuit.

It was white.

A giant rattling sound filled the room suddenly.

A massive steel door raised upward, the sound of chains grating through pulleys. Dim sunlight hit the cement floor and spread outward as the door opened. As it did, the view was filled by one thing, framed in the doorway.

A *wheel*.

A massive wheel. So big it blocked the view of everything else.

There was no doubt which vehicle it belonged to . . .

Flynn could make out the hydraulics attached to the wheel. He knew by studying the shock absorption system that the vehicle was a Series 7 SMV. He knew that because he had designed the system himself.

Flynn smiled, fondly.

Then he saw the man standing in the huge doorway.

Small, unassuming, bookish even. No armor, just a gray uniform with the same spinning twin-circle hologram, but his presence somehow seemed to dwarf the armored men who flanked him. The man studied the group of new arrivals, and they stared back warily. His demeanor, combined with the lack of a physical presence, was confusing to them, Flynn guessed. In their world, it was usually one or the other.

"There is a phrase stenciled on the floor here," the small man said. Somehow his soft voice filled the room. The inmates went quiet. "'Cooperation means reward. Resistance means punishment.' It is a phrase that means *nothing* to me."

It must be the captain of the *Charon*, Flynn guessed. Braga.

"Every statute written in every Prisoners' Rights edict means nothing to me," Braga continued, "because there's no one on my Crawler who's going to discount *my* version of what happens. Accidentally taking a fall off the top deck looks just like being pushed off intentionally. Being left outside in the Cinder when the heat locks seal looks just like a heat suit malfunction. Getting keelhauled looks just like a hydraulics accident. You see the pattern."

The room of killers and thieves was silent. They had no reply.

"This world and its mining rights belong to the Maas-Dorian Corporation," Braga said. "All they care about is regular shipments of the most refined Xytrilium in the galaxy. *Their* Xytrilium. They don't care how many of you die getting it for them. And neither do I. On the *Charon*, resistance means *death*. And cooperation means *survival*. Learn this lesson. Because a hundred more of you show up on a train here next month."

Braga saved one last gaze for the crowd, and then his eyes settled on Flynn.

Flynn stared back, feeling a growing sense of unease. The man's look was more than curiosity. It was *recognition*.

"Board them," Braga ordered, holding Flynn's gaze a moment more. Then he turned and moved off. The guards in the room advanced.

"You heard him, scumbags," an amplified voice said. The rail rumbled back to life. The chains went taut and Flynn was jerked forward with everyone else. Straight ahead. Out the big access door and into the dim, brown light from the sun hanging on the horizon.

The *Charon*, now fully revealed, towered over everything. Something about seeing a Surface Mining Vehicle out in the open and away from the factory floor made it seem even larger, even more imposing.

There was a loud thud behind him.

Flynn turned around. Maddox lay on the protocarbon floor, his body twisted and held in place by the shackles on the rail.

He'd finally passed out.

SIX

THEM BONES

It was always the same in his memory. Scattergun in his hands. The muzzle trained on Major Canek. The look on the asshole's face while he took another sip of Scotch from a coffee mug.

"You do this, Maddox, they'll throw you to the Razor," the major told him. They were standing in his kitchen, in an orbital Kronos apartment no one at his pay grade could ever afford. "No one'll believe you. Hell, no one'll care."

Maddox was still ashamed by how long it took to pull the trigger. Even after everything he'd seen. He'd almost put his own miserable life above all the misery this bastard would keep causing. Just like he'd done before.

But he did pull. He sprayed the life of Canek, a man he'd once thought of as a father, all over his kitchen stove. The major had been right, though. They did throw him back to the Razor. And no one had cared.

Tiny slivers of something began to swirl and push the darkness away. It took a while for him to realize it was pain. His eyes opened. More pain. Everything was bright and hazy.

He was in a bed with raised side rails. There were three other beds in the room. Everything was white, almost too white. Cabinets lined the walls, stocked with all kinds of supplies. Surgical and examination equipment hummed. It was an infirmary. And judging by the small size of it, probably the one on the Crawler he'd been assigned to.

A set of eyes appeared above him, staring down. They belonged to a woman.

Bright blue, like the scrubs she wore under her gray lab coat. There was a medical scanner on her belt, worn from use. Maddox had seen them before; it was the kind doctors used. She was early thirties, he guessed. Her hair was thick and full and tied into a bun on the back of her head. It seemed to waver between different shades of brown and red. The lines of her face were . . . wrong. For her age. Deeper than they should have been. Pale skin, but not just from lack of sun. She was burdened.

Maddox knew a lot about that.

From behind her, somewhere else in the room, came a strange sound. Like small, rounded, dull objects hitting the floor and scattering apart.

"I'm sorry," the girl whispered to him then.

Maddox knew the sound. He'd heard it many times. The look of the girl, the slight look of desperation in her eyes, suddenly made sense.

Maddox held her look. "I'm sorry too."

The doctor studied him a second more, then moved out of view.

Maddox saw other figures now.

Two prison guards, helmets on, keeping their identities secret. Smart, given just how bought-and-paid-for they must be to get a gang leader up this far from GenPop.

Another man was crouched, and he wasn't looking at Maddox. He was staring at the floor, at a dozen little things scattered there. Maddox knew what they were. Bone dice. Twelve of them. Each marked with runes. Like all Bloodclan, the man was superstitious.

Whistler was his name. He was where Maddox's road finally ended. Strangely, he didn't feel trepidation or fear. He was just glad to get it over with.

"Augury of the Adders," the big man said in a low voice, the *S* at the end hissing out from his lips, hanging in the air. His accent was thick Obeah. Warm, colorful, with a singsong tone that moved up and down. It was a strange sound in Whistler's deep, rumbling voice.

"You know what that mean, boss man? Means time be running short. And don't that seem just about right?"

Maddox swallowed. His voice came out hoarse and ragged. "Short for me? Or short for you?"

Whistler chuckled deep and low.

He swooped up the bone dice with one quick gesture, and it struck Maddox that the Bloodclan's arm moved like an adder itself. The big man slowly stood up to his full height. He was huge, like most Bloodclan, heavily muscled, dreadlocks trailing down the back of his black jumpsuit. Voodoo tats wound up and down his arms.

The two guards behind him, even on the take, watched him warily.

"Ah, boss man. You got any notion what it take to get you here? Any at all?" Maddox kept his mouth shut. "Nothing, brother. Truly fucking nothing. Your boys, they just serve you up to Whistler like a big steaming plate of plantains." Whistler's eyes moved over what he could see of Maddox, bound to the medical gurney. "Work you over first, eh? That okay. Still plenty left."

"Two minutes," one of the guards said, his voice electrified under his helmet. "Need to be back for RCP."

Roll call precheck. Guards had to check in before a GenPop prisoner roll call, which happened before a shift change. If they were worried about not being back before then, then that meant they were worried about getting busted for being in Whistler's pocket. Not because it was unethical; that didn't mean much on the Razor. But because they probably weren't cutting the captain in on their profit.

In some ways, the Razor was more locked down than most prisons. Only three people had ever managed to escape it in the forty-seven years it had been active, but as far as what went down surface-side, it wasn't much different than any other lockdown colony. If a prisoner had the ability and resources to benefit guards or captains, they could make all kinds of deals, and Whistler certainly had that ability. The Bloodclan were the biggest narcotics runners in the galaxy, with supply lines stretching from the Trident all the way to Earth. The fact that Whistler was up on the *Charon*'s top level, above GenPop, an area completely off-limits to inmates, was a pretty good sign just how much influence he wielded here.

And just how screwed Maddox was.

Still, all the influence in the galaxy couldn't get you a shuttle ride through the ionosphere back home. A certain amount of corruption within Corrections Council worlds was allowed. The kind that remained out of sight and out of news broadcasts. Anything that drew unwanted attention was explicitly prohibited. That meant once you were here, you stayed.

"Just do it, Whistler," Maddox said. He struggled to stay awake, to keep his eyes on the man who was going to kill him. Oddly, he realized, he *wanted* to be awake for it. "*Do it.*"

Whistler laughed again. Low and deep. Not a pleasant sound.

"What you expecting, brother?" Whistler nodded slightly behind him, toward the guards. "One put a hole in you and that be that? No, boss man. Whistler been thinking on this a long time. No bullet, no shank. Gonna be an angel. *Whistler's* angel."

Whistler looked to his right. The doctor from before stood there, leaning against a medical cabinet, staring at the floor. She looked miserable.

"She *your* angel too." Whistler kept his gaze on the doctor. "But no angel of mercy, that for sure."

The doctor said nothing, just swallowed and kept her eyes down.

"*Right*, angel?" Whistler's voice took on a dark edge.

"Right . . ." she said, her voice barely audible. The girl forced herself to look at the big man.

Maddox felt anger rise in him. Whistler could toy with him all he wanted, but the doctor didn't have anything to do with it. "I stopped it, Whistler. I shut it all down."

Whistler's giant fists clenched. His eyes glowed like coals.

"None of that why Whistler come to you," he snarled. "Whistler come to you because you the only one on this whole pile of ash who be righteous. Who *care*. Or so Whistler thought. But he was wrong. Dead wrong."

The man's eyes bored into Maddox's. Maddox tried to hold the look, but failed. He closed his eyes. In the dark he saw her again, staring at him, in the cargo container.

"Dead slaver Ranger." Whistler's voice was suppressed rage. "Narcs losing some creds, what that matter to Whistler? *She* still gone, ain't she? That all Whistler care about. At the end, it all *you* gonna care about too. Whistler promise. Whistler *guarantee*."

Maddox couldn't open his eyes, couldn't look at Whistler. "I see her every time I close my eyes."

He heard Whistler step closer. The guards tensed.

Then the floor rattled, shaking up through the bed. There was a hiss from the air vents in the room as the interior began to pressurize and the oxygen recyclers kicked in. The *Charon* had disconnected from its berth; the Xytrilium reactors, the X-Cores, were coming online.

They were about to head toward the Cindersphere.

Maddox opened his eyes and stared at Whistler, just feet away now.

"Whistler," the guard spoke again, his voice nervous. "Gotta go. Now."

The smile returned to Whistler's lips as he stared into Maddox. "Whistler likes that, brother. Whistler likes it, because that mean she's the last thing you ever gonna see. That much, you and Whistler got in common."

The big man held Maddox's eyes a moment longer, then he turned and moved for the door out of the medical bay, the guards following. When he was gone the air inside seemed to go with him.

Maddox coughed harshly, his body spasming. He couldn't catch his breath. Everything seemed to hurt. And he was filled with desperation.

Why couldn't it be over? Why couldn't it be done with?

Then she was there. Looking down on him again. Her blue eyes filled everything. She placed a hand on his chest, gently. His coughing slowed and then stopped.

"I'm sorry," she said. Her hand was warm where it touched him.

No angel of mercy . . .

Maddox's eyes followed the line of her neck to her shoulder, to her arm, to her wrist—and there he saw something strange. Under the hem of her coat, where her skin met the stale air of the medical bay, was a slight glowing, like the embers from a dying fire.

Maddox nodded. He understood now.

"What's your name?" he managed to ask, staring at the glowing on her skin.

"Raelyn," the girl finally answered. Her voice was calming.

"Well, Raelyn," he managed to say, looking back up at her, "you already said that."

And then the world faded away again, and there was nothing but black.

SEVEN

INTAKE

Flynn could feel the vibrations from the Crawler's turbines rumbling up through the superstructure and into his feet. Every once in a while the whole room shifted as the *Charon* moved over uneven terrain, heading toward the Cindersphere.

Outside, the planet's sun would be rising, ever so slightly, as the craft moved west. Because of the Razor's improbable orbit, the farther you went west, the higher the sun rose.

But, of course, he couldn't watch the sun. The new inmates were crammed into a square, metallic room with barriers of clear polysteel separating everything into "pens." The pens were divided by jumpsuit color. Above them, guards watched from a railing.

Flynn knew where he was; he'd seen the SMV schematics enough times. Everyone else in the room seemed to know too, judging by how they stared at the big doors in front of them. The holding tank. On the other side was GenPop, the main area of the prison level.

A muted thud sounded next to Flynn. He turned instinctively and stared into the eyes of an inmate on the other side of the polysteel. Younger than Flynn, but much worse for wear. Tall, incredibly thin, so pale his blue veins crisscrossed under his skin, his eyes bloodshot and wired. He was dressed in yellow, like everyone else there, maybe a dozen prisoners.

The man stared at Flynn intensely, opened his mouth, and breathed on the polysteel, clouding it. His finger raised. He drew on the glass.

He drew a heart.

Flynn's veins turned to ice.

The man smiled, holes where numerous teeth should have been. His eyes had a strange, primal look Flynn had never seen before, hungry almost.

Flynn looked away, locked his eyes on the door.

The muted thuds again. Flynn went rigid, just kept staring straight ahead and didn't look back.

This would *not* be his life.

Everyone in the tank jumped as an alarm blared, three grating pulses of sound. The white lights in the metallic ceiling flashed off and everything went yellow.

The mood in the tank became electrically bipolar. Insane cheering competed with whimpering and vomiting. It was time. They were joining GenPop.

The first door opened, cranking slowly up and out of the way.

It was the pen for the yellows, next to Flynn.

The screech of the inmates was loud enough to hear through the polysteel. The yellows surged forward, pushing through while the other prisoners watched. Flynn risked a look at the pale man as he moved. To his relief, the man never looked back.

As the yellows disappeared, Flynn heard the sound of voices from beyond. A kind of strange, volatile roar that was primal and raw. He shrank back from the sound. And he wasn't the only one.

One after the other, the doors at the end of the polysteel pens opened, emptying each one of its prisoners. Every pen went, until only Flynn's was left. The white jumpsuits. Those without a gang or a crew. It occurred to Flynn then, listening to the roar outside, just how precarious that might be.

The door cranked open. Flynn's heart thudded.

Through the door, he could see more metallic walls. Flynn remembered when he'd worked on the thermal capacitors for GenPop, and he had noted even then how every wall in the level was bare metal. More cost effective. Who cared if the prisoners had wall colors? They were there to die mining Xytrilium.

Flynn was pulled forward as the rail jerked to life, yanking him and the rest of the whites ahead.

When he passed through, the sound was deafening.

A deep, rhythmic thudding filled the interior of the giant metallic room beyond the door, loud and forceful. Flynn could feel it in his chest. The roar of hundreds of voices. Chants of various kinds blended in with and were lost amid the yells and screams.

GenPop was a giant, open level, extending a thousand feet straight ahead. Stretching into the distance, Flynn could see the various sections of the prison level, all designed for the inmates themselves. Food distribution, showers and washrooms, the exercise center, mining preparation, various heat locks, the communal and recreation zones with basketball and starflare courts. All of them divided by the same thick, clear walls of polysteel.

And hanging in the air above it all, as far as he could see, attached end to end on the walls and ceiling, were the cell blocks themselves.

Huge metallic trapezoids suspended in the air, holding sixteen cells each. A massive rack system maneuvered the blocks three dimensionally, up and down the length of GenPop and in and out of one another. Guards could move groups of prisoners using the blocks anywhere they wanted, yet still keep the inmates divided.

Each cell, in every single cell block, had its own polysteel wall that looked out onto GenPop. And the inmates, hundreds of them, stood at those polysteel walls, watching as Flynn and everyone else was jerked inside by their chains.

The eyes of every inmate were on the group being led in now. To Flynn, it felt like they were staring at *him*. They chanted inane slogans and cries, pounded rhythmically against the walls with their fists.

The sound shook the floor. Flynn just kept moving, trying his best not to fall.

The rail stopped them in the middle of GenPop, clicked and hummed, switching to a different track.

The pounding kept coming. The prisoners behind their invisible walls, all of them yelling down at him, jumping and snarling, hundreds of them. His eyes moved from one container to the next, trying to control his fear, trying to fight the urge to bolt, not that there was anywhere to run. He was in GenPop now. This was it.

Then he saw a cell block above and to his left, on the third row at the top of the wall.

His eyes thinned in surprise.

Two female inmates stared back. Red jumpsuits. One's head was a mottled mess of pink and purple, flaring brightly in the harsh light. But Flynn's eyes almost immediately settled on the other woman. Her head was shaved; a thin cover of black was all that was left of her hair. She leaned on her elbows against the clear wall, forehead pressed against the glass. She was too high up for him to really be sure, but it felt like she was staring right at him.

Flynn stared back. There was something about her . . .

"Keep moving," a guard barked. The rail jerked forward again, pulling

Flynn along. The rail moved him and the other whites to the edge of a cell block that had been lowered to the floor. The prisoners in front of him were yanked inside. Flynn followed.

He could feel the cell block sway under his feet as it loaded up new inmates. Faded red symbols were stenciled onto the scratched metal walls between the polysteel doors that led to each cell. The designator of his cell block.

M8.

Flynn watched the inmates detach from the rail and enter cell after cell in pairs. No one had to tell them, they just knew. No one argued their cell or roommate assignments; no one said anything. They just passed through their doors and disappeared.

The rail pulled Flynn forward. He was the last prisoner in line. He came to a stop between two open cell doors. The first cell looked like the others he'd seen: two bunks, lockers, toilet, sink, rusty metal walls, crazy, haphazard scrawling all over them.

The other, though, was very different.

One bed, much bigger than the bunks. Lockers, toilet, sink, like the other cell, but there was also a shower, a desk, empty bookshelves, and a small fridge. The walls were clean and free of ramblings. The sight was so surreal, Flynn froze as he studied it.

"What would you say is the thing that defines a man?" a soft voice behind him asked.

Flynn turned, as best he could, still on the rail. A man stood there, hands in his pockets, studying him inquisitively.

It was the captain of the *Charon*. Braga. Dressed in the same gray uniform from outside. "Genetics? Experience?"

Flynn stared back, thinking. The answer came to him immediately. Most answers did.

"Their choices."

Braga smiled. "Quite right, Dr. Flynn." He spoke Flynn's name and title with familiarity, and it was disconcerting. "Quite right."

EIGHT

CHOICES

Braga walked slowly down the hallway. The cells were all sealed now. No matter how loud the prisoners yelled, or how hard they hit the walls, there was no sound. It was unsettling, watching them scream and pound without any of the noise to go with it.

Braga, for his part, seemed immune to it all. "Did it seem as if the furor outside increased when you entered GenPop?"

The question was blunt and direct, in a tone that implied Braga expected no answer. So Flynn said nothing.

"The yells for the white jumpsuits are always the most energized. The pounding and the yelling, it's more than a random display of fervor. It's done to intimidate you. It's the one time, other than mining X, where the different gangs and syndicates on this vessel cooperate. Personally, I find the affair useful, in that it quickly acclimates new inmates to the reality here. That they are alone, and that this is a very unadvantageous position to be in. Normally, you would have to choose, if you wanted to live. This cell block, for instance, will be empty in a week. The white jumpsuits will have been exchanged for colors."

Braga moved past Flynn, staring into the first cell, the one like all the others.

"Not that long ago, there was an inmate here," the man said. "Much like you. Not equipped to deal with this environment. Not strong. Weak. Easily overcome." Flynn felt a slight sense of anger, but he said nothing. "His cellmate was his exact opposite. And . . . depraved. As many are. The first night he was in this cell, the stronger one began to 'purse' the weaker. It means to dominate. Well . . . that's not exactly right. It means to break someone so completely that they will do whatever they are asked. It means to crush them. Physically, through pain. Through humiliation. Through sexual depravity. Through actions that there are no real words for. Over and over again. Every night. Until all that's left is a shell of the original person."

Flynn tried to keep his composure. It was a fairly accurate summary of every worst-case scenario his mind had generated since his sentencing. It was a tactic, obviously. Not much different from the banging and yelling outside. But that didn't make Flynn feel any better.

"Inmates call that type of person a Skivvy." Braga finally turned and looked at Flynn. "The last time I saw this inmate was in the ship's morgue. He had disconnected his suit and walked through the heat shields outside. It takes fifteen seconds for the rads in the Cindersphere to cook you in your suit. Many people here make that choice." Braga studied Flynn as he spoke. "I could have helped him. Given him protection, a cell transfer, any number of things. Do you know why I didn't, Dr. Flynn?"

Flynn finally spoke. The answer seemed clear. "Because it wasn't in your interest."

A slight smile formed on the captain's face. "He profited me nothing . . . and so to me he did not exist. As you said, life is about choices. I will allow you to *choose* which cell you would like. Pick the one behind me"— Flynn looked past him to the cell like all the others—"and you and I will never see each other again. Choose the other, and you and I will become fast friends."

"As long as it's in your interest," Flynn said, holding the captain's gaze as best he could.

The smile faded from Braga's face. "I wonder, Dr. Flynn, if you have any thoughts on that?"

Flynn made himself slowly stick his hands into his pockets so the captain couldn't see them shake. Maddox's words replayed in his mind.

Whatever deal you offer, you only get to offer once.

Flynn swallowed, thinking fast. One possibility came to mind.

"The *Charon* is a Series Seven SMV." Flynn managed to keep the tremor out of his voice.

"Yes."

"Because of the Rudberg Accord, your heat shields were upgraded to the G4 variant."

"Yes."

"One thing about G4s," Flynn told him, "they use the same BIOS as the G3s. Which means their frequency output can be manually tuned."

At that, Braga's eyes thinned. "There are no controls for that in the admin panel. I would have seen them."

Flynn almost smiled. Braga didn't know everything. "The *BIOS*, not the admin panel. They don't want Crawler captains overclocking their shields; that would exceed the mining regulations. After all, with overclocked heat shields, an SMV could go another fifty, sixty miles into the radiation. The Xytrilium veins you'd find there would be a lot richer."

Richer X veins meant filling the *Charon*'s stores faster, which meant heftier bonuses for Braga.

The captain's hands slipped into his pockets. "And how would one manually regulate the heat shield frequencies on a G4 system?"

"On the regulator outside. You just need a portable monitor tap to access the BIOS."

Slowly, very slowly, the smile returned to Braga's face. "Does this mean, Dr. Flynn, you've chosen your cell?"

Flynn turned and looked behind him, into the solitary cell, at the empty shelving along the wall.

"Books," Flynn said. "I'd like books. And journals. Scientific, engineering. I can be more useful if I stay up to date."

Braga considered Flynn a moment. The glint in his eye was worrisome. Flynn understood. The moment he stopped being useful was the moment he ended up just like every other prisoner on this rig.

But risk, Flynn guessed, was his new reality. And he had ideas on how to extend his usefulness.

Braga hit a button on his wrist control. The chains of the rail clicked as they disconnected from Flynn's ankle bracelets. It was a relief. The captain nodded into Flynn's new quarters.

"Welcome home, Dr. Flynn."

And yet, the words were not comforting. His new cell was nicer than the other, by far. It came with perks. But a cell was still a cell. It still felt like a defeat.

NINE

RAELYN

The generic beeps and tones from monitoring equipment mixed with drums and a bass line and biting, sharp pulses from something that sounded metallic and airy all at once. Maddox could almost remember the name of the instrument. A kind they didn't play anymore.

The strange combination of sounds was jarring. It took a moment for him to remember where he was and why, and when he did he let his eyes blink open. He winced at the room's harsh light. Above him, the same plain, white ceiling tiles. Under him the same bed. The same shackles on his wrists and ankles.

It all came back. The *Charon*. Whistler. The doctor . . .

She was there, standing above and to his right, plugging into a new IV bag the hoses running to his arm. The liquid inside was purple.

Purple. What the hell kind of medicine is purple?

Maybe it wasn't medicine at all, it occurred to him. What had Whistler called the doctor?

Your angel.

Raelyn.

She wasn't looking at him, hadn't seen his eyes force open and blink. Her hair wasn't tied in a bun now; she'd left it free to hang, and it trailed down the lines of her shoulder and upper back. Brown and red, all at once, like a painting.

The music hit hard then, the drums like punches in his gut.

"What is this?" Maddox asked. His voice was impossibly hoarse. It hurt to talk.

The doctor's head turned, slowly, so she could look down at him. Her eyes were just as blue as before. "Hank Mobley. Old Earth." Her gaze made a quick circuit, studying all the parts of him not hidden by his blanket, before returning back to the IV. Her look was odd. She seemed frightened and sympathetic at the same time. "I can turn it off—"

"No," Maddox stopped her, clearing his throat. "My mom used to listen to this."

"Mobley?"

"I don't know. I guess, maybe. Just . . . She said jazz was the only kind of music she could fully concentrate on. Probably why she listened to it whenever she wanted to forget something."

"I know the feeling," Raelyn said. She reached and hit a button on a control panel. The music faded.

Maddox coughed. "Can I . . ."

Raelyn held the straw from a water bottle up to his lips. Maddox sucked the liquid in, drinking heavily, feeling it coat his throat. The water tasted like chlorine and metal but he didn't care. She took the bottle away.

"Doctor?" he asked. He figured she wasn't a nurse. No reason for the scanner on her belt, no reason for the way she articulated every word like it was some kind of medical term.

She studied him thoughtfully. "Couldn't really say any more."

Maddox got it. He'd had titles too, ones he'd cared about. Titles that marked periods of his life, good and bad. They'd all been fleeting.

"Is"—Maddox looked to the purple IV bag—"that it?"

Raelyn tried to hold his stare, but failed. She looked down, past the bed, to the floor. Maddox got that too. The frankness of a man talking to his executioner was more than she could handle, apparently. He felt sorry for her.

"Shouldn't have said anything," he told her. "Makes it harder."

Raelyn shut her eyes tight. "God damn it."

She could lie to him, of course. Tell him it was grape-flavored saline or something. But they both knew that once things got under way the truth would be pretty obvious.

"Saroxetine and Vassalatin," Raelyn said tightly, with more conviction than he expected. She still didn't look at him, though. "It should rapidly deteriorate your arteries and . . . all the surrounding tissue with them. I've—" Her voice broke, but she kept going. "I think it will take three sessions."

Maddox was surprised by the slight apprehension he felt. Three sessions. "Don't guess you could just slip me a tranquilizer?"

Raelyn looked to her left, toward something there. A camera, set up on a tripod, pointing at Maddox on the bed.

It was all the answer he needed. Whistler wanted to watch.

"Why does he hate you so much?" Raelyn asked. Whistler hadn't shared the details with Raelyn, and it said a lot about whatever the big man had on her that he didn't *need* to.

"Because I made him just like everyone else on this planet," he said. "Someone with nothing to live for."

Raelyn's eyes thinned. She opened her mouth to ask more, but the lights in the ceiling flashed off suddenly, plunging everything into blackness.

A single jarring alarm tone sounded inside the medical ward. Maddox could hear it echoing in the halls outside too.

He knew what it meant. The *Charon* was passing through the SMV gate on the Barrier, the giant, fortified wall that sealed off the Cinder-sphere side of the Razor from the rest.

Navigating something as big as a Crawler through the cramped space of an SMV gate was dangerous. All crew were at stations. All prisoners were on lockdown. All noncritical systems were shut down . . . including things like environment lighting inside the medical ward.

Raelyn was just a shadow now, the lights from the medical equipment inside the lab the only source of illumination.

The bed under Maddox rocked slightly as Raelyn gripped it. He could hear her breathing quicken.

"It's normal," Maddox told her. "We're going through the—"

"I know what we're doing," she cut him off tightly.

From above, the sounds of groaning metal echoed through the ship as the giant craft passed through the tight confines.

Maddox studied Raelyn's shadow. "You don't like the dark."

"It's not my favorite thing."

As his eyes adjusted, Maddox saw a new source of illumination. The strange glowing coming from underneath Raelyn's coat sleeve. If she were to slide it up, he knew what he would see.

Thin, vein-like lines curling up the forearm toward her bicep. They would glow and pulse with faint red light, like simmering coals.

"I'm sorry," Maddox said.

"About what? My nyctophobia?"

"The Slow Burn."

Raelyn clamped down on the sleeve of her gray lab coat. The glowing vanished.

"I've seen a lot of it," Maddox said. "Met a lot of synth addicts who weren't—"

"I'm not an addict," she cut him off again.

Maddox paused before answering. He couldn't keep the note of skepticism out of his voice. "Okay."

"I'm *not*." Her tone was insistent. And defensive.

"*Okay . . .*"

Synth was a powerful neurostimulant. Fairly affordable, easily produced, delivered by stealth hypos, it was the drug of choice for users seeking an intense high without much tolerance falloff, and it had spread through the galaxy's slums like wildfire. The downside, though, was its final effect.

Slow Burn.

Synth acted directly on the human somatosensory system by flooding it with neuroreactors. The reactors were synthetic, so the body couldn't break them down; they just clung to the sensory nerve pathways. The more you used, the more the pathways were inundated with synth, until, finally, they overloaded. When that happened the reactors combusted, and the combustion spread through the nervous system. Slowly.

You could see it when it began, under the skin, the pathways all lighting up and burning, slowly spreading as more of the built-up reactors ignited. The reaction spread, and as it did, so did the pain. Real pain.

Maddox had heard it felt like every nerve ending was on fire, and every day, more and more of your body was covered in the glowing vein-like marks as your nerves burned and burned.

Most people killed themselves long before their entire body was consumed.

"Whistler has something I need," Raelyn told him. "And if I don't get it back . . ."

"Things get grim," he finished for her.

"Things get grim," she repeated.

The groaning from outside ceased. The alarm tone went silent. The lights in the ceiling flashed back on, filling the lab with light again.

Raelyn's fists were white, she was gripping the bed so hard.

"You can open your eyes now," Maddox said.

Raelyn did, and looked right at him. Maddox didn't know her story. She said she wasn't an addict, but most addicts said the same thing. And, as far he knew, it was the only way to get Slow Burn.

Maddox didn't know what Whistler had to make her do what she was doing, but what he did know was that if she didn't do it, things would get even worse for her.

"I deserve what he wants you to do," he told her, his hoarse voice taking on a new tone. "In fact, you'll be doing me a favor. So whatever guilt you're feeling, you should just let that go."

Tears formed in Raelyn's eyes. Slowly at first, just a glistening reflection off the harsh lights in the ceiling, before finally leaking out and down her face. She wiped them away quickly, looked at the IV next to both of them, the purple mixture inside.

"Do you believe in second chances?" Raelyn asked, her voice lower, darker.

Maddox cleared his throat. The handcuffs tying him to the bed rattled. "My recent experience is that life is now or never. Do or die."

Her breathing was audible. Quick, long bursts of air. Maddox thought he could almost hear her heart.

Raelyn wiped the tears away. She reached for the camera and flipped it on. A red light flashed as it recorded.

"Session number one, with patie—" Raelyn stopped, correcting herself. "*Subject* Maddox. Administering . . . first dose . . ."

Maddox felt his pulse begin to race, watching her hand move toward the IV.

The line was ready. She just had to turn the flow knob. Her hand hovered over it, shaking. She stared at the IV like it was a viper.

Maddox was actually rooting for her now. For her to turn it on, for her to let the acid flow into his veins and fill him with pain. Rooting for her to finish the job. To give him what he deserved. To end it.

Raelyn's fingers touched the knob. Maddox held his breath.

Her hand dropped away. She shook her head, stepped back from the IV, almost fearfully.

Maddox exhaled. He was so tired. Of everything. "Raelyn, if you don't do this, they'll just send me to GenPop and I'll be dead anyway. And then they'll come after *you*. Whatever you need from Whistler and the Bloodclan, you won't get it. Do you understand—"

"Whistler wants me to kill you because you hurt him somehow." Her voice was venomous now, angry. "But *you* want me to kill you because you're too much of a coward to do it yourself. You don't want to live with whatever it is, but you're perfectly happy letting *me* live with it, aren't you? Letting me live knowing I killed someone to save my own skin."

The words were like slaps—hard, stinging ones. She was right. Maddox hadn't thought of her feelings once.

"They'll just kill you anyway?" Raelyn kept on. "I say, let them." Even before she finished the sentence, she had already turned away.

"Raelyn . . ." Maddox managed, but anything else was beyond him. He didn't know what to say, how to even start.

She didn't look back as the med bay door automatically opened for her, revealing the hallway of the science wing outside.

"You're a real son of a bitch."

She disappeared through the door, and it closed behind her, leaving Maddox alone again. Back in limbo. Back in purgatory.

TEN

TERMINUS

The low-pitched alarm tone finally shut off, the last of it echoing between the shaking metal walls of GenPop.

"Ain't that a sound?" Barnes asked, in front of the line of inmates in the training room. He had his body armor on, but no helmet. Probably so he could enjoy his cigar. The smoke hung around his head in a cloud that followed him wherever he moved. "The Terminus alarm. Gonna fill you with dread, another week or two. Any of you scrubs know why?"

Flynn did, but he said nothing.

The Cindersphere had no clear border. The closest thing was the Terminus, the point where radiation levels became lethal. That line wavered back and forth depending on weather patterns, solar storms from the planet's star, and the geography of the Razor. Now that that alarm had silenced, it meant one thing . . .

"We are inside hell, ladies." Barnes kept going with his speech, an oration he'd probably given hundreds of times yet still seemed to enjoy. "A balmy three hundred and fifty degrees and climbing fast. Another thirty minutes heading west, a gulp of oh-two will melt your lungs, if the air pressure doesn't pop your eyes out of their sockets first."

Barnes looked like he was midfifties, but he was clearly still in shape. Under the armor, Flynn guessed his muscles were as big as any of the prison tough guys'. Black skin, gray hair, face clean-shaven except for two long sideburns that trailed down either edge of his jaw.

Flynn was in a line of inmates, two dozen or so. They all stood shoulder to shoulder, wearing jumpsuits of various colors, listening to Barnes drone on. Flynn's hands were magnetically attached together, hanging loosely at his crotch, but his ankles and legs were free. It was the first time outside of his cell when he wasn't attached to the rail, which was probably the reason for the extra guards.

The training room was at the far end of the Crawler, a big, wide-open space with racks of Maas-Dorian–designed heat suits of different types hanging from the walls. Nearby, Flynn saw mock-ups of extractor and scanner controls, and a roller pod, a heat-shielded and reinforced spherical ATV used for moving around the Cindersphere. Roller pods could survive outside a Crawler's heat shields for an hour or two before the tread melted off the struts.

The equipment, of course, was all designed for one thing.

"Mining X, no bones about it, is the most dangerous thing you will ever do." Barnes blew a puff of smoke down the front of his armor. "You may doubt that, badasses you all are, but you will come to believe. The JSCC grants you *one* training session per piece of equipment. Means you get just one chance to learn what you need to not die, so I'd listen good. Today's lesson is this . . ."

Barnes leaned against a large mock-up of machinery inside the training room, part battle tank, part construction vehicle. A pinpoint miner. Thirty-one and a half feet long, 5,897 kilograms, with a treaded wheel system that pushed a fifteen-foot focused plasma beam generator wherever it needed to go.

Flynn knew it was a mock-up. The beam on a real one would punch a hole straight through the *Charon*'s hull, which is why they were mounted externally, along with all the other dangerous machines the Crawler carried into the Cinder.

"The pinpoint is the one thing none of you idiots get to directly operate," Barnes continued. "Guess no one trusts a convict with a giant, focused beam of atomically ionized gas. Go figure. It gets run from the control deck, by people who didn't murder and steal their way onto this planet. You get to be outside, clearing away all the rock and X crystals so the pinpoint can do its work."

Barnes moved to the rear of the machine. As he did, Flynn risked a look down the line of prisoners. Interestingly, Flynn noted, Maddox, the one he'd met on his first day, was nowhere to be seen.

"So why do you need to know about this thing if you ain't gonna be operating it?" Barnes asked, coming to a stop at the end of the pinpoint. "How about the fact that you have twenty seconds to get clear of the blast site once the coordinates are confirmed. Why twenty seconds? Because that's the most time the JSCC gives their most expendable tools, yourselves. Anything longer, and Maas-Dorian starts losing credits."

Flynn could hear the nervous shuffling from the inmates on either side of him.

"How about that the plasma stream is six feet in diameter? That's wider than most of you are tall. So stand the *fuck* back when it fires. How far back? How about thirty feet? That's the average distance in any direction from a pinpoint hit where the eruption is going to occur. Anywhere in that zone, you're going to take a Xytrilium crystal up the ass. When the eruption ends, you can move back in and start collecting all the highly volatile, newly solidified Xytrilium on the surface. We'll talk about collecting at another session, but—"

"I'm sorry, sir," Flynn cut Barnes off. It had been almost automatic, a leftover from years of design review scrums and pitching executive boards, and he instantly regretted it.

Barnes blinked, confused, studying Flynn like he was some kind of lesser animal, a squirrel or a hamster maybe, that had just discovered the power of speech. "What?"

Flynn swallowed. Too late now.

"The part about being able to move back in once the eruption ends. With the newer plasma beam temperatures, secondary eruptions can continue for up to thirty seconds after—"

"*What?*" Barnes stepped toward him now, pulling the stun baton from his belt. The inmates on either side of Flynn stepped away. The guards on the railing above peered down with piqued interest.

"Look," Flynn said, trying to sound as docile as he could, "I'm not disagreeing, it's just—"

"But you did," Barnes cut him off. "You *did* disagree." The baton sparked in the man's hands. "What else should I know, professor?"

Flynn made himself look at Barnes. "With the wrong information, people could get hurt. That's all I'm saying."

"You're right. They really can . . ."

He felt the sharp pain and spark of the baton as it rammed into his ribs. Flynn fell to the floor.

"Wherever you're from, clear to me you're used to telling people what's what. Well, you ain't *there* anymore."

Flynn groaned again as a kick from Barnes's boot found his stomach.

"You know how many ways there are to die outside?"

Another hit with the baton, more electricity. Pain flared through him. Flynn tried to crawl away, but there was nowhere to go.

"You know how many of those ways I can personally *arrange*?"

Another kick. Laughter from the guards. Snickers from the inmates. Flynn braced himself.

"Do you—"

"That'll do, Trainer."

Everything stopped.

Standing behind Barnes was a guard, her helmet concealing her face. Her voice was low, distorted by the helmet's speaker, but the Colonial accent came through from the other side.

"Now what?" Barnes asked, angry and focused on the guard. Flynn felt thankful for that.

"This one's being pulled off the training line," the guard said.

"Why the hell's that?"

"Because the captain's got other plans for him. And none of the captain's plans are possible if he's *hurt*."

Barnes stared heatedly at the guard through her helmet. "Then get him the fuck out of my sight."

The guard motioned Flynn to stand. It wasn't easy with all the pain, but he made it up.

The guard nodded to her right. Flynn started moving, past the other inmates. Some of them chuckled as he did, or whispered threats. One even spit. But Flynn just kept moving.

Up ahead was where he guessed he was being taken.

Two large pressurized doors, inset into the wall. Flynn knew what it was. The forward deployment zone, one of three areas that held the *Charon*'s heat locks, pressurized and insulated ports for deploying mining teams outside.

"Best policy around here is never show you're smarter than someone else," the guard's filtered voice said behind him as they moved.

Flynn felt his aching ribs. "That's not what it was about."

"Still got you a baton in the gut, didn't it?" the guard retorted. Her voice was different than that of the other guards. There was something more approachable about it. "Most guards take this job so they can feel like big shots, the one place people have to listen to them. Upset that order at your own risk."

"Why did I get pulled off the line?"

"Because you don't need mining training. Because you're special and smart and you found an angle."

Flynn stiffened. The guard sensed it.

"I don't know any details," she continued. "I don't *want* to know any details. Cut a deal with the captain? Good for you."

The pressurized doors in front of them groaned open and they stepped through. As in the training room outside, the walls of Forward Deployment were lined with equipment and heat suits, but these were faded and worn, some even blackened. The real deal.

The guard, however, led Flynn toward another set of pressurized doors. A small window looked in, and faded letters were stenciled across them in yellow.

**CAUTION: PRESSURIZED CONTAINMENT.
HIGH RADIATION. HIGH HEAT.
SHIELDED SUITS REQUIRED BEYOND THIS POINT.**

"The heat lock?" Flynn asked, a little unnerved.

"You're getting trained in heat suits. That's all I know."

It made sense. His arrangement with Braga meant going out onto the hull, the very top of the Crawler, where the heat shield emitters were, and he'd have to do it while the SMV was inside the Cindersphere. It was a crazy scenario, dangerous and foolish, but he'd take it any day over the other cell he'd been offered.

Still, it was a sobering thing, moving into the heat lock.

The doors opened slowly, revealing the small white room beyond. On the other side of it sat another pressure door. A single heat suit hung on a rack in the center of the room.

Flynn and the guard moved inside. The heat lock was cramped, with handles circling the walls for the inmates to hold on to during depressurization. That's all they got, a pair of handles, the only thing to keep them from being sucked out with the rest of the air inside when the pressure vented.

A single light in the ceiling flickered. Flynn's eyes settled on the door at the opposite end of the room. He could almost feel the heat coming off it. The floor under him shook as the Crawler forced itself over something tall and hard outside.

"Wakes you up really quick, doesn't it?" the guard said behind him. "Right outside there, nothing but death."

Flynn blinked and turned to her. She didn't talk like any guard he'd ever encountered. To Flynn, most just seemed like they were looking to find any excuse to beat you down. This one, though . . . she talked to him like he was real, not just someone waiting to burn up or be forgotten.

"Get in," she said, motioning to the suit on the rack. "We'll work on using the door controls."

Flynn grabbed the suit from the rack—and almost fell over when it came loose.

It must have weighed sixty pounds, without the helmet. He couldn't imagine having to work in one, outside, with the heat and the radiation.

He stuck his legs inside, started attaching the connectors and sealers.

"You've done this before," the guard said, watching him.

Flynn shook his head. "No. I'm just familiar with the suit designs."

If that impressed the guard, she didn't say anything, just kept watching as he buckled up. He was feeling less mobile and more constrained by the second.

As Flynn kept strapping on the suit, the woman started disconnecting the ports and plugs that kept her helmet in place.

"You said people take this job to feel on top," Flynn said. "Is that why you took it?"

The last of the connectors come loose from the guard's helmet. There was a hiss of air as the oxygen vented.

"This job?" Her voice was no longer filtered through the helmet, the Colonial accent coming through clear now. When the armor came off, Flynn's eyes widened.

He knew her.

Or rather, he'd *seen* her. His first day. When he was ushered into Gen-Pop with all the fanfare, with the rest of the whites.

She'd been the one he had looked up and found. The woman with the shaved head. Staring down at him.

"Believe it or not," she said, and it was only then that Flynn realized she wasn't a guard at all, "today's my very first day."

She swung the helmet so fast Flynn didn't have time to react. It connected with his head and he dropped in a daze of swirling, buzzing sound. All he could tell was that he was on the floor now.

"How does anyone *breathe* in this thing?" The woman dropped the helmet, rolled her head on her shoulders.

Flynn looked up at her, watched her pull out something wedged into the material between the belt and the armor around her waist. If he'd seen it sooner, he would have known right then she wasn't a guard.

A knife. If you could call it that.

Made of various pieces of things a prisoner might have access to. Toothbrush, a piece of cut metal from an air vent, rubber bands.

Flynn tried to make himself move, to get up, but the girl's boot stepped on his stomach, pinned him back down.

"I know it's kind of a cliché, but that doesn't make it not true." Her voice was soft and casual, the accent thick, and she rubbed a hand over the shaved fuzz of hair on her head. "But this isn't fucking personal."

The knife gleamed in her hand.

ELEVEN

YELLOW LIGHTS

The plan hadn't been simple, but it had worked.

Whenever Flynn was going through mining training, Drake would get Key assigned work duty to clean the carbon filters, a task that would tie her ID up all day in the system. He also got her a guard's outfit, and she'd used it to walk right into the training center and lead Mr. Shit-Out-of-Luck off and inside the heat lock.

Once he was dead, Key would just flush him and the guard's armor out the heat lock, take the maintenance tunnel back to Work Central, and punch out.

It had gone flawlessly so far. So why were her wings itching?

Key took a step toward Flynn, twirling the shank in her hand, watching him crawl away from her slowly, half out of it, hands fumbling underneath him. Key almost pitied the guy.

"Jesus," she spat. "You wouldn't have lasted a month here. It's like I'm doing you a goddamn favor."

"Such . . . a humanitarian . . ." Something about the way he said it, the tone, made her wings itch even more.

There was a humming from behind the walls suddenly.

Key knew that sound, knew what it meant. Her eyes widened . . ."What did you—"

The shank flew out of her hands and slammed into the wall, sticking magnetically in place with a giant spark.

Flynn rolled onto his back with a level of dexterity that showed he wasn't as hurt as she had thought. Key could see what his hands had been doing under his frame. Manipulating the controls on his wrist.

He'd activated the heat lock's EM scrubber, a big electromagnetic wave the room projected to depolarize suits coming out of the Cindersphere. A side effect was that anything metallic inside the lock became a flying hazard. Which made it a pretty good way to get a shank out of someone's hands if you had to.

Flynn, whoever he was, knew heat suits, knew their controls. It would have been impressive, if he hadn't just killed them both.

"You idiot!" Key turned for the door back into Deployment, but Flynn was already on his feet. He slammed into her, and the weight of the heat suit was enough to send them both crashing down. It was also enough to pin her in place. "You *idiot!*"

The heat lock door slammed shut with a heavy thud. Lights flashed in the ceiling. A buzzer sounded.

The heat lock was activated, pressurizing itself right now, and in ninety seconds the other end would open. Even if the air pressure venting didn't rip them right out of the lock, they'd be dead in two or three minutes, cooked alive inside the small metallic space.

"The scrubbers start the heat lock vent," Flynn said, staring at the room with an annoying mix of confusion and curiosity. "Didn't know that."

"Clearly," Key said, pissed off, still pinned by him. The weight of the suit was starting to hurt. She felt the anger build, but it was more at herself than anything else. Flynn wasn't the easy mark she'd figured him for. And now . . .

The EM scrubber whined as it died down. The shank fell to the floor. The buzzers and alarms kept sounding, though.

Flynn looked around, studying the room. Something flashed behind his eyes. An intense focus. He had a plan, she could tell.

He hefted himself off her. "I think you should get your helmet on."

Key stared at him oddly. "What the fuck for?"

"Because we're going outside."

"Outside?" Key was aghast. "The heat shields aren't up."

Not strictly true. An SMV could project its heat shield in a bubble four or five hundred feet around itself when it was stationary, to protect the mining crews on the surface. When it was moving, like now, a Crawler still had its shields up, but they only projected about three feet from the hull.

"Your guard armor's insulated for emergencies," Flynn said, fastening the rest of the clasps on his suit. "If we hug the hull, we'll stay within the shields."

"Hug the *hull*," she replied back, stunned. Who *was* this guy? "Then what?"

He looked at her oddly. "Once you . . . killed me, how were you getting back to GenPop?"

"Maintenance hatch," she said. "A guard gave me filter duty." She could see what he was thinking now. "But there aren't any maintenance hatches on the hull."

Flynn slid the helmet onto his head, muffling his voice. "No, but there *is* a carbon vent from the reactor right above us," he said, fastening the helmet in place, typing on the control panel on his wrist. "We crawl through that, we can reach a maintenance hatch."

"The carbon vent only opens when it needs to purge. How are you—"

"Can you open the hatch if we get inside, or not?"

Key stared at him. "Yeah."

"Then, you know, put your helmet on."

The yellow lights flashed a few more times, then went solid red. The buzzing became a single loud, jarring tone. She only had seconds. Flynn stared at her. She could just see his eyes through the transparent slit of a visor.

"Look, I get it," Flynn's electrified voice said from behind his helmet. "Things didn't go the way you expected. But you're not dead yet."

The moron had a point, she thought.

"Fuck it," Key said, and slammed the guard helmet back onto her head. She felt the blast of air fill up the suit as it pressurized.

Then the exterior heat door opened, and the maelstrom blew inside and almost took her off her feet.

TWELVE

STORM

Even through the polymer-reinforced stitching of the suit and its electro-magnetic protection, Flynn could feel the heat that howled inside the lock.

The gauges in the helmet's HUD all spiked, and the screen flickered before it corrected and adjusted to the intense brightness streaming through the door. And when Flynn looked outside, he forgot to breathe.

He'd heard its description numerous times, seen VRs and holograms, but it was all a pale comparison to the real thing.

The Cindersphere's landscape was burned clean of anything remotely alive. Jagged mesas and canyons stretched into the far distance, red silhouettes against a darker red sky. The star hung far above the horizon now, a giant orb of blazing red energy, and it felt ominous, like it was alive and staring through him.

As a kid, Flynn remembered watching the engines on Jeremiah's ship, staring at the patterns the heat made in the air. Everything in front of him was filled with the same kind of wavering thickness, and it was dizzying.

Inmates called the disorientation "heat goggles," and it was a dangerous phenomenon. Besides the obvious problems—difficulty seeing, having your equilibrium thrown off—the wavering air could also produce a hypnotic effect. Miners had been known to freeze on their feet, staring through the haze. And mining Xytrilium was not a good time to freeze.

"And here I thought we were pressed for fucking time," Key's staticky, sarcastic voice came through his helmet's speakers. She stood right behind him, suited up again in the guard armor. Her posture suggested deep annoyance.

As much as the Cindersphere distracted him, so too did the sight of her. She'd just tried to kill him. With a homemade *knife*. Now he was relying on her to help save his life.

Flynn remembered looking up at her from the bottom of GenPop.

He had a pretty good idea now why she'd been staring at him so intently. But that didn't explain why he'd been staring back, did it?

It also didn't answer the larger question. Why try and kill him? Why go through all this trouble for someone she didn't know? There was really only one explanation, one possibility of who might go through this much trouble.

What'd you think they were gonna do? he asked himself bitterly. *Forget?*

Another blast of heat ripped through his suit. Flynn's gauges showed that the spike had been close to five hundred degrees. His integrity alarm wasn't going off yet, but it would soon.

"The ladder. Outside," he told Key. "It's a hundred-foot climb."

"Is that all?" she shot back. "With the Crawler bouncing everywhere, and radiation gusts?"

"You have a real tendency to look on the glass half empty side, huh?"

"Kept me alive this long. How about we start moving before I suffocate?"

For her, that was a real problem. Flynn had liquid oxygen tanks to keep him breathing. The only air Key had was what was already in her suit.

Flynn turned and pushed through another blast of heat.

The landscape spread out before him dramatically; fire and ash and melting mountains all behind thick fields of shimmering air. It rushed by as the *Charon* thundered over the ground, which, looking down, was very, very far below.

Flynn looked away quickly, his head spinning. He wasn't a fan of heights.

Next to the door, on the hull, the tiny rungs of the access ladder climbed upward. Flynn stared at them and swallowed.

"Christ on a stick, should I go first?" Key's voice again.

Flynn didn't look, just made himself move. He grabbed a rung, put one booted foot on another rung, swung out from the door into the superheated air, and started to climb.

His instruments spiked again. The Crawler's shields were hugging the hull. Not enough to keep him and Key alive for very long. If either of them stuck an arm out, it would pass through the shields and the exposed suit would melt in a few seconds, followed quickly by flesh and bone.

Flynn felt the vibration through his gloves as Key, below him, started climbing. Even without looking, he could sense how much easier this was for her.

Her helmet hit his boot. "Have you not climbed a ladder before?"

"Not on a *moving* SMV," Flynn retorted into his comm.

The integrity alarm on his suit had begun to flash at about the third rung. Eighty-nine percent. His mind did the calculations. Five minutes. That's all he had.

"Fuck me sideways," Key said below him. Her voice was tight, with a hint of fear.

Flynn looked over. The Razor's sun was a giant crimson orb in the sky, and Flynn winced as the HUD darkened itself automatically to compensate. When it did, he saw what Key was talking about.

A huge, swirling mass of haze and flame filling the sky. A hundred miles away, and coming fast.

"Radiation storm . . ." Flynn said in awe.

Back on Earth, when Sol hiccuped it was called a solar flare. But Earth was forty million miles farther away from its star than the Razor. Here, those same kind of flares produced towering, gigantic funnels of lethal radiation and heat that moved over the surface. Dust clouds that would shred anything that didn't have an SMV's protective shield and reinforced hull.

"Move your legs!" Key yelled below him.

Flynn climbed as fast as possible. He could see the temperature and radiation measurements on his helmet's HUD starting to rise.

Looking up, he saw the carbon vent. Another few seconds and Flynn reached it, climbing past to give Key access to it from underneath him.

He looked down and watched her climb. She didn't even seem winded. It was impressive.

A blast of heated air slammed into them, running at the front of the approaching radiation storm. Key cursed as she was ripped off the ladder. Flynn barely managed to hold on, then he, too, flailed when she grabbed his feet.

The shift sent Key slamming into the hull, and she reached out for the ladder. She flailed once, twice, then grabbed hold, yanked herself back onto it.

She stared up at him. Flynn stared back, angry now. "Is it worth it if we *both* die?"

"I don't know," her voice answered in his helmet, "but I'd feel better."

The storm bearing down on them eclipsed the sky. Inside the Crawler, proximity alarms would be going off, prisoners put back on lockdown, crew sealing ports. They had a minute, maybe two, then Flynn and Key were going to be toast.

Flynn pulled himself back up, Key followed after him. They reached the vent. A six-foot-square grille of thick metal, its teeth blackened by the carbon bleed from the X-Core. The edge of it was so black he had to wipe it with a glove, but underneath he saw what he was looking for: four sets of bolts, holding it to the hull.

"Whatever this plan is," Key's voice said in his comm, "I hope it leans to the simplistic side."

Flynn ran a hand along his suit until he found the protective strip on the bottom. He ripped it off, exposing the tubing there, found the pressure hose, then yanked it off too.

The hose jerked as liquid oxygen streamed out of its frayed end. It took Flynn a second to wrangle the thing down. When he did, he held it up to one of the carbon vent's bolts. The white stream shooting out of the hose coated the bolt, flash freezing it. He pulled the hose back, counted to three, then hit it as hard as he could.

The bolt shattered. The grate was coming loose.

Flynn couldn't help it. He looked at Key and smiled through his helmet.

She looked back, decidedly unimpressed. "You're kidding, right?" Key motioned into the distance. The radiation storm had almost doubled in size.

Flynn gripped the hissing hose again. "If we can freeze the bottom bolts, we can bend the edge up to—"

"Fuck *that*." Key took another step on the ladder.

Flynn felt the protective fabric around his suit's alternator and oxygen tanks ripped free. His eyes widened. "Wait, what are—"

Key grabbed the main liquid oxygen hose and pulled hard.

There was a violent rush of air, so loud that Flynn could hear it through his helmet.

The gauges in his HUD spiked. Alarms started ringing. He watched the digital needle for his oxygen begin to sink. White mist sprayed everywhere, filling the view of his helmet.

Key had yanked off his main air supply, and the liquid O_2 was spraying everywhere.

"You psychotic—" He was cut off as Key climbed on top of him, straddling him from behind.

"Hold on real tight, smart guy," her voice told him.

Flynn could feel her body pressed against his back, even through his suit. Normally he might have liked it. But everything he had left to breathe was funneling out into the superheated atmosphere in a white cloud, so the effect was lost on him.

Key held up the main oxygen hose. The plume of liquid coated the vent grate instantly, filling in all the spaces, freezing everything it touched.

His eyes widened as he realized what she was doing.

"I can tell you're about to say something that's gonna fucking bug me." Key's voice stopped him before he said anything. He felt her free hand on the back of his helmet. "So don't." She rammed his neck forward. Hard.

The helmet slammed into the grate. Coated in liquid oxygen, it burst, spraying pieces of frozen, jagged metal everywhere.

"Guess your brain *is* good for something," Key said, as she started to climb over him again.

Flynn scowled. "If you had told me what you were—"

"Aw, don't be fucking hurt. It was a team effort."

He watched as Key shoved herself into the opening, wiggling inside and disappearing.

Once she was in, Flynn started to climb after her, and as he did his eyes glanced down the length of the *Charon*'s massive hull, toward its rear, toward east and the Razor. When he did, he froze. In spite of everything.

Something was there. In the distance, several hundred miles away. Flashing straight into the sky. A bright red, wavering beam of energy.

It stood out even amid the glare coming off Flynn's viewscreen and shone through the heat waves rising from the Cindersphere floor. It was so bright, it might even have shot into orbit.

Everything was forgotten as he looked at the giant pillar of energy in the sky.

His mind raced. He'd never heard of anything like this on the planet. It definitely wasn't naturally occurring. A distress beacon, maybe? But those were satellite transmitted, not visual. Why would the Corrections Council or M-D need—

"Moron!" Key's voice rattled in his helmet, jarring him back to reality. "*Hello?*"

The wind was blowing everywhere around him, threatening to tear him off. Every gauge in his HUD had redlined. He risked another look behind him, and saw the solar storm had consumed the entire horizon.

Flynn shoved himself through the ruined grate.

His suit caught and ripped. Heat burned his skin, and he yelled in pain. But it spurred him forward and he slid inside on his hands and knees.

Key was ahead of him, entering a code into a keypad next to what must have been the access shaft for the carbon vent.

It beeped, then slid open.

In spite of everything, Flynn smiled when he saw her. She'd waited for him. When she could have just left him to burn.

"Sorry you had to cut your sightseeing short," she said, glaring at him through her helmet. Then she dived through the access shaft.

Flame filled everything behind Flynn as the storm hit, rushing toward him. Wide-eyed, he lunged after Key and through the access shaft.

He barely heard it close behind him, sealing out the fireball, and then he was falling and sliding wildly until he finally hit something solid and everything went quiet.

"Ouch," Flynn moaned, rolling over and grabbing the connectors and removing his helmet. The HUD died as he did.

Lying on his back, he opened his eyes, breathing heavy, face covered in sweat and grime.

A figure stared down at him. A man. Short hair combed neatly and parted to the left.

Captain Braga, surrounded by his guards.

Across from him, on her knees, hands behind her head, was Key. Across the room, in the same position, was someone Flynn didn't recognize. A guard, in his armor, but without a helmet. Pale skin, a goatee, balding hair in a widow's peak. He looked terrified.

They'd made it, Flynn realized. They were back in the deployment zone. But staring up at Braga, he didn't feel much relief.

"Dr. Flynn," Braga stated darkly, "I'm so very relieved to see you."

THIRTEEN

ALL

The first time Key killed a man was the day after her eleventh birthday.

Nothing to get a tattoo over, just some synth addict looking for a score. He'd jumped her in an alley behind the starport on Fudomyo, a nice secluded, dark area where she sold her contraband—vids, stims, the occasional external biotech—and even though it had never happened to her before, she'd been ready. You'd be an idiot, selling in a place like that, not expecting to get jumped, so she kept two old single-shot ballistics out of sight. The first was under her messenger bag, but he'd gotten on top of her too fast for her to reach that one. That's why she kept the other one in a storm grate, wrapped in foil to keep the water out.

She'd rammed her hand into the grimy concrete hole while the junkie went for her throat.

The blast from the gun was muffled in his stomach, but it was still messy. Most of what he'd eaten that day splattered across the Dumpster behind them, and he'd slid off her and rolled into a fetal position on the cracked, wet pavement.

She got back to her feet and drew the second gun from under her bag and aimed it right at the junkie's head. She would have pulled the trigger immediately—pulled it, grabbed her merch, and gotten the hell up the fire escape while the shuttles and transports hovered in the airspace above. Except . . . he'd looked at her. And the look made her pause.

There was emotion in his eyes. It looked like . . . relief.

Key got it, even at that age. He'd reached the end. He was grateful. No more running, no more scrounging. No more fear.

Key studied him a moment more, knowing something about it was important. Then she pulled the trigger and ended him right there and grabbed her merch and ran.

Key had a feeling that Captain Braga, staring down at her right now, saw the same look in her own eyes. She hadn't quit. She'd lost, no doubt, but she hadn't *quit*. Now she could be done with it too.

"Your name?" Braga asked. He'd moved close, the guards surrounding her. Alarms were sounding in the deployment zone, the monitors around the room flashing warnings about the solar storm outside. As massive as it was, the effects inside the *Charon* were minimal. The Crawler rocked a little more than usual, but the shields and inertia dampeners were doing their jobs.

"Fuck. You." Key thought she might need to clarify. "*Miss* Fuck You."

The guards tensed. She expected blows from stun batons, boots in her ribs. "Manner teaching," they called it. But none of that happened. Braga just looked past her, to some guard out of her sight line, and nodded.

Someone fell next to her. In his guard uniform.

Drake.

His face bruised and bloody, tears and snot staining his face. They'd worked him over pretty good, even though they didn't need to. He probably gave her up after the first hit.

Braga let the reality sink in, then held something up in his chubby little hands.

The metallic box she'd gotten from the Suit.

The one with the Vid on it, the one with the proposal. Kill Flynn, save Nia. Key felt whatever hope she still had vanish.

Fine. Fuck it.

"Guard Sergeant Drake was attempting to destroy this box when we found him," Braga said, his voice severe. "The recorded video, whatever it was, had deleted itself, but the guard sergeant was forthcoming. He says you were offered a contract by an off-world third party. A contract to kill Dr. Flynn."

Across from her, Flynn kept looking between the captain and her, as if he was trying to figure a way to get them out of this. He was smart, no question, but he didn't know shit about how the galaxy worked. All *he* had to do was keep his mouth shut, but there was no way out of this for her.

"I would like to know more about the contents of this message," Braga said.

Key cleared her throat. "I already told you my name. You want me to repeat it?"

Braga smiled thinly, nodded again. A pulse pistol appeared next to Drake's head. He whimpered and shut his eyes.

"I don't imagine," Braga continued, "that threatening the guard sergeant would encourage you in any way to reveal the details of the video?"

Key held it together. "Wow. I mean, if the situation wasn't what it was, I'd probably laugh out loud."

"As I figured." Braga nodded again. The blast from the pulse pistol rang in Key's ears. Flynn jumped.

Blood sprayed all over the floor. Drake collapsed in a quivering heap right next to Key. For her part, she barely flinched, just kept holding Braga's eyes. Executions weren't anything she wasn't used to.

The captain took a few steps to his left, studying the ceiling as he talked. "That was an illustration of the seriousness I attribute to this moment. It will help for what is to come."

Key could hear the door to the deployment zone slide open. Heard boots on the floor, someone being shoved forward. Saw Flynn's eyes thin in confusion.

For the first time in the encounter, her wings itched.

There was a spark from a baton and a dull thud. Someone collapsed beside Key. She didn't have to look to know who it was. She caught a glimpse of short pink and purple hair.

Key felt her veins turn to ice.

"Let's begin again," Braga said, and this time the tone had a singular lack of patience. "Your *name*."

"You can go—" Nia began, snarling, but Key quickly cut her off.

"Key," she interjected quickly. The girl had to stay quiet. Maybe there was still a way. Not for herself, but maybe for Nia. After all, she hadn't even known about this.

Braga nodded slowly. His eyes drifted down Key's red jumpsuit, dirty and frayed from the experience outside.

"Red," he noted, almost bored. "Ice pirates out of Norstar. There were more of you once. What happened to them?"

Key felt anger and shame, but forced it down. The only hope Nia had was for her to stay focused. "Two joined Grimm. Three more got shanked."

"That's out of order, I believe," Braga said. "Three were killed, and when it became clear you were incompetent as a leader, the others left. Am I right?"

Key's fists clenched at her side.

"Am I *right*?"

"Yeah," Key said in a low voice. "Spot on, mother fucker."

"What was the deal you made with the third party on this Vid?"

Key said nothing. She had no idea if telling this bastard the truth would help or hurt Nia's chances.

"This one has Lucord's." The voice was one of the guards behind them.

Braga's gaze shifted to Nia. "What stage?"

Nia stared back defiantly at the captain.

"Two, probably," she spat, "you fucking shithead."

The girl rocked forward as a baton slammed into the back of her neck. Another kick sent her all the way to the floor. Key shut her eyes. The situation was spiraling.

"Ah," Braga said, still bored. "So you were offered Doxypaxoline-190 in exchange for killing Dr. Flynn."

Key couldn't guess what Flynn might be feeling, but who cared? He knew the score the moment she led him into that heat lock. There weren't many surprises left.

"I have no real compassion for your situation," Braga continued, looking back at Key, "but I do admire your tenacity. Unfortunately, rules were broken today. Serious ones. And that cannot go unpunished. How severe the punishment, however, depends on how cooperative you are."

The guards moved for them. It took three to hold Nia down. Key didn't move, even when their hands grabbed her shoulders. She just stared at Braga.

"She didn't have anything to do with this," Key moaned.

"What does that matter?" Braga asked back. "I'll ask again. Who hired you?"

"I don't know," Key answered. She could hear her voice crack.

Braga nodded to the guards. Nia fought hard as they dragged her away, toward the heat lock.

Nia, who used to steal her socks. Nia, who'd only had time to see the worst of the galaxy. Nia . . . who was the last of those Key had gotten thrown into this hellhole, the last she'd failed. Shame and guilt blossomed in her stomach.

"He didn't say his name!" Key cried desperately, eyes moving between Braga and Nia. "He wouldn't even say *my* name, why would he tell me *his*?"

"Why, then?" Braga asked. "Why so much effort to kill *one* prisoner?"

"I don't know . . ." Key's voice was almost a whisper now.

"Put her in," Braga ordered. Nia screamed, tried to bite the leg of a guard as he shoved her through the heat lock door, but her teeth couldn't get through the plate. They kicked her hard, collapsed her on the floor. A guard stood at the control panel, ready to seal the door.

It was going to happen, Key realized. She was going to fail again. And this time, she'd get to *watch*.

"*Please!*" The frustration and fear boiled over. "I can't lose them *all*!"

The exclamation surprised even her. She locked eyes with Nia, on the floor of the heat lock. The look the girl gave her back was sympathetic. Which only made the pain worse.

"Oh, my dear," Braga said quietly. "You most certainly can." He held Key's eyes another weighted moment . . . then nodded to the guard at the control panel.

"Wait!" It was a new voice, one that had been silent until now. The last voice Key expected. Flynn's voice.

Braga, the guards, Key, even Nia, bleeding inside the heat lock, turned toward Flynn, on his knees in the center of the room.

"I'll tell you," he said, more calmly than Key expected. More calm than anyone else. "Just don't kill her."

"Don't . . . kill her?" Braga slowly turned to face Flynn. "They were both behind the attempt to kill *you*. You do understand that?"

Flynn nodded. "I have a feeling this place makes people do really desperate things."

Braga considered Flynn. And he seemed . . . disappointed. "Speak."

"It was probably an aerospace firm," Flynn said. "Gemini or Corinth Logic, if I had to guess."

Braga's eyes thinned. "But you worked for Maas-Dorian."

Key raised an eyebrow. Maas-Dorian? The ones who owned the lovely hellscape outside the *Charon*? The most powerful corporation in the galaxy?

"The last thing M-D wants is me dead," Flynn told Braga.

"Why?"

"Because then all my patents revert to public domain."

Braga's head cocked on his short neck. That meant something to the captain. Key, however, was totally lost.

"If a competing corporation were to kill you," Braga stated, thinking out loud, "then they could use your research as they wished. Research, I assume, that is highly lucrative." Braga nodded, as if it made sense to him.

"Right," Flynn said, his eyes shifting from Braga to Key. "She didn't have a choice. It's not her fault."

Key studied Flynn. Those were the last words she expected to hear from someone whose throat she'd been planning to slit less than an hour ago. Whoever Flynn was, he wasn't much like anyone she'd met before. It didn't matter, though . . .

"No, Dr. Flynn, you're right," Braga stated. "It isn't her fault. It's yours." Braga looked at the guard running the heat lock . . . and nodded one last time.

Flynn's eyes widened as the guard keyed in the sequence on the controls. "What? *Wait!*"

Braga studied Flynn almost pityingly. "I did tell you, Dr. Flynn, that our relationship would be built on trust. That wasn't strictly informational, I'm afraid. It was . . . a warning."

Key tried to get to her feet, but her body jolted hard as the electricity from a baton lanced through her.

She tried again, but her muscles were done. She just fell to the floor.

Nia looked at her over the distance. Key looked back.

"No one else can be what you can be," Nia said, holding her gaze. Key stopped breathing. The words were unlike anything the girl had ever said before. She had no idea where they'd come from.

And she never would.

The door to the heat lock slammed shut. Yellow lights began to flash in the ceiling as the pressurization process began inside.

Key didn't move. She just shut her eyes. She wanted to die.

"You're a monster," she heard Flynn say somewhere close by.

"Yes," Braga replied. "And now we have a new conundrum. Our arrangement is in question. Whoever wants you eliminated will likely try again. That means more resources to keep you protected, and I'm unsure if that would be worth the effort. It's all become quite complicated, hasn't it, Dr. Flynn?

Key kept her eyes shut. She didn't want to see the yellow lights on the ceiling turn red. The sign that the lock was open. The sign that Nia was gone.

"I grew up on Dermeer," Braga said casually. "One of the older colony worlds, far away from its star. Very, very harsh winters. Colonists there use dog sleds for short trips in the snow. It's actually more efficient than firing up a shuttle or snowcat. My father raised his own dogs, and I remember one of them . . . well, it just wouldn't do its job. It wouldn't pull the line. It didn't have the heart, I suppose."

Key could hear Braga's feet move as he spoke.

"Do you know what my father did? He put it and one of the older, sicker dogs in a pen by themselves. He turned the heat off. He left them there while the temperatures dropped. It was days before enough hunger set in, but when it did, that dog, the weak one . . . it *killed* the other. Killed and ate it. After that, whenever it was hooked up to the line, that dog *pulled*. With *all* its strength. It better appreciated what it *had*."

Something metallic skittered across the floor. Key's eyes opened. She saw the shank, the one she'd brought to kill Flynn, come to rest in front of Flynn's knees. He looked down at it uncertainly.

"Restrain them both," Braga said as he turned and walked back toward the exit. "And restrain them *together*. Give Dr. Flynn the knife. When there's only one of them left, send me word."

And then Braga was gone. Flynn looked up from the shank to Key. She stared back, tears forming in her eyes.

Beyond them, the yellow lights stopped flashing. They turned red. There was a slight rumble as the heat lock opened on the other side, and what remained of the solar storm ripped inside and tore whatever was there into flaming pieces.

FOURTEEN

SHANK

Flynn walked through a landscape on fire. His feet were burning coals underneath him, flames blazed everywhere he could see.

Through the fire was a figure.

Flynn recognized him immediately.

Jeremiah. His father.

Wearing the same leather jacket he always did, the one that hid the ballistic 10mm he always wore.

The heat and the radiation from the massive sun in the sky didn't seem to touch him.

"Boy," Jeremiah said. It seemed like ages since Flynn had heard his voice. "You got darkness in you, no matter what you say. You wanna survive here . . . you gotta let it *out*."

Something appeared behind Jeremiah then. Something in the sky beyond the flames.

A giant, red column of energy, shooting straight upward. Powerful and bright. Flynn stared at it, curious, confused.

"You belong here, kid," his father said. "You always did."

Then Jeremiah's face began to melt.

Flynn's eyes snapped open and he winced from the pain in his head. They'd beaten him good, once Braga left.

Just a trickle of orange seeped in from the bottom of what looked like a large door near his feet. And sound echoed everywhere. Pressurized hisses, the grinding of metal on metal, explosive, percussive hammering. One loud noise after another.

He rolled over on his side, trying to study the small, square room as his eyes adjusted. He could just make out pipes, vents on the walls, and a glowing readout panel in the ceiling. The room rocked as the *Charon* hit uneven terrain outside.

"Who's Jeremiah?"

Flynn startled. It was Key's voice.

She sat next to him, cross-legged, back against the grimy wall. Her eyes were closed, but she was lightly hitting the back of her head against the wall, over and over. The sound of it blended in with all the others.

"What?" Flynn asked.

"Kept saying his name," Key said, continuing to hit her head.

Jeremiah. His father. The dream from before played vaguely in his mind. He remembered the red beam of energy. It had looked like the same thing he saw outside the *Charon*, in the far distance, toward the east.

"All the fucking noise . . ." Key moaned. She meant the mechanical sounds all around them.

Where were they?

Flynn sat up from the floor and immediately felt something strange on his left wrist. Something cold and heavy hung from it, and he pulled his arm back. Whatever it was bit into his skin, and Key's right arm was jerked toward him at the same time.

"Please don't," Key said testily, without opening her eyes, continuing her rhythmic assault on the back of her skull.

Flynn figured it out then. He was bound to her, handcuffs on their wrists, linked by heavy chain.

At Flynn's feet, something shined slightly in the light from the glowing ceiling panel. It was the knife from earlier, the one Key had intended to kill him with. The guards had left it. He felt a chill remembering Braga's last words.

When there's only one of them left . . .

Flynn looked at her, next to him, the chain binding them running along the floor. He guessed it let them have a maximum of four feet between them. It would keep them close.

"So who is it?" Key asked again. "Jeremiah."

"My father," Flynn said.

"He an uppity prick too?"

Flynn frowned. "Actually, he was a lot like you."

He studied the room again, listened to its sounds, looked at the pipes and conduits and vents and flashing panels. He realized where they were, and it made little sense.

"I thought we were in solitary."

"We are," Key replied.

"This is the engine level," Flynn said.

The sounds were consistent with the *Charon*'s massive mechanical infrastructure. Positron hydraulics, Xytrilium distributors, carbon gearing.

"Braga made the storage closets on this level into *special* solitary," Key clarified sarcastically. "He thinks all the noise, twenty-four seven, makes it more torturous. He ain't wrong. People come out of here very different than when they went in."

Flynn listened again to the sounds, feeling the vibrations, imagined having to cope with it for days on end. Unable to sleep. Unable to think.

"I can show you how to do it," Key said, her voice a different tone now.

Flynn blinked, uncertain.

"So it's quick," she clarified. "Otherwise, you'll bleed me out or hit a nerve cluster or some other dumb-ass thing. No disrespect, but it's obviously not your specialty."

Flynn realized she meant the knife. She meant using it to kill her. He felt a weird, misplaced sense of defensiveness. "I bet I can figure it out."

Key smirked. "What are you in for anyway?"

"Murder," Flynn said pointedly.

Key snorted. "You never killed anyone in your life."

Flynn couldn't help it. He was more than a little offended. "Why do you think that?"

"First time you kill someone—I mean on purpose—it's in the eyes." She paused. "That's not totally right. I mean . . . the eyes *lose* something. And you can see it's gone." She kept hitting her head against the wall. "Still there, in yours. You've never killed anyone. But you're gonna have to if you wanna survive. I'll show you how."

Flynn stared at her. His mouth moved to respond, but he couldn't think of anything to say back to that.

"What are *you* in for?" he managed, still flustered.

Key's eyes finally opened. She looked at him and smiled. "*Everything.*"

The smile was disconcerting. Flynn studied her eyes, looking for the missing piece. They just looked like any other set of eyes to him.

"Why did you help me?" Flynn asked. "You knew there wasn't a way out. You knew you were screwed either way."

Key shook her head, annoyed. "See? This is what I'm talking about. It's not a *knife*. It's a *shank*. You gotta start learning what's what. You're not on Earth anymore."

"You didn't answer the question," he pointed out.

"Why did I help? Fuck if I know," Key said, and looked down. "Maybe I'm just a prideful bitch that doesn't like the idea of losing, even though being on this Crawler means I already have. Or maybe I just didn't have anything better to do right then."

Flynn's eyes moved to the knife on the floor, just visible in the dim light.

"They said I killed someone," he said out loud as he studied the knife. "But I didn't. You're the only person who ever believed me, and I didn't even tell you."

"So, what? You got framed?" Key asked. "Because of what you told Braga? Your stupid patents?"

Flynn nodded. They did seem stupid now. "I had a new one. I hadn't filed it yet. I was going to take it and start my own firm."

"You scared them," Key said. "So they put a gun in your hand."

Flynn looked up at her, surprised.

"What?" Key asked with a sneer. "Shocked the punk lowlife gets corporate intrigue? Fuck off. Slums on Mars, shiny-ass boardrooms in a place like Maas-Dorian—it's all the same. People want power. All they can take. What people *don't* want is competition. And you were gonna be competition. So now your ass is here." She closed her eyes and started tapping her head into the wall again. "You're just like everyone else. How's that feel?"

Flynn had never met anyone who spoke as bluntly as Key. Everyone in his world kept their real thoughts under wraps, either for fear of offending someone or because they were playing an angle. Key, for all her faults, had no interest in angles, and she definitely didn't care about offending anyone. Odd as it was, Flynn liked her. A woman who had tried to kill him.

And now he was supposed to kill *her.*

The idea of it, that to survive here Flynn would have to actually do the thing he'd been accused of, that after everything, the people who framed him would really and genuinely make him a murderer, made Flynn angry. Angry in a way he hadn't been since any of this began.

"No," he said and kicked the knife away from him. "I won't do it."

"You have to," Key said with intensity. "Braga means what he says."

Flynn shook his head. "I'll figure something out."

"No. You'll die. Take the shank."

"*No.*"

Key's eyes slimmed. "Take the goddamn shank—"

"Why?" Flynn could hear the edge in his voice. He was even angrier now. "What's this really about? Get me to do it because *you* can't?"

Key's expression changed, deflated into something duller and darker. She stared at him dangerously, but Flynn didn't care.

"You talk like a badass," he kept going, "but the truth is you're just as scared as everyone else. Just as scared as *me*. What did you mean before? 'I can't lose them all'?"

Key tensed. "Stop."

"Who? All the other red jumpsuits? Your gang? That girl, Nia, she was one, wasn't she?"

"Stop . . ."

"You sit there feeling sorry for yourself and want me to put a knife in you to make it all stop."

"Shut the fuck—"

"And you'll even show me *how*, so it doesn't *hurt* so much! Yeah, you're the real deal, Key. *I'm* not special? Screw you. *You're* not spe—"

Key lunged forward so quickly Flynn didn't even have time to react. She slammed into him, the chain that connected them rattling, and drove him to the ground.

Her hand reached out, grabbed the knife from the floor and held it to his throat. Flynn froze, eyes wide.

Key's eyes were filled with fury—and with pain.

"You don't know anything," Key snarled, knife in hand. "You don't know *anything*. I *told* them when we got here. I *warned* them . . ." Her voice seemed to deflate then. The grip on the knife lessened. "Mace was gone. They took him . . . wherever they took him. So they trusted *me*. Like I knew what I was doing. Like *anyone* knows what to do in a fucking place like *this*." Her voice turned bitter again. "Yeah, they're all gone. You're right. Every one of them. So just take the fucking knife . . . and do it."

Key turned the knife in her hand and held it out to Flynn, still on top of him. Her eyes looked desperate.

Flynn studied the knife, then looked back up at her. "I thought it was called a *shank*."

Key's green eyes refocused on him. She shook her head. Her eyes glistened. "You won't survive here."

"You're probably right," Flynn admitted.

He looked around at the dismal room, felt the cuff on his wrist attaching him to Key. The dim orange light from under the door wavered on the metal walls.

"I've been telling myself since I got here that this won't be my life, but . . . it is. Isn't it?"

Key's eyes studied him behind an unreadable expression. There was no way to know what she was thinking, but the anger was gone now. She just seem tired. And sad. Slowly, she rolled off of him, let the knife fall to the floor.

"Yeah," she said in a low voice. "It is." The chain linking them rattled as she lay down next to him. Flynn could hear her breathing. "But if it makes you feel any better, it's my life too."

Flynn found, to his surprise, that it did . . .

A blast of sound suddenly filled the room.

An alarm tone. A loud one.

Blue lights in the ceiling lit up. They flashed strobically, bright and piercing, in time with the jarring alarm tone.

Flynn and Key looked at each other, stunned and confused.

And then the automatic door in the wall groaned and hissed as its hydraulics slid open.

There were no guards outside. No movement at all. Just more blue lights in the hall.

Their cell was open. And there was no indication why.

FIFTEEN

DEALS

Maddox was torn from his sleep by an abrasive high-pitched sound that felt like a drill bit boring into his head.

When he snapped open his eyes, he saw that it was the heart rate monitor from one of the beds next to his. Raelyn was there, in her scrubs. So was a nurse.

They were working on someone. Maddox couldn't see who it was, other than that his lower half was covered by guard armor. The way his hand hung limply off the gurney, and the dire tone from the monitor, suggested he wasn't doing well.

Raelyn pumped on his chest a few more times, then tore off her surgical mask and took a step back.

"Should we . . . call it?" the nurse asked. She was young, barely twenty, had already let the pressure off the man's wounds, what was left of his life flowing freely out now, while the cardiac alarms kept sounding.

Raelyn exhaled. "What for?" She threw her gloves in a waste bin. "Go clean up."

"Yes, Doctor," the nurse said, turning and moving for the door. As she did, the girl's eyes found Maddox's. Fear played in them. "He's awake."

Raelyn turned to him as the door slid shut behind the nurse. The two stared at each other.

"Bad day?" Maddox asked. His voice was still hoarse, but the fluids he was getting seemed to have helped.

"Dead inmates go straight to the morgue," Raelyn said, her voice tense. "But when a guard gets killed, they send them up here anyway. Protocol. And I work on them every goddamn time."

"Why?"

"Because my first patient here was an engineer who got himself chewed up in a set of turbine blades. Total flatline, severe trauma, but you have to try. So I tried. Life support, agitate the heart, twenty cc's noxycyline. Two seconds later, he's breathing. Floundering around like no one told him he was supposed to be dead. Sealed him up, took off the limbs. M-D employee, so he gets biotics free of charge. Guy still works in a supply depot somewhere. Running autoloaders. So now, every time they send me a flatline, I think about *that* guy. I mean, who knows? If I hadn't seen that, my first week, maybe I'd just not try. Like every other doctor on this planet."

Maddox looked at the body on the table. "Who was that?"

Raelyn rubbed her eyes wearily. "Guard sergeant. Name was Drake. That's all I know."

"Inmate killed him?"

"Last time I checked, inmates didn't carry pulse weapons."

The door to the med bay slid open again, revealing two guards, these very much alive. Their helmets were off, and their eyes both went to Maddox as they entered.

The guards were about the same height, but one was clearly older. He had the same military-style short-cropped hair most guards had, only his was almost completely silver, and his hazel eyes were cold and without emotion.

The younger one could have been his clone—same haircut, same build, a twenty-year flashback. They walked into the med bay without even using the intercom, just overrode the security protocol to the room.

"Doctor," the older guard said, almost monotone.

Maddox recognized his voice. It was the one who'd spoken when Whistler was here. They were Bloodclan dogs. Bought and paid for. And Maddox only needed one guess why they were here.

"Paying your respects, York?" Raelyn asked, moving out of the way of the table.

The eyes of the older man shifted to the dead guard. He shrugged and moved farther into the med bay with his younger clone.

"All kinds of deals on this planet," York said. "Not my problem someone makes a bad one. But you know what *is* my problem? You. *You* made a deal. When you agree to something, you follow through. You don't, it creates complications. It's the only rule that matters on the Razor."

"I don't care what your boss thinks," Raelyn said harshly. "If Whistler wants him dead so bad, he can do it himself."

The guards just kept looking at Maddox, and he could see it in their eyes. A tension, a gearing up. Things were about to get violent.

"But that wasn't the deal, Doctor." York said impatiently. "The deal was *you* would kill him. You agreed."

Maddox watched the younger guard move to the room's main control panel, near the door. He held up his hand, accessing the security protocols, which materialized in the air as a holopanel. His fingers typed on the illusory buttons. Seconds later, the illumination flashed off in the room, replaced by red emergency lights, the various control panels flickering and dying.

"What are you doing?" Raelyn asked, her eyes thinning.

What they were doing, Maddox could tell, was disconnecting them from the *Charon*'s network. Anything that went on in here now wouldn't be monitored. They were completely cut off.

"I don't think you get how things work here, Doctor," York said.

The back of his hand arced outward. Raelyn gasped as it struck her. She almost fell.

Instinctively, Maddox tried to rise, but the shackles and the pain shoved him right back down.

"*Raelyn*," he said. "Just do what they want."

The advice seemed lost on her. The sting from the slap had infuriated Raelyn. She flung herself right at York, clawed and hit, kicked too. If it wasn't futile, it would have been impressive, but her blows didn't do much against the guard armor.

The younger guard, meanwhile, moved to Maddox. "Been looking forward to this all day."

Maddox saw it coming, but he couldn't even raise his hands to block. The kid's armored fist punched Maddox in the face. Then punched again. The world went fuzzy.

One of the guard's hands grabbed Maddox's throat, pinning him to the bed. The other slammed into his stomach, knocked the air out of him.

"Let me go!" he heard Raelyn yell, furious. Maddox could see her struggling, but it didn't last long. A few more hits from York calmed the doctor down. Then he grabbed her by the hair and shoved her forward.

"Do what you said you'd do," York said, slow and pointed. "Either that or I kill you and put a slug in his head myself."

"And how would that look?" Raelyn asked venomously, breathing hard. It was the wrong question, Maddox knew.

"On the *Charon*?" York's voice had a hint of amusement in it now. "It would look just fine. Rat Fink gets loose, kills his pretty doctor. We got here too late. No one gives a damn."

Maddox breathed as best he could with the younger guard's hand on his throat, squirming, trying to get free. Through a haze, he saw Raelyn, hair in York's palm, look up at him.

It was in her eyes. Maddox saw it, clear as day. He couldn't speak, could barely breathe, but he shook his head anyway. Trying to signal her to stop. Pleading with her with his own eyes. She was going to do something very, very stupid . . .

"*Do it,*" York told Raelyn, scowling, breathing into her ear. His grip tightened on her hair. "Do it now."

"Fine," she said, still holding Maddox's gaze. "He's a piece of shit anyway."

Raelyn groaned as York pulled her close. "I mean it. Don't fuck with me."

"You want it done? Then let me go. Stick around and watch if that's what it takes."

York held her close a moment longer, then let her loose. Raelyn slowly, painfully, stepped toward the IV, the one with the purple liquid, the lethal concoction Raelyn had made just for Maddox and that was still wired into his arm.

Maddox still couldn't speak, just shook his head as hard as he could. Raelyn ignored him.

Through the blurry haze, Maddox saw the doctor do the exact thing he'd feared she would.

She whipped something out from her lab coat—and jammed it into York's neck.

An autohypo.

York yelled in pain, cursed, yanked the needle from his neck, then full-on punched Raelyn in the stomach. She staggered back and crashed through a table full of supplies.

It was too late, though.

Whatever was in the hypo, it was strong. York's knees buckled and he fell forward, grabbing for Raelyn. The two of them collapsed onto the floor of the med bay in a heap.

"Fucking . . . *whore* . . ." York moaned, grabbing the doctor, pulling her under him.

The younger guard stared at the whole thing, surprised, caught off guard.

Maddox felt the hand on his throat loosen and lift off.

His vision returned. So did oxygen.

Maddox's hands were shackled, but he had just enough slack to grab the wrist of the younger guard. He twisted inward, a tai chi move, and snapped the kid's wrist.

The kid yelled and tried to pull away, trying to get loose, jerking the gurney back with him. The whole bed tipped and fell over.

When it slammed to the floor, it crashed right on top of the kid. He yelled in pain as the weight clipped his kneecaps, pinning him.

Maddox saw that Raelyn was still struggling with York. Whatever she'd hit him with had had its effect, he was fading, but he was still stronger. He'd pinned her, hands circling her throat.

"Whore . . ." he breathed weakly.

The railing of the bed, where it was attached to his shackles, was broken from the impact. Maddox ripped what was left of it loose and grabbed the guard's wrist, pulled it toward the pulse pistol on the kid's belt.

The guard resisted, even with the snapped wrist, groaning in pain.

The kid reached for the IV bottle, on the floor now with everything else. The one with the purple liquid, the tubes running right to Maddox's veins.

The guard's fingers found the knob on the IV bottle, brushed it, turning it, slowly . . .

Maddox shoved the kid's hand downward, forced it onto the pistol.

The holster beeped, acknowledging the biometrics, and a light glowed green. The gun came loose.

Maddox ripped it free, twisted it, used the kid's hand to pull the trigger. The gun flashed.

Blood painted the walls. The kid went lifeless.

Maddox raised the gun back up, toward York, still on top of Raelyn.

The older guard froze, staring at Maddox over the distance. Maddox stared back.

York opened his mouth to talk. "Now look—"

The gun fired again. York's blood sprayed everywhere. His body tumbled off Raelyn, slid to the floor, then went still.

Raelyn gulped great gasps of air, breathing again. She looked over at Maddox with wide eyes. Maddox looked back.

Two guards dead, blood all over the walls. There weren't many ways to spin this. They could come up with a story, but the only ones that would work, involved him taking the blame. That was fine. But they had to do it quick. Who knows who would have heard the shots.

Maddox coughed, pushed away from the bed, trying to get the weight off his ribs. "Reconnect the med bay to the network."

Raelyn stood up, moved for the control panel near the door and the floating holo display next to it. She tapped it. And when she did, alarms suddenly blared to life inside the med bay. Triple pulses of short, high-pitched sound. Lights flashed in the ceiling, bright and sharp, in exact time with the alarm.

The lights were *blue.*

A protocol alarm, ship-wide, and who knew how long it had been going off.

"Is that for us?" Raelyn asked. "They're coming?"

Maddox shook his head. "York disconnected the room. Whatever it is, it happened while we were logged off."

The blue lights kept strobing in the ceiling.

Maddox's brow furrowed. *Blue* lights . . .

He'd only heard one mention of blue-coded lights during Ranger training, from the very back of a small, forgotten chapter of the field manual. It couldn't be that . . .

"On the screen," Maddox instructed, "at the top, there should be a protocol warning."

Raelyn looked back at the control panel. She swiped the holo display. It flashed.

"Lost Prophet," Raelyn said. Maddox felt a rock form in his stomach. "It says Lost Prophet."

SIXTEEN

LOST PROPHET

Flynn and Key stared in confusion at the open door to the cell. There was nothing but shadows and flashing blue lights beyond, while the alarm kept on blaring.

It had been a full five minutes, and no one had come through. No guards. No engineers. No inmates. No one.

"Never seen blue lights before," Key said, a strange note in her voice. "Never even *heard* of them."

Neither had Flynn. He knew the default color codes on the SMVs from his days at M-D. Red for fire. Yellow for decompression. Orange for heat shield failure. Blue wasn't one of the originals, which meant it had been added to the *Charon*'s systems after the fact. But for *what*?

"Let's go," Flynn said, starting to move toward the door. The chain linking him with Key went taut, and yanked him to a stop before he got moving.

Key stared at him like he was insane. "*What*?"

"What else are we going to do?"

"Stay the fuck *here*. Do you realize where you are?"

"Engineering."

"*Solitary* engineering," Key corrected pointedly. Whatever she was implying was lost on Flynn. "Idiot, if *our* door is open . . ."

Flynn got it then. She meant it was possible the door of any other prisoner who was in solitary was open as well.

"We can't reseal the door," he told her. "Would you rather be boxed in, or able to run?"

"I'd rather not be chained to *you*."

"The feeling's mutual, but that doesn't change the facts."

Key frowned, but after a moment she got to her feet with him. Together they moved toward the door.

When they looked outside, there was no movement in the hall. Just the flashing blue lights and the jarring alarm.

"See?" Flynn quipped. "All clear."

Then the floor and the walls shook around them. Hard. Flynn almost lost his footing from the vibrations that rattled through the bulkheads.

"That was a goddamned explosion," Key stated, staring up at the ceiling.

Flynn felt the inertia of the shock move downward. It had to be an explosion. From *above*.

Flynn headed quickly down the hall and Key followed, the chain rattling between them. He was pretty sure he knew where he was—a maintenance hallway off one of the third-level engine compartments. Another few steps confirmed it as they stepped into a large room.

Rumbling hydraulics and gears towered over Flynn's head, connected to three massive shafts of metal that spun in the dark, passing through holes in the bulkhead. Those shafts were turning the Crawler's giant wheels outside, and they were turning very fast. Whatever was going on, the *Charon* was moving at full speed.

They were in one of the drive shaft maintenance pockets, where engineering crews could access and tune the SMV's gigantic differential system. In addition to the hydraulics and spinning gears, there were rows of computer terminals, the monitors all flashing and showing different data, the only other source of light in the room besides the flashing blue lights.

The *Charon* rocked again, and Flynn struggled to hold on. Another blast, this time from underneath.

"What the hell's going on?" Key asked, unnerved. There was no one else here, no engineers or crew. It was eerie.

They moved to the terminals and Flynn scanned them. He tapped on the first screen he came to, scrolling until he found the General Ship Status menu. The user interface was just like he remembered. Information scrolled in front of him:

Heat Shield Integrity: 29%
Heat Shield Failure Imminent
Improper Course Alignment

That was an understatement. According to the GPS, the *Charon* had been turned west, directly *into* the Cindersphere. The temperature readings outside were off the scale. So were the radiation counters. If they kept going like this, the shields would fail and the SMV would implode. Violently.

In the time he had been studying the monitor, the integrity was already down to 27 percent. There was only one possibility.

"They're *scuttling* the *Charon*," Flynn said.

"Why would they do that?"

Flynn had no idea.

Something else flashed on the screen. At the top right corner. A protocol alert. Flynn tapped on it.

System-Wide Protocol
LOST PROPHET

The words had no meaning to him.

"Do you know what means?" he asked Key.

She shook her head. He could hear her breathing over the alarms; it was growing quicker, more frightened. Flynn didn't blame her.

He tapped the monitor again. The local controls for the drive shaft pocket came up and he found the status he was looking for.

AEV Status: Locked/Compliant

Key moved in close to him. "There's an AEV here?" Her voice was surprised.

"Yeah," Flynn said.

Automated extrication vehicles were computer-guided escape pods, with their own heat shields, designed to evacuate people out of the Cindersphere and back to the Razor in case of an emergency. AEVs were generally deployed from the crew decks, in large banks of hundreds, depending on the size of the SMV. But additional pods were put in place on the lower decks, in case anyone there couldn't make it back up to the crew deck.

Unsurprisingly, the only deck on the *Charon* that didn't have AEVs was GenPop. Prisoners, in the case of a catastrophic systems failure, were expendable.

Flynn looked left, saw the small, circular access port set into the bulkhead, which marked the location of the AEV. As the computer indicated, it was still here.

Flynn stepped toward the port, pulling Key with him.

That's when he saw the bodies lying on the floor, revealed in strobing flashes of blue.

They wore crew uniforms, not inmate jumpsuits. Even in the dim light, he could see the blood that had pooled underneath the bodies.

Key grabbed Flynn and shoved him back against the wall. He started to complain, but she clamped down on his mouth. Her eyes were focused, studying the shadows.

Flynn heard a slight sound over the hydraulics and the alarm. Movement appeared in the corner of his eye.

Both Key and Flynn turned toward it.

A figure emerged from the dark. Key tensed. So did Flynn.

His hands fumbled around on a nearby workbench, grabbed the first thing he could find as a weapon. It felt thin and light in his hand, but he held it up defensively between them and the shadow all the same.

It was a stylus pen. For writing on the terminal monitors. It didn't have one sharp edge to speak of.

Key studied the useless pen in Flynn's hands, then looked back at him with an extreme level of annoyance.

"If we survive this, I'm going to kill *you* with that *myself*."

Then the figure moved for them.

Maddox stared at Raelyn over the bodies of the guards he'd just killed. The alarms were still sounding, piercing and loud. Blue lights flashed in the ceiling. The sound of explosions echoed from underneath them, the shock waves rattling the supplies in the cabinets.

"You have to hurry," he told Raelyn.

The doctor stared back, frightened and unsure. "What's happening?"

"They're scuttling the ship."

"That's what the blue lights are?"

No. They meant a lot more than that. Maddox still couldn't believe it, but Raelyn had said it herself. *Lost Prophet*.

"All that matters is the Crawler's being evacuated," he told her. "You have to get to the crew deck before the AEVs are gone or the heat shields fail."

Her eyes thinned. "What about the prisoners?"

Maddox's fists clenched in impatience. "They're not leaving! And neither are you if you don't hurry. You have to *go*, Raelyn!"

He could read what was in her eyes. She was bothered by it, didn't like the idea of leaving him. Nice gesture, but he didn't deserve it. Not anymore.

"Just go," he told her.

Raelyn stared at him, her eyes starting to glisten.

The Crawler rocked again as another blast tore through the interior. The glass shelves of the supply cabinets shattered. One of the gurneys fell over.

The ship was dying.

"*Go!*" Maddox yelled.

Raelyn got to her feet, turned for the door.

And then new alarms sounded on top of the first. Green lights flashed along with the blue. It made a chaotic mash-up of sound and color, both frightening and disorienting.

Raelyn's eyes widened. This alarm code she knew. "They're *out*."

She was right. Green lights on a Crawler meant GenPop was overrun. The prisoners were loose. *All* of them. And when they were done killing and maiming one another, they would be making their way upward. One particular gang, Maddox knew, was surely already on the way.

There wasn't a choice now. Maddox sighed.

"Unhook me." He pushed away from the gurney as best he could, his ankles and wrists still attached.

Raelyn stared at him, unsure now.

"You won't make it otherwise," he told her. "Not now."

She studied him seriously, maybe even skeptically. "But you don't believe in second chances."

"That's not what this is. Unhook me."

Outside the med bay, filtering in over the alarms, came a new sound. A high-pitched whine. Most likely a high-impact torque drill, the kind the inmates used when mining. They would have gotten it from one of the deployment zones as they passed through from GenPop. And they'd know how to use it—enough to drill out the bolts that held the bulkhead security doors in place.

Raelyn moved for him. In a few seconds he was unsecured from the bed. His muscles, however, didn't cooperate. He fell to the metal floor on his first attempt to stand.

"My savior," Raelyn said, gripping him under the shoulders, dragging him to his feet. He grabbed a gas grenade off the dead guard's belt as he stood, and tossed the gun. It was useless now. Guns on the Razor were biometrically linked. Only the owners could fire them.

"Do you have Doxypropenol?" Maddox asked. Raelyn looked at him curiously, then nodded. "We need it," he said, swallowing, trying not to black out. "And tape too."

Raelyn helped him hobble until they reached the storage cabinets along the far wall. He balanced against them as she ripped them open and searched. When she was done, she had a bunch of vials of clear liquid and a roll of silver tape.

Maddox took it all, placed the vials on the gas grenade, and started wrapping the tape around all of it, combining it all into one.

"Are we going to get out of here?" Raelyn asked next to him.

Maddox finished with the grenade, and looked up at her. She was scared. He could see it in her eyes.

The situation, if he were honest, seemed near impossible. Maddox nodded all the same. "We are."

The answer was more for her benefit than anything else. He had to try. He couldn't do nothing. Not again.

Raelyn held his gaze, studying him, looking for something in him to believe in. "Okay," she said.

They made it into the hall outside the med bay. The *Charon* science wing was torn apart. Refuse, papers, bags, equipment of all kinds, all tossed everywhere.

Toward the bow was the crew elevator, but it would be locked down now. If they went aft, the cargo elevator would still be operational—those didn't get locked during a protocol alarm. It was their best shot at getting to the crew decks before the AEVs were gone.

Maddox nodded toward it.

They started hobbling. Everything on Maddox's body hurt, and he wasn't entirely sure he could even feel the lower half of his legs.

It didn't matter. All he had to do was get Raelyn off the ship. It wouldn't make up for anything, he knew. But maybe it implied, at least, that he was different now. That was something. Wasn't it?

Ahead of them, the sound of the whining drill stopped as the giant steel security door slammed to the floor with a massive crash.

Raelyn screamed. Her grip on him intensified.

In the flashing blue and green lights, a giant figure emerged, flanked by a dozen more. They all wore black jumpsuits.

"Boss man," Whistler stated casually, in spite of everything going on around them. "Up and around. Feeling better. Whistler so glad."

Maddox sagged against the wall. He felt his stomach go hollow. It was too late.

The figure moved for them out of the shadows with a strange, disturbing, jerking walk.

Key could just see the soiled white jumpsuit. Horribly long hair that fell down his shoulders, a weird, angular shape to the head.

An inmate. Forgotten down here for who knew how long, amid the dark and endless sound.

He breathed heavily as he moved right at them.

"Hey, man . . ." Key knew what was coming. She tried anyway. "I didn't put you in here. Okay? I didn't—"

The figure kept coming.

"God damn it . . ."

It slammed into her and Flynn, grunting and groaning, no speech.

All three of them went down, twisted around one another.

The inmate smelled like urine; his breath was like rotted meat. Dark fingernails dug into her. His mouth opened to take a bite out of her.

Key was really starting to get pissed off. "No way!"

She slammed her forehead into his grimy face. The shadow groaned again. Another strike with her knee rolled him off of her.

Key rolled over on top of the man. Punched him hard in the throat, then the nose, then the throat again. She was more crazed than he was, but that was just how she fought. "No fucking way!"

It wasn't enough.

The inmate was too strong, full of adrenaline and who knew what else. He flipped her over with some kind of inhuman moan.

He bit Key's shoulder. She screamed in pain—then she bit him right back, through all the grime and dirt and germs. She didn't give a fuck. He roared, backed off. Key punched him again. She wasn't going out like this, killed by some fucking whack job.

Above her, Flynn got to his knees, pulling her arm with him. He reached for a toolbox next to one of the hydraulics hubs, came back with a hammer. An upgrade from the stupid pencil he'd gotten before.

The inmate's hands clamped down on her throat. She gurgled, her eyes bulged.

Flynn raised the hammer, ready to strike down.

Then she saw it. The light in his eyes. It didn't die, it flared up. She knew what was going on in his mind. He was realizing what he was about to do. Analyzing every in and out of it like a total fucking civilian . . .

The hammer just hung there in the air. Refusing to strike. While Key's lungs burned . . .

The hammer hung in Flynn's hand like it was wired to the ceiling. It wouldn't strike. *He* wouldn't strike.

In spite of the dirty inmate's hands around Key's throat. In spite of the way she spasmed underneath him. In spite of the way her eyes glared into his.

He heard his father's warning again: *If you draw, you* pull!

But all Flynn could see was the inmate's head splitting open in front of him. The blood spraying up like a fountain. And the hammer just . . . wouldn't . . . come down . . .

Key's hand shot up, grabbed the hammer out of his hand.

It sunk into the crazed inmate's skull with a sickening *thunk*.

Then it did it again. And again.

Flynn shut his eyes tight, trying not to vomit at the sound of the thick, wet blows.

When he finally did look, the inmate was draped over Key, his body spasming and covering her red jumpsuit in blood. His first thought was that at least it wouldn't show much.

"If you don't too fucking terribly mind," Key began, breathing heavy, "get this asshole *off* me!"

Together they pushed the dirty, spasming body off of Key and let it collapse next to them in a pool of blood.

Key glared at Flynn with barely contained fury.

"Okay, okay . . ." he started, trying to push away from her. The chain that connected them, though, made that difficult. "I could have done more there—"

A new alarm tone blared to life, as if the first weren't nerve-fraying enough. Green strobing lights flashed and mixed with the blue.

Flynn knew this one. GenPop was overrun. Apparently, Key knew it too.

"Fucking hell," she spat, under him.

They both got to their feet, moved to the control terminal. Flynn tapped it, bringing up the camera system for GenPop. When the image appeared, he quickly looked away, breathing heavily. "Jesus . . ."

"Yeah," Key said, watching the camera feeds. Killing. Blood. Body parts. Large-scale horror. Another explosion, this one farther away, echoed around them. It sounded ominously like thunder. "Scores are being settled up there. All of them. At once."

That was one way to put it. To Flynn, it had been every horror movie he'd ever seen combined into one image. He refused to look at the terminal again, moved away quick and pulled Key to the AEV port on the wall, the one with the magnetic seal. He tried not to look at the bodies underneath it. It was hard, when he was sliding around in their blood.

"They'll be coming," Key said.

"Here?" Flynn asked. "Why?"

"Inmates pull cleanup duty all the time; they get sent to places like this. They would have seen the AEV."

Flynn pulled an electric driver from a toolbox on a workbench. It whined as he started unscrewing the control panel to the locked AEV door. "Great."

She was right, most likely. But the GenPop alarm had just gone off. There was no way they could get down here before—

The sound of something slamming into metal echoed behind them.

Flynn froze, waiting.

It came again. Louder.

Both he and Key turned and looked. The door to the main engineering hall rocked on its hinges.

Someone was hammering it with something big. It wasn't a secured door; the main bulkhead was back the other way. If they had gotten through that, then there wasn't much to stop them from getting into the maintenance pocket.

Flynn's breathing quickened. "What if they get in?"

"You saw the monitors."

Flynn had. His hands shook. And the control panel broke off from the wall, wires snapping loose. The power on the LED screen died.

Flynn stared at the broken panel in his hands, frozen, eyes wide. So did Key. "You meant to do that, *right*?"

Flynn looked back. "It's . . . not ideal." Her eyes lit on fire. "Hacking the panel isn't the only way to open the port," he shouted, dropping the panel on the floor.

"No," Key snarled, "just the *easiest*."

The door rocked again. Key looked back at it. "How much time do you need?"

Flynn looked around, his mind whirling, cataloging what he saw. A fire axe on the wall. A toolbox. Drill presses and saws. The sealed, garage-style door to a supply closet.

"*Flynn!*"

"A few minutes," he lied. He actually had no idea how he was going to do this.

One of the hinges on the door separated from the wall in a spray of debris. The inmates outside kept pounding it, about to break through . . .

Halfway down the hall stood Whistler and the Bloodclan, their black jumpsuits strained by giant muscles, dreadlocks running down their backs, blocking the way to the cargo elevator.

Maddox held the gas grenade in front of him so Whistler and his men could see it.

"Gas bomb?" Whistler asked, unimpressed. "Really, boss man? You know how many times Whistler been gassed?"

A lot, Maddox reckoned. NC gas was used pretty heavily on Crawlers to put down all kinds of misbehavior. The Bloodclan would have no real reason to be intimidated. Then again, they couldn't see the glass vials under the tape.

There were seven Bloodclan, bunched together by the door they'd drilled through. Maddox would have to time the throw perfectly—assuming he didn't black out first. He was barely standing as it was.

"Trying to save your sweet angel?" Whistler hadn't moved, but he was ready to spring. So were the other Bloodclan. "She not that kinda angel. She something different. You got no idea." Next to him, Maddox felt Raelyn tense. "How you fix your problem now, butterfly?" Whistler asked in his deep, gentle voice. "You know the pain waiting on you."

"I'll figure something out." Raelyn's voice was hard.

"No doubt," Whistler said, chuckling low. "You good at that, Whistler reckon."

With his thumb, Maddox primed the grenade. It detonated at seven seconds. Maddox counted to himself as he slowly started backing up. Raelyn went with him.

One . . . two . . .

The Bloodclan still hadn't moved; they were waiting for Whistler to give the signal.

"Where you think you go?" Whistler asked, watching Maddox and Raelyn back up. The *Charon* shook violently. Lights in the ceiling exploded in sparks. "You hear the alarms. See the lights. All of us, every one, brother . . . we gonna burn."

Three . . . four . . .

"You got one part of that right," Maddox said.

Maddox threw the grenade, aiming at the wall just to the right of the Bloodclan.

When it hit, there was a crunching sound as the vials of Doxy shattered, releasing their fumes.

It was an old marine trick, a low-rent solution when you needed to make a real grenade and all you had was riot gear and a first aid kit.

Sparks sprayed as the grenade aerified the naranocarbon. By itself, it wasn't flammable. Add in liquid Doxypropenol, though, and the effect was all the way different.

Whistler's eyes went wide. He understood. But too late. "Back! *Get ba—*"

A plume of green flame exploded around them. The walls were immediately ablaze. Fire filled the corridor. There were screams from the Bloodclan as they were engulfed, and Maddox could just make out their huge shapes, flailing around, burning in seconds.

"Go!" Maddox yelled at Raelyn, and she supported him as they moved down the hall as fast as they could. The screams behind them intensified.

Flynn stared at the fire axe resting in its case on the wall. It was heavy, made of composite steel, which made it nearly unbreakable.

Problem, Flynn thought to himself. *Opening an electromagnetic lock without a control panel.*

Flynn grabbed the axe, pulled it loose. The blade gleamed in the flashing blue and green lights.

Solution: use the electromagnetics against themselves.

"You gotta be fucking kidding me," Key moaned next to him, staring at the axe in his hands with intense skepticism. "You won't even be able to dent the—"

Another explosion ripped through the ship. Everything vibrated and groaned. The door into the engineering hall continued to pound, the inmates on the other side almost broken through.

"Instead of complaining," Flynn said, moving back toward to the AEV port door, dragging Key with him by the wrist chain, "how about helping?"

"How?"

Flynn hefted the axe. It was noticeably top-heavy. "We have to swing it together." It was true. With the chain binding their arms together, it was the only the way to do it with two hands.

"Swing it at a reinforced metal door?" Key was flustered.

So was Flynn. The door into the room kept pounding, almost torn completely loose from the wall.

Key glared at him, took the axe with her hand. "When this bounces back at us, it better hit *you*."

"It's not going to bounce."

They raised the axe above their heads, gripped it with their hands bound by the chains. "Now!" They swung the axe down, hard. It was a crazy swing, not guided by coordination or strength. It didn't matter.

The moment the blade got within two feet of the door, the magnetics grabbed it and brought it home.

The blade sank deep into the small gap between the two half-circle doors of the port. It was now wedged and held in place by a magnetic field with a pull force somewhere near two thousand pounds.

Key stared at the axe, sunk almost to the handle between the giant steel doors. "Fucking A," she said.

Another alarm joined the symphony. A new light flashed. Orange. A bad one, Flynn recalled. *Heat shield failure.*

The floor rocked under them. Sparks sprayed from the EM drivers. The monitors for the terminals exploded in blasts of glass and circuits.

It was happening. They were out of time.

Flynn and Key had already cut and yanked out the chains that moved one of the room's garage-like supply closet doors. He attached the C-clip from one end of the chain into the hole on the axe handle and dragged the rest of the length toward one of the big drive shafts that turned the *Charon*'s massive wheels.

It was stuttering and grinding. The wheels outside were probably melting. The whole thing was about to fail.

Key looked from the chain running to the axe in the doors, then back to the spinning drive shaft.

She got the plan. Her eyes widened. "Christ on a dinner plate . . ."

Flynn grabbed the end of the chain and tossed it into the driveshaft above his head.

"Wait!" Key yelled, but it was too late.

The geared teeth grabbed the chain, wrapping it around itself in a blur. On the floor, the chain was ripped forward.

The polysteel axe stuck in the door stayed in place. The tension on the chain kept ratcheting up.

Physics only allowed for one option.

The door broke through its supports with a giant spark and flew through the air.

Key rammed into Flynn and drove him to the ground just as the door flew through where their heads would have been.

All two hundred pounds of it slammed into the floor and slid crazily, blowing through supply containers and workbenches, snapping the chain.

Flynn exhaled, breathed deep, looked at Key on top of him.

She stared down hotly. "As smart a son of a bitch as you are, you really should think things *all* the way through."

Flynn nodded. "I don't disagree."

The door to the engineering hall blew apart. Figures, a dozen, poured through and into the flashing lights of the room. Flynn could see they were all covered in blood, their eyes crazed.

"Come on, professor!" Key yelled, dragging Flynn up.

Key's wings itched like crazy. The inmates ran for her as she pulled Flynn toward the open AEV port.

The ship rocked violently. Two of the drives exploded, spraying debris everywhere, and the blast flattened three of the inmates. The rest, though, kept running.

The alarms and flashing lights all died, leaving just red emergency lighting. Everything around them began to shake and tear itself apart.

Key climbed inside the small cockpit of the AEV, pulling Flynn with her. It was perfectly round, like a ball . . . and there was just one seat: a rounded, padded shape that circled up one side of the wall. Everything else was piping, oxygen canisters, a computer monitor, controls, and switches.

Key fell on top of Flynn as another explosion flared behind them. Fire began to spread.

Through the open port, she could see the inmates rushing toward them. They were screaming and shouting and frothing at the—

Flynn reached around her, flipped a switch. The door to the AEV shut tight. She could hear the pod beginning to whine, powering up.

Key pushed up enough so that she could see Flynn's face. It was right in front of hers.

He wore a mask of concentration as he manipulated the controls behind her. The AEV started to rumble.

And then the AEV door pounded loudly—the inmates desperately trying to get inside, their last chance at survival.

Key stared warily at the door, cramped into the small space, on top of Flynn.

"These things all go to the same place, right?" she asked. "I mean, they're programmed to a course."

Flynn nodded. "A staging area. You can't steer it, if that's what you're asking."

"So we're going straight to where all the other assholes went."

"Would you rather stay *here*?" He didn't look at her, just kept working the control panel. The AEV shook as it disconnected from whatever rack held it to the *Charon*, and, mercifully, the pounding on the door ceased.

A voice on the small pod's speakers began to count down. "Ejection protocol in five . . . four . . . three . . ."

Flynn finally looked at Key. He was inches away. Her body was pressed against him. Key looked back.

"Your hand's on my ass," she told him.

Flynn's look softened. He seemed . . . embarrassed almost. Something about it—the softness, in spite of everything they'd just been through—made Key want to smile. But she didn't.

"AEVs are made for one person," he said, staring up at her.

". . . two . . . one." the countdown voice continued.

"It doesn't have to be on my ass, though," Key said back. "Does it?"

The pod shook hard as the thrusters shot it through the *Charon*'s super-structure. Everything rocked as it slammed to the ground. The world went haywire as the AEV's engines activated and it began to roll, end over end, faster and faster, taking them away from the dying Crawler where Key had lived for the last nine months.

Flynn's second hand joined the first. Key found, right then, that she didn't care.

Maddox sucked wind as he and Raelyn reached the bottom of the stairs.

There was a door there. A heavy, fortified one, with an access panel.

"Scanner . . ." Maddox breathed.

He hoped it was still online. Everything in the ship seemed to be in its last throes. Just like him.

Raelyn held a hand to the scanner. It beeped. A small red light turned green. The door clicked and hissed open.

Above, not far at all, Maddox could hear the sound of furious movement. People rushing down the stairs after them.

"*Maddox!*" Whistler's voice, full of anger and hate. And it sounded odd somehow. Wrong. But there wasn't time to think about it.

He and Raelyn pushed through the door and let it slide closed behind them. Maddox heard the lock click into place.

It would help, but it wouldn't keep Whistler out for long.

The *Charon*'s X-Core wasn't all that big. That was part of the wonder, how small a Xytrilium reactor actually was. It sat within an interior compartment, blast doors open, allowing a glimpse inside. The X-Core itself was a cylinder made out of composite and polysteel. Purple energy flickered inside, throbbing and pulsing all over the clear container.

Surrounding the reactor compartment were banks of controls, holo displays spinning in the air above them, all abandoned now. A utility area off one of the blast doors was lined with several heavy-duty rad-suits, for when workers needed to do maintenance in the X-Core itself. The suits hung from a rack system built into the wall.

"Oh, God," Raelyn moaned. Maddox turned to her and saw that she was staring at one of the computer terminals. It showed a camera feed from the bow of the *Charon*, looking straight ahead.

The view was nothing but mesas and cliff faces and flame. The screen flashed and flickered. The camera was probably starting to melt. Maddox stared at the display in awe. He'd never heard of any Crawler going this far into the Cinder and coming out. They were almost finished.

Raelyn looked at him. With her blue eyes.

Maddox had only met her a day ago, but she had refused to kill him when it would have been better for her to do so. And now she would die, if he didn't get them out of here.

But for what? He didn't believe in second chances. He'd told her as much. And they would still be trapped in the middle of a world on fire.

Behind them, the door to the X-Core pounded. It was Whistler and the Bloodclan. From behind it came the whine of the torque drill again.

"Come on." Maddox pointed to the rad-suits hanging from the rack in the wall.

"What are we going to do?" Raelyn asked as they moved for them. "Jump?"

"Not exactly," he said. "But close."

Raelyn hurried to the nearest suit, started to pull it off the rack.

"No," Maddox stopped her. "Climb in, keep it attached."

"*Why?*"

"Because there are no seat belts in here," he said pointedly.

Raelyn's face dropped as she figured out what he intended. The terror in her eyes grew.

"Hurry!" he yelled, struggling to balance as he moved for the nearest controls.

The whine kept growing outside, the drill getting closer to tearing through the door.

"*Maddox!*" Whistler's voice, full of fury and pain, somehow roared through the door and over all the sound.

Maddox swiped on a touch screen in the control bank, found the menu he was looking for. A very rarely used one.

Emergency Reactor Ejection Protocol

"Jesus," Maddox said under his breath, hands hovering over the screen and the initiation button, the implications of what he was about to do hitting him.

An X-Core meltdown was a very serious incident, which, fortunately, didn't happen all that often. But when it did, it could not only kill everyone on board an SMV but also destroy the machine itself. Crawlers were pricey pieces of machinery, so, in a last-ditch effort to save one, later models were designed with the ability to eject the entire X-Core.

The process would launch the reactor high into the air and away from the Crawler before it imploded in on itself. The ejection system had most definitely not been designed for passengers. There were no restraints, no inertia dampening inside the X-Core, nothing that would soften the landing, and the landing was going to be hard and real.

Whistler's voice yelled again from outside. It sounded slurred and pained. The drill kept whining, almost through.

There wasn't any other choice, Maddox knew. This was a crazy plan, but it was the only one they had.

Maddox hit the Init button. New lights flashed with all the others. Red ones. Joined by new alarms. A timer started.

30 . . . 29 . . . 28 . . .

Maddox ran back to the rad-suits on the wall, secured in their harnesses.

The process would launch the reactor high into the air and away from the Crawler before it imploded in on itself. Being inside the suits, tied to the walls, was the only thing that had a chance of stopping Maddox and Raelyn from being thrown around like rag dolls on impact.

And it was a slim chance.

"Maddox," Raelyn said, fastening the last of her suit's connectors, hanging from the wall. She was looking at him guiltily.

Maddox knew what she was thinking, and he shook his head, slipped inside the suit next to her. "Don't."

23 . . . 22 . . . 21 . . .

"You didn't have to do this," she said.

Maddox felt heat rush through him. "You're wrong."

"You don't know what I've done," she said.

"I don't need to know," Maddox said, strapping into his own suit. The drill kept whining. Everything shook and flashed around them as the *Charon* began to melt. "People do what they do, they live with it, and that's all there is."

19 . . . 18 . . . 17 . . .

Raelyn stared at him with emotion. It comforted her, maybe, his words, but that's not why he'd said them. He said them because he was the last person who had any right to judge.

They both slipped the rad-suit helmets over their heads. There was a hiss of compressed air as Maddox's suit locked into place. The HUD flashed to life in his viewscreen.

There wasn't anything to do now but wait. Well, maybe one thing . . .

"You the praying type?" Maddox asked grimly.

"Not until about thirty seconds ago," she replied in a tight voice, over the suit's comm system.

The polymer had melted off the wheels by now, and the giant vessel shuddered as what was left of them dug hard into the scalding, ashen ground outside. It was about to explode.

10 . . . 9 . . . 8 . . .

The computer terminals blew outward in showers of sparks, one at a time. The flashing lights—blue, green, orange—all went dark. The alarms stopped. A horrible groaning, the sound of rending metal, echoed from the decks of the giant Crawler below them.

"I'm scared . . ." Raelyn said.

Maddox wasn't sure why he did it. Maybe it was the terror in her voice; maybe it bothered him how alone she sounded. But he reached and took her hand, the thick gloves they wore barely allowing him to squeeze hard enough to hold on.

There was only one sound now. The whining from the impact drill, even now boring through the door.

"Maddox!" The voice filtered in through the suit's comm system. "I will *never* let you go!"

Whistler. Still trying to get to him. To make him pay. To kill him.

If only Whistler understood. There wasn't anything left to kill. Maddox was already gone.

3 . . . 2 . . . 1.

And then he and Raelyn jolted violently in the suits as everything roared and shook and the X-Core launched free and into the air and left the *Charon* behind.

SITE ELEVEN

SEVENTEEN

LUCKY DAYS

Ironic thing was, this had all been part of the plan.

At least before the blue lights started flashing outside the reinforced plastic cube they'd secured him in, plus shackles and a muzzle, attached by thick rubber bindings to the railing. No metal anywhere; nothing for him to use. Smart.

He'd freed his gun arm about twenty minutes after they'd left him alone.

The plastic shackles weren't a big deal, if, like him, you didn't mind dislocating a wrist or a thumb to get out of them.

When the Rangers came back to check on him, they couldn't see his arm was free. He was just a big, hulking shadow to them, face covered by the muzzle, turned away like a bogeyman they'd managed to capture and seal away.

He dropped one with a side strike to the pterion, a spot an inch or so back from the eyebrows, a structural weak point in the skull. He was probably dead, but there was no way to tell.

He could have snapped the second one's neck, but he needed him, so he drew him in instead, broke his nose to keep him disoriented, and yanked the scattergun off his back holster and tossed it away. No reason to keep it, with the biometrics. It wouldn't fire for him.

The one he was holding was young, just a kid, razored hair, probably right out of Colonial.

He didn't even bother to struggle against the hand around his throat. He was a Ranger, kid or no kid, and he knew what was what, which meant he knew he wasn't going to be the one to resolve this.

Two more Rangers had their guns drawn in the entry to the cell, all aimed at him. But he already had their boy held up as a shield. He didn't need a gun; the hand around the throat was enough. He could crush a larynx as fast as they could pull their triggers.

"There's a set way things like this go, but it doesn't have to," an older Ranger said, a captain. Midforties, still strong, still lean, not as quick as he used to be, but he had experience to fill in the gaps. The handle of his gun was faded and worn; it didn't shake in his hand. The man's voice was level, even with one of his men lying still on the cell floor. He was a pro. "This isn't going to change anything. You're going where you're going, end of the day. You know that."

"It changes everything," the prisoner corrected him. His voice was even, deep and smooth, filtered strangely from under the plastic muzzle they'd fitted him with. "Right about one thing, though. It doesn't have to go the set way."

The prisoner's eyes moved slowly up and around, reverifying the situation. One hand still locked to the rail above. Contained compartment. One exit. Two locks to get loose. Three Rangers left. Better odds than he'd been expecting. Things were looking up . . .

The prisoner's eyes settled back on the captain. He might have to kill all three of them to get out of here.

"Here's how it should play," the prisoner said slowly. "Unlock me, I let your boy go, take a dive out the bulkhead door, hit the ground running. No doubt our paths cross after that, but by then it won't matter. And *then* you get your shot."

The Ranger's eyes thinned. So did the eyes of the one next to him. A little younger, rising up the ranks, he'd heard the captain refer to him as lieutenant. There was fire in that one's eyes. That one would blast away if it were any other day—or any other prisoner.

The problem, for everyone involved, was that he wasn't any other prisoner. This particular prisoner had a No Kill order stenciled in bright, flashing red letters across his holographic file.

The powers that be wanted him alive. They wanted their weapon back. The prisoner had been disappointing them for years. Today wouldn't be an exception.

The kid in his grip tensed, blood still pouring out his nose. "Captain, don't—"

"Shut up, Scott," the captain cut him off.

"You drew bad cards, Cap'," the prisoner said. "Not your fault."

The two men locked eyes. One from behind the barrel of a gun, the other from behind the scalp of a hostage. Men like this captain, they were open to propositions. Not because they were any smarter but because they'd seen so much. The more darkness a man lived through, the fewer lines he was willing to cross. The Reaper takes his toll on the living as much as the dead.

The captain licked his lips, eyes narrowing. The prisoner had him right where he—

Alarm tones suddenly blared outside the reinforced cell.

Blue lights strobed in the ceiling.

The Rangers all stared at each other, stunned, but kept their guns up.

"Gotta be fucking kidding me," the lieutenant said.

The older man's grip on his sidearm stayed tight. "Confirm it."

The lieutenant touched his earpiece, spoke into his comms. "Skybird, Fallen Angel Three. Confirm active protocols." He waited a moment, listening to what some other voice on the other end of the radio told him. Judging by his look, he didn't like it.

"Confirmed," the lieutenant said, his voice tight. "Lost Prophet."

"Why?" The captain's voice was just as tight. His gun hovered in the air like a rock.

"All I heard was one hour until extraction. We make an evac point or we ride it out planet-side."

The captain's demeanor darkened. Something serious was happening, more serious than the prisoner being loose. And that said a lot.

"Well, Zane," the captain said. It was the first time he'd used the prisoner's name since they'd met. "It's someone's lucky day. Just not sure if it's mine or yours."

"If it makes you feel better," the prisoner named Zane said, "there's no such thing as luck."

The captain's eyes shifted to the kid in Zane's arms, kept them there as he told the lieutenant what to do. "Overjack the X-Core, lock the navigation, blow the terminal."

Zane's eyes thinned just slightly. That wasn't what he'd expected.

The lieutenant stared hard at the captain. "We're leaving Scott to—"

"Do it," the captain replied.

The younger one hesitated a moment, then stepped to the left, out of sight.

The captain noticed Zane's look. "Still thought they wanted you alive?"

Zane didn't react, just kept his massive hand on the kid's throat.

"They didn't bring you home to dissect," the captain continued. "They brought you home to die."

The captain looked at the kid one last time. Zane felt the Ranger's muscles tense in his grip.

"I'm sorry, Scott," was all the captain said.

"Me too, sir." The kid knew his role, knew this kind of shit came with the job. His ticket was punched.

But like the captain said, things didn't have to go a set way. Zane loosened his grip, and the kid pulled away instantly, wide-eyed, stunned. The captain stared back, unsure.

Zane shrugged. "It's all on the wheel, Cap'. It all comes around."

The Ranger captain smiled slightly, then nodded.

The kid grabbed the body of the motionless Ranger, dragged him out the door of the plastic cell. When he was clear, the captain slapped a button on the wall. The armored door slammed shut, separating them and plunging everything to darkness, except for the flashing blue lights that filtered in through the tiny observation window.

Zane stared at the strobing blue, and laughed.

It was a dark and booming laugh that overpowered the sounds of the engines and the alarms and the rumbling walls. He was genuinely amused. He guessed, all things considered, it made sense. That he would finally outgrow his own worth, even to the UEG.

Under his feet, he could feel the train rumbling harder, could feel the inertia pushing him back against the wall. The Rangers had set full throttle, had probably bailed out already. He was on a runaway train now, headed who knows where.

Zane kept laughing. The irony was hilarious.

EIGHTEEN

ALONE

"When I pull my foot out of my ear, I'm going to rip your balls off."

Key's voice sounded particularly displeased, but Flynn didn't care.

As the AEV rolled on its gyros through the Cindersphere, it tossed them around everywhere inside. Bound to each other by the wrists, the end result was that by the time the machine finally rolled to a stop, they were completely tangled around each other.

"Would you rather be back on the *Charon*?" Flynn's voice was muffled by Key's kneecap in his mouth, but it sounded testy all the same. She was alive after all. She could show some appreciation.

"I'd rather not be chained to you inside a giant metal ball," she replied. "Why would you make an escape pod as a *giant metal ball*?"

"Well, engineering-wise, it solves a lot of problems for a—"

"The question was fucking rhetorical. Move your arm, I can't breathe."

Flynn tried.

"Your other arm."

He tried again.

"Move it the *other* way!"

Flynn groaned in pain as she yanked at him. "Hey! I want out of here as bad as you."

But where was "here"? The AEV had stopped, and there was no clue where.

Flynn studied the small sphere's interior. Pipes and electrical conduits, a few handles, and a small computer terminal near the door. He'd need to reach it.

He lifted up. The irons cut into his wrist, and he lay back. "I can't reach . . . the . . . Can you move your—"

"No."

Flynn sighed. "Can you just cooperate?"

"I mean no, I can't move *anything*. Your knee is wedged somewhere it shouldn't be, and my hand's pinned behind your head."

"Let me . . ." He lifted his leg, tried to push Key's body forward.

"Ouch!"

Flynn stopped trying. This was insane. They were wedged together inside this tin can, and maneuvering out of it seemed impossible.

"Aren't you some kind of scientist?" Key asked. "Shouldn't there be a math formula to get us out of this?"

"I'm an engineer, not a mathematician, though one of my degrees was in—"

"Jesus, you and rhetorical fucking questions."

"Maybe if you stopped complaining and started helping."

"What do you want me to do?"

Flynn's eyes moved around the sphere again, studying how he and Key were lying—sideways, apparently, on the AEV's seat.

"Push with your right hand."

"On what?"

"The *bulkhead*."

"Why?"

"Just . . ." Flynn gritted his teeth. "Just push on the bulkhead so I can get leverage."

Key did. He felt her weight lift slightly.

"This hurts," she said.

"Good." He slid down and slowly turned around, felt the chain on his wrist start to twist the cuff into his skin.

"That hurts *more*."

"*Hold* on . . ."

He kept turning, then managed to slide around Key, pulling her onto her side. They were still wrapped around each other, but not as badly. And now Flynn could move his free hand.

He smiled. Key glared at him.

Her face was inches from his now. So were her green eyes.

"Now what?" she asked pointedly.

Flynn looked away from her, back up at the monitor. He stretched upward and it lit up when he got close, showing the AEV's stats and modes. He tapped through the menu screens, looking for the information he wanted.

The environment sensors.

The information scrolled across the readout.

"Good news. Normal oxygen, even if the temp's on the high side. It won't be comfortable, but we'll live. Better news, nonlethal rads. We must be past the Terminus."

"At the same place every other fucking AEV on the *Charon* went."

She was right. The coordinates on AEVs were programmed beforehand, so when a crew evacuated a Crawler, they all ended up in the same spot for rescue.

Once they went outside, they'd be greeted by everyone else who'd escaped, and none of them would be wearing colored jumpsuits. They'd be recaptured, and everything they'd managed to escape just now would start all over again.

But they'd be alive. That mattered. Didn't it?

"How come no welcoming party?" Key asked.

Flynn paused. They'd been here a few minutes now. Why *hadn't* a tech or someone else opened their hatch? Shouldn't that be protocol?

"Either we open the door ourselves . . ." Key said.

"Or we stay in the pretzel machine," Flynn finished for her. He looked up at the pressure handle on the AEV's round door. Unlike the computer terminal, it was out of reach.

"You'll have to help," Flynn told her, making his choice.

"Oh, joy."

He pulled her toward him. "Roll over."

Key twisted around until she was lying on her back on top of him.

"Can you reach the handle?" he asked.

Flynn felt her weight shift as she tried, saw the lines of her neck angle up and away, the lines moving down to the skin of her shoulder.

"No," Key said above him, her body relaxing.

He raised the hand that was shackled to hers up around his head to give her room. "Slide up."

Key did, her body moving toward the door above, sliding over him as it did.

Her scent washed over him. An aggressive mix of leather and sweat and oil, not altogether unpleasant. Flynn cleared his throat.

Jesus, what was wrong with him?

This woman had tried to kill him not all that long ago, had probably killed who knows how many people in her life. And he was—

"Moron?"

Flynn blinked. He looked up at her.

She stared back impatiently. "Now what?"

"Turn the handle clockwise. It'll vent, then I can release it."

There was a high-pitched hiss as Key shoved the handle to the right. He tapped the screen and found the menu he wanted. He swiped the controls. Buttons flashed and dimmed. The screen scrolled again:

Decompression Request Initiated
Time to Decompression: 1:15 . . . 1:14 . . . 1:13 . . .

Outside Flynn heard the hiss as the intense pressure they'd brought with them from the Cindersphere vented out into the air beyond.

The timer on the monitor continued.

1:11 . . . 1:10 . . . 1:09 . . .

"Is that it?" Key asked above him.

He nodded. "Once we depressurize, we're out."

She slid back down him and rolled over, her face was across from his again.

He looked at her. "I have a name, you know. It's not Moron."

Key shook her head. "No fucking way. I start calling you your name, next thing you think we're friends. I can tell. You're like a little lost puppy, and I don't like little puppies."

"I'm shocked."

"You helped *me* out back there, I helped *you* out back there. That's it."

"We can't *keep* helping each other?"

"Jesus Christ in a saddlebag." Key studied him like some alien life form. "Get in fucking step, man. Everyone on this planet is out for themselves. Why do you think that is? They're just giant scary assholes who hate everybody? Don't get me wrong, they *are*, but there's more to it. It's what keeps you alive. You and I are better off without each other. We're better off alone. Because then we can't fuck each other's plans up. We can't let each other *down*."

Flynn stared back at her. "Who let *you* down?"

Key held his gaze a second, then looked back up at the timer. "Where do I start?"

"It doesn't matter," she said. "When this thing pops open, you're getting carted off to some other Crawler and you can make a deal with some other captain, get your fancy cell back, try to scramble up some pathetic version of how things used to be. Just like everyone else here."

She was right. Flynn knew. He hadn't really escaped anything.

"What about you?" he asked.

Key breathed in and slowly exhaled. "I'm not going back."

Flynn looked at her again. The way she said the words made it clear that she wasn't thinking about escaping. The opposite, really.

With a burst of air, the hatch to the AEV snapped open.

Sunlight poured in, bright and harsh and hot.

Flynn and Key pushed up and through the pod's hatch, barely fitting through the hole, pressed together, half in, half out of the big metallic sphere.

Neither of them spoke as they took in their surroundings.

AEVs. Like theirs.

Thousands of them.

All around. Stretching into the distance as far as they could see.

Far more AEVs than would be on the *Charon*. Far more AEVs than would be on *four Charons*.

And among all of them, no matter where they looked, one thing was missing.

Guards. Engineers. Techs. Medical personnel.

No one. The field of AEVs was empty. *Abandoned.*

Flynn and Key stared, stunned, as the sunlight poured down everywhere.

NINETEEN

ROCKETS

When they landed on the ground outside the craft, they were surrounded. AEVs were about eight feet tall, which meant that they blocked the view in every direction. It was like being in a maze of giant orbs.

This far out, the Razor resembled something like the deserts of the old American southwest, only on a much more epic scale. Rocks and sand, towering cliffs and mesas stretching away on either side. The burned red sand was soft under their boots.

They moved toward what Flynn hoped was the center of the AEV field. He felt Key's shackles bite into his wrist as they walked.

"Why are there so many?" Her voice was quiet, slightly unnerved.

"It's got to be AEVs from . . . at least six different Crawlers," Flynn said.

"That would make it every SMV assigned to our depot. Why would they scuttle that many at once?"

Flynn didn't have an answer. A single SMV, at their current iteration, cost Maas-Dorian a hundred million or more. They were tremendous investments, and crucial to the corporation's business model. After all, the Razor was the source of M-D's power: the purest Xytrilium in the galaxy. And without Crawlers, there was no way to get it.

"Bigger question is . . ." Key started, and Flynn knew what she was thinking.

"Where's everyone else?"

Given the number of AEVs in the canyon, there should have been thousands of people roaming around, boarding other Crawlers or trains or some kind of rescue craft. But there was no one. No sounds of humanity. Just the hot wind whipping through the AEVs.

They kept moving, twisting past and around the metallic spheres, and as they did they noticed something ahead. Smoke. Thick black smoke, rising up into the sky.

Flynn and Key moved through the AEVs until their boots hit something hard. A pad of concrete, spreading out ahead of them in a circular shape, about two hundred yards along the canyon floor. There were only two things of note on top of it: a large two-story metallic structure. It was burning. The source of the smoke.

And a huge hatch in the ground. It took up about half the total girth of the concrete field, a giant square in a larger circle.

"What the hell?" Key stared at the giant hole in the ground, then started pulling Flynn toward it.

He stopped her. "Wait."

Everything around the giant hatch was charred black.

Smoke and waves of heat rose everywhere in the air. He knelt down, put his hand on the concrete.

Then instantly pulled it away.

Key looked at him oddly.

"Hot," Flynn replied. "Really hot."

They stood where they were, resisting the impulse to move forward. Flynn had a feeling the heat coming off the concrete would melt their boots, the closer they got to that giant hole. The lone building kept burning in the distance.

Flynn could guess what they would see if they approached the huge hatch. A sheer drop-off, metallic walls sinking into pitch-blackness. Giant rails running straight down its walls, designed to guide something up and out of the shaft.

"A blast pad," he murmured.

Blast pads deflected the engine blast from a rocket, prevented the energy from being absorbed, and thus increased its thrust for escape velocity.

The hatch covered a rocket silo. And the rocket was *gone*.

Judging by how hot the pad was, it hadn't left all that long ago, either. Flynn felt a sense of dread begin to fill him.

"A rocket?" Key mused. "Why not use another SMV or the rail system or . . ."

Her voice faded away as the same thing occurring to Flynn occurred to her too.

From above, far above, came a low rumbling, almost like distant, sustained thunder. Flynn and Key looked up.

Thin black streaks crisscrossed the sky, dozens of them, as numerous objects flew through the air. Engine exhaust, and it was growing thinner.

Rockets. Heading into *orbit*.

"The ionosphere," he said quietly.

It made sense. The only way to get a craft on or off the Razor was through the EM corridor right above the starport—basically a demagnetized portion of the sky that occurred naturally in the ionosphere. Trying to take a ship, no matter how electromagnetically shielded, through the atmosphere any other way was a bad idea.

But what if you needed to get people who weren't at the starport off the planet? What if you needed to get *lots* of people off the planet? Something simple would be the best choice. Something more mechanical than electronic.

"The only thing that could make it out of the ionosphere is rockets," Flynn finished his thought.

"They're . . . abandoning the Razor," Key said.

Flynn stared back up into the sky, watched the black streaks becoming thinner and smaller.

Scuttling five SMVs was one thing. But evacuating the entire planet?

The Razor was M-D's greatest resource, the purest Xytrilium in the galaxy, the thing that gave it all its power. And the UEG government ran on X-Cores powered by the same fuel. For both institutions to sign off on this . . .

"What's happening?" Key asked, unnerved.

Flynn couldn't think of anything to say.

A strange sound suddenly filtered through the air, from nearby. Sharp and full of static. Flynn and Key almost jumped. There had been no sound at all since they'd stepped out of the AEV.

They turned toward the sound, to their right. It came again, louder, more fragmented, cutting in and out. Their eyes followed the rounded edge of the concrete pad, stretching away from them, past rows of AEVs lined up against it, to the one thing that was different from everything else.

A canopy tent that had been erected at the edge of the pad. Under it sat a single workbench. There was equipment on it, abandoned like everything else. The sound was coming from there.

Bound together, Flynn and Key moved for the tent. When they reached it, they saw what was arrayed on the workbench.

A few tablets, still glowing and turned on, with lists of names on them, sorted alphabetically. Flynn's eyes scanned one instinctively. Each name had either a check mark or a bold *X* next to it.

Brent Bardos, Guard, Sergeant, SMV *Warlock*
Eric Barton, Guard, Lieutenant, SMV *Charon*
Jona Benjamin, Engineering, SMV *Ambassador*
Richard Best, Command Crew, Piloting, SMV *Warlock*
Anton Braga, Command Crew, Captain, SMV *Charon*

The last name made Flynn freeze where he stood. Next to Braga's name, there was no check mark. There was an *X*.

"Douchebag didn't make it." Key smiled. "Give it enough time, and the universe actually gets it right."

A spark of sound came from an unassuming metallic box on the table. Communications gear. It had a glowing touchscreen, monitoring twenty different comm channels. On top of the device lay a wireless handset.

The sounds coming from the box were indecipherable. Bursts of static and noise, solid tones of sound, abruptly cutting off.

Key tapped a different channel on the screen. The device cycled over, picking it up.

"Six two . . . six one four, copy . . ." voices behind bursts of static said, and cut off. Then came again. "Prophet prot— . . . all birds in the air. Repeat last . . ."

More static, the voice fading. Flynn touched another channel.

Bursts of noise, another tone of sound, then, "Starport Ops, Orbit One, please respond . . . Starport Ops, Orbit One, respond . . ."

The voice was easier to make out, the signal stronger. Whoever it was sounded like they were trying to raise the starport. Over and over. They were only getting static in response.

"Starport Ops, Orbit One, resp—"

Orbit 1 cut out as a new signal took over. It was brief, hard to hear, but the words came through. The voice sounded weak. It sounded off. And something about it was unnerving.

"Orbit One . . ." More static filtered through the signal. "Quarantine fail. Breach not contain—" More static. ". . . no one. No one left. Keep quarantine. Keep *away* . . ."

The voiced faded away. The other voice, Orbit 1, wasn't heard again either.

Key breathed next to him. Flynn could feel the bonds of their shackles sag against his wrist. "They were talking about the starport," she said, almost whispering.

No one left, the voice said. Flynn felt an involuntary chill.

"We have to get there," she said. "We have to get there fast." It took a moment for the words to sink in, but when they did, Flynn stared at her like she was crazy.

"Did we hear different transmissions? Because to me it sounds like the starport is the opposite of anywhere we want to go."

"If the starport is damaged or there's an Xytrilium leak, then no one will *be* there," Key said pointedly, moving closer. When Flynn tried to step away, she yanked him back. "But every ship that's made Razorfall *will* be. Just sitting there. It's the only chance we have to—"

A loud, high-pitched *ping* echoed from next to them.

They turned their heads toward the sound.

On one of the tablets, the screen had gone completely black, with the exception of simple, flashing white words.

Hello, Dr. Flynn.

Flynn stared at the words, frozen. The heat in the air seemed to vanish.

TWENTY

PULSE

Red dust swirled around Key's boots as she stared at the words on the tablet.

The wings on her back itched. Badly. Bringing with it a severity of feeling that made her want to bolt and run. That was going to be hard, of course, tethered to Professor Obvious, but she'd find a fucking way. She'd get off this rock if she had to rip his arm off.

Flynn, for his part, just stared at the terminal, confused.

Hello, Dr. Flynn.

"Who is this?" Flynn finally asked.

This is no time for questions.

Apparently, Key figured, whoever was on the other end of the connection could hear them just fine.

You have until the last rocket enters orbit. After that, we will not be able to communicate from this terminal.

"How do you know who I am?"

Focus, Dr. Flynn. The coordination signal will initiate soon.

Key's wings itched harder. Things were spinning further out of control, and she was starting to feel boxed in.

"Coordination signal?" Flynn asked. His voice had a different tone to it now. It was laced with something else. Curiosity.

Key wanted to punch him in the balls.

"What coordination signal?"

A single, blaring tone of sound emitted from the communications unit. Flynn and Key both jumped.

A second blast. Another. Then another.

The gaps in between the tones, Key could tell, were diminishing. They were coming closer together, the more times the tone repeated.

Something about that seemed bad. Key's wings practically burned.

That coordination signal, Dr. Flynn.

The strange tones kept sounding out of the comm unit. They were growing shorter and shorter . . .

From your current location, travel northeast approximately seven miles. You will intersect a rail line. Follow it north another two miles, until it splits into two tracks. Continue northeast. The rail line will terminate at a facility. Remember the following: 66119. When you enter the facility, we will talk further.

Above them, the sounds of the rumbling rocket engines finally ceased. Key looked up. The black contrails from the giant engines were still in the sky, spreading out and disappearing. But the rockets themselves, the little pinpricks, were gone.

What was it the tablet had said? *Until the last rocket enters orbit . . .*

Not following these directions, very likely, will result in your death.
The Razor is about to become even more precarious.

Good luck, Dr. Flynn. Sincerely.

Next to them, the tones of sound finally merged into one long, sustained high-pitched squeal that split the air.

Key felt her heart racing. Something was coming, but she had no idea what.

"Wait," Flynn said to the tablet. "I don't—"

The tablet's previous screen returned, showing the personnel checklist. Flynn looked at Key. She looked back.

"Do you," Key began darkly, "have any fucking clue what's going on?"

The sky flashed above them.

Not just a piece of it; the entire thing. The horizon lit up, piercing and bright, whiting out everything above and around them.

"We should get under something," Flynn announced.

The blast wave hit like a bomb exploding. There was a thick wall of sound, and the force of it was like being kicked in the gut.

Both Key and Flynn were thrown to the ground, rolling on the red sand.

The tablets on the workbench, and the communications unit, exploded in a shower of sparks that sprayed everywhere. Behind them, a wave of fire raced through the giant collection of AEVs, one after the other. Flames shot out of their panels. Glass and metal and circuits shot into the air and then rained shards down everywhere around them, like a shower of razor-sharp hailstones.

Key pulled Flynn underneath the workbench as it all thundered down around them.

The chaos lasted a moment longer. The last of the debris and sparks fell and clanked on the concrete. Then it was over.

Nothing but the sound of the wind and the flames spreading on the burning structure in the middle of the blast pad.

Key looked at Flynn. He stared back, eyes wide, and he seemed . . . mesmerized. He seemed to be enjoying himself.

She shoved him over, straddled him, and her hands shot around his throat. They started to squeeze.

His eyes bulged.

Key was pissed off and done. The more she'd let him yank her around, the more complicated and grim the situation had gotten.

"I. Don't. Like. This."

Key accentuated every word with a harder clamp on Flynn's throat. It wasn't completely homicidal. If it were, she'd be dragging his carcass across the Razor. But she did want to make a point.

The debris lay everywhere around them, some of it still smoldering. Something had just blown the hell out of everything electronic around them, and it had come from the sky. Where the rockets had gone. Where they'd disappeared.

Flynn gurgled below her. Key kept squeezing.

"I am not a happy fucking camper. Do you know why?"

Flynn shook his head as best he could.

"Because I don't understand what's happening. And that makes me angry."

"It . . . it was . . ."

Flynn struggled to speak, but it came out as hoarse gasps of air. Key loosened her grip just enough.

"It must have been . . . a pulse . . ."

Key froze. Pulse? "An EMP?"

Flynn nodded, then coughed and gulped air. "They waited until their people . . . were clear, then they fried everything electronic on the surface."

"Why the fuck would they do that?"

"Because it's a really good way to make sure a million-plus homicidal maniacs stay right where they are."

Key thought it through, and she had to admit it made sense. A pulse would take out anything that wasn't magnetically shielded. X-Cores would still work, but all the electronics running from them would be useless. No transports, no shuttles, no weapons. Shit, even coffeemakers wouldn't work.

She stared at Flynn, feeling the trepidation growing in her stomach. Her wings kept itching.

"It pisses me off that you're the only one who knows what's going on right now," she said, her hands going around his throat again. "It makes me want to break things."

"*Knows what's going on?*" Flynn shoved her hands off him. "Nothing's made sense since I got here!"

She stared down at him curiously. The anger in his eyes and face didn't really seem to fit. She kind of liked it.

"I don't have any clue what's happening on this planet," Flynn said. "But it sounds like whoever was on the other end of that tablet does."

Key stared back. "Am I supposed to pull the point you're trying to make out of your ass for you?"

"Whoever it was knew about the pulse before it happened. They *warned* us. They're trying to help."

"No," Key said, shaking her head. "No, no, no, *Doctor*. Your worldview needs a fucking adjustment. No one ever *helps* anyone, unless they want something. Especially on the Razor."

Flynn stared at her. "Then we have an advantage."

Key's eyes thinned.

"If they want something from us," he told her, "then we have leverage. And I have a feeling no one left on this planet has much of that right now."

Key looked at him. His point was a fragile one, but a point nonetheless. Besides, what was their other option? If they made it to the starport, some of the deep space freighters might be sitting there. Those wouldn't have been affected by the pulse, since they were shielded. But how were they going to get there? Walk hand in hand all the way, scale the Barrier hand-cuffed? Maybe, at least, wherever the tablet wanted them to go might have a way to cut them loose from each other. Then the good doctor could follow whatever voices he heard next. And she would be somewhere else. Anywhere else.

A new sound came from the top of the table then. It sounded like static, but with other, stranger sounds mixed in. Scratchy, unsettling high-pitched squeals.

Key and Flynn stood up and stared at the table.

It was covered in debris from the explosion. The radio was still there, knocked over, the digital screen blown out. Even so . . . the sounds were coming from *it*. Somehow, it was transmitting a signal.

"That's . . . not normal," Flynn observed, his voice unnerved.

The sounds coming out of the blown speaker didn't sound random, either. They sounded organized. Almost like voices. High-pitched scratches and whines, but clearly voices. Many, many voices.

Key grabbed the radio, smashed it into the side of the table. Again and again, until it finally broke apart.

The sounds, whatever they were, died. There was nothing but the sound of wind whipping through the canyon and the flames from the burning building.

"Just a charge left in the wires, feedback . . ." Flynn offered unconvincingly. Key stared at the broken comm unit darkly.

"Let's find that rail line," she said.

Flynn offered no objection. Seconds later, they were moving. Northeast. Just like the tablet had told them to.

TWENTY-ONE

BURDENS

It had happened months ago, but Maddox could still see all the details in his head.

The starport hangar, brightly lit by LEDs. Fifty yards square, made of steel and polycarbon, like all the other buildings on the Razor. The dim light of permanent dusk filtering in through the ventilation fans in the ceiling, stripes of shadow and light painting shapes on the walls and the floor as the blades spun.

Maddox didn't notice any of that.

His scattergun was heavy in his hands as he stood surrounded by the men in his Ranger unit. They all had their scatterguns out, too, and they were all aiming at him.

Reed, Jericho, Mars, the rest of them. Most of them he'd served with in Colonial Force Recon. The JSCC tended to offer contracts to entire units for Ranger duty on hard labor planets, after they deactivated. He remembered when they'd all signed on, how they'd toasted all the credits to come.

It was ironic, all things considered.

Maddox wasn't looking at them, though. He was looking at the only other man inside the circle with him. And the only man who was unarmed.

Captain Canek. His commander, then and now. A man he'd bled with, one he'd come to trust, one who'd saved his life more than once.

"Explain it to me then," Maddox said, staring at Canek in a way he never thought he would. With open hostility.

The captain just shook his head. "What's to explain? It should be obvious."

"You're not helping your case, sir," Maddox replied. The scattergun shook slightly. He felt rage. And shame. He'd come here hoping to find it was all bullshit. Instead, he'd learned the opposite.

There was only one thing in the hangar besides themselves. An automated 6211 cargo container, the kind meant to load onto the big intersystem transports. It was already attached to the rail system, which would lift it up and through the ceiling hatch, to the big ship on the platform above.

Its door was open. Inside were a dozen female prisoners. All in their jumpsuits. Bound together in shackles, and mag-locked to a railing system in the container's ceiling and walls.

They all stared out through the door, wide-eyed, scared.

Among them was the one Maddox had come looking for.

Deep black skin, dreadlocks, lithe muscles covered by tattoos.

Marcias. Whistler's woman. The leader of the Bloodclan.

She stared back at him calmly, like she knew her fate was sealed either way.

"Fuck's sake, Maddox, put the gun down," Canek said.

He was about the same height as Maddox, so their eyes were aligned. Canek's stare was firm but not hard, like his demeanor. Maddox had seen Canek stay calm through far tenser situations than a scattergun pointed at his chest.

"I don't think I can do that, sir," Maddox replied. "I think I have to arrest you."

Some of the Rangers around Maddox chuckled. The rest kept silent and their guns pointed.

"Christ," Canek spat, disappointed. "The world's so black and white to you, isn't it?"

Maddox's grip tightened on his gun. "How is this *anything* other than black and white?" His anger was growing. "You took oaths. To uphold laws. I took the same ones; we *all* did. You're a *slaver*."

The word fell out of his mouth, coated with venom. Canek's look, however, softened. He nodded, resolved, took a moment before responding.

"There's the title," he finally said. "You're right. I'm selling these prisoners into slavery. They will go to some remote, far-off planet, where they will live in cramped, horrible conditions." As he spoke, his tone became more and more sarcastic. "No access to things like medical care, or the extraweb, or proper food and water. And they'll be forced to work at hard, dangerous labor until they finally die. That's what I'm sentencing them to, you're right. Which is exactly the same goddamned fate the UEG sentenced them to on whatever colony world or station they got busted on."

Maddox swallowed, shook his head slowly.

"Lifetime incarceration here, lifetime incarceration somewhere else," Canek went on. "You know what the difference is? It's who *profits*. Here, on the Razor, it's Maas-Dorian. Shit, they profit on a scale so big, you need a different word for it. Who else? The United Earth Governments. And whatever other private Earth enterprises buy their tech from M-D, which is pretty much everyone these days."

"So, what then?" Maddox shot back, trying hard to not pull the trigger. "You're getting rich, so all's fair?"

"No!" Canek's voice was abrupt, angry. "Christ . . . *No*. You know Jameson's kid has Geery disorder. You know how expensive that is to treat."

Maddox's glare softened, he couldn't help it. Jameson was just to his right, staring at him down the barrel of his 10mm.

"Mars's parents have been stuck in a crime-ridden district on Titan for the last twenty years, and now he's moving them into a retirement facility on Opus Major. Every one of these men, *your* men, is doing it to take care of theirs. Because who else is going to? Evelyn fucking *Maas*? The *UEG*? Fuck . . . You were in the Outlier; you saw where we ranked on the priority list. How many guys did we bury back then? How many farmers toting pulse rifles did we take away from their kids? It's no different on this planet. It's no different anywhere."

Maddox felt his grip begin to loosen on his gun. He swallowed again.

"These prisoners made a choice, Maddox," the captain said, motioning behind him to the cargo container. Maddox glanced there, to the women inside it, and to the dark-skinned woman specifically. Marcias was still staring at him. "They killed and stole their way into getting incarcerated here. None of us had anything to do with that. At least with my way, they still get what's theirs, and then, finally, we get what's *ours* too. What we should have gotten all along."

Maddox tore his eyes away from the woman. "That doesn't make it right, sir."

"That's true," Canek said evenly, nodding. "It doesn't. But it doesn't make it wrong either. And if you're going to judge us with that kind of polarity, that's how you need to see it. You have a son . . ."

Maddox sighed, looked down. He felt the same emotions he did every time he thought of his boy. Two years old now, and he'd never even met him. Not for lack of trying, but his son had been born during the Revolution, at the beginning of his second tour. Allie had already wanted nothing to do with Maddox by then, and when his child support transfers started bouncing back, she wanted even less.

"You told me about your father, the kind of man he was," Canek said. "What would you do to give your son the opposite kind? How much is that worth? Is it worth *that*?"

Canek gestured behind him again. This time Maddox didn't look. He couldn't.

"Sending them to the *same* fate . . . just a few more light-years away?"

Maddox looked back up at his captain. His muscles had lost their tension; the scattergun hung limply in his hands. He felt tears starting to form. His mind was changing, and it hurt.

"Back in the Outlier," Canek said, his voice softer now, "we followed a lot of orders. You didn't know the specifics. The why of it. There's a reason for that. You couldn't live with the knowledge. Not because you're weak, Maddox, but because you're a good man. So I took that on for you, let you go on without knowing. Because I love you, like I love every man in this room. And that's what you should do for your son, right now. You should take it on, too."

Maddox shut his eyes, feeling the emotions wash over him, emotions that eclipsed all the other ones he had come in here with. His eyes stung.

"That's what men do. That's what fathers do. You're not my blood . . . but you are my son."

Maddox shook his head, eyes still closed. He knew if he opened them, the tears would flow.

"Put the gun down, Maddox," Canek said, in his softest voice yet. "Put it down, son."

Slowly, Maddox did. He let the barrel tilt toward the floor.

Laughter filled the room. The tension broke.

The Rangers, his unit, his brothers, they all holstered their weapons, they all moved for him. Their arms were on him, hugging him. Ruffling his hair. Slugging him on the shoulder and the back.

"Hey," Canek said, lifting Maddox's eyes up to his. "You can always kill me later."

More laughter. Canek hugged Maddox.

Maddox hugged him back, but over the man's shoulder he stared into the supply container, at the woman there. At Marcias. Standing with all the others. Her look never wavered, never changed.

He held her look until the door to the container closed and it started to lift up and away.

TWENTY-TWO

X-CORE

Maddox woke from the past into the present and found he couldn't move.

Through the visor of the rad-suit's helmet, he could see the sheet of warped polysteel that had burst through the containment doors and rammed against his legs and chest as he hung in the harness. He could feel the thick bulkhead wall pressed against his back on the other side.

Blinking, he got a better idea of what had happened.

The support beams of the doorway into the X-Core had shot straight through the containment door, blowing it apart, probably from the impact of the landing, pinning him in place. It was a miracle he hadn't been crushed.

There was no way to know how high up the ejection had shot them, but even with the parachutes that deployed, something as heavy as an SMV X-Core would hit hard when it landed.

He found a way to move his arms and hands, got them up to where the rad-suit was harnessed. He searched with his fingers, found the clips, disconnected them.

The suit fell and he went with it, crashing to the floor but free of the debris. He wiggled loose. The rad-suit was bulky and heavy, not made for this kind of environment. Then again, nothing probably was. He pushed clear of the wreckage.

Smoke was thick in the air; flashing lights lit it up in strange, prismatic silhouettes of red light. Through the debris, he could see what was left of the containment door. As expected, everything past it was full of hardened carbon foam. It would have deployed before impact, sealing the core in place, with the goal of preventing it from breaching. All the easier for a recovery team to deal with.

Of course, there wasn't going to be a recovery team this time.

He could just glimpse the metallic ceiling, caved in at odd angles. The polycarbon walls around him were rippled badly. Shockingly, even buried in twenty square feet of carbon foam, the core still seemed to be power-ing itself. Lights flashed. Alarms sounded. Sparks sprayed constantly from power conduits that had ripped loose.

He was still alive. He and . . .

Raelyn.

Maddox quickly found the spot where her suit had hung next to his. It was blocked by more debris, and he couldn't tell what was there now.

Desperation set in. She was buried, could be crushed, for all he knew.

Maddox moved for it, tried to shove the debris out of the way. In the suit it wasn't easy, but he ignored the pain and pushed with his legs.

The metal groaned, the walls shaking dangerously.

He saw her. In her suit, strapped to the wall, hanging lifelessly, the glass visor of the helmet fogged so he couldn't see through to her face.

He felt even more desperate. Which was, he knew, ridiculous. All he'd been doing this entire time, since he'd killed those guards, was forestall-ing the inevitable. The situation was just too severe. But still, the idea of failing her, of failing someone else . . .

Maddox clawed at the metal, pushing it away, and when he finally cleared enough of it, Raelyn's body slumped forward into his arms.

He still couldn't see into her helmet, couldn't tell if she was alive.

The alarms continued to blare, more and more smoke filling the tiny interior as his gloved hands found the clips that held the helmet to Rae-lyn's neck brace. The clips snapped loose, the suit vented, and he pulled the helmet off.

Her neck lolled downward limply. It was a good sign. Dead people's necks didn't do that.

"Doctor?" Maddox shook her slightly. "Raelyn?"

He searched for a pulse, could barely feel it through the thick gloves, but it was there. She was alive. Maddox sighed in relief.

But she was unconscious. Looking down, Maddox saw why.

The beams from the crumpled doorway had missed him when the bulkhead collapsed, but Raelyn hadn't been so lucky. A shard of metal had pierced straight through her leg, puncturing the composite material of the rad-suit.

Blood seeped out of the jagged hole, coating the floor, staining the legs of her suit, and it was still running free, dripping onto his boots.

The doctor might not be dead. But she was about to be.

Panic battled against exhaustion and apathy. What was he doing? It would have been faster to just let the guards do them both in, back on the *Charon*.

But he hadn't. He'd gotten involved. The very thing he swore he wasn't doing anymore. And why?

Because it would have been another one, a voice in his head said. *Someone else you failed by doing* nothing.

He saw Marcias again. The women in the cargo container. Saw them lifting up and away while the rest of his unit laughed around him.

Maddox barely had enough energy to stand, but he pulled Raelyn free of the debris, careful not to rip her suit any more than he had to. They were going to need it. When she was clear, he laid her gently down on the floor.

"Hold on, Doctor," he told her. "Hold on for me."

Raelyn's body contorted as she coughed, her breathing erratic. Maddox reattached her helmet, clicking it back in place, then scanned what was left of the X-Core's radiation lock. He found what he wanted, amid the spilled contents of the supply lockers, scattered across the floor.

An automated first aid device. Maddox grabbed the kit. It reacted to his hand, lit up and flashed, the screen on the side scrolling its status.

It was still functional.

Maddox brought it back to the doctor—and froze. It wasn't just the leg of her suit that was ripped; the forearm was too. Standing out under the material, he could see, fully revealed, what he had guessed was there before. Thin, vein-like lines curling up her forearm toward her bicep, glowing with faint red light, like simmering coals.

Slow Burn.

Maddox knew the basics of the disease, that medication couldn't reverse it, could only halt it. Whistler no doubt had taken her meds back on the Charon, in his bid to make her kill Maddox. She'd likely been without them for some time now. The longer she went without, the more it would spread, and the more pain she would deal with.

It was one more reason to get her out of here.

Maddox ripped open the suit around her leg. Blood gushed just above her kneecap. The rod had plunged several inches into the meat of her thigh.

Maddox hefted the AFAD. It was circular in shape, about the size of a small briefcase, with numerous ports and plugs and a small touch screen on the front. It was designed to treat injuries sustained in dangerous mechanical environments, and it had a host of features.

Maddox activated the touch screen, scrolled through the menus, finding the item he wanted.

The head of a tiny blowtorch poked out and ignited a thin, focused, hissing blue flame.

Sparks flew as Maddox cut what remained of the rod in Raelyn's leg in half, making it more manageable. He grabbed an end of it.

"Sorry," he told the comatose doctor.

The rod was smooth and still straight; it came out easily. So did the blood, pouring out of the leg wound.

"Fuck." Maddox's heart beat wildly, watching the wound gush. If he didn't stop the bleeding . . .

He tapped the AFAD control screen, smearing it with blood. He wiped it off, and the menus all changed when he did, resetting.

"*Fuck!*"

He could barely make out the screen now, but he finally found what he wanted, tapped it.

A rounded, flexible, metallic instrument rattled out. Maddox had used it before, mainly on gunshot wounds.

The doctor moaned on the floor. "Words . . . only words, Dad . . ."

She was speaking, at least. Even if it was delirious, it was a good sign.

Maddox pulled the wound taut on the doctor's leg, then pressed the device against it. The machine beeped twice and the screen flashed, indicating to hold still.

There was a sizzling sound. Smoke wafted up from Raelyn's leg.

She moaned again, shifted, but Maddox held the thing in place.

After almost a minute, the machine beeped again, the flashing stopped.

He checked the wound. Fresh, dark red scar tissue ran in an ugly line across the entire line that had been ripped open. It was flash-cauterized and, as far as Maddox could tell, not bleeding anymore.

Maddox didn't let himself relax. Even with the bleeding under control, there was still only so much time people could survive in an ejected SMV X-Core in the middle of the Cindersphere.

How the hell was he going to get Raelyn back to the Razor?

Really, Maddox knew, there was only one answer. And the survivability of it depended on where they'd landed inside the Cinder. If the winds and heat patterns had carried them toward the Razor, they might make it. If not . . .

He felt incredibly, completely exhausted.

When could he just . . . *stop*? It had been the one, solitary thing that had comforted him. Once he got to the Razor, he could let go. He could let things *end*.

The universe, as usual, had had other ideas.

Maddox swiped the control screen on the AFAD, finding what he wanted.

The same device as before, the cauterizer, appeared from its port.

Maddox gathered up the material of Raelyn's suit. He placed the device over it. It beeped and the screen flashed, then more smoke, followed by the hissing sound.

When he pulled it away, the rip in the suit was fused back together, just like the skin of the doctor's leg. The AFAD had been designed for a mining environment, where radiation and heat suit malfunctions and damage were commonplace. Its equipment was multifunctional.

Maddox repeated the process on the tear in the arm. It was a temporary fix, probably wouldn't hold up long but, then again, the doctor wasn't going to be moving much.

He dropped the AFAD and stood up, found the pieces of what he needed. More rods from the containment door. Some plexisteel from where the bulkhead had been ripped apart. It was light but strong, just what he needed. He used the welder from the AFAD to fuse it together, then yanked out as much insulation from behind the walls as he could, for cushioning.

When it was done, Maddox lay Raelyn on top of the hastily created sled and unhooked the rad-suit harness from the wall, using it to strap her securely to the sled. With the helmet on, he still couldn't see her face, but he *could* see her chest rising and falling under the suit.

Maddox grabbed the makeshift handles he'd made and pulled Raelyn toward the radiation lock door, the one that used to lead back into the *Charon*'s interior and now led right to hell.

He reached for the controls.

Maddox waited for the usual hesitation, the self-doubt, the skepticism. But it didn't come this time. Instead, he felt something decidedly different.

There were no second chances, he knew that. But something about what he was doing filled him with emotion. He felt . . . hopeful. It was the last thing he expected.

He looked back at Raelyn, on the sled, lying still.

"You and me, kid."

He selected a button on his rad-suit's controls and the visor on his helmet darkened automatically. He hit the panel to the door, and it slid open.

Waves of heat and wind blew inside, almost knocking him over. He caught brief glimpses of canyons and mesas, burning in intense heat. The warning instruments in his HUD spiked.

Maddox pushed forward into it, pulling the weight of the sled, feeling the pain in his legs and arms. He didn't know how far he would get, but that wasn't the point.

Maddox smiled for the first time in forever.

TWENTY-THREE

BEACON

Maddox went down in stages. Knees first, then all the way, the helmet of his rad-suit indenting the burning sand. He could feel the heat soak through the material.

He'd made it. Again. Into the shade cast by one of the Cindersphere's giant mesas. Right now it towered above him, along with all the other strange, angular, wind-carved rock formations.

A good sign. Go too far into the Cinder, there were no formations at all. It meant they were close to the Terminus. But in the Cindersphere, "close" was a dangerously relative term.

The HUD in his helmet had digital gauges. Radiation. Heat. Air pressure. They were slowly winding down, out of the redline, back to levels that wouldn't kill him. Or at least not immediately.

Since he'd dragged Raelyn out of the ejected X-Core, he'd been moving between pockets of shade in the landscape. As fast as he could.

The temperature and radiation differences between the shade and the full sun were the difference between a suit failure and barely surviving. And there wasn't much shade.

Maddox slowly rolled over onto his back. His body was soaked with sweat. The air coming through the air filter felt like engine exhaust, but he breathed it in greedily.

The sky was almost white above him, no blue in sight. The atmosphere burned away.

The makeshift sled dug into the ground behind him, holding Raelyn. She hadn't moved since they'd walked out of the X-Core. The visor on the helmet was completely fogged. He couldn't even tell if she was breathing.

What if she was already dead inside that suit?

Maddox exhaled, his breathing pained. He arched his neck and looked east, where he needed to go. He only knew it was the right direction because of a needle-sharp, supremely bright column of energy that shot straight into the sky there.

He'd gotten his bearings off the X-Core's computer when he'd stepped outside, and the energy line was the first thing he'd noticed. Even this deep into the Cindersphere, it stood out.

Whatever it was, it was behind the mountains he could make out in the distance, mountains he knew were not in the Cindersphere.

If he'd figured it right, that would make the line of energy, the beacon, in the Razor somewhere.

Maddox had never seen or heard of anything like it on the planet. One more mystery to add to the rest. And one more thing he didn't have time to worry about.

Maddox studied the landscape ahead. Just shimmering heat and death in between rare spots of shade from mesas and outcroppings. It was a maze of towering needle columns of rock and slot canyons, carved out by wind and solar storms.

It would be easy to get lost in these canyons. Even easier to hit a dead end and have to backtrack—which would be the end of them, most likely.

Maddox sighed. It was better not to think about it. He would keep going. He wouldn't do nothing ever again.

Maddox groaned, pushed to his feet, hefted the makeshift handles of Raelyn's sled, spotted the next bit of shade he wanted to hit, ahead of them.

Probably sixty yards away. He would have to be fast. Fast as he could, anyway.

His shoulders jolted as he started to pull the sled. It slid through the sand easily enough, but it was probably close to two hundred pounds.

He stepped clear of the shade, into the full fury of the planet's sun. His instruments spiked. He felt the heat push through his suit and sear into his skin. But he kept moving.

Lights flashed. Alarms blared.

One foot after another, over and over, the weight of Raelyn behind him bending his arms and shoulders.

He fell again into the shade, this time from an outcrop, a huge column of rock towering into the burning air, casting probably only about fifteen feet worth of shade. But it was enough.

The alarms quieted. The digital needles sank out of the redline on the screen in front of his eyes.

Everything hurt.

Old wounds. New wounds.

Even so, Maddox was surprised by the energy coursing through him. The old kind, the kind that had always driven him before.

The kind that came when he had a purpose.

It felt good. It felt like he was coming back to life. The feelings surprised him.

He was supposed to be done. He was supposed to have been gone long before this. But here he was.

He raised up, looked at the girl on the sled. Her form unmoving. He felt resentment. And somewhere under that, he felt gratitude.

"Fuck you," he whispered, the breathy sound of it filling his helmet.

Maddox stood up, faster than he had before. He grabbed the sled, started moving.

Pain lanced through his shoulders and back. But he kept moving, stepped into the sun.

The needles spiked in his HUD; the heat burrowed through the suit.

Lights flashed. Alarms blared. The old ones, from before. But a new one now, too. One he hadn't seen before.

Proximity Alert: Weather Anomaly

Maddox glanced behind him. The view there was mesmerizing.

Giant clouds of dust, spiraling upward, filling the horizon, blocking out the sun. Barreling down on him at hundreds of miles an hour.

A solar storm.

Full of razor-sharp particles of dust and Xytrilium crystals that would shred their suits if the impact from the blast didn't smash them to pieces first.

It would be on them in a minute. Maddox could already feel the vibrations from it rumbling up through his boots.

He had to get Raelyn to safety, and fast.

Maddox scanned the immediate area, looking for something specific.

He found it, about a hundred yards to his right. A slot canyon. It might not be the closest one, but he didn't have time to be picky.

He turned hard, dragging Raelyn's sled behind him.

The sliver of open space carved out of the rocky side of a mesa by wind and by the kind of storm that was bearing down on them could lead anywhere—or nowhere.

It might protect them. It might not. But it was their best chance.

There was a lot of sun between them and the canyon, and not much time to cross it. Maddox pulled harder, the pain increasing.

He felt the heat burn past the suit. The gauges in his HUD kept rising, moving closer to the redline.

Maddox breathed heavily, kept moving, his arms burning, sweat pouring down his chest.

Alarms sounded. Lights flashed.

Through the suit he could hear the sound of the rushing storm. Dust began to blow everywhere, the precursor of the onslaught, coming fast.

Maddox felt his feet leave the ground.

Felt the handles of the sled ripped loose from his hands.

The storm slammed into him with the force of a train.

Maddox clipped the edge of the entrance wall, flipped into the canyon, hit the ground and rolled.

The storm thundered outside. The sound was overpowering.

Maddox raised his head up and saw Raelyn's sled hurtling toward him.

He braced himself. It hit. Hard. Tossing them both backward, twisting and spinning. Together, they rolled as the storm rammed the canyon.

Dust and darkness filled everything. Alarms blared in his helmet.

Pain flashed like lightning in his legs and shoulders, but somehow he pushed himself up out of the dirt. He felt what was left of the metal sled crack and break apart as he pushed it off him.

Dirt cascaded off the sides of his helmet.

The storm raged outside the canyon, but it was deflected by the wall of the mesa. They were protected. Barely.

Looking around, he found Raelyn.

She was bent at a weird angle, the sled completely shattered. He felt his heart sink. He wouldn't be able to pull her anymore. If he was going to get them out of here now, he would have to carry her.

Maddox almost laughed. It was insane. Anyone with a normal amount of sense would just take off their helmet and let the rads do their worst.

"Fuck you," he breathed, bending down, hefting Raelyn up, draping her over his shoulder. The weight of her buckled his knees, shot pain down his back. Still, he felt more alive than he had in weeks, and he hated her for it. "*Fuck* you."

When he made it out of the canyon, back into the open, everything was dark. The storm had swirled a tremendous amount of dust into the air, so thick that it blocked out the sun. The instruments in his HUD showed the result.

A plus, but it came with a problem. The dust was so thick that Maddox couldn't see more than ten feet ahead of him. There was no way he could navigate now.

Then he saw it.

Blurred, but he could still make out the glow, emanating to his right. Somehow, impossibly, the beacon that shot into the sky cut right through the haze.

What was that thing?

The gauges in his HUD were rising again. The air was lightening. The dust was blocking the sun for the moment, but it wouldn't last long.

Raelyn stirred on his shoulders. "You and me, kid," she moaned deliriously through her helmet, repeating what he'd said before.

Maddox felt new strength. His boots sank into the soft red sand, but it was like walking over coals. He could feel the heat radiating up his legs, one step after the other.

He walked straight for the beacon, the only thing he had to guide him.

When the sun finally burned away the dust, there'd be no more moving between shade pockets. This was the end of the line, and it would all be decided in the next few moments.

Maddox collapsed to his knees, pushed himself back up, balancing Raelyn, groaning with the pain of it. He forced himself forward.

The air kept lightening, the gauges still rising. It would be over soon. The Terminus was just too far away. It was okay, though. He hadn't quit. Hadn't done nothing.

Then he saw something in the thinning haze.

Lights. Sharp, small ones. Dozens of them, pushing through the dust cloud.

They blinked and flashed. Rhythmically. In grids.

As he slowly got closer, he saw more. The outline of something big and rectangular. Human-made. A *facility*.

The dust finally burned away and the sun shone through full force. Maddox fell to the sand. Raelyn tumbled to the ground with him. He felt the heat of it on his back. The gauges spiked. Alarms sounded.

Maddox grabbed Raelyn's arms and pushed with his legs, backward through the sand, half a body length at a time. Toward the facility behind him. Dragging her . . .

It was powered. It would have heat shields.

He kept pushing. One leg length at a time. His arms and legs screamed, sweat poured off his face. His strength was fading. This was it.

Then the air shimmered as he passed through the edge of the heat shields. The gauges on his instruments all slumped to Nominal.

Maddox fell back, coughed and gasped. Weakly, slowly, barely conscious, he unlocked his helmet, peeled it off, and looked around.

A mining facility. An old one. A gridwork of metal and polycarbon, sheltering access tunnels and exhaust towers, all arrayed in a perfect square. Vehicles, sandcats, power loaders, all sat lined up on the concrete pad outside the main entrance door.

The place had been built before Crawlers, sent mined Xytrilium in storage pods along conveyors that ran east to refineries just past the Terminus. They could ride in those pods, Maddox knew, ride them all the way back to the Razor. They could make it.

Maddox thought it through.

There were only eleven of these facilities, up and down the entire length of the Terminus, and he had somehow crawled right toward one.

His eyes moved up, found the beacon again, a sharp, red line shooting into the sky. It was almost dead center behind the facility.

If it hadn't been there for him to navigate by . . .

Raelyn moved, just barely, on top of him.

Maddox yanked her helmet off. She was covered in sweat, her hair stuck to her face. So wet, it looked black now. He brushed it away, out of her eyes, felt her breath on his fingers. Maddox exhaled in relief.

Her blue eyes flickered open. They were like deep pools, he thought. She stared up at him. Weakly, but she stared.

"You . . . made it." Her voice was barely audible.

Maddox smiled, shook his head. How the hell had he gotten here?

"You and me, kid."

TWENTY-FOUR

STRIPE

The ride lasted all of three minutes, but it was intense, their pods darting on mag-rails, in a tunnel carved straight through the mountains to the east that bordered the Terminus. The pods were made to transport Xytrilium, not humans. Smaller than coffins, but similarly shaped, with a triple-hinged lid that vacuum sealed in place. Since there wasn't enough to room to lie flat, Maddox and Raelyn would have to curl into fetal positions in order to fit. And it would be dark inside.

Maddox sealed Raelyn in her pod. She'd been terrified, he could read it in her eyes.

"It's just the dark," Maddox told her. "The dark can't hurt you."

"Are you sure?"

He stared down at her, tried to smile comfortingly. He held her blue eyes as he shut the lid, listening to it seal.

She had about fifteen minutes of oxygen inside the pod. The ride would take a fraction of that—the mag-rails moved at about eighty miles an hour—but if anything went wrong . . .

Maddox put it out of his mind, set the deployment timer on the automated track, gave himself sixty seconds, and climbed into his own pod. His he couldn't seal; not if he wanted to open it from the inside.

He'd rigged up a handle of sorts, from a chain and a door hinge, and attached it by removing two of the pod's bulkhead screws.

It was nerve-racking. A Lost Prophet protocol came with one final kick in the balls for everyone who was left planet-side. An EMP, fired into the atmosphere, that took out all the Razor's electronics.

It still hadn't gone off, but it had to be imminent now. There'd been enough time for the rockets to make orbit. If it hit while they were in the pod, they would be trapped in the middle of a mountain, in a transport tunnel too cramped to even open the pod lid. They would die there. Buried alive.

Maddox climbed in, pulled the pod door shut, felt the thing start to move, and held on.

At eighty miles an hour, the gravity wanted to yank the lid up and off, and it hurt trying to hold it down.

Eventually, Maddox felt the pod come to a stop, the mag-rails underneath them powering down.

A few seconds later, he had the lid open and was looking up at the sharp, blunt light from LED installations in the ceiling of the receiving center.

Just like at the mining facility at the other end, the lights were flashing blue, the alarms sounding. The indicators of the ongoing Lost Prophet. They'd made it. They were past the Terminus. They were back in the Razor.

There were no sounds other than the alarms, and he didn't see any movement. It looked safe.

The building was a large open space with two huge metal doors on either end. Dozens of giant refining tanks lined the center, running out of sight away from the tracks the pods came in on. The tanks were highly pressurized units that compacted Xytrilium crystals, over time, into the incredibly dense spheres that would eventually be placed inside the X-Cores, once charged and processed.

Railway tracks came in underneath a giant closed door in a far wall, and automated grappling arms sat in the middle, for loading the refinery tanks onto train cars that would then carry them back to the starport for transport off-world.

Maddox crawled out and fell to the floor. It was concrete, not polycarbon, which showed how old the place was.

He sat back against the pod, resting on the automated track, and breathed deeply. The temperature was cool and the air was absent the strange hum found in the Cindersphere.

He felt a wave of relief.

Maddox needed to get Raelyn out of her pod. He started to stand, when the alarms suddenly stopped sounding. The protocol lights kept flashing, but the pulses went away. It was odd, everything going silent just like that.

"Got it!" a voice yelled, somewhere not far away. "Got the damn thing off."

Maddox froze. He wasn't alone after all.

He scanned everything again, and this time his eyes went to the ceiling. There, where he hadn't seen it before, in the rafters lined with LED lights and power conduits, hung the bodies of probably a dozen guards.

Limp and lifeless, still in their armor, helmets removed, electrical cables around their necks. The features of their faces were totally gone. Bloody. Cut. Hammered.

They'd died badly.

He saw more bodies then, on the ground, yards away. Engineers. Civilians. Blood everywhere. Their throats slit.

If those voices were the ones who—

He felt the sharp, cold bite of a blade push into his temple right as he sensed the people moving in around him.

Maddox didn't move. The pain vanished. So did the exhaustion.

He slowly looked up. Prisoners. Five of them. All wearing purple jumpsuits.

Maddox swallowed. So far, they hadn't paid any attention to Raelyn's pod. So far . . .

"Well, lookie." One of the purples moved in front of him. His voice was harsh and tight, slightly accented. "A quandary. Ain't it?"

The guy was tall, thin as a rail, the veins standing out under his pale skin. His head was shaved on the sides, leaving a crop of wiry white hair running down the middle in a stripe. His eyes darted around wildly, unable to focus. High, Maddox guessed.

This Stripe was probably the leader. He held the knife against Maddox's head, but his underlings all had pulse pistols. They didn't seem to get that guns on this planet were tied to biometrics; they wouldn't fire. But that didn't matter with these kinds of numbers. They could just beat Raelyn and him to death. Or worse.

"He's white," one said, referencing Maddox's jumpsuit. It was visible underneath the rad-suit.

"White," a third one echoed with disdain.

"That makes us nervous," Stripe stated. He had a weird habit of chewing on his lower lip as he talked. "Makes us wonder."

The pale man's eyes darted over his features. Maddox stared past him, back to the bodies up top, hanging from the rafters.

Something had gone down here, in the receiving center, probably when the Lost Prophet had gone off. The guards never made it out.

"You like?" Stripe asked, following Maddox's gaze. "Might be up there too, play your cards wrong. Where you from?"

Maddox saw one of the purples, to his right, a hefty one, step closer—which also brought him closer to Raelyn's pod. She was terrified of the dark, by her own admission, and it was pitch-black inside that pod. If she pounded on the lid . . .

Stripe's fingers lifted Maddox's chin up. "Where you *from*?"

"The *Charon*," Maddox said.

That took them by surprise. "A Crawler? How'd you get on the track?"

"Just kill him," another purple stated. "We need to bail before the deployment teams respond. No one's checked in for more than an hour."

"Take a sandcat outside and go," said another.

Maddox took stock. Two on either side, all with their useless guns raised. The others behind him, on the other side of the track. Stripe was right in front of him, knife he'd gotten somewhere. There was a tool chest, with socket wrenches, just out of reach on the left. Big socket wrenches.

Maddox saw his play. It was a bad one. Him versus five prisoners with just some wrenches. But if he could take a few of them before they figured out their guns were useless . . .

"The cats aren't going to work much longer," Maddox said. "You guys are going to need a new plan."

All five of them stared at him intently. "The fuck you talking about?" the hefty one next to Raelyn's pod asked.

"See the blue flashing lights?" They looked up. Maddox kept his eyes on Stripe in front of him. "Those aren't for Christmas. Those are protocol lights. The color means a Lost Prophet order. Means the Razor's being *abandoned*."

More silence as they took that in. Apparently the gears in these guys' heads turned slowly.

"Abandoned?" It was Stripe. The concept seemed like a tough one.

"Everyone except prisoners, which is the problem. Can't have us running around with leftover pulse pistols, can they? So they're going to fire an EMP in the atmosphere."

"What's that?" the hefty one asked.

"An electromagnetic pulse, you fat fuck," one of the others answered.

"That's right," Maddox said. "It'll fry everything with a circuit, X-Core or no X-Core. That cat outside. The rail system. The lights in the ceiling. Everything."

Stripe looked back down at him, his eyes thinning. "How you know all this?"

Before Maddox could answer, one of them yanked down the neckline of his rad-suit. It revealed the brand there, shaped like the symbol of the Razor.

"Fucking Fink," Stripe spat. "You a guard, Fink? That how you know this?"

Maddox shook his head. "Ranger."

"Fucking A," another purple said. The group moved in closer. "God-damn Ranger."

Maddox swallowed.

"How'd you cross the tracks, Ranger?" Stripe again. "How'd you get on this side?"

"Kill him and quit fucking around."

"What if he's right? What if—"

"He ain't right, he ain't even—"

"Then we're the luckiest *bastards* this side of the Barrier." Stripe cut everyone else off, smiling broad with yellow teeth. "The whole planet. The whole goddamned thing—"

The pod above Maddox suddenly rocked. Something rattled it on the inside. It was Raelyn. She had finally panicked.

Maddox felt a knot form hard in his stomach.

"What the hell?" the fat purple said, tapping a few buttons on the pod's controls. The lid opened, rising up on its compressed hinges.

Maddox, and everyone else, heard a deep, intense intake of breath from the pod.

Another purple looked inside. His eyes glistened at what he saw. Maddox could hear a yelp as the thug grabbed a handful of hair, yanking Raelyn up and out and onto the floor.

Her eyes were wild, terrified. They found Maddox. He stared back.

"Lookie," Stripe breathed, excited. "A honey. A beautiful honey. Ripe."

Maddox's eyes darted to the tool chest. He could go for it, but not before Raelyn got grabbed, was used against him. There were too many.

Maddox felt the muzzle of a gun press into his temple again. Harder this time.

"Gonna have fun with you," Stripe's hoarse voice said above him. "With you and the girl. A long time. Make you watch, too, all our turns. Make you watch the light go outta her. Then, after that, we'll start on you."

Maddox didn't look at him, just stared at Raelyn. The one he'd failed. The latest one.

He should have quit earlier, but he hadn't, and now they were here.

Raelyn screamed as the purples yanked her out of the pod. Maddox tensed, looked at the toolbox. He might as well—

A rumbling filled the room.

Growing louder, more powerful. Shaking the pillars of the building.

Everything stopped. Maddox and the purples and Raelyn all looked toward the sound. In the center of the room were the railroad tracks, running from under the giant doors in the far wall.

The rumbling grew. Maddox's eyes widened.

"Sick fucking joke," a purple said, barely audible.

The entire building rocked as the train exploded through the wall in a maelstrom of fire, blowing debris everywhere like a hurricane.

It barreled into the center of everything, then tipped and slammed to the floor, digging a trench straight through the concrete like it wasn't even there. Metal snapped and frayed. Flame and rock blew forward, slamming into the rows of refining units, tearing them to pieces.

Everyone—Maddox, the purples, Raelyn—lunged for cover as the massive machine ripped the refinery to shreds.

TWENTY-FIVE

ZANE

The impact was hard core. But he'd been expecting it.

When he felt the gravity tugging, he braced himself. Zane was big—two fifty or so—and solid. The inertia when he got thrown, as he'd hoped, ripped the carbon thread bonds right off the ceiling.

They'd made the room to contain him, which meant no metal, and he'd bounced back and forth like a pinball inside it. The walls were softer than metal, but it still broke ribs, dislocated a shoulder.

The train car split in half with a piercing screech. Then the fire exploded inward, filling the room with white heat.

They'd never done anything to dull his pain response. Zane had always appreciated that. Nothing motivated you like pain. And right now the searing pain from the fire was pissing him off.

With a roar, he ran forward, slammed into the back side of what was left of the door to his cell. It was split in two and groaned as he forced it open. The X burned in his muscles, hotter than the fire, adding to his strength.

He moved into the hall, saw the tear in the exterior wall, more fire beyond it. It was the only way out.

He leaped forward and busted through. Jagged metal scratched a gash in his back, adding its pain to the rest.

He hit cement on the outside, rolled and slid.

The flames were here too. It hurt bad. But he was obscured in them, and he'd take strategic advantage at the cost of pain any day.

It was a large facility, older. He could sense the rust coating the metal, but it was still strong. Blue lights, like the ones in the train, flashed in the ceiling. Giant pressure tanks thrown everywhere. Conveyor belts. Storage pods. Forklift bots, powered down. Rafters in the ceiling, next to spinning vent fans.

And bodies. Hung by the neck, swinging limply.

Guards, judging by the armor.

More bodies nearby. No armor, regular clothes. Engineers and miners, civilians.

Whoever had made the mess, he could feel stirring through the metal support rods that lay in the floor. Their vibrations were like faint sonar pings echoing up his legs.

Seven of them. Coming out from cover now. He could see them through the flames.

"What the hell is up with this planet?" The exclamation came from a purple jumpsuit. Tall and thin, wiry muscles without much strength. White hair razored into a stripe.

The stripe shoved one of the others to the ground. Rad-suit over a white jumpsuit. This one was shorter, but strong. Hard edge in his eyes, the kind you got from learning to block out all the things you've seen.

A girl screamed next, yanked up by her hair. She wore another tattered rad-suit, but this one looked like it covered doctor's scrubs.

The rad-suits put those two in a group. They'd escaped something, then ran into the purples.

Bad luck. Also not his problem.

There wasn't anything here he couldn't handle, so Zane stepped out from the flames, into plain sight. The reaction was what he expected.

"Holy . . . fucking . . . *shit!*" a purple exclaimed.

Hugely muscled, clothes burned to ash, muzzle on his face, stepping out of a flaming train wreck that was warped to slag. He was a sight. Then again, he always was. They'd designed him to be intimidating.

Zane ignored them, stepped toward one of the forklift utility bots and touched its metallic arm.

The X burned in his veins. The metal smoked slightly as it blackened and charred. He felt it absorb into him, felt the rib repair, the shoulder realign, the pain lessen.

All this while the others watched, shocked to silence.

When he'd taken in enough, he let go of the arm, felt the Charge withdraw and spread through his muscles. It hurt, like always, burned through him, but he liked it all the same. It still gave him a rise like nothing else.

Zane stepped toward the dead engineers, ignoring the others in the room. They weren't anything to him. He found the biggest body on the floor, not as large as he was, but close enough.

He took off the man's clothes. Work pants, boots, a black T-shirt, orange vest. It all barely held his girth.

"Big man . . ." It was Stripe. He'd taken a step forward. "Someone who walks out of that kind of wreck without a scratch . . . well, shit, that's the kind of someone I say can just keep walking, no hassle from me."

Zane slipped the vest over his back, and scanned the room, one person at a time. He looked at Stripe and said nothing. Most men found it hard to keep Zane's stare, and this one was no different.

The man in the white jumpsuit, though—when Zane's eyes found him, that one stared back evenly. It wasn't bravado or strength. Something had hollowed him out inside. Removed the softness, left all the hard parts.

The girl was shaking, wide-eyed, true terror. She was right to feel that. Men like these were simplistic and predictable. They would rape her. And then she'd take a blade.

Again, not his problem.

"You heard the news?" Stripe again. "No more chains. No more guards. They abandoned the whole fucking planet."

Zane cocked an eyebrow. The UEG abandoned the Razor? It explained a lot. The Rangers' tension, how they'd left him on the train. If it were true, then the real question was did it help him or hurt him? He needed to find out . . .

Zane turned and headed for the gaping hole of twisted metal the train had made. He heard the girl whimper behind him.

"Big man, wait," Stripe called out.

Zane kept walking.

"Could use someone like you. Lots of carnage to come. We got scores. Sure you have, too."

Zane didn't stop.

"Stay and you can have a turn with the honey. Or even kill you a Ranger."

Zane's feet froze on the concrete. The X burned inside him, like it was hungry.

"Ranger?" he asked. His voice was deep and low and somehow filled the entire building. Zane turned his head slightly, back toward the prisoner in white. "That what you are?"

It took a moment for the white jumpsuit to realize he was being addressed. "I . . . used to be."

Zane turned farther around. "Used to be. What are you now?"

"Nothing," the man said without hesitation.

Zane smiled behind his muzzle. He turned all the way, let his eyes slowly drift up from the Ranger to the doctor. The look in her eyes was intense.

"The girl. With you?"

The Ranger nodded tightly. As he did, the Stripe looked between them.

"You don't need to be talking to him," Stripe yelled out. There was an edge in his voice now, a tension. "You talk to me. I'm the one with the juice, eh?"

Zane ignored him. Rangers had access. Rangers knew things. Like the UEG most wanted list, for instance.

"You know what kind of train this is?" Zane asked slowly. "What kind of prisoners it carries?"

The Ranger nodded again.

"You have any idea then who *I* am?"

Zane could see the Ranger swallow over the distance. "An idea, yeah."

"Then you know what you need to do."

A new look formed in the Ranger's eyes. Not fear; more an awareness. That things were turning. Instinctively, the man looked at the doctor. She looked back at him, confused.

A life like this Ranger had led, it either dulled you or it sharpened you. It was clear which way this one had gone. He'd been honed. That was good.

"*Hey!*" Stripe yelled over the distance. He took a step forward, his fists shaking, gripping the knife tightly in his hand. "Either you talking to me, or you getting the *fuck* out of—"

"You talk really loud, friend." Zane cut him off, finally letting his gaze settle on the thin, pale man. "Why is it that the ones who talk the loudest always got the least to say?"

Stripe paused, his eyes thinning. "What did you just say?"

Zane closed his eyes and rubbed his temples. His head hurt. Partly from the X, partly from this waste's jarring voice. "The Ranger comes with me."

Stripe looked back and forth uncomfortably. "You don't—"

"The girl, too. Men like him function better when they have someone to protect. And I need him to function well."

Stripe was breathing faster. He looked like he was going to explode. His gang sensed it.

"Sal . . ." one of the purples warned. The others, at least, had a sense of the reality here. It likely wouldn't matter.

"Shut the fuck up," Stripe responded, his voice on edge. "This guy wants to play? We can play. Goddamn right we can play."

Zane could see it in Stripe's expression. Fear mixing with insecurity. So many men were like him. Either tortured or ignored. It led them here, to dead ends they couldn't avoid. Still, he deserved a chance . . .

"There's a piece of us," Zane said, holding Stripe's gaze, "that knows when it stands at the edge of the tempest. Not many listen to it. What about you, friend? You listening?"

Another purple spoke up. "Boss, I really think—"

Stripe struck the man across his face, staggering him backward. The others stared, wide-eyed.

Stripe looked back at Zane. "That answer your question?"

Zane shook his head, smiled slightly, clenched a fist. "It was never really a question."

It only took a moment after that. They moved for him. Most of them were hesitant, but they'd been around enough to know that when things started, you were better off in a group. Usually, anyway.

The Ranger was on his feet in a flash, running, diving over the storage pods, grabbing the doctor and shoving her to the floor, covering her.

The Charge from the forklift was still flowing through Zane. It burned. It hurt. It felt fucking amazing. He didn't feel their blows as they jumped him; he'd been designed to take much, much worse.

Zane twisted the neck of one almost all the way around. He fell. Zane grabbed the socket wrench the man had had in his hand, used it to dismantle the rest of them. One at a time, blood spraying patterns on the floor, until only Stripe was left.

The guy charged and thrust his knife forward

Zane didn't even move, just let the blade plunge deep into his stomach. The pain was sharp and biting. He liked it.

One of his huge hands grabbed Stripe's skinny throat, squeezed. The other grabbed the knife, but instead of pulling it out, Zane pushed it farther *in*.

Stripe, terrified, tried to pull away, but he didn't have anywhere near the strength for that. Zane pulled him closer. The knife sank deeper. The pain felt good.

Zane could see the fear in the man's eyes—and the shame.

"You rode the tempest," Zane told him, his voice calm. The knife started to smoke and heat, dissolving, blackening, absorbing into the Charge, absorbing into Zane. Stripe stared down at it, eyes wide. "Rode it and lost."

Zane kept the man's hand on the knife as it melted and burned. Stripe screamed in pain.

"But you *rode* it," Zane whispered. He squeezed Stripe's throat. His screams cut off. Zane kept squeezing, harder and harder, until the man went still.

Zane let him fall.

The knife's blade finished absorbing, blending into his skin, and the wooden handle fell to the floor with a hollow sound against the concrete.

Zane stepped over the bodies and moved until he stood above the Ranger, lying on top of the doctor, staring back up, his eyes intense.

"If it makes you feel better," Zane told the man, "we can call it a negotiation."

The Ranger swallowed, shook his head. "I don't see the point in that."

Zane smiled behind his muzzle. "Your name?"

"Maddox," the Ranger answered.

Zane looked at the doctor. "Yours?"

"Rae . . . Raelyn . . ." Her voice was shaky and frightened.

"Site Eleven," Zane said to the Ranger. "You know it?"

The Ranger, Maddox, nodded.

"This side of the Barrier?"

Maddox nodded again.

"Take me there. Then you and Raelyn can go free. Hinder me in any way, and she dies." Zane's voice was matter-of-fact. There was no reason to make it any other way. Maddox knew who Zane was. "Not gruesomely. No point in that. But she will die, and it will be your fault. Do we understand each other?"

Maddox stared back, and there was something new in his look. Something . . . haunted. "More than you know," he said.

Zane nodded. He didn't care what demons this Ranger had, just that he got him where he needed to be.

"I know your names," Zane said. "Just so I know you understand, say *mine.*"

The doctor looked back, confused, scared. Maddox stared back intently, hesitating, as if saying the word was an acknowledgment of the reality.

"Zane," he finally said. And then the air caught fire.

Everything electronic blew apart. The lights in the ceiling. The control panels. Computer monitors. Every single one of the huge refining tanks. The air was full of sparks and flying debris and noise.

When it was over, the room was dark and full of smoke. The only light and sound came from the fire from the train, spreading through the building. The building's power had gone dark.

Zane studied it all slowly.

"We live in strange times," he said quietly. Maddox and Raelyn, on the ground below, said nothing.

TWENTY-SIX

BONEYARD

It felt like the train tracks went on ten miles before they hit anything noteworthy. But what they did hit made Flynn's heart beat faster.

Crawlers stretched into the distance, hundreds of the giant machines, piled and stuck together. All models, all eras, sitting in the bottom of a huge meteor crater, rusting in the heat.

Flynn and Key lay at its rim, staring down at all the machinery.

"It's a boneyard," Key said, shielding her eyes from the sun with her free hand. The cuffs rattled on their wrists. "If I had a ship, I'd strip this place bare."

"Defunct M-D Crawlers are valuable?" Flynn asked.

"Defunct M-D anything is valuable. Conduit circuitry alone. Christ, it feels *hotter*."

She was right. It did feel hotter. The sun beat down and Flynn saw Key's skin was drenched with sweat. She had rolled the top of her jumpsuit down and tied it, leaving just the tank top she wore underneath, revealing the curve of her lower back . . .

Flynn swallowed and looked east, back toward the Cindersphere and the Terminus, back where they'd managed, somehow, to escape.

There was something odd there, far away, on the horizon. It looked like smoke, wavering in the air, probably fifty miles away or more. Flynn stared at it.

"Why would they want us to go *here*?" Key asked.

Flynn looked back at her. "He just said follow the tracks."

"Oh, it's a *he* now?" Key sounded annoyed.

Flynn sighed. "I didn't mean anything by it. I just—"

"It told us what to do, it sounded in charge, so it must have a fucking cock."

Flynn stared back at her. "Is it impossible for you to not use profanity?"

"Jesus," Key spat. "It's like being chained to a housewife. Or . . . a monk. Should I just start saying 'F-word' instead? 'C-word'? 'G-word'?"

Flynn's brow wrinkled. "There's a G-word?"

"Fuck me. Look, this is why we need to be *disconnected*," she emphasized. "We are not compatible, you and I."

"I don't disagree," Flynn said, "which is why we should go down there. With all those parts, I can probably find a way to cut us loose."

She gave him a severe look. "You don't know who's down there."

"It doesn't look like *anyone's* down there."

"It wouldn't be much of an ambush if it did, would it?" Her tone dripped sarcasm. "You need to be a lot more paranoid."

"You mean more like *you*," Flynn shot back.

"Exactly," Key said, almost pleased. "There's no order here anymore, Professor. We're on our *own*. Whoever we run into from now on, if they've survived to this fucking point, they're gonna be very scary and very dangerous."

Flynn stared back down at the boneyard again. The wind picked up in the crater, whipping up dust in a little funnel that moved between the Crawler wrecks. It was the only thing he could see moving below.

Key was right; he should be paranoid.

Flynn remembered the monitors in the *Charion's* engineering pocket, before the SMV. The gangs fighting, tearing each other to pieces. That level of brutality wasn't anything he'd ever imagined, and those same kinds of people were all that were left on the planet now.

At the same time, what were they supposed to do? Sit here and sweat in the heat? This was where the words on the monitor told them to go. This was the only path Flynn could see.

"You want to cut loose of each other, right?" Flynn asked.

"More than I can express," Key replied sharply.

"Then going down there is the only way. I understand there's risks, but we're going to have to take some if we want to escape."

Key studied him pathetically. "You really don't get it, do you? No one gets off the Razor, Doc. You're not escaping anything."

Flynn stared back at her. "We're closer than we were yesterday. Aren't we?"

Her look turned dark, pitying almost, then she shook her head and looked back down at all the rusting machinery. "Come on . . ."

They followed the tracks as they wound down the crater. When they reached the bottom, they shadowed the line as it moved through the wrecks.

Flynn's eyes moved between the silent machines, towering over them. He recognized them all, one model after another. The Series 6 SMV. A Series 3. Two Series 4s—always his favorite, with their dual-action torque compressors and giant solar array.

And a Series 2.

A six-axle monstrosity, one of the largest Crawler models ever built. Back before plasma suspensions tripled the top speed of the machines. After that, the giant Crawlers, with cargo holds of a thousand-ton capacity, weren't necessary anymore. The newer models could do two sorties in the time it took the older versions to do one.

But Flynn had fond feelings for the S2. After all, it was the first Crawler he had ever worked on at Maas-Dorian. The first *anything* he had ever worked on.

Key was a pace or two ahead of him—as far as she could get before the chain went tight. She stopped, turned, stared at him, decidedly annoyed, watched him staring up at the Crawler.

"Now what?"

"It's . . . Look." Flynn pulled Key toward the machine, found a panel in the side, near the axle of one of the giant, rotting wheels. Flynn tore it loose, revealing the circuitry and the electronics. Most of it was rusting, but he could still see the mechanics behind it. The plasma solenoids and the vacuum seal. The wiring.

"I designed that," Flynn said, motioning to the arrangement of parts and pieces. "It was the first thing I *ever* designed. On my own."

Key pushed in. She actually seemed intrigued. "What is it?"

"An overload inhibitor," Flynn said. Key's eyes shifted to him. "It stops the bleed-out of electrical pressure in the case of an overload."

"A *fuse*?" Key looked decidedly unimpressed now. "You made . . . a fuse?"

"Well," Flynn replied, "I mean, it's more than just that. It's—"

"A fuse."

"It's a *powerful* fuse," Flynn said, feeling defensive.

Key turned away. "I'm sure it is."

Flynn felt angry. "I had to rethink the entire electric dispersal system, on a Crawler model that wasn't even supported anymore. It extended the profitability of—"

"I'm sure it did," Key replied, motioning ahead of them. "Here's something else you can rethink."

Ahead of them sat one of the Razor's transport trains, about two dozen cars' worth, headed by an engine. All useless now, after the pulse. The X-Core would still work, but none of the circuitry would transmit the power, and all the controls would be dead.

The main thing, though, was that the train tracks the machine sat on continued another ten feet . . . then stopped altogether. Pretty much right next to the Series 2.

"Huh," Flynn said, his anger forgotten.

"Yeah," Key replied. "Fucking 'huh.'"

The tracks ended *here*? It didn't make any sense. Why would they have been led here? For that matter, why did the *trains* come here? To transport *Crawler parts*? Maas-Dorian serviced their Crawlers with new parts, fabricated on Mars or Segundis 7; there wasn't any need to scavenge parts from old SMVs.

So why the tracks? Why stop *here*? At this Series 2 that, unlike every other SMV in this boneyard, sat by *itself*?

It had to be intentional. It had to be by *design*.

Flynn studied the exterior of the Crawler. Everything was as it should be: bulkheads, gears, axles, shock absorbers, vents.

Then Flynn saw it. Near the S2's middle wheel, perfectly inset into the rusted hull. Something that shouldn't be there. Something not part of any Series 2 design.

A large, smooth, silver door. With a small keypad inset next to it. He stared at it.

"What?" Key asked, staring at the door now too.

The door had been added to the hull intentionally. More than that, it had been made to look just as aged as every other part of the Crawler.

He moved his hand to the control panel next to it. It lit up, information scrolling on its display in bright, flashing colors.

"Whoa," Key intoned next to him, moving closer.

The panel was much newer than the Crawler itself, in spite of how it had been artificially aged. But more than that, it was powered. Which meant it was electromagnetically shielded.

"Six six one one nine," Key said behind him.

Flynn looked at her. "What?"

"What the tablet said." Key reached for the pad and entered the digits with a series of beeps.

The door slid up and out of the way, revealing nothing but pitch-blackness beyond.

Flynn and Key stared inside warily.

"Shit," Key said.

TWENTY-SEVEN

SUITS AND LADDERS

The door slammed shut behind them, sealing away the heat and the brightness. Everything went black.

Then Flynn winced as bright red laser light filled the small room. Two projectors in the corners combined beams into a grid in the air and slowly tilted it downward.

The scanner passed over Key and Flynn. When it reached their feet, it shut off and the room went dark again.

There was a beep. A door slid open in the far wall. Inside, a ladder led *down*, not up, into the SMV.

"Where are we?" Flynn asked.

"The place you wanted to find," Key said, pushing him forward. The chain rattled at their sides. "At least it's cooler."

She was right. The interior was climate controlled.

The ladder disappeared into pitch-blackness below. They stopped and stared down at it.

As perplexing as the blackness was, there was another, more immediate issue.

"How are we supposed to get down a goddamn ladder?" Key asked. It was a good point. Ladders got tough when you were handcuffed to someone else. Even with his hand stretched up, it still wouldn't give Key enough slack to follow after Flynn in the normal way.

"You could go upside down," he said, partly sarcastic.

"Very funny."

An idea occurred to him. He moved for the hole in the floor, and Key knelt down, giving him slack enough to climb the first few rungs.

"Get on my back," he told her.

She studied him skeptically.

"What's the worst that could happen?"

"We fucking fall?" Key climbed down behind him, until she was on his back.

"Can't be that far down," Flynn said, pinning his feet on the outside rail of the ladder. "If it was, there'd be an elevator."

He loosened his grip on the ladder, let them both start to slide. Their combined weight pulled them downward, faster and faster. The blackness quickly surrounded them.

Flynn waited for them to touch down, but they didn't. They just kept falling.

"Hey!" Key shouted. "I thought it wasn't supposed to be far?"

Flynn swallowed, clamped down on the railing again. The descent slowed, but he wasn't wearing gloves, and his hands began to heat from the friction. Fast.

They kept sliding downward fast into the dark, Key holding on to Flynn's back, his palms starting to burn . . .

And then their feet hit what felt like plate metal. Flynn's knees buckled under Key's weight, but he held on to the ladder, didn't fall.

When Key stepped away, Flynn rubbed his burning hands together and grimaced, thankful for the dark.

"You okay?" Key asked suspiciously, somewhere to his left.

"Yeah, sure," Flynn managed, wincing.

And then LEDs flickered to life, lighting up a tiny, circular, metallic room.

Key saw him standing there, rubbing his hands saw the look on his face. She snickered knowingly.

"Shut up," Flynn said defensively.

Then terminals on the walls activated, flashing to life. Four of them, at angles from each other in a cramped, octagon-shaped room, showing digital readouts and schematics. Computers began to hum. A holo-display flickered to life on top of a long illuminated control panel.

The room was some kind of control center, but for what exactly was unclear. But it had four doors, set into the walls at compass points, across from each other.

Before Flynn could study the layout further, the face of a man appeared on one of the screens.

Sixty-plus years. Thin, pale, bald; small black wireframe glasses. A gray suit, gray tie. There was nothing particularly striking about him at all. Except the look in his eyes. Calm. Thoughtful. Predatory.

"Dr. Flynn," the man said in a voice without any accent at all. "Can you hear me? This signal is quite truncated, I'm told."

"Fuck," Key said. Her eyes were wide, her breathing shallow. Flynn looked at her oddly.

"Your associate and I have interacted before," the man explained.

"One way to put it," Key replied. "This suit's the one who wanted you dead."

Flynn's own eyes widened now, he turned back to the monitor.

"I won't waste time denying it," the Suit replied, his voice even. "You're certainly aware of the value of your patent portfolio, Dr Flynn. We have both worked for the same kinds of men. For them, profit is like oxygen."

Flynn nodded, his mood darkening. "Just business . . ."

"Indeed," the Suit said without irony. "Which brings us full circle. Events transpiring on the Razor may make you even more valuable alive. It is why I wish to speak to you."

"That was you on that tablet at the rocket pad?" Key asked.

"It was."

"Why should I listen to anything you have to say?" Flynn asked.

"Because I can give you your life back," the man answered plainly.

Flynn's eyes narrowed.

"I can extricate you off the Razor. There is ample confusion right now to accommodate it. Your Crawler is melting in the Cindersphere; who's to say who escaped it and who did not? Provided we can come to a mutual agreement, of course."

Time seemed to stop. Flynn slid his hands in his pockets so the man couldn't see them shake.

Extricate. Off the planet.

The thing he'd been told to forget about, to not hope for. And now it was being offered right to him. A chip in some kind of bargain.

"Time is short, Dr. Flynn," the Suit's voice brought Flynn back to reality.

"What do you want?" Flynn asked. He couldn't be sure, but it looked like a slight smile formed on the Suit's lips.

"The facility you are in is called Site Eleven," the Suit said, "one of several black sites the UEG maintains on the Razor for the holding of exceptionally dangerous prisoners."

"Lovely," Key moaned.

"As well as the conducting of exceptionally dangerous research."

"Fantastic . . ." she moaned again.

"We believe something occurred inside Site Eleven, something that triggered the order to abandon the planet."

Flynn stared at the man on the monitor. "How do you know that?"

"Because," Key almost spat, "he's got someone on the inside."

"*Had* someone," the Suit corrected her. "Contact with our operative was lost at about the same time the Lost Prophet was initiated. What we do know, is that the facility underneath you is divided into four laboratories, with tunnels connecting each. We are specifically interested in what occurred in the 'hot labs,' *here*."

The image of the Suit was replaced with a design schematic. It showed tunnels forming a square. At each corner was another square, representing one of the four laboratories. They were all labeled.

REVERSE ENGINEERING LABS

MEDICAL LABS

HOT LABS

DEFENSE LABS

Flynn guessed the room in the very center of the square structure was the control room they were in now, and each of its four doors opened to one of the four tunnels leading to the various labs.

"We would like a download of that lab's entire research collective," the Suit said pointedly.

"That's it?" Key asked skeptically. It did seem a fairly easy task, for such a large reward.

The image of the Suit returned to the screen. His stare was harder now.

"There are complications. For one, the facility is currently under a quarantine lockdown."

"Quarantine?" Key sounded unsettled. "Like viruses and shit?"

"I'm afraid we're not sure. The elevator will take you to the laboratory level, but due to the lockdown, the doors will seal behind you. You will likely have to figure out a way to either shut down the quarantine alarm or open the doors some other way."

"Open them how?" Flynn asked.

"I don't know, Dr. Flynn. I'm not an engineer, am I?" The Suit studied Flynn with impatience. "However you do it, bring us the data drive, and we can free you. No one will ever know you are still alive. My employers can be quite accommodating to those who prove themselves valuable."

There it was again. Everything he'd been told not to hope for. But one question still bothered Flynn.

"Why me?" Flynn asked. "You could get any inmate to do this."

The Suit nodded, as if anticipating the question. "Right now, strange events are transpiring on the Razor. Events we cannot explain. The data drive below may go a long way to answering them, but it is only the first piece of the puzzle. You are one of the foremost engineering minds in the galaxy, and you happen to be incarcerated on *this* planet at *this* moment. The odds of it are infinitesimal, yet here we are."

Flynn wasn't sure if those words were calculated or not, but they couldn't have captured his imagination any more. Problems and mysteries were what he lived for. But there was one other thing.

"Key, too?" Flynn asked.

The question seemed to surprise Key, because he felt her gaze snap to him. The Suit studied him strangely as well.

"You are in a position to demand a great deal," the man stated.

"I guess it's lucky you didn't kill me, then," Flynn retorted.

"For us both, Dr. Flynn. Recover the research, proceed to the starport. You will be contacted with further instructions there. And Dr. Flynn . . . whatever has occurred below in the labs, I would not trust anyone I met, were I you."

"No fucking worries there," Key said. "Not trusting people's my specialty."

"I'm certain," the Suit replied. Then, almost immediately, his image flashed off.

Flynn looked at Key. "What do you think?"

Key looked back. "I think it's lucky I didn't kill you either."

TWENTY-EIGHT

VOICES

The monitors in the control room flashed now that the Suit's image had disappeared, and they all showed the same thing.

> Quarantine lockdown in effect
> Dual verification required to unseal labs
> WARNING: Doors reseal after exiting control center

Two terminals on either end of the small room showed imprints of hands, indicating they were touch screens. Intentionally, they were too far away for one person to reach by themselves. Flynn and Key had to stretch out in the small room, the chain going taut between them, in order to put their hands on top of the imprints.

There was an acknowledgment tone.

The control center's four doors groaned as they started to lift upward, revealing dark tunnels beyond, just as Flynn figured. One of them, however, sparked almost immediately, rumbled a little bit, then refused to budge. There was no way through it.

Flynn stared at it, perplexed.

"Wild guess," Key remarked. "The door we need?"

Flynn nodded. It was the door to the hot labs.

"At least our luck's consistent," Key observed.

Flynn replayed in his head the schematic of the facility he saw earlier.

"We can go through the RE labs."

"How?"

"Each lab is a corner of the facility, so each lab has two doors. The second door in RE takes us to the hot labs."

"And *RE* stands for?"

"Reverse engineering."

At that, Key looked very displeased.

Flynn ignored her, looked through the door to the left of the broken one. It was pitch-black beyond, with the exception of dim red lights running along the floor, stretching into the dark distance.

Unlike Key, he couldn't help but feel excited. He had a chance now, a chance to get back to where he came from. Whatever was happening inside this place, he would figure it out. He had to.

Flynn stared into the hall on the other side of the door, remembering the Suit's warning about the quarantine lockdown.

Problem: How to reenter a room that closes its doors behind you.

Solution: Don't let the doors close.

Barely visible in the reddish glow, a fire repressor hung on the wall. A thick, electronic foam dispersal system that could be removed and automated in case of a fire. It might work . . .

"See the repressor?" Flynn asked. Key nodded. "We're going to wedge the door with it."

"Is it strong enough?"

"It'll work," Flynn said.

She studied him skeptically, but didn't argue. From her, that meant something.

"Three . . ." Flynn started. "Two . . . one . . ."

They dashed out of the elevator.

It beeped. The doors whined again, descending downward behind them.

Key grabbed the repressor with both hands and yanked it off the wall, then the two ran back for the elevator.

The doors were almost shut.

Key dropped to her knees and slid, shoving the thing forward as she did.

It fit right under the door as it slammed down. The repressor dented under its weight, buckled and shook . . . but it held.

The door groaned horribly as it froze about two feet from the floor. The hydraulics whined loudly another second, then eventually gave up and powered down. Everything went quiet again. The door didn't move again.

"Good job," Key said, standing up, brushing herself off.

Flynn felt a twinge of pride. It was the first time he could remember her praising him. He didn't say anything, though. Why push it?

They started moving down the hall, leaving the LED light from the cracked elevator door behind. Everything quickly became just red-tinted shadows.

Key studied the dark warily. "You said this place was shielded."

"Has to be," Flynn's voice was low. "Military grade."

"Then why aren't the lights on?"

It was a good question. The red lights on the floor were clearly emergency lights, but those were generally used in the case of a power failure. The working control center behind them proved there was power, so why the red lights?

Flynn touched one of the walls. If the X-Core were running in a facility this compact, he would feel its vibration, even hear the hum behind the walls. He felt nothing; the wall was cold.

"Reactor must be powered down," he said. "Everything's on battery power."

Something about that possibility, mundane as it was, in this environment, was unsettling.

A sound suddenly bounced back and forth around them.

A wet, slimy rattling. Faint and distant, but definitely there. A few seconds later, it came again. But farther away.

"I want a gun," Key announced.

They both jumped as a flash of sparks lit up the hall a dozen feet away.

The image burned into Flynn's retinas showed the hall branching left and right ahead. Flynn replayed the schematic again, led them forward, then turned right. The RE labs should be at the end of the hall.

But everything was just as dark ahead, no sign of any lab. They pushed forward, the only sounds the echoes of their footfalls, nothing else.

Key went stiff next to him suddenly. "What was *that*?"

"What was what?"

"What you just did."

Flynn went stiff too, realizing where his hand was. He pulled it away.

"Did you just . . . try to hold my hand?" Key demanded.

"No . . ."

"Yes, you did," Key insisted, a hard edge to her voice. "You just tried to *hold*—"

"It was instinct," he admitted.

"Well, the instinct was *wrong*."

"Okay, I'm sorry."

"Don't do that again," she emphasized.

"I won't," Flynn replied, his voice taking on its own edge. "Believe me."

They started walking again through the dark.

"Holding hands is not my thing," Key informed him after a few steps.

"I'm shocked."

More sparks lit up the reddish-black hall behind them. They moved quicker, until the hall dead-ended at a set of thick, heavy blast doors. Two monitors on either side showed the same thing as back at the elevator: outlines of hands.

It looked like, during a quarantine, every door took two people to open.

Neither of them moved for the monitors; they just stared at the big, heavy doors.

"Reverse engineering," Key said. "Whatever it is, it's probably bad, right?"

Flynn didn't answer either way, just stared at the doors warily.

"*You're* going in first," she told him.

"We're tied *together*," Flynn reminded her. "I can go ahead of you, like, a foot."

"I'll take it," Key told him sternly.

Flynn frowned and put his hand on one of the monitors. Key did the same.

The big door hummed loudly, then started to rise, slowly and loudly, the sound echoing up and down the tight hallway behind them in a way that Flynn didn't really appreciate.

As the big door slid open, Flynn saw there was a second door behind it, just as big and thick, sliding up along with the first. In between was a space of probably ten feet, with another terminal screen on the wall.

Beyond that, the reverse engineering lab glittered.

Its lights were off too, but computer monitors glowed, scrolling information throughout, casting harsh shadows through the rest of the lab. A workbench lined one wall, full of equipment that looked medical or biology oriented. In the center of the room was a large chair with leg braces and straps, and tables next to it lined with syringes and IVs.

Even though it was dark, Flynn felt somehow at ease. The instruments, the computers, the lab equipment. He felt at home. He wanted all this back . . .

He and Key stepped through, chain rattling between them, and his enthusiasm melted away at the macabre scene inside.

One entire wall was sealed with clear polysteel, blocking the contents of another small room beyond, which soon became clear, was a *cell*.

It had a bed, a nightstand, toilet, shower. The back wall was nothing but shelves full of books. Real books. An unusual sight these days, when most people read from tablets, but there must have been two hundred tomes on the wall.

Inside the front of the cell, against the back side of the polysteel, a woman—young, Asian, long black hair, wearing a lab coat—sat, staring blankly out.

And behind her, by the bookshelves, stood another woman.

Much older, maybe in her sixties, with a white jumpsuit just like his, and silvery long hair tied in a tight braid that fell down her back. She had a book in her hands, and as they entered, the woman's eyes drifted up from its pages to Flynn and Key.

Her gaze did not seem surprised. But it did seem curious.

The woman snapped the book closed, but it made no sound behind the thick polysteel. She hit a button on the wall. Speakers inside the laboratory crackled.

"You're not an evac team," the woman's voice echoed in the lab. It was smooth, slightly accented, and she spoke every syllable with perfect clarity and weight. "I was expecting an evac team. Where did you come from?"

"We were—" Flynn started, but then felt Key's fingers grip his hand hard. He went quiet.

Without looking away from him, the woman motioned to a nearby wall. "The intercom."

Flynn saw them, all around the lab, inset into the walls. Red panels with single buttons. The monitors in the room showed the feed from a variety of cameras inside the cell. Whatever this place was, the female prisoner seemed to be the main focus. It didn't explain the woman in the lab coat inside with her, however. She just sat against the clear wall, staring blankly, as if dazed.

"Fuck *this*," Key said. The cuff dug into Flynn's wrist as she pulled him away. The second door out of the RE lab was at the opposite end, and it had apparently opened with the first set.

Flynn and Key rounded the corner of a lab table . . . and froze all over again.

Just visible in the flashing monitor light were black marks running from a spot on the floor to the second set of doors. They moved through it and out beyond, into the darkness of the hallway.

Five black marks, blending and twisting around each other. And each mark was about the size of a human . . .

"I've seen it kill," the woman's voice echoed in the room.

When Flynn turned around, he jumped.

She had moved, unseen and quick, from the back of the cell to the front. She was inches away now, standing next to the Asian scientist on the floor. The clear polysteel made it look like nothing separated her from Flynn.

Flynn, instinctively, took a step away. So did Key.

"You are in a great deal of danger," she said, stroking the hair of the scientist under her. As she did, Flynn noticed something else. The tip of each of her fingers was covered by a metallic cap. Even the thumbs. "I could help you."

Key's face twisted into a scowl. She slapped one of the nearby intercom buttons.

"You're locked away," Key said. "How the hell are you going to help us?"

"Isn't it obvious?" the woman said patiently. "You're going to release me."

Key laughed out loud, but Flynn just felt uneasy. The woman's voice was far too calm. And there was a slight smile on her lips now.

"There's two types of people in this world, lady," Key said. "Ones in cages, and ones not. Whichever place people are, they tend to stay there."

The woman's eyes drifted down to the cuff on Key's wrist, the chain linking her to Flynn. "And which are you?"

A sound echoed in the room.

It sounded like static, with scratchy, high-pitched squeals mixed in. And behind all the sounds was something like voices. Many voices. Chattering and stirring.

It was coming from speakers in the computers and walls . . . but somehow, it seemed, only the ones near the door that led to the hot labs.

And whatever they were, the sounds were almost identical to what they'd heard back at the rocket pad. From the radio that shouldn't have worked. Flynn felt a chill.

"Ah," the woman said. "There it is."

Flynn and Key both stared at the hot labs door, wide open, nothing but shadows beyond.

The voices on the speakers were growing louder. As if their source was coming closer.

"It has sensed you, like it sensed the others," the old woman said. "You should seal the lab, quickly."

Key didn't hesitate. She jerked Flynn along after her like he wasn't even there toward the big fortified doors to the hot labs and put her hand on the terminal on one side, like before. Flynn did the same.

This time, however, nothing happened. The doors didn't move.

"Did I forget to mention?" The woman's voice mixed with the swirling, scratchy sounds on the speakers. "There is a security code to reseal a laboratory once it's been reopened after a lockdown. You wouldn't know that code, would you?"

Key turned back to the woman, glared at her over the distance.

"I have seen the scientists, like Sedona here, enter the code many times." The woman's fingers and their metallic caps twirled through the girl's hair. "I could seal it for you."

If she were out of her cell, Flynn thought. Static sparked in the speakers. The scratchings and the hisses and the voices kept growing louder.

"If it's so fucking big and bad, why didn't it get *you*?" Key asked into an intercom.

"It tried," the silver-haired woman said. "But it couldn't penetrate the polysteel. A protection you do not have." Her gaze settled hard on Key. "One benefit to being in a 'cage,' I suppose."

Flynn's heart beat hard. He pulled Key back toward the door they'd entered from.

As he did, the computer and wall speakers near that door crackled to life too. The same sounds, the same scratches. Even louder now . . .

Flynn and Key stopped dead in the middle of the lab.

"On all sides," the silver-haired woman said. "It does move quickly, doesn't it?"

Flynn stared into the darkness outside the big doors. He couldn't see anything but the reddish haze of the emergency lights.

"Let her out," Key said. Flynn turned to her, stunned. She looked back sternly. "If the polysteel really did protect her, then she wouldn't want out of it unless she was going to seal the doors. Let her out."

"So logical," the woman said, and pulled her capped fingers free of the scientist's hair. "What is the code, dear Sedona? For my cell?"

"Two nine one four," the scientist said, almost immediately. Her voice was as dead as her gaze. It occurred to Flynn that she was staring at the black drag marks on the floor.

"I would hurry," the woman said to them.

Key and Flynn dashed forward. The speakers in the room were full of sound now, buried voices muttering imperceptible sounds. They reached the control panel next to the cell door. It beeped four times as they entered the code.

There was a clicking sound. The door unlocked and swung open.

The woman exited the cell, and Flynn and Key gave her a wide berth. Her gait was like a predator's.

"Once I activate the panels," she said, moving for the nearest door, "you will have to press the terminals at the same time, one on each side of the first door, just as before."

Flynn saw what she meant. There were touch screens on either side of the big door—one on the lab side and one just outside, before the second door.

"Then get on with it," Key said, moving around the door, stretching the chain connecting her and Flynn, leaving Flynn in the lab.

The voices and the hissing became almost unbearably loud. The speakers shuddered in the walls.

The woman keyed a series of codes into a control panel, using the caps on her fingers. The monitors next to Flynn and Key lit up again, showing the imprints of hands.

"Now, please," the woman commanded.

Flynn and Key touched their monitors.

As the woman had described, the big doors slammed shut. Just not the second, exterior doors. They were the *interior* ones. They came down with a powerful burst of force, right onto the chain running between Key and Flynn, slamming them both onto the floor.

Dazed, Flynn tried to stand, but the chain on his wrist was wedged in between the door and the floor, pinning him where he lay.

Above him, through a polysteel observation window, Key's face peered in, wide-eyed.

When the door came down, it must have severed their chain. Key, at least, was free.

She stared at him for a second, eyes full of fear. Then she looked to her right.

The silver-haired woman was there. She pushed a button on a wall, spoke into another intercom.

"I will give you one word of warning," the woman told Key through the sealed door. "Don't turn on the lights."

Key looked back at Flynn. There was emotion in her eyes, conflicting ones. Then she was gone. Running.

He couldn't help it. He felt . . . what? Hurt? Betrayed? Flynn had been tied to her since the *Charon*, and now she was gone. And he was finally alone.

Or, almost alone.

"Did you expect differently?" the woman said, moving slowly toward him. Her eyes fixed on him with an unsettling intensity. "Survival here, as anywhere, is everything."

She knelt down when she reached him, studying him with curiosity. Like some kind of interesting puzzle.

Flynn couldn't get up, couldn't run. He was trapped. "Who *are* you?" he asked, his voice hoarse.

"Those who know me best, call me Gable," the woman answered. "As for who I am, that is a long story."

TWENTY-NINE

GABLE

Twelve hours earlier, Gable had held Sedona's throat with one hand. In the other, she had nothing.

In spite of how they had capped her fingers, and all the instruments on the lab table—torch cutters, scalpels, molecular fusers—her palm carried all the threat needed. For the moment.

"Gable . . ." John said, in the lab outside her polysteel cell, his voice shaky. "*Think* about this . . ."

He was the lone person there now, the last of the science team. The soldiers were in the defense zone, between the two security doors.

"John . . ." Gable clucked her tongue. "Have you ever known me to do anything that was not thought out?"

"Just . . ." He held up his hands. They shook. His eyes were wide, staring at Sedona in Gable's grip. "Don't hurt her. Don't . . ."

So contemptible . . .

"John," Gable said with forced patience, "*listen*, please."

"Harris!" A voice echoed over the intercom. Rough and stern. Older. "Don't listen to one word that bitch says!"

The other part of the equation. Lieutenant Anderson. The head of her lab's security detail.

The alarms had begun almost five minutes ago. A specific alarm: three short tones, one long one. A quarantine lockdown alarm.

Gable knew, because she listened, she observed. It was amazing what you could pick up, once your captors became used to you, once they no longer feared you. They ran drills. They entered and exited doors. They talked and revealed their feelings for each other.

Gable filed it all away, in anticipation of the moment it could be used. And that moment had come.

The soldiers, led by Anderson, were in the defense zone, in between doors three and four. From what Gable had gleaned, in the event of a quarantine lockdown, each lab's security detail took positions there, in between the scientists and whatever might have gotten loose in one of the other labs.

And it appeared something had indeed gotten loose.

"Mute her cell right now!" Anderson's voice demanded. He was clearly listening in on their conversation.

"Is that what you want to do, John?" Gable asked, turning Sedona's lovely young neck just so. "Mute me?"

Relationships between coworkers on black sites were strictly forbidden, probably for this exact reason. They kept it secret, John and Sedona. But Gable had deduced it. She had listened and observed.

"John . . ." Sedona moaned, her eyes locked on the man on the other side of the polysteel.

"Let's try something different," Gable said, her voice a musing tone. "Let's mute *Anderson* instead."

John froze at the directive, staring at her. It was the first realization, Gable knew. Until now, everything had been instinct, primal fear. Now he was coming to understand the reality. That she had the one thing he would do almost anything to protect.

"Harris!" Anderson shouted over the intercom. "You fucking do what I say!"

John just stared at Sedona, unsure.

"Mute him, John," Gable told him.

"Harris," Anderson yelled, "whatever the fuck is loose in this place, it is nowhere *near* as bad as she is!"

Gable smiled. Anderson was absolutely correct.

"*Now* John," Gable said softly. "Mute him . . . or I will drain her blood."

"Harr—"

The lieutenant's voice cut off as John hit a button on the closest computer. Gable smiled, pleased, enjoying the silence. Now they could talk. Now they could bargain.

"Okay," John said, holding his hands up. "You got what you wanted."

Gable raised an eyebrow. "Did I, John?"

"Please . . ." Sedona whispered. Gable could feel her young body shaking.

"Do you remember the first time we met, John?" Gable looked down at Sedona. Her perfect skin, her black hair, dark like a raven's feathers. She smelled lovely. Even here, even in this place. "Before you came to know me better, back when you still believed simple *pain* could get you what you wanted?"

"Gable, please," John said, taking a step closer, desperately. Were there tears in his eyes?

Her free hand slid toward the tray with the medical instruments, the ones they had used on her over and over again. The caps on her fingers scraped against the metal.

"Do you remember . . . the laser torch, John?" Gable lifted the instrument up so that John could see.

"Jesus," John said, his voice breaking.

Sedona tensed, started to squirm. Gable squeezed her neck until she went still again.

"I remember it explicitly," Gable said. "All the lovely little sensations."

"Please . . ."

"Do you remember what I told you then? That, one day, we would revisit every moment we've spent together?"

"Gable . . ."

"And you laughed, John. You laughed." She flicked a button on the device in her hand. The laser torch burned to life with a hiss, a little sliver of superheated plasma at its end. "Are you laughing *now*?"

"Gable, please!"

"Please, what, John? Please don't kill her?"

The lockdown alarm continued to sound everywhere. And Sedona began to cry in Gable's arms.

"Sedona has always been kind to me." Gable pulled her closer, brought the laser torch to where she could see it. "Haven't you, blossom? While the others cut and burned me, or did their tests to try and figure out how I had made myself into what I am . . . Sedona fed me. Sedona cleaned me. Sedona *bandaged* me. And so . . . I am inclined to let her live. But nothing is ever free, John."

"What do you want?"

"Something very, very simple. I want you to use the security panel. I want you to enter your override code. And I want you to deactivate the internal quarantine lockdown for this lab."

John's eyes widened. "*What?* For God's sake, why?"

"Because something . . . interesting has escaped its confinement. I want to *see* it."

The lights in the lab suddenly went dark. Emergency lighting lit up along the floor, painting everything in black and red shadows. Someone had shut down the facility reactor, it seemed. Interesting . . .

New sounds filtered in through the security doors, from the hallway outside. Gable could barely hear them over the intercom in her cell.

Gunfire. Rapid. Violent. Frantic.

"Goodness," Gable breathed. Things were escalating quickly.

John could see the implications now. He looked tortured. "If I override the internal lock . . ."

"Yes," Gable agreed sympathetically. "You and the security team will likely die. Whatever is out there, it doesn't seem very friendly, does it?"

John looked back at her. "You'll just kill her anyway."

Gable clucked her tongue, pulled Sedona closer. Her scent was truly lovely. "John, you can trust every word I say. Do you know why? Because one of you is going to die here in this lab. Her. Or *you*. And if it is you, as I'm confident it will be, I will make Sedona *watch*. Every second of what is to come. I will pry her eyes open if I must, and she will live with it. See it every time she closes her eyes. For the rest of her life. And knowing that, John . . . makes me feel *warm*." She let the words sink in, glared hard into John's eyes. "*That* is how you can trust me. Because we've come to know each other so well these last six years, haven't we?"

John stared back at her, shaking, eyes moving between Gable and Sedona.

"Do we have a deal then?" Gable asked, bringing the laser torch up to her hostage's neck. Sedona tried to push away, but Gable pulled her close. "Or should I start sculpting her."

"Don't, John—" Sedona started, but Gable squeezed her throat shut. John stared back at her through the glass, tortured.

"You don't have to say yes, John," Gable said. "I can see the answer in your eyes. Shall we tell the good lieutenant? It's only fair, isn't it? I think it's best if it comes from you. Unmute his channel."

"John . . ." Sedona moaned, her voice barely audible.

"*Now*," Gable told him.

John's hands moved lifelessly back to the computer, pressed buttons. Immediately, Anderson's grating voice broke in.

"—lying! Whatever she's told you, she's—"

"Tell him you have no choice, John," Gable said. "Tell him . . . you're *sorry*."

"Harris!" Anderson yelled over the speaker. "You cannot let her loose!"

"Tell him," Gable said again. "It will make you feel better."

"I'm sorry," John said, his voice monotone. Dead.

"*Harris!*" Anderson shouted.

John's hands moved to a new set of controls. He looked up at Sedona. "I love you . . ."

Sedona struggled. Gable let her.

The doors at either end of the lab opened as John entered his override code.

New sounds broke the air, almost overpowering the gunfire filtering in from outside.

Hissing. Scratching. Static. And . . . voices. Underneath it all. Lovely voices. The sounds, Gable noticed, were somehow coming from her cell's speakers, filling the interior with their music. It gave her chills.

"Oh my . . ." she moaned.

John moved toward the polysteel between him and Sedona, didn't even look behind him at the open doors. He placed his hand on the wall.

Gable let the girl do the same, let their palms mirror each other. It would only make the memories sweeter.

Stroboscopic flashes lit everything up.

The security detail; Anderson, four others, retreated back into the lab, pulse rifles firing.

Everything electric in the room suddenly flickered. The lights from the computers and the machines and the tools, they all dimmed, as if they were hooked up to the same switch.

Only muzzle flashes lit the lab now.

Then a surge of blackness exploded inside the room.

Gable's eyes let her see far more than ordinary men. She saw the swirls, the formations . . . the tendrils. She saw *it*. And she smiled, watching it move, watching it grab and take them, drag them out and back into the hall, one at a time, kicking and screaming and dying.

John was the last. When he was ripped away, Sedona screamed.

When it was all over and done, the scientist sank against the polysteel, fell to the floor with a dazed look, shaking.

"Beautiful . . ." Gable whispered, staring after the force that had swept through the room.

THIRTY

POINTS

Flynn immediately recognized the device Gable pulled from a pocket, and his pulse quickened at the sight. It was a laser torch.

"Now. Tell me," Gable said. "Tell me who you are and why you're here. Use as few words as possible. I grow bored easily."

There was no malice in her voice, but the threat was implicit. Flynn was still trapped by the chain on his wrist, which was pinned under the security door. There was no escape.

"I'm Marcus . . . Flynn. Dr. Flynn. I, uh—"

"Doctor. Point *added*. I am also a doctor. I have a great deal of respect for those who pursue the ways of the mind. Doctor of what?"

"I have PhDs in mechanical . . . and Xytrilium engineering."

"Point added. A rarity on the Razor. The bargains you must have been able to make. How did you get here, Dr. Flynn?"

"I was sentenced for—"

"Point *deducted*," Gable said, cutting him off sharply. "Please listen more carefully. How did you get into this *facility*. You entered it voluntarily, and without escort."

She didn't know about the surface, apparently. "The . . . planet's been abandoned. We've all been left behind."

Gable's eyes narrowed. "Explain."

"There were blue lights," Flynn began with a nervous start, "and an alarm. We were on a Crawler, in solitary, only it wasn't really solitary. The captain, Braga, he made a solitary cell out of rooms in the engine level—"

Flynn stopped as the cutting torch ignited in Gable's hand. It wasn't close, but he could still feel the heat from it.

"Point deducted," she told him. "Fewer. Words."

"The guards are all gone," Flynn said quickly. "Everyone who worked for the JSCC or Maas-Dorian. Only the prisoners are left."

Gable studied him a moment. "The entire planet. Why?"

"I don't know," Flynn said. Gable frowned slightly. "I swear! But someone who does know, he sent us here."

"Explain."

"I don't know who he is, but he knows *me*," he said, and then told her the rest. The deal he'd struck. To find the hot labs and recover the research there. How he and Key had gotten to the RE labs.

"How generous of this man," Gable said. "The research in the hot lab must be very valuable."

"He tried to kill me," Flynn blurted, then immediately regretted it, as Gable's eyes narrowed curiously.

"Explain."

"On the Crawler, the one I was assigned to. He made a deal with Key to kill me."

"The one you were bound to?"

Flynn nodded.

Gable studied him even closer. It was disconcerting. "You have had an interesting few days, haven't you, Dr. Flynn?"

"Um . . . yeah."

"And you've managed to survive. Point added," the strange woman said. Her eyes raked over him again, narrowing in thought for a long moment. She nodded, as if reaching some internal conclusion. "Well then . . ."

The blowtorch descended. Flynn squirmed, tried to get away, but the chain pulled taut against his wrist. "Wait! Don't!"

There was a popping sound. The tension in the chain fell away.

The plasma of the laser torch had cut straight through the chain between Flynn and the door. The cuff was still on his wrist . . . but he was free. Flynn stared down at the severed chain, stunned.

"Come, Dr. Flynn," Gable said, standing and leaving him there without a second look. "We have much to do."

Flynn, dumbfounded, watched her move through the lab to a workbench, watched her start gathering tools. Pliers. A blade. Some sort of drill.

He pushed to his feet and immediately looked through the observation window on the door.

He could only see blackness outside, the faint accent of red from the emergency lights.

Key was gone. There was no way to know if she was still alive or not.

Instinctively, he looked behind him, to the black drag marks on the floor . . .

Key had been nothing but a pain in the ass since he'd been chained to her. Not to mention she'd tried to kill him. But she'd saved his life, too. Kept him alive.

It probably didn't make a lot of sense, but Flynn was worried about Key.

Flynn jolted as a high-pitched whine filled the room. It was a power drill. A small one. He turned to see Gable working at the bench, couldn't tell what she was doing, with her back to him, but the drill whined louder.

Then blood sprayed the wall in front of her.

Flynn's eyes widened. He felt a chill go through him. The sound of the drill kept going. More blood sprayed.

Gable didn't even flinch.

He had to get out of here. Now.

Flynn looked back to where the drag marks were—and to the two pulse pistols lying on the hard floor.

When the drill sounded again, he used the sound for cover, moved and grabbed one of the guns from the floor, raised it at Gable's back. It felt odd in his hands, foreign. He couldn't help but remember the only other time in his life he'd held a gun.

If you draw, you pull.

"Goodness. Dr. Flynn." Gable seemed to know he had raised the weapon, but didn't seem particularly concerned. She didn't even turn around, just set the drill down, grabbed a pair of pliers, kept working. He could see her hands were bloody now. "Do you even know how to use that?"

Flynn swallowed. "I'll figure it out."

"Yes, I imagine you're quite mechanically inclined." She still didn't look at him, just worked with the pliers. More blood sprayed.

Flynn winced.

"Open the door," he told her, trying to keep his voice firm, trying not to look at all the blood.

"Did you say your first name was Marcus?" Gable kept twisting the pliers. "I had a cat named Marcus once, when I was very young. He was my . . . first experiment, you could say. He didn't last long, I'm afraid."

Flynn gripped the gun tighter. "I said open the door." *Sound like you mean it*, he told himself. *Sound like Key.* "I'm not . . . fucking around here." The words came out awkwardly.

"Which door, Marcus?"

The question stopped him. It was a good one.

The first door, the one they'd come through initially, that was where Key had gone. The other door, the one that led to the hot labs, that was where he needed to go if he wanted to escape this planet.

"Open both," Flynn told her, splitting the difference. "Right now."

Gable set the pliers down and finally, slowly turned around. When she did, Flynn saw what she'd been doing. Removing the metallic caps on her fingers.

They must have been bolted into the bone, because there was blood all over from where she'd torn them loose. Her right hand was clean of the caps, and the skin at the ends of her digits was torn and frayed.

Flynn stared, shocked that she hadn't even flinched—yet curious why they were capped in the first place.

Gable took a step forward, eyes raking over him.

"Why both doors?" Gable asked. She seemed genuinely interested. "To save *her*? The one who tried to kill you?"

"She didn't have a choice," Flynn answered back.

Gable shook her head, clucked her tongue. "Petal. *All* we have are choices."

"Look . . . I'm not . . . I'm not kidding around." He leveled the gun. "Open the door. *Now.*"

Gable looked at the gun in Flynn's hand. Then she took another step forwad. "No."

Flynn fought the urge to retreat. "I was convicted for murder."

Gable smiled. Took another step. Blood dripped from her hand onto the floor. "Then you should definitely not hesitate, Marcus. The door code is two eight four four four. It will open both sets of doors. But you will have to kill me to use it."

Flynn didn't say anything this time, just kept the gun pointed.

If you draw, you pull.

"You can still save her," Gable told him, taking another step. She was a few feet away now. Her eyes bored into his. "There is still time."

The gun shook in Flynn's hand.

If you draw, you pull.

"Do what you must." Gable took another step.

Then he squeezed the trigger.

There was a hollow clicking sound. The gun didn't fire.

Flynn's eyes widened. He tried again. Same result. Same empty clicking.

Gable looked at him approvingly. "Point added."

Flynn had never seen anyone, young or old, move as fast. She was a blur. In front of him one second, on top of him the next.

She slammed him into the polysteel of her old cell, hard, one hand pinning the gun in his hand against the clear wall, the other gripping his throat. The one free of caps. He felt the blood drip onto his throat. Her grip was like a vise, like steel.

"You just had a moment," Gable said, studying him, "didn't you?"

She twisted his wrist inward. He tried to fight back, but it was impossible. She was *strong*. She kept twisting his wrist until the gun was pointed at his own head.

There was another click from the trigger as Gable pulled it. Flynn flinched. It didn't fire.

"The weapons on this planet are linked by biometrics to their owners," Gable told him. "They won't fire for anyone else."

Flynn studied the woman, inches from her face. She studied him back. And then, without warning or explanation, he saw something impossibly strange. It looked like a glowing sliver of light moving, *swimming*, from one of Gable's eyes to the next.

Flynn's breath caught in his throat. "Who *are* you?" He could barely speak; her grip was incredibly firm.

Gable studied him sympathetically. "Look at you, Dr. Flynn. You must feel so out of sorts. Lost and trapped on a world full of predators."

The grip tightened on his throat. He coughed raggedly. He felt his feet leave the floor, felt himself lifted up, seemingly without any effort at all. Gable held him in the air with one arm, against the polysteel wall.

"Who am *I*?" she continued, as if the answer should be obvious. "I am the *worst* of them."

Flynn coughed, staring down at her, trying to breathe, helpless. Gable let the words sink in . . . then she let go.

Flynn dropped to the floor, collapsing in a heap. His breaths came in ragged gasps. His throat burned.

"Now," Gable said, moving away, back to the workbench she had left. "We are pressed for time, I think."

THIRTY-ONE

WALLS

Maddox had seen the Barrier dozens of times, and it always made an impression.

A giant wall of concrete and steel and polycarbon circumnavigating the entire circumference of the planet, except in a few spots where the oceans made it unnecessary. It rose six hundred feet into the air, rimmed with guard towers and drone pads and gun emplacements, built between the center of the Razor and the Cindersphere.

The purpose was obvious. Seal off the Cindersphere side of the Razor from the rest. If a Crawler was lost to a riot, or a supply depot's prisoners managed to escape, they would have to find a way past the Barrier before they could reach the starport or any other part of the Razor's vital infrastructure. Ninety percent of Maddox's Ranger assignments had taken place on this side of the Barrier.

It was a testament to something—though, to what, Maddox wasn't sure. Human ingenuity? Maas-Dorian's commitment to its profit center? Whatever it was, it had produced one of the more impressive engineering feats this side of the Rift.

"I've never seen it from the outside," Raelyn said, lying next to him.

They were on the edge of a bluff, staring down at a valley where the Barrier stretched north and south as far as they could see, disappearing on both horizons.

The Barrier had SMV gates, big enough to accommodate the Crawlers, every fifty miles or so. When the machines passed through, the entire vehicle was on lockdown; prisoners in their cells, crew in their quarters. It made sense that Raelyn had never seen it like this.

Of course, Maddox had never seen it like this either.

One of the huge gates rested in the wall below, flanked by guard towers. A hundred yards next to it was a much smaller gate, also sealed. Train tracks led out from it, moving north, following the Barrier until they disappeared on the horizon with the giant wall.

Everything in front of those two gates was chaos. Two burning SMVs sat facing the Barrier, smoke billowing off them and into the air. Prisoners waged war in front of them, clashing with each other in large groups, like medieval armies.

"Rival gangs?" Raelyn asked.

"Fighting over the SMV gate," Maddox guessed, watching the action below. "Each probably took over their Crawlers when the Lost Prophet went active, probably thinking to ram through. EMP took care of that."

Occasionally, tracer fire from the guard towers streaked down toward prisoners who got too close to the SMV gate.

Tracer fire meant guns. And guns meant guards. Still manning the towers.

"The guards stayed?" Raelyn was confused.

"Barrier detail. Only group that doesn't get pulled out after a Lost Prophet. Their armory's EM shielded, so their guns work. Anyone wanting to get to the starport has to go through them. Luckily, the gangs hate each other as much as they want to escape. The detail can just sit up there while the prisoners thin their own numbers."

The guards here were severely outnumbered, though. There were almost two thousand prisoners on the ground down there, and maybe a dozen guards in the towers. Guns or not, if the gangs got their act together, the guards were going to have a tough time stopping them.

Maddox looked back to Raelyn as she moaned next to him suddenly.

"How you doing?" he asked. She mostly kept the pain she was going through to herself. She'd had a while to get used to the Slow Burn, but it was spreading now. And, of course, there were her other injuries, the ones she'd gotten in their escape from the *Charon*.

She smiled slightly, looking down to where Maddox had cauterized the gash in her leg. "Nice sutures."

"Combat level," Maddox said, straight-faced. "Should scar up real nice, look macho."

"That's what I was hoping . . ."

"Can I see?"

Raelyn knew he didn't mean the wound on her leg. She slid the sleeve of her coat up. The orange, glowing, vein-like lines stretched from the forearm almost all the way to the bicep now.

"Pain?"

"Only hurts every other second," she said, making light of it, but Maddox could tell it was becoming very real.

He felt for her, wished he could do something.

It was a shift, after not feeling much of anything for so long. A trend, if he was honest, that Raelyn had started.

Maddox reached out and took her opposite arm, massaged it, deep as he could.

Raelyn looked at him oddly.

"Soldier trick," he told her. "Makes you forget about the other arm."

"It isn't working," she told him bluntly.

Her skin felt nice, Maddox thought. It was soft, even in the heated air, with tiny hairs that were almost invisible. His hands started to slide up her forearm, to the bicep, but he stopped himself, kept focused.

"Why did you save me?" Raelyn asked as he massaged her arm. She was staring at him intently now.

Maddox looked at her, suddenly uncomfortable. "I saved *us*."

"No, it's more than that. If it was just you, I don't think you would have done anything."

Maddox felt a sense of darkness creep back inside. She was probably right.

"People suffered because of me," Maddox said. Almost immediately, the image of the women in that transport unit filled his mind, the doors closing. "I didn't do anything to stop it."

"So you're making up for it?"

Maddox shook his head. "There's no taking back the things we do."

"No second chances," Raelyn said, quoting him from before. "My father always said we're the split difference between who we are and who we want to be."

Maddox thought about it, nodded. It sounded right to him. "What if you can't be what you want to be?"

"It's the wanting that matters," Raelyn said.

Maddox held her gaze a moment, unsure of what to say. Like the Razor, he had his own Barrier, his own walls. And there wasn't any scaling them.

Instead, he looked back down to where the Slow Burn was spreading on her arm, burning through her nerve endings one millimeter at a time.

"How's it feel now?" he asked, kept massaging the clean arm.

She smiled again. He liked her smile. "Better."

The sound of more gunfire below, tracer fire shooting downward. Screams and yells, fury, as the gangs clashed again in their grim, futile dance.

"Can't we run?" Raelyn asked as she watched, her voice low.

Maddox shook his head. "He would find us."

"Who *is* he?"

That was a complicated question. Rangers were briefed on the JSCC most wanted list. In a galaxy as big and bad as this one, it was a tough list to make. The man named Zane—the Gray Man—was number three.

Who he was, though, was the subject of only rumor. UEG operative? Failed science experiment? His file had no last name; it just said "Gray Man." No background. No birth date. Nothing beyond a huge confirmed kill list and a string of crimes ranging from arson to destroying space installations. His reputation had become such that he was almost a ghost story in criminal circles. Some even thought the Gray Man was just a story dreamed up by crime syndicates to keep the UEG off their backs.

But, for a ghost, he'd been the target of one hell a massive manhunt for the past year and a half. An unsuccessful one. Any group that managed to track him down, task force or bounty hunter, always ended up dead. Frankly, Maddox was surprised the man had actually been subdued and brought in alive. He could still see the sight of the big man walking calmly out of the flames from that train crash.

"The knife," Raelyn said, her voice haunted, remembering the same experience it seemed. "It looked like it . . ."

"Absorbed into him," Maddox finished for her.

There were rumors of that too. Scary ones. Of Zane's . . . abilities. And they all had to do with metal. But there was no real consensus on how they worked or where they came from.

"I don't know how that could be possible," Raelyn murmured.

"Everything's impossible," a deep voice said, distorted, as if through a filter. "Until it isn't."

Maddox and Raelyn turned as a shadow appeared over them.

Zane stood behind them, a hulking silhouette that blocked the sun. He was easily the biggest man Maddox had ever seen, and he'd seen plenty. Six foot four, probably 275, all muscle. Either he kept himself in amazing shape or he didn't need to. It was impossible to tell nationality or colony from his skin, because, just the like the stories said, it had an ashen quality to it. It was almost gray.

The security muzzle was still on his face. Maddox couldn't see his mouth move behind it, couldn't see smiles or frowns, all he had to go on were Zane's dark eyes, and it made him all the more imposing.

Maddox forced himself to hold Zane's gaze as he dropped three bags of different kinds onto the ground. It wasn't easy.

"Food. Water." Zane's dark eyes moved to Raelyn. She looked away. "No meds."

Maddox studied the packs. "You got them where?"

Zane nodded to the battle going on below. "From people who won't miss them. Or anything, ever again."

Maddox had no doubt. "What gangs are they?"

"Scorps were all I saw," Zane answered.

Scorpios. Gunrunners out of Solisto, bionics, one of the larger gangs, one of the nastier ones too. Then again, whoever was still alive at this point was going to be nasty. The best strategy was just to avoid them, if possible.

"Gonna be there awhile," the Gray Man continued, "fighting at a stalemate like that. And the guards are armed. I don't think anyone's getting through the Barrier anytime soon."

"We'll have to, if we want to escape," Maddox said.

"I'm not interested in escaping," Zane said, watching the fighting below.

Maddox studied him. What did that mean? If he didn't want to escape, that put him in the vast minority on this world. Then again, Maddox thought, he didn't much care about escaping either, did he?

Zane knelt down to Raelyn, reached for her arm. She pulled away instantly. Maddox tensed.

"Don't mean any harm," Zane told her. The tone was firm, but somehow believable.

Slowly, Raelyn let him have her arm. His giant hands slid the coat up, revealing the Slow Burn again, glowing, pulsing vein-like lines up and down her skin.

"She'll need meds soon," Zane said, looking from the arm to Maddox. "Slow Burn spreads exponentially. Slows down just the same."

"Don't talk like I'm not here," Raelyn told him in a tight voice.

"You're here," Zane replied. "But *he* needs to know, if he's going to keep looking after you."

Maddox felt a twinge of discomfort at the idea of looking after anyone. But only a twinge. A week ago, it would have been much worse.

"The longer you wait to get meds in her, the faster it spreads before it stops. More pain she'll have to deal with, now and later."

"I can deal with pain," Raelyn told him firmly.

Zane's eyes hardened at the word, studied her in a different way then. "You'd do better than most, I guess. But the Burn catches up with everyone. When it does, if we're still together, I can end it for you. I can make it easy. No shame in it."

Raelyn swallowed as the meaning of Zane's words sunk in, but, now, she didn't look away from the big man. She studied him in a different way too.

Maddox felt his blood run hot. "You just back the *fuck* off," he told the Gray Man.

Zane didn't take his gaze from Raelyn. "Just calling it how it is. You both might prefer I be the one." He held the doctor's look a second more, then stood, rising back to his full height, blocking the hot sun again. "Once we get where we're going, you can do what you want after that."

Maddox stared at the big man, unsure. "What do you want at the black site?"

Zane was quiet a moment, looked back to the Barrier, to the battle going on below. The prisoners waded into each other again. It was savage, brutal, even from afar. "What we all want. Answers."

Beyond the giant wall, in the distance, still shining brightly, piercing the sky, was the red beacon. The same one that had guided Maddox out of the Cindersphere and back to safety. Relatively, anyway. Maddox stared at it, along with Zane.

"Strange times," the Gray Man said again. He grabbed two packs, leaving one for Maddox.

"I can carry my own," Raelyn said, grabbing one from the Gray Man, and starting to stand. Zane looked at her, and it seemed like maybe he was smiling under the muzzle. Just a little.

"Whatever you say." He turned and moved, started following the rim of the bluff.

Maddox and Raelyn looked at each other, then moved after him.

THIRTY-TWO

SECOND CHANCES

Maddox found the rail line from the Barrier tunnel a few miles later. The giant wall continued straight north, but the tracks took them west. Eventually, even the giant structure disappeared from view.

The air was oppressively hot. Hotter than it should be this far into the Razor, but Maddox chalked it up to strain, to injuries. He'd been through more in the last week than maybe both his tours. And yet, somehow, he felt energized. Felt alive.

Raelyn walked next to him, hefting the pack Zane had given her. Her hair was slick on her forehead, but she was doing a good job keeping the strain and the pain off her face. Maddox wasn't sure whose benefit the show was for, hers or his, but she was tough.

Maddox liked her. More than he should. He turned his eyes back to the tracks before she caught him looking.

Eventually, the tracks led them to a drop-off that appeared out of nowhere, the rim of a giant crater. At the bottom sat the Crawler graveyard—and Site Eleven, hidden in the middle.

Maddox had been here three times. Escort duty, all for prisoners being transferred to the black site, either for safekeeping or for study. Every one of those inmates had been scary, in their own special way.

Zane crossed his massive arms, staring down at the crater and all the rusting machinery. "Where?"

"See the Crawler in the center?" Maddox asked. "The big one?"

"What's the layout?" Zane asked.

"I don't know for sure. I never went past the first checkpoint. Internal security took over from there, but I'd always heard it had three labs. And a med bay."

It was that last one that interested Maddox. If it was fully stocked, hopefully Raelyn could get the medicine she needed. She rubbed her burning arm next to him, as if thinking the same thing.

They made it down to the floor of the crater and followed the tracks to where they ended: a huge, decrepit Crawler in the center. There was a transport train there too, sitting unused and unpowered.

Maddox keyed in the security code he remembered from the last time he'd been here, and the door in the SMV bulkhead slid upward, revealing only darkness beyond. Raelyn stared at it hesitantly, not liking those shadows. She stepped inside with them regardless.

Security scanner beams moved over them, then another door opened, revealing the ladder to the control room. When they got there, the monitors and holo-displays lit up when they sensed their presence.

Quarantine lockdown in effect
Dual verification required to unseal labs
WARNING: Doors reseal after exiting lift

Only, the odd thing was, the doors weren't all sealed. Three of them were, set solidly into their frames, but the fourth one, the one that led toward the RE and medical labs, was cracked open, about two feet. Someone had wedged a fire repressor there, keeping it accessible.

"Someone's here," Zane observed.

"Someone smart," Maddox said. Whoever it was, they were using the repressor to prop the door open, for when they needed to leave.

They all looked under the small gap between the propped-open door and the floor. Everything beyond was pitch-black, with the exception of the red emergency lights along the floor.

Raelyn's breathing quickened. More dark, more shadows. Again, she followed them, crawling under the door and into the darkness beyond.

When the end of the first hall branched in two directions they moved left, toward the med lab, away from RE, the only sound their footfalls on the metallic floor. If something had happened here, there was no sign, except that the facility's X-Core had been powered down.

The doors to the medical lab appeared out of the shadows ahead. Big, fortified ones. Monitors on either side, with hand imprints.

He and Zane put one hand each on the monitors. The doors slid upward powerfully. Beyond them was the med lab.

The ceiling lights were off, just like the halls. But computer monitors flickered and flashed, instruments and medical equipment glowing, all of it lighting the environment in a harsh bluish white.

There were no people inside; no bodies either.

But that didn't mean there weren't things to see.

The first Maddox noticed were the blackish marks, like dried oil or cinder stain, on the floor.

Several of them, all about the width of a human, leading across the floor, through the medical equipment, and disappearing through the lab's other door.

The second thing he noticed was much less cryptic. Empty shell casings littered the floor. A lot of shell casings.

"Spent ammo," Maddox said. The guns were there too, ballistics, no pulses, tossed about through the room.

"People got dragged out of here," Zane said, touching the black marks on the floor with the toe of his boot. "Several somethings."

"That's not blood," Raelyn said, her voice unnerved.

"What do you think?" Maddox asked Zane.

"I think whatever set off the quarantine wasn't friendly," Zane answered. He knelt down, picked up one of the 10mm pistols. It might as well have been a rock. "Can you reset the biometrics?"

"We'd need a security terminal," Maddox said. "And they don't have those on this side of the Barrier."

Zane thought for a moment, his brow furrowed, then he nodded and looked up at Maddox. "Here, we part ways."

Maddox studied Zane. "Just like that?"

"Just like that," the Gray Man replied. "You look surprised, Ranger."

"More . . . cautious, I'd say."

Zane touched the floor. Like everywhere else, it was made of metal. The Gray Man's hand ran along it slowly, feeling the creases and folds, all the rust.

"Do what you need to do, quick," Zane told them, hand on the floor. He was almost caressing it. "There's movement. All around. And it doesn't move like a human."

Maddox's eyes narrowed, wondering how the hell he could know that from touching the floor.

Raelyn seemed to be wondering the same thing. "What made you like this?"

Zane ran his hand along the floor a moment longer, then stood up and looked at Raelyn over the rim of the muzzle.

"Nothing mysterious," he said. "Just men."

Then he moved to the doorway at the other end, stepped through it into the shadows and was gone.

Maddox exhaled. It had been one problem after another since Maddox had killed the two guards, and he'd stepped out of the *Charon*'s X-Core, dragging Raelyn behind him. Zane was the last of those complications, and when he disappeared it felt like a weight had been lifted.

In Maddox's experience, that was usually the time to watch your back the most.

Do what you need to do, quick, Zane's words echoed in Maddox's mind.

"Let's hurry," he told Raelyn. She didn't argue.

Maybe all med bays were arranged in the same way; Maddox had no way of knowing. But Raelyn looked at home in it, went to certain cabinets, pulled specific medication and equipment, started stuffing it into her pack. An autosyringe and a box of needle tips, about a dozen vials of different meds.

She picked several vials of chemicals and started mixing them in a larger vial, making a reddish-yellow concoction, then shook it hard and attached it to an IV stand.

It was impressive, the way she blended the liquids, even just the way she moved around the equipment. Maddox watched how her hair moved down her back. In the dark, it looked more brown than red.

"Maddox?" Raelyn asked.

He blinked, realized he'd been staring at her. Raelyn was looking at him with a slight smile.

"Here." She offered him the needle tip to the IV and started wrapping a rubber cord around her arm, making the veins stand out. "You do it."

"Do what?" Maddox asked.

"Put the IV in," she said. "I pass out when I do it, sometimes. When I see blood."

Maddox took the tip from her. "You pass out when you see *blood*? You're a doctor."

"My *own* blood. Your blood wouldn't bother me."

"Well, I guess that's a positive." Maddox studied the tube, unsure what to do with it.

"See the vein?" Raelyn asked. "Just push it in. I'll do the rest."

Maddox had to admit the idea made him a little uneasy too, but he did what she said, pushed the needle tip into her vein as gently as he could.

Raelyn flinched, but that was it. "Okay . . ." She attached the end of the tube to the needle and held it in place with her fingers. "Turn on the IV. It's the red knob."

Maddox turned the knob clockwise a full turn. The liquid inside started flowing, down through the tube, into her arm. As it did, Raelyn shut her eyes, leaned back. Her breathing was quick at first, then started to slow.

"Well?" Maddox asked.

"It's a start. After I saturate with the IV, I can start injecting daily to slow the momentum. Then it's just one injection a week."

"But it'll keep spreading until then," Maddox said, remembering Zane's warning.

Raelyn nodded. The meds would stop the spread, but it wouldn't reverse it. Whatever growth happened in the interim was permanent. And so would be the pain.

As he watched the fluid fill her veins, he finally gave voice to the question he'd been wondering about since he'd first seen the glowing lines on her arm. "How did you get this? You don't look like a synth addict."

"I gave it to myself," Raelyn said matter-of-factly. "We all did."

It wasn't the answer he expected. "We?"

"We were working on a cure."

"For Slow Burn?"

Raelyn nodded, eyes still shut. "It didn't go well."

"How not well?"

Her voice was grim. "I'm the only one left?"

Maddox didn't know what to say.

"Slow Burn only affects humans," she continued. "Which means your only choice is human trials."

Maddox had heard that before. One of the reasons the disease was so difficult to cure.

"We knew we could crack it," Raelyn said with bitterness. "So we took grant money for a made-up project to work on it in secret. We were going to be the ones. We got close, too. Really close. But not close enough."

Her eyes opened and looked down at the glowing vein-like marks spreading up her arm. She never stared at them with hostility, Maddox realized. Just acceptance.

"They died because of me," she said, almost too soft to hear. "I convinced them, told them we could do it. They believed me. They believed in me. All five of them." Her eyes glistened in the dim light from the monitors. "I deserve this."

At that moment, Maddox felt more connected to her than he had to anyone since the loading docks. He wasn't sure if it was the words themselves, so similar to his own, or just the thought that he wasn't alone in believing them. It made him want to take her hand. But he didn't.

"Medical license revoked," Raelyn said, voice bitter again. "Felony charges. I was infected then, though, so they let me off easy, I guess. JSCC contract was only thing I could get. The Razor. I didn't care. I just needed a place where I could requisition chemicals, where I could finish it. Where I could make it all right." Her voice dropped off. "But then . . ."

"Whistler," Maddox said.

She nodded. "The Bloodclan ran the supply intake for the *Charon*. When they started seeing my chemical orders come in, they took them."

It made sense. Anything unusual like that, the Bloodclan would stockpile. It was easy, with their loading dock access. They'd know that whoever owned it couldn't go to the *Charon* officers about it being missing. After all, what Raelyn was doing was illegal. Once Whistler had something on her, he used her, the only doctor on the *Charon*, the one who would treat Maddox once he showed up. A convenient instrument of revenge.

Maddox suddenly understood all her trepidation, all her fear. And he admired her ultimate choice even more. She had broken her deal with Whistler, in spite of everything at stake. In spite of everything she was trying to make up for.

"I'm . . ." Her voice cracked as she looked up at him. "I'm really . . ."

Maddox finally took her hand. "I'm going to get you off this planet," he told her. He meant it, too, he realized. Meant it more than anything in a long time.

She wiped tears away with her free hand, studied him gravely. "But what about *you*?"

The question filled Maddox with a hollowness. He said nothing, just stared back into her blue eyes.

"Maybe . . ." Raelyn said carefully, "maybe we can be each other's second chance."

Maddox kept staring. He felt a strange sensation, foreign for so long. Desire. For this woman who had done so much for him. He wanted to tell Raelyn everything, about what he had done, or not done. He wanted to tell her *yes*.

But a strange sound interrupted his thoughts before he could. Not from the air, but from somewhere close. It took a moment for him to figure out where.

The room's speakers. In the walls. In the computers.

The sounds were disturbing. Scratches and hisses, buried in static.

And underneath it all, something dark. Voices, it sounded like. Nothing he could make sense of, but it sounded frightening all the same.

Raelyn's hands began to shake.

"What is it?" she asked.

The sounds seemed to grow louder.

Maddox wasn't sure, but he knew one thing. "We need to get out of here."

THIRTY-THREE

WHO YOU ARE

The old scientist had seven bodyguards at any one time, probably more rotating on and off. And all of them hired to protect the man named Jovenheimer from Zane.

It hadn't been enough. Less than a month ago, Zane had killed every single one of them.

All of them had pulse rifles, like Zane had anticipated. If they knew anything, they knew that shooting bullets at *him* was a bad decision. Jovenheimer had purchased the top two floors of a superscraper in New Miami, back on Earth, and had every piece of metal in the place covered or replaced with plastic or polysteel.

That hadn't mattered either. Zane had brought his own.

A couple of handfuls of rebar he'd pulled out of a junkyard and stuffed in a pack. It wasn't until the end when he'd finally had to use it.

The last merc had been the toughest. Probably the leader. Older, more experienced, he fought smarter, even got a few blasts in with his pistol before he switched over to a plasma blade.

Zane pulled one of the rebar rods out of the pack, let the Charge flow into it, watched as it started to glow. He felt the wounds heal, the pain subside, except for the pounding in his head. That pain never dulled . . .

The merc fought as well as he could. Didn't give up.

Even with the red-hot glowing rod shoved through his throat and his blood spraying all over the ceiling, the man still kept coming. Kept coming until his knees buckled and he fell to the floor with the rest of the guys Jovenheimer had paid to die.

Zane admired him. But he'd killed him all the same.

Then he kicked open the door to the condo's master bedroom, while the alarms ripped the air, and stepped inside.

Luxurious as the rest of the two-story place. Paintings Zane was sure were originals, nice sheets, a Buddhist altar against a wall, some weird polysteel sculpture in a corner.

The bed was between him and an entire wall of glass, and beyond that a balcony that looked out on New Miami below. A man stood at the railing there, staring out over the twinkling lights of the city and the streaks from intersystem shuttles and atmosphere transports that crisscrossed the sky.

Zane moved out onto the balcony with the man, looking at the expanse of color and technology stretching away to the horizon. It was a hell of a sight.

The superscraper they were in was over five thousand feet tall. Zane could see the autocars, millions of them, moving back and forth below, could see the airships, the glittering holograms on the streets.

It was cold, this high up. Breathing in the air was like breathing in ice crystals. It felt good.

"Hello, Zane," Jovenheimer said, his voice bending up and down, his Markatum accent thick. "I made it as hard as I could."

"Not hard enough," Zane replied. "How long has it been?"

"Year and a half."

Zane looked at Jovenheimer, a little surprised. Had it really been that long since they'd made the decision to run?

"Surprising?" The man had a drink in his hand, bourbon it looked like. He looked older, Zane thought. Lines under the eyes, hair fully gray now. He looked almost frail. Zane guessed that constantly looking over your shoulder for the bogeyman took a toll.

"Road didn't have to end here," Zane said. There was a finality to his tone. "For the most part, I liked my work."

The glass shook in Jovenheimer's hand. "We did good things . . ."

"Sometimes," Zane replied.

"I can't honestly say I knew this day would come," the man said, finally turning to look at Zane. His eyes were icy and blue. Eyes that had seen much, hands that had done much. "I hoped you weren't all you were supposed to be. But you are. Ironically, I feel proud."

He held Zane's gaze evenly. Not many men could.

"I'm sorry you lost her," Jovenheimer said.

It was only then that Zane felt the first stirrings of anger. "I didn't lose her. You *took* her."

Jovenheimer shook his head. "I was never part of her Book. *You* were my focus."

Zane stared at Jovenheimer, confused. "Book?"

"The Book project was an ambitious UEG endeavor," Jovenheimer told him. "Gray Book—you—was one. But there were more. Blue Book. Black Book. Red Book. Astoria was someone else's life's work, not mine."

The anger flared hot now. For this man who had participated in his creation, who had made him do all the things he'd done, and who, directly or indirectly, played a role in the loss of the one person who had ever really understood him.

His hand shot forward, grabbed the old man by his shirt collar, and lifted him off the balcony until his feet dangled in the open air, the city streets five thousand feet straight down.

The glass fell and tumbled into the void, vanishing almost immediately. Jovenheimer's shirt ripped at the neck.

"She was no one's *work*," Zane snarled. "She was real. She was perfect."

"If you think that"—Jovenheimer's voice shook in terror—"you don't understand anything."

"Where is she?"

"I don't know!" Jovenheimer's shirt ripped again. "I can only tell you where to start."

"*Where?*"

Jovenheimer struggled. The shirt ripped further. The abyss waited underneath him. "Site Eleven. On the Razor."

"The Razor . . ." The idea seemed strange. A prison planet? *The* prison planet?

"If you survive it, you will find your answers," Jovenheimer said. "You may even find who you are."

Zane's stare fixed on the man. Jovenheimer stared back. His voice was strangled. There was a strange, misplaced pride in his eyes.

"In many ways, you are my son. And, as a father, I—"

Zane let go. Jovenheimer screamed as he fell, twisting and turning in the dark air, disappearing below.

"Feeling isn't mutual." Zane watched until the sound of the old man's screams faded away, then he turned and headed back out of the condo. He knew where he needed to go now. To get there, though, Zane would have to do something strange. Something out of character.

He would have to get caught.

THIRTY-FOUR

DUST AND DARKNESS

Zane moved through one of Site Eleven's cramped halls. Sparks lit up the dark occasionally, before everything went back to the reddish black.

Through his boots, he could feel the metal from the floor spread out, feel it connect to the supports in the walls. It was good metal. Strong. No rust, just a few impurities.

He could feel the Ranger and the doctor behind him too, still where he'd left them. That was bad. He could feel the other things in this place. Different sizes, different forms.

They could sense things in their own way, too. And they were coming.

Zane hoped, for their sake, they didn't get in his way.

Giant double doors appeared ahead, like the ones from the med lab. These, though, were permanently sealed, a steel bar running across their length. The monitors on either side were dark. A sign had been affixed to the doors.

SEALED BY ORDER OF UEG DEFENSE INITIATIVE

DANGEROUS MATERIALS. SENSITIVE INFORMATION.

Strange sounds echoed from the dark distance. A rattling noise from far off.

Zane felt through the metal again. The movements were coming closer. It was all but certain now, there would be a confrontation. But he was used to that.

Zane touched the thick steel bar over the doors, let the Charge bleed through his fingers and into the metal. He felt it heat, felt it begin to dissolve, saw it warp and twist. The Charge grew in him, the heat and the power, and the pain in his head swelled.

He kept drawing, pulling more and more out of the metal bar, filling himself, until finally it snapped apart.

The X burned. He groaned with the pain, punctured the gap between the doors with his hands. He gripped, strained, pulled in both directions.

The doors were metal. Thick metal. But nowhere near enough to stop him. They snapped and frayed apart, tore open violently as sparks sprayed the air.

When it was done, there was a warped gap where they'd buckled in on themselves. Zane squeezed through it and into the lab on the other side.

Inside the defense labs, there wasn't even the red emergency lighting. The dim light from the hall revealed a few outlines, tables and chairs mostly. Aluminum, he sensed. Perfect.

He snapped one of the legs off a seat and let the Charge trickle in, just a little. Not enough to absorb the metal, but enough to heat the tip of the aluminum. It grew hotter and hotter, until it began to glow, a piercing end of bright orange.

No flashlight, but in the dark room, it cast just enough light.

Zane shined it around the room.

Desks, workbenches, cabinets. All covered by plastic tarps, which in turn were covered by a thick layer of dust.

Under the tarps, Zane could see the outline of holo terminals. He swept a tarp off, let it float to the floor. Surprisingly, the computer hummed to life when he hit the switch. The screen flashed, booting up, beginning to scroll information. Zane let it finish and moved farther into the room.

Everything seemed to be centered around a large, shadowy object in the center. He funneled more Charge into the chair leg and moved closer.

The shape was a giant upright canister of clear polysteel, framed with metal. Above it hung a hydraulic rack, with clips for ankles and wrists, to lower a person down into whatever substance would have been waiting there.

And the far wall was lined with a system of big cabinets.

Zane recognized them for what they were. He'd seen enough in other places.

Coroner cabinets.

But why have those here?

He moved to them, shining the light from the chair leg. There were spots for name tags, but they were all empty now.

He opened one of the cabinets. There was nothing inside it.

Zane looked around the room again, all of it at once. All of it covered in dust and darkness.

Was this where they made her? Where they stripped and replaced the humanity inside her with their own version, a version much more useful to them? Zane felt the anger begin to form as he pictured Astoria, stuck in this dark, hostile place, while they did their work.

Zane felt emotion he hadn't felt in a long time. Rage. He wanted to let the Charge fill him, wanted to destroy everything here, every person who had been involved, every single piece of this place.

The computer beeped on the other side of the room as it finished its boot. From across the room he could read the screen.

Enter Data Card

Zane's eyes narrowed. He looked around, saw the series of file cabinets nearby. He moved for them, opened one. There were file folders inside. And each folder contained the same things: a data sheet, a data card, and a picture.

He had no way of knowing what Astoria's real name might have been, but more than likely her face hadn't changed all that much. He would recognize her.

Zane flipped through the first few files. None of the pictures was her.

He kept flipping, scanning each. There were at least a hundred cabinet doors; it would take him hours to go through them all. He didn't care. This was what he'd come for. This was what he'd killed for.

Zane tore open each file, one at a time. Cabinet after cabinet, name after name, face after face, until a pattern began to emerge, an obvious one. A very disturbing one.

None of the pictures were of girls the age Astoria would have been while she was here. In fact, none of the pictures were of women at all. They were of men. Large, muscular ones.

Just like Zane.

Something occurred to him. He'd been so intent on the pictures, he hadn't bothered to look at the files themselves. Zane scanned the data sheet of the one he was holding and saw the words there.

Project Gray Book. The name Joveheimer had given to *his* project. Not Astoria's.

The file and its contents hit the floor.

He looked around at the room in a very different way, back to the giant polysteel canister in the center of it all, the rack hanging above it. It should have been his first clue. The contraption was far too large for someone Astoria's size.

But it would fit *him* perfectly.

If you survive, you will find your answers, Jovenheimer told him. *You may even find who you are.*

Zane turned back to the files with renewed energy. Ripping open more and more, scanning image after image, throwing them away after each perusal. Soon they littered the floor. Hundreds of them. Hundreds of faces.

Zane kept flipping, looking. Then, there it was.

His face. On a file.

Zane stared at the picture. And there was no recognition.

He could tell it was him. The features were the same. All things he had seen in the mirror countless times. What he had not seen before was the hair. Thick and wavy, black.

Zane's head was smooth now. He had no memory of it being anything else, had always assumed it was how it always had been. After all, it never grew. He didn't need to shave it.

It seemed trivial, all things considered, but now that he'd seen the picture, it didn't add up.

Zane scanned the data sheet.

"Adrian Gannon," the name read.

Gannon . . .

His name? Like everything here—the room, the black site, the giant vat—it all meant nothing, stirred no emotion. If he had been here, he had no memory of it.

Zane studied the rest of the file.

Physical description, birth date, no aliases.

And then he froze.

Near the bottom, stenciled in red, was one single line:

Date of Death: October 4, 2137

His eyes scanned the line over and over again.

It was too intentional to be a typo. But . . . how could that be right?

Instinctively, his eyes stared through the dark, back to the far wall. The wall full of corpse cabinets.

Zane's heart pounded then . . .

He ripped the data card off the file, moved back to the computer, shoved it toward the slot—and froze again.

His huge hand shook, the card just inches from the reader.

Why the hesitation? he asked himself. *Haven't you always wanted to know?*

Zane had only one real memory from before he woke up, eleven years ago, and even it was vague and uncertain. The men he'd worked for, government suits and scientists like Jovenheimer, they never told him anything about who he used to be. For most of that time, he hadn't cared. Astoria, though, had changed that. She'd changed lots of things. He'd come here looking for her, and instead he'd found the last thing he'd expected.

Himself.

The data card hovered in front of the slot on the computer. One push and he could know it all.

But this wasn't why he'd come. And yet, it was the path Jovenheimer had put him on. He wouldn't have done it if there wasn't some connection to Astoria here in the lab.

Zane flipped over the file folder, looked at the logo printed there— something else he'd ignored in his haste earlier. It was an arrangement of icons in a circular pattern. The icons were books. And each book was a different color.

Zane hit a button on the computer and the terminal flashed.

"Voice commands," he said through his muzzle. The terminal flashed again. "Query. List parallel research projects to Gray Book conducted on the Razor."

Words scrolled across the screen in response.

The requested information is not available from this terminal

"Why?" Zane asked back.

The information is UEG-DI CLASSIFIED

Zane felt the anger returning. At every step, they tried to stop him. "What terminal could the information be accessed from?"

All information on UEG-DI projects can be accessed from the White Room data archive

Zane stared at the screen like it was transmitting Greek. "Where is the White Room data archive?"

The White Room data archive is located at the planetary starport

The starport.

The first place he'd seen on this planet, where he'd let them cuff and muzzle him and believe anything they wanted—except for the truth: that he'd let himself be caught, that he *wanted* to be on this world. And he did. He'd already found more than he'd expected, and he felt energized by it now. He felt renewed.

All he had to do was get back to where he began.

Through the metal of the floor, he suddenly sensed movement. Close and coming fast.

Zane turned just in time to see a figure push through the doors. A woman, he noted. Red prisoner jumpsuit, the top rolled down and tied around her waist. And he could just make out the outline of tattoos on her back.

Wings.

Her eyes found him then, and she went still.

On the smaller side, but not tiny. Lithe muscles, shaved head, a look in her eyes that spoke of experience and hard knocks.

Zane gripped the data card in his hand as he studied her. She held his look without hesitation.

"I can already fucking tell . . ." the woman said, her Colonial accent dripping attitude. "I'm gonna have to kill you, aren't I, tough guy?"

Zane smiled behind the muzzle. He liked her instantly.

THIRTY-FIVE

SURVIVAL

"I will give you one word of warning," the silver-haired woman's voice said over the intercom. "Don't turn on the lights."

And then those horrible sounds cut the woman off and took over the speaker.

Scratches and hisses, static. And the voices. Dark, frantic ones. Growing louder.

Key lashed out with a fist, hit the speaker next to the door hard. It knocked loose from the wall in a burst of sparks, hit the floor.

Everything went silent.

Key looked at Flynn through the observation window, one last time, then pulled away and looked back down the dark hallway.

Nothing there. Just the red-tinged blackness.

Her wings itched really fucking bad.

She could make it back to the elevator, as long as nothing was in between her and—

The voices came again. Even louder now. Sounds of static. Hissing.

With wide eyes, Key slowly looked to the speaker on the floor, broken and disconnected.

The sounds were coming from it. Even broken . . .

Something shot down from the shadows on the ceiling.

Something black and fibrous.

Key dodged and hit the wall behind her.

Another tendril shot toward her. Then another one.

Just broken shadows, but they looked like *appendages*, with no indication of what they were attached to.

One went for her throat. She ducked, slipped, hit the floor.

The other grazed her arm. And when it did, Key screamed.

It burned. Like acid.

Key kicked the thing away, rolled, got to her feet, and ran.

The voices and the hisses swelled from the broken speaker on the floor.

Looking behind her, she saw something fall to the floor in front of the security door she'd just been at.

Whatever was after her, it was on the floor now.

She ran harder, could still feel the pain in her arm from where it had grazed her.

The hall branch appeared out of the shadows and Key made a hard left toward the control center, slipped, kept running, her breathing and footfalls the only sounds.

She made it to the door, the repressor still wedged underneath it, holding it open. Right where Flynn had left it.

Looking at it, Key felt something that always pissed her off. Emotion. Shame. Maybe guilt.

She had left him, after all, left him with that witch, which was, without question, a bad place to be.

Most people, even in Key's world, were just pretenders. Faking being bad, being hard, when they were really just as scared as everybody else. More so, maybe. After all, they'd seen all the dark shit people did, up close.

The silver-haired woman, though, she was *not* pretending.

She was on the other fucking end of that spectrum. The look in her eyes wasn't fiery or volatile. It was icy. Muted. She had looked at Key like she was barely even there.

Key had a feeling she looked at everyone like that. And Flynn was trapped with her.

"Tough shit," she said, ducking under the door. The controls detected her presence. The monitors and the panels lit up. The big doors all groaned and rose back up.

Above her, the ladder extended down, within easy reach. She could pull herself up, start climbing, be gone from this nightmare in minutes.

Instead, she froze.

"Goddamn it," she whispered, almost in pain. *Just start climbing,* she scolded herself. *It's about survival now.*

The chain still hung from her wrist, the one that had attached her to Flynn. It felt wrong now, without him absorbing half the weight.

It felt a lot heavier.

What was her *problem*? Jesus Christ.

Nothing had made sense since that asshole showed up. In fact, it had been a fucking downhill slide. She wouldn't even be in this horror factory if it hadn't been for him.

Of course, without him, she'd probably be dead.

Key stared at the ladder. Nothing about starting up it felt right. In fact, it filled her with fear.

And that was fucked. Because this was what she should have wanted. Freedom. To be on her own. No one to drag her down. No one to fail. And of what she'd seen of *this* place, up that ladder was definitely the least scary option. Somehow, though, it didn't matter.

"Well, fucking A," she said, and stepped back from the ladder, making her choice.

It wasn't entirely pathetic, she told herself. Flynn did have a line, however thin, on getting off this rock. Maybe it was actually smart staying here, not an indication of anything worrisome—like, for instance, her developing a conscience.

Her wings itched suddenly. She turned too late.

Key jumped as something ripped the repressor back into the shadows of the hall, something black and oily.

Hisses and scratches exploded over the speakers in the control center.

Key stumbled, tripped, fell through a different door. As she did, the controls beeped.

The doors began to close.

Something lunged out of the darkness then, on the other side. Something big and contorted, something that moved like—

The doors slammed shut, sealing it away. Everything went black.

Key got to her feet again, ran down the new hall, her footsteps pounding the metal floor.

Just wonderful. The repressor was gone and the control center was sealed. She was done. Her wings itched badly. The fear, the fucking fear, was intense.

Calm down, she told herself. It just meant she had to find Flynn now. He would know what to do, how to get the doors open again.

There had to be a way back to the RE lab. This whole place was just one big loop. She would find something sharp and hard, find that silver-haired bitch and ram it into her chest, then drag Flynn out of here by his ass.

She ran faster. Her hall hit a fork, like at the other end, one hall going right, the other left. Key slid to a halt, looked around.

Now what?

She heard a sound. From her right.

Key peered into the darkness there, and the darkness stirred. Something moved. About half her size, crawling on three legs, and it seemed to be dragging something with it.

In the faint red light, Key could just make out what it was.

Two bodies. In lab coats. Their skin blackening and leaving drag marks behind them as the three-legged horror pulled them along.

Key felt terror start to crawl up her throat.

She turned and ran in the opposite direction, reached another set of doors in the hall. More fortified ones, only these were completely ripped open. Like someone had used a hydraulic jack on them. Not exactly encouraging.

Behind her, she heard something scamper closer.

"Fuck it," she said, and pushed through the gap in the door.

Tables, workbenches, some really creepy vat in the center. Another lab. She could see all of it because there was a light source.

A giant man, standing next to a computer, held a piece of metal, the top part glowing bright orange.

When he turned toward her, Key froze where she stood.

The guy was huge, pure muscle, and he wasn't wearing a jumpsuit. He had on work pants and a black T-shirt, covered by an orange vest that barely held his girth. The skin she could see looked almost . . . gray. Something about that raised a red flag, but it was too dark in this fucking place to really be sure.

Strangest of all, though, was the muzzle on his face. It covered his mouth, was made of leather and plastic, and was wrapped around his lower jaw. It gave the guy a really unsettling look. Key dug it.

"I can already fucking tell . . ." she said, taking a step farther inside and keeping her eyes on him, watching him turn to face her. "I'm gonna have to kill you, aren't I, tough guy?"

The big man's eyes lit up, like he was smiling behind the muzzle.

It was a bluff, as they both surely knew. No way she was even denting this fucking guy.

Maybe the thing outside, whatever it was, would go for the big man first. That was her hope, anyway, if she could just stall long enough for it to make its appearance.

"Can't kill what's already dead," the man said. His voice was low, deep, smooth, but it seemed to Key that it somehow held a hint of bitterness.

"Well, that's fucking morbid," Key said. "You work here or something?"

The big man thought about it. "I may have used to."

"Huh. Well. Does that mean you *are* or are *not* aware of the upside-down oil slick monster outside?"

Sounds came to life in the room, filtering in over whatever speakers were there, powered or not.

The man's eyes narrowed, listening to it all.

Scratches. Hisses. Voices.

"Yeah, it talks," Key said. "Sort of."

If the man was unnerved in the slightest, he didn't show it.

Key turned and looked behind her, into the dark hall, through the hole in the doors.

"You broke these doors, huh?"

"I did." He took a step closer, staring out into the shadows curiously. Key, though, took a step *back*.

"Not a long-term thinker are you?"

The voices and the static began to build in the speakers, louder and louder . . .

THIRTY-SIX

HOT LABS

Sharp pain lanced through the tip of her thumb as she pulled off the last of the metallic caps.

They had attached them well, drilled them into the bone. She had to drill each screw out, then rip them loose. Blood was everywhere.

Gable smiled.

People feared pain for its own sake, of course, but they also feared it because it was a precursor to losing control. She had found pain could become lovely, when death was no longer a factor. It was just one more sensation, one more source of information. All too short-lived.

The wounds on her right fingers had already healed, the others would quickly follow, and the sensations would all fade away.

Flynn was still there, pushed against the clear polysteel wall, at the opposite end of the room, where Sedona lay.

Gable had only known the man a short time, but she could already tell he was unique. She could hear the rhythm of Flynn's heart in his chest. He was scared, of course. He should be. But when most people met her dark side, their fear was primal.

Flynn's was different. It was focused. It was the kind of fear that spurred action.

And that kind of fear was learned. Not instinctual. So where had a Maas-Dorian engineer learned it? Who had he been *before*?

Perhaps she would learn. Perhaps not.

All that mattered now was that Flynn had a way off this planet. She intended to see that his deal became *her* deal. Then she would decide what to do with him. Only two types of people ever survived meeting her: those of use. And those of interest.

Instinctively, she looked back at Sedona. The blank stare in her eyes . . .

It made Gable feel warm.

"Come, Marcus," she said, leaving the workbench, turning her back to him. She could detect any aggressive actions, but she was confident he wouldn't make that mistake again. He would wait now, look for an opportunity.

She wished him luck.

When Gable reached it, she keyed in the code again. The giant doors reopened. All that waited beyond was reddish black.

Flynn stood beside her, staring into the darkness beyond the door. "Why is the reactor off-line?"

Gable studied him. He was a scientist, like her, but unlike other scientists he seemed to have a trait she found very valuable. His curiosity could override his fear.

Gable noted it.

"What do you think?" she asked back.

He was silent a moment. "I think someone turned it off."

"And why would they do that, Marcus?"

"Because . . . it's a weakness."

Gable had already reached the same conclusion. She could see it in his eyes, the satisfaction that came with putting pieces of a puzzle together. Gable liked it. Gable could *use* it.

"Let's find out," she said, and took a step into the hall. Flynn followed right after, curiosity still overriding apprehension. "But stay behind me."

As they moved, Gable studied the floor. For her, the emergency lights provided plenty of illumination. She could see the drag marks stretching ahead, where Flynn could not.

They seemed to get darker—and thicker. Gable kept following them, into the dark, followed by Flynn.

Eventually they reached a new set of doors, sealed like all the others, leading to the hot labs. The drag marks disappeared under them.

"If the labs are sealed from a quarantine lockdown . . ." Flynn mused.

"Then how is it moving bodies between them?" Gable finished his thought.

The terminals with the handprints were on either side of the big door. Gable moved to one. Flynn, however, did not. He just stared at Gable.

"Marcus," she said patiently, "you look like you have something to say." The response he gave was the predictable one. So boring.

Point deducted.

"You may have killed my friend," Flynn said, "when you sealed her off from the lab."

"You certainly are concerned for her," Gable said. "Tell me, do you think she's as concerned about *you*?"

Flynn's face dropped. Slightly. "That's not the point."

"What *is* the point, Marcus?"

"Something's bringing people to this lab." His voice had a hard edge to it. "If we find her in here . . . with the rest . . ."

"You'll do what? Kill me?"

"You showed me something before. You showed me—"

"That you had it in you, after all," Gable cut him off. "That you *could* pull the trigger. Even if it were to a gun that wouldn't fire. Pulling a trigger, for whatever reason, is very important to you, isn't it, Marcus? Did someone tell you that you couldn't?" Something else occurred to her, a different option. "Or did you need to, once . . . and failed?"

The look that passed over Flynn's face showed that she'd guessed right. Another button to push. Gable noted it.

Flynn, for his part, stared at her, perplexed.

"Yes, my precious petal," she told him with disdain. "You are *that* easy to read. Do you think you're special, Marcus? Do you think you're the only one crippled by self-doubt? It must be comforting to think that way. How long have you been doing it? Telling yourself these stories? When did you decide to play this role?"

"It's not a role," he said, his voice defensive.

"I think it is. And it's really quite boring. So you pulled a trigger. Bravo. Unfortunately, Marcus, you're still nowhere near what you need to be to survive this world, much less to survive *me*. But I do hope I'm there when you finally pull the trigger for real." She let her words sink in, held his gaze without blinking. "Now. Put your hand on the terminal, or I will cut it off your arm and put it there *for* you."

Flynn stared back with fire. He didn't like being told who he was.

Even so, placed his hand on the terminal, and when he did the door to the hot labs opened. More buttons. More information. Gable noted it. They followed the drag marks inside.

The interior of the lab was as chaotic and nightmarish as Gable had hoped.

Instruments and equipment and computers thrown everywhere. Ammo casings littering the floor, bullet holes in the walls. The lights were out here as well, and the computer screens that still functioned flickered on and off strobically.

Three hazard suits lay on the floor, big and bulky, with metallic helmets, designed to keep contagions and other dangerous environmental components out.

Apparently they had failed.

The viewscreens on the suit helmets were broken, their glass littering the floor. Black marks, like the ones from Gable's lab, stretched out from them, as if whoever had been inside had simply been yanked out.

The marks from the suits joined with the rest, blending together into a thick, nondescript sludge smeared across the floor to one of the walls. And then the trail moved *upward*.

Gable followed it with her eyes, saw where it ended, in the center of the lab, on the ceiling.

She smiled at the artistry of it. At the function and form. The design. The intention.

"What is it?" Flynn asked. He didn't have her eyes. For him, the shadows on the ceiling were too dark to see through.

"I sense you would rather not know," Gable said, and meant it.

She tore her gaze away from the sight on the ceiling, looked at the room's most dominant feature. A containment area, similar to her own, a wall of clear polysteel separating it from the rest of the lab.

What was in it, however, was impossible to tell.

The glass had completely fogged over, was dripping with condensation. There was a dull glowing behind the fog, but what it was, even Gable's eyes couldn't tell.

They heard a voice then. Weak, hoarse, full of fluid. From their left.

"Purge . . ." it breathed.

Gable heard Flynn's heart beat faster in his chest, sensed his breathing grow heavy.

She slowly turned to the source of the sound.

There was a desk there, crumpled. On the floor, on the other side, lay a man in a lab coat.

Gable had never seen him before, but that wasn't abnormal. The teams that worked in the different labs in Site Eleven rarely interacted.

Appendages—that was all Gable could label them—almost like tentacles or an insect's legs, dripped down from the ceiling toward the man. They weren't just wrapped around him; they were burrowed *into* him.

And his body was almost completely black. It looked nearly liquefied.

It throbbed and pulsed. And yet there was a hardness to it as well. Like liquid metal.

Only the man's neck and head were still normal. But the blackness seemed to be spreading. Upward.

The scientist's eyes locked with Gable's. "Purge . . ."

"Holy God," Flynn breathed, looking away. His heart beat even faster.

Gable looked back to the containment area, to one of its several control panels. On each there was an identical large red button, covered by a plastic cover. It read, "Purge Containment."

However the button worked, Gable guessed the effect would likely kill whatever was in the containment area. It would purge it . . .

"Don't . . . turn on . . . power . . ." the man moaned.

The black spread towards the man's head. The appendages began to pull him upward.

Flynn shut his eyes tighter.

"Why?" Gable asked.

"Tapped . . . into reactor . . ."

"So you cut the power," Gable said. She could tell that Flynn's heart rate had slowed suddenly. So had his breathing. His curiosity began to override his fear. Yet again.

"Killed . . . it . . . I killed . . ." the man managed. Black liquid began to seep out of his nose and ears. He was slowly being dragged upward.

"How?" Gable wanted to know. "By turning off the reactor?"

"Killed it . . ."

He was losing himself fast. She got to the pertinent question. "And what *is* it?"

"Purge . . ."

Gable frowned, watching the black spread almost to the man's neck, bubbling and throbbing. His breaths were gasps and gurgles.

"While . . . you still . . . can . . ."

A mass of thick liquid rolled out of the man's mouth. His head seemed to wither, blackening and bubbling.

And then the appendages dragged him up into the shadows along the ceiling.

Flynn was clearly trying not to vomit on the spot. For Gable, it had all mostly been a waste of time. Very little had been learned, very little had—

Flynn moved to one of the control panels, for one of the red buttons.

That would not do. Not at all.

In a blur, Gable grabbed Flynn's arm and yanked him back.

He stared at her, wild-eyed, shocked.

"What are you doing?" he asked.

Gable sighed. "What I always do, Marcus. Thinking things through."

"This thing . . ."

"Fascinating, isn't it? Certainly, it deserves *contemplation*."

"It killed everyone here!"

"So would I, given the chance," she said slowly, squeezing his arm painfully for emphasis. "Very unpleasant things are done in this lab, Marcus."

Flynn just stared back, confused and torn. He didn't see the world the way she did. But, who did?

Sounds erupted over the speakers in the lab. The ones she'd heard before. Scratches and hisses, static, and something like . . . voices.

Flynn's eyes widened as he saw something behind her.

Gable turned. There was a shadow behind the fog on the polysteel. From something on the other side. Something big and hulking. Something dark.

There . . . can . . . be . . . bargains . . .

Gable's head hurt suddenly. The voices, the ones under the static on the speakers, she could . . . understand them? Was that the right phrase?

There . . . can . . . be . . . bargains . . .

"Bargains." Gable said the word out loud, tasting it on her tongue, and found she liked it. Pain flared in her temples.

"What?" Flynn asked, staring at her, confused.

Gable let him go, took a few steps toward the polysteel, where the shadow stood. It towered over her, almost to the ceiling.

She reached up, wiped away the condensation.

Behind it, the shadow was revealed. And it was glorious.

"Goodness . . ." Gable whispered.

THIRTY-SEVEN

WASTED FEAR

Flynn could see the containment area was full of a strange fog-like mist that made everything inside difficult to make out, with the exception of the horrible thing standing against the polysteel.

It was almost insect-like, like a spider with just a torso, no head, and four thick, angular legs that looked triple-jointed. Its skin was fibrous and pitch-black, flaky and wet. No face, no eyes, nothing that even looked like a head. It stood perfectly, rock-solid still, towering over them both. Flynn had to crane his neck to look up at it.

He recoiled. It was . . . *inhuman*. And wrong. And surely deserved to be destroyed, just the way the scientist had warned them. If this thing had gotten *Key* . . .

Flynn stepped back. He wanted away from it. Wanted to run, wanted to be anywhere else.

Gable's hand clamped down on his arm again. Her grip was like a vise.

"Look at it," she hissed, holding him, keeping her eyes on the creature. Flynn refused. This . . . *monster* was the last thing he wanted to look at. He felt like he would go insane if he did.

"Ignore your fear," Gable instructed, pulling him closer. He tried to fight her, but couldn't. How was she so strong? "Fear is a wasted emotion. Look at it. Become *more*."

Gable dragged him closer. The thing was right in front of him now, right on the other side of the glass, inches away.

"There was a time I was like you," Gable said into his ear. "But I made myself, *forced* myself, to be comfortable walking in the dark. It took blood and pain and lives, but I did it, and do you know why? Because I realized that if you fear death, you can never truly live. Look. At. *It*."

Flynn couldn't move, couldn't run. So he did what she told him. He looked at the horrible thing. Studied it. Tried to stare at it objectively.

The first thing he noticed was its skin, which wasn't skin at all, actually. It looked slimy, but he could tell it was *hard*, like wet metal. Was it like that all the way through? Or was it some kind of exoskeleton?

Flynn's fear receded as he studied the situation more intently.

Past the creature, where the mist was thin enough to see through, Flynn saw something else. Attached to the walls, things were growing. Dozens of them. Round, made of the same metallic-like substance, and yet they throbbed and bulged.

They looked like eggs. Or . . . nests.

He felt the fear again, but muted now. He was fascinated.

"Created by simple people," Gable said suddenly next to him. "What are we to do?"

Flynn looked at her, confused. She was staring intently at the thing on the other side of the polysteel, not at him. Were the words meant for the thing in front of them? The sounds were still coming through the speakers. Could she understand them—or, more disturbingly, *it*?

Gable let go of his arm, stepped to the right, toward a small metallic door in the polysteel, with a control panel next to it. It was a pass-through into the containment area.

Flynn's eyes widened as she tapped the panel.

"What are you *doing*?" Flynn asked, shocked. Surely she wasn't . . .

"Calm yourself, Marcus." The pass-through door slid open.

Flynn rushed her. Gable's hand moved in a blur and slammed him against the polysteel, squeezing his throat. The thing was right in front of him now, its faceless black torso standing in the mist on the other side, towering above him.

He gasped as she held him, tried to squirm loose.

"*Calm*," she reiterated.

Flynn looked sideways, watched as she reached through the polysteel—and *touched* the creature.

The sounds from the speakers intensified.

Gable jolted. Her muscles tensed, fingers clamping down on his throat. It felt like Flynn's larynx was about to rupture.

He struggled, squirming and bending, pushing against the silver-haired woman as hard as he could. Somehow he pulled loose of her grip, fell to the floor, coughing and gasping.

Gable stood where she'd been like a statue, her eyes rolled back in her head, hand still outstretched into the containment area and touching the horrible creature on the other side.

Lights flickered. A computer monitor exploded. The horrible sounds grew louder and louder. It all felt like it was building.

Flynn did the first thing his instincts told him.

He stood up and ran full force at Gable, slamming into her with all his weight.

It was enough.

She was dislodged from the creature. Together they fell to the floor, hard, rolled, slammed into a workbench.

The sounds from the speakers died—the static, the hisses, the voices— it all went silent.

There was a strange rattling sound from inside the containment area.

Flynn watched, wide-eyed, as the creature on the other side began to contort and tremble. Seconds later, it crumbled in on itself, the hardness of its skin collapsing in a pool of horrible blackness that spread, thick and gelatinous, all over the floor.

Flynn exhaled gratefully. The thing was gone. Dead.

"Thank you, Marcus," Gable said. She looked dazed. "That was almost too much for me."

"*What* was almost too much?" Flynn demanded, looking away from the sickening pool of black the creature had dissolved into. "What did you *do*?"

Her eyes focused on him. "I need you to reactivate the facility's reactor."

Flynn stared at her like she was insane. "The scientist said—"

"I know what he said, Marcus. I found his arguments uncompelling."

Something occurred to him then. "What are you doing? Are you . . . trying to *help* it?"

"Help it how, Marcus? It's quite dead."

She was talking in circles now. Flynn steeled himself. "I'm not reconnecting the X-Core."

"Yes," she said. "You are."

"No," Flynn said. Even though the woman next to him looked old, she had proven herself to be extremely dangerous. It didn't matter; he wasn't reconnecting the reactor. "I don't care what you do."

Gable studied him intently. "Believe me, Marcus, you *would*. But I don't have to convince you. If you don't, neither one of us will escape this facility alive."

Flynn paused. "Why?"

The lights from the computer monitors flickered. One of the computers died. Then another.

The room began to darken.

And Flynn noticed something else. Something new inside the containment area, just visible in the thick mist there. The nests on the walls had started to shudder.

"Isn't life fascinating," Gable said, taking it all in, "the way one thing leads to the next?"

Flynn had an idea what was happening. There was really only one possibility.

"The batteries are dying," he said.

"So it would seem."

"But they're quadripolar, at least. They should last—"

"*It* is draining them," Gable said. She meant the creature. The nests on the walls vibrated. "It seems to drain a great deal of power."

Another computer died in the room. If the batteries in the facility went, he would never be able to get the data the Suit wanted. And if he didn't get the data . . .

"You do still wish to leave the Razor, I presume?" Gable asked, with a knowing tone.

Flynn looked back at her. "Yes."

Gable smiled. "Then reconnect the reactor."

Whatever hesitation he had felt previously was dissipating.

What did he care about releasing a possible threat on the Razor? He hated this world. It was a cesspool of violence and horror. Maybe this thing would cleanse it completely. It wouldn't matter to him. He wouldn't be here to see it.

This will not be my life.

Flynn was up, moving toward something he'd seen earlier. A metallic box in the wall, hanging open. There was a large handle inside it, shoved down. Next to it was a simple numeric keypad.

The box was an emergency reactor deactivation switch, probably wired directly into the power relays. Flynn could see it wasn't original to this lab; it had been installed not all that long ago.

If the creature could tap into the facility's power and use it, then it made sense that someone would have added a shutoff valve in this lab, to counteract the possibility of that threat.

The keypad meant that the system had been designed, wisely, to be shut off by anyone who worked in the lab, but to require a specific code to allow it to be reactivated.

"Can you reconnect the power?" Gable asked, next to him.

"Yes," he said, studying the keypad. It was true. He just had to pass through the power. The problem was that the wiring and circuitry he needed was all behind the keypad, and it was bolted in place.

"I need a screwdriver," he said, "or a drill to—"

Gable yanked the entire enclosure straight off the wall. The screws and bolts flew through the air like bullets. The wiring on the other side was exposed.

"Or . . . Okay . . ." Flynn said. Gable stared at him impatiently.

From here, it was a pretty simple override. He found the wires he needed, polarity and ground wires, twisted them together.

There was a click as the lock on the handle disconnected.

Flynn shoved it upward.

Sparks flew from computers and lab equipment. Lights flashed to life in the ceiling—LED light, harsh and bright, wiping away the room's shadows.

It took a second for his eyes to adjust, but when they did, the ceiling was revealed. In all its horrible glory.

Bodies. *Dozens* of them.

Blackened. Just like the wet, metallic skin of the creature.

All blended and morphed together into one giant tapestry of regurgitated DNA, somehow stuck on the ceiling.

Eyes stared. Mouths hung open. Hands clenched in pain. Faces and legs and chests and tongues, all blended together.

It was the most gruesome, horrifying thing Flynn had ever seen in his life. It made his brain want to shut completely off. It made him want to—

Gable's fingers took Flynn's chin, pulled his eyes back down to hers.

"Fear," she reminded him, "is *wasted*."

She was right.

Flynn forced himself not to look up, studied the lab, found what he wanted next. At the back of the room was a single, rectangular data server, about six by six. All the computers in the lab would feed into it. If Flynn wanted a complete collection of the data in this lab, that was where it would be.

The nest-like things in the containment area bulged almost as one, seemed to be expanding. Something unpleasant was about to happen.

The speakers around Flynn filled with sound again. Static. And hissing.

"Time is short," Gable told him.

Flynn believed her. Whether it was a result of touching that thing or
not, she seemed to know a lot more than him. He ripped open the doors
of the data server.

Inside, wires and circuitry ran everywhere. Flynn scanned the interior,
following the data conduits to their logical destinations. They all came
together at a large blue-cased device in the center.

The main drive.

He felt a rush of emotion, looking at it. The thing he needed. The thing
that would make this nightmare end. He just had to—

Inside the containment area, the nests suddenly exploded.

From each, a swarm of darkness surged outward, and the interior filled
with putrid blackness in seconds, devouring the mist and the fog.

Flynn stared at it all, eyes wide, watching the swarm grow and spread,
filling the cramped confines of the containment area until it was pure
black.

"Marcus." Flynn felt Gable's hand on his shoulder, felt it squeeze tight.

He turned back to the server, studied it quickly. It was attached by bolts,
but that was the least of the complications.

He could see the two thick purple wires attached to those screws. And
the third purple wire running to the drive itself.

Flynn knew what they were. Fail-safes. If someone pulled the drive out,
it would auto-erase. And that meant losing all the data. And Flynn's one
hope of escaping the Razor.

"I need wire cutters," Flynn said.

Gable grabbed a pair of cutters from a table, handed them to Flynn.

Flynn looked back to the drive . . . which is when the polysteel of the
containment area began to *crack*.

The sound of it echoed sharply in the lab, from wall to wall. Flynn
jumped.

He stared at the polysteel, watching the cracks grow—and the black
swarm pressed against it. He couldn't believe what he was seeing.

"It's . . . breaking through!" he exclaimed. Polysteel, in spite of its clarity, was one of the most molecularly strong substances mankind had ever
produced. And yet, whatever was in the containment was breaking right
through it.

"It is the least of your worries," Gable whispered.

Flynn wasn't sure how that could be true, but he turned back to the drive, nonetheless. He snipped a red wire, deeper inside, buried within the others.

Flynn took the wire, frayed and twisted it, exposed the metal, and routed it to the screws on the drive, where the purple wires were connected.

"Can you pull it loose?" Flynn asked. "In one pull? Clean?" Gable gave him a stern look, reached for the drive.

"Now?" she asked impatiently.

Flynn breathed, thought his engineering through. It should work.

He nodded.

The bolts broke apart as Gable yanked the drive loose from the server in one straight pull. She handed it to Flynn.

He could feel the warmth from its internal power. It was still operational.

"Well done," Gable told him, a note of approval in her voice.

In spite of everything, Flynn felt satisfied. He felt . . . pride. *Point added*, he could almost hear in Gable's voice.

Then she dragged him away, through the lab, by the back of the neck.

The polysteel kept breaking, cracks spreading through its surface.

Whatever the hell the swarm was, it was about to burst through.

Gable yanked open a supply locker along one of the walls, threw the contents on the floor, then shoved Flynn inside it.

"Hey!" he yelled.

Gable studied Flynn from the outside. There was a strange look in her eyes, one that Flynn couldn't read.

"They will let you pass," she told him.

Flynn stared back. "*What?*"

"When you escape this facility," she said, ignoring him, "head for the starport as quickly as you can. There are issues there that require your attention—and *your* attention only. Like here, I'm afraid, you have very little time. Things have changed on the surface."

"What are you talk—"

"It will make sense when you are outside."

Gable closed one door of the locker, started to close the other and seal him in.

Flynn felt fear beginning to rise. "*Wait!* Where are *you* going?"

"Don't worry, Marcus," Gable said, with a smile. "I have a feeling we shall do terrible things together."

Behind her, the polysteel finally shattered in a maelstrom of sound.

The blackness, a giant swarm of it, flowed forward, filling the lab.

Gable slammed shut the door as she turned to face it. Darkness covered Flynn. And then the alarms began to blare.

THIRTY-EIGHT

THE DARK

The sounds grew louder, coming out of every speaker in the room.

"Maddox . . ." Raelyn said behind him, still plugged into the IV. She sounded scared. He didn't blame her.

Something was coming.

He remembered Zane's last words. *It doesn't move like a man.*

Maddox headed for the control panel next to the room's big door, where they'd entered from. "How much longer?"

Raelyn looked up at the IV bottle, at the remaining liquid inside it.

"A minute," she said, "maybe two."

That might be too long. He reached the controls on the wall, found the button for the fortified doors, pressed it. Nothing happened. Except on the terminal, where a digital numbered keypad appeared.

"It needs a code," Maddox said. He looked back at Raelyn sitting on the stool, the IV plugged into her arm. They couldn't leave until the infusion finished, or coming down here had been for nothing.

The sounds kept growing louder.

"I'm scared," Raelyn told him.

Maddox nodded. "I could use a weapon." He moved for a line of storage lockers, past one of the medical gurneys.

"There aren't any weapons here," Raelyn said.

Maddox yanked open a locker. Nothing useful, just meds. Pills and vials.

He opened another. Basic supplies, bandages, alcohol.

Another. Equipment—surgical maybe, judging by the size.

Maddox started pulling things out, showing them to Raelyn.

He held up a scalpel.

"Nothing bigger?" she asked skeptically.

He grabbed something that looked like a giant set of pliers with serrated teeth.

"Rib splitter. Not bad."

Maddox looked again. Attached to the inner wall of the locker was a small gleaming silver chainsaw. It was about half the size of a baseball bat, with sharpened teeth running in an arc along the top half.

He showed it to Raelyn.

She nodded. "Bone saw."

"We have a winner," he said.

The sounds, the static and hissing, the voices, all of it swelled loudly in the dark—then suddenly silenced. The only sound was their breathing now. Raelyn's was heavy. Maddox could hear it from across the room.

He gripped the saw, put himself between Raelyn and the door they'd entered.

There was nothing beyond but reddish darkness. Nothing moved.

Then something exploded into the lab from the *opposite* door.

Maddox spun just in time to see a strangely shaped shadow, about four feet tall, blow over a table. Equipment hit the floor, sprayed everywhere.

It rushed at Raelyn with a strange rattling sound, like rocks bouncing around inside a bag. She screamed.

Maddox moved to block the thing, whatever the hell it was. The saw whirred to life. The thing was big and thick, yet somehow incredibly fast.

It turned on a dime, closed the distance in a blur, and rammed into him before he could connect with the saw.

It hit hard. The thing felt like it was made of metal.

Maddox crashed into one of the gurneys, flipped over it, hit the floor. The breath burst from his lungs.

The thing rattled, turned . . . and moved for Raelyn.

She fell off the chair, pulled over the IV as the thing moved for her. The bottle smashed on the floor. She raised her arm up instinctively, the one with Slow Burn glowing in the dark, as the thing advanced.

Something on the sides of the creature, like appendages, lashed forward and wrapped around her arm—

And then the sounds on the speakers flared, loud and painful. Maddox winced.

The creature recoiled. The appendages let Raelyn go. It stumbled backward.

Maddox saw a stunned look on Raelyn's face. There was something about the Slow Burn that the thing clearly did not like.

There wasn't time to think about it now, though.

Maddox moved. The saw whirred loudly.

Sparks sprayed from the top of the creature and the saw bounced off it. It was like hitting steel.

It did its job, though. The thing was distracted. The sounds and voices on the speakers swelled as it turned toward Maddox.

He could see it a little better now. Totally black, a wet-looking sheen all over it. Triangular body, three legs, two appendages on top, insect-like, no head that he could see . . . but there was a mouth.

It opened, black fangs ready, as it rushed Maddox.

Raelyn was on her feet, pulling the IV out of her arm. She grabbed her pack, ran for the door. It was the opposite door from the one they'd entered.

"Raelyn!" Maddox yelled. She was panicking, didn't listen.

The thing slammed into Maddox and drove him to the floor. The smell coming off it was almost chemical. Not organic. And sickeningly intense.

Its mouth opened, the appendages reaching for him.

Maddox jammed the saw into its mouth, pulled the trigger.

A torrent of black, thick liquid sprayed everywhere.

The sounds on the speakers flared so loudly it hurt.

The thing backed off, took a few steps, collapsed.

Maddox was up fast. The bone saw was ruined, the teeth popped out of their tracks. He let it fall to the floor and ran.

In the flickering light that lit up the shadows, Maddox saw something when he looked behind him.

The creature, whatever it was, was dissolving.

It flattened on the floor as more and more of the black liquid drained out of it, coating everything.

While he watched, stunned, the black stuff reached the walls . . . then started to spread *up* them, showing no signs of slowing down.

It was mesmerizing, watching it cover the entire room. But Maddox made himself break away and run after Raelyn, through the door. He found her outside, paralyzed.

It was darker in the halls, almost pitch-black.

Her breathing was coming in shocked gasps.

"Hey!" he yelled, grabbing her, pulling her close. She was terrified, shaking. Her eyes focused, found him. "Are you okay?"

She nodded. Maddox took her arm, studied where the creature had touched her. There was no mark. Just the Slow Burn, glowing in the dark like coals on her skin.

They looked at each other, both confused.

Then bright lights flashed on up and down the hallway. Alarms began to blare through the halls. Maddox and Raelyn winced.

"What's going on?" Raelyn asked, shielding her eyes from the brightness.

"Someone just turned on the reactor," Maddox said. "And it's going haywire."

He grabbed her arm and pulled her along. They had to find a way back to the control center.

THIRTY-NINE

PAIN

Zane had been around, seen and killed pretty much one of everything. Men. Creatures. Things you couldn't even put in those categories. Whatever was coming for him in the hall outside, he didn't have a quarrel with it. But if it fucked with him, it was going to die.

The girl, though, she stared at the darkness in the hall decidedly differently. She had seen something out there, something that had stuck with her.

Whoever she was, she talked tough. Zane guessed she could handle herself, too, but underneath, she was scared. And fear was a bad variable for this equation.

"What's your name?" Zane asked.

"Key," she said. He could just make out the wings on her back.

The strange sounds filtering out of the room's dead speakers seemed to be growing louder. Static. Hissing. Scratching. And something like voices, underneath it all.

"What are you thinking, Key?" Zane asked.

"That I either need a fucking drink or a fucking knife," she said. He could hear the tremor in her voice.

Zane turned and moved through the lab, studied the lockers along the back wall, looking for one he'd seen earlier labeled "Prototype Storage." It had a large digital combination lock on the front.

Zane grabbed the lock, let the Charge flow through it.

The lock heated in his palm until it glowed orange. Then it blackened, as the Charge transmitted the metal into Zane's body. The X burned. His head hurt. He dealt with it like always.

"Who the hell *are* you?" Key asked, watching the lock heat in his hand and glow.

"My name is Zane," he told her through the muzzle. He could feel her tense through the metal floor.

"Zane's a campfire story," she stated. "I've met a million guys claiming to be Zane."

"And where are they now?"

"Dead. Mostly."

Zane squeezed. The lock burst apart in his hand.

"Exactly."

He yanked open the locker. It was lined with rifles and pistols in a rack in the back, all useless without biometrics. Cases of different shapes and sizes were stacked on the bottom.

"You said a knife," Zane reiterated, pulling out a specific case from the back and snapping it open. Inside rested two long, sharp knives, packed in foam.

They should work nicely.

"I have this memory," Zane said, turning back to Key, "of being in the desert. It's night. There's hills, big ones, all around me. I can see storm clouds nearby, and I can see the lights of a city shining on the clouds from underneath. Every once in a while there's lightning, but no thunder."

Zane pulled the two knives from the foam and showed them to Key. Her eyes widened lustfully at the sight.

"I feel like I'm a kid in this memory, but I'm not sure," Zane continued. "It's the only memory I have from before I woke up. And it's the only memory I have, before or after, of being scared."

Zane flipped the switches on the hilts of the knives and their blades began to glow with orange light. When activated, the blades were coated with superheated plasma, which let them slice right through things a normal knife would just bounce off of.

"Maybe I'm lost, maybe something's hunting me, I don't know. What I do know is it's also the only memory I have of not being in pain. I feel pain all the time. In my head and in my veins. Burning. I have the feeling most people would find it excruciating."

Zane offered the knives to Key. She hesitated a moment, then moved to him, eager to take them.

When she got close enough, Zane twisted one of the blades and let it rake, flat edge down, across the skin of her arm.

Key yelled out in pain, jumped back as the plasma scarred her skin.

Her face contorted in anger. She yanked one of the knives free, raised it to strike. Exactly the reaction Zane was hoping for.

He grabbed her wrist, spun and slammed her into the lockers, pinning her against the metal, still holding one of the glowing knives.

"*What the fuck?*" Key yelled, furious.

"The point is," Zane said easily, "the reason very little frightens me . . . is *because* of the pain."

Key's chest rose up and down violently. She glared at him over her shoulder. There was a nasty cauterized wound on her arm. It had to hurt bad.

"Pain is useful," he told her pointedly. "Pain focuses you. It's just one more sensation, and either you learn to use it to become stronger . . . or you don't. In which case, I promise, there won't be anything to fear *then*. Because you'll be dead."

Zane held her furious eyes a moment more, then slammed the other glowing plasma blade through the metal lockers, an inch from Key's face. The voices on the speakers kept growing, louder, more intense.

"Are you still scared?" Zane asked over them.

"No," Key told him in a tight voice.

"What are you?"

"Pissed off."

"Perfect." Zane let her go and turned back to the door leading to the hall and the shadows outside. Then suddenly, the voices faded away, plunging the lab back into silence.

Zane planted himself in front of the door, made himself visible. For him, it was better to be noticed, better if whatever it was came right at him. He checked where the closest metal was. Two workbenches, he saw. The floor, even, if he needed it.

Behind him, Key ripped the blade out of the locker, twirled it with the second one in her hands, testing their weight. They glowed hot, bright orange. She stood next to him now, rubbing the burned spot on her arm. She still looked pissed

"Are all the stories about you real?" Key asked, staring out the door with him.

"Some of them," Zane answered.

"Which ones?"

"The scary ones."

Then the shadows exploded. A creature raced inside. The sounds and the voices and the static flared over the speakers.

Whatever it was, it had three legs, some kind of appendages on top, and no head. Its surface was black and oily and it moved fast.

Zane was planted in place. Let it come.

It slammed into him with one hell of an impact. So much so, he slid back a few feet.

Interesting . . .

Zane moved quickly, grabbed whatever it was, and released some of the Charge.

He hefted it up into the air . . . then slammed it right back down. The sound was loud. The impact was harder. He felt the tremors shake through the floor and into the walls.

Whatever it was, it wasn't soft, even if it looked like it was. It was hard. Like metal.

Zane didn't care. It wasn't getting back up.

He raised his fist, channeled, and—

Appendages lashed upward, like tentacles. One wrapped around his fist. Another, his neck. Both of them pulled hard.

Zane groaned, surprised, pushed back against it. The thing was strong. Too strong for even him. First time for everything.

He crashed down, and when he did, the creature flipped him over like he weighed nothing. Its appendage tightened around his wrist and he felt a searing pain there. Not a burn; more like intense cold.

Zane looked at his wrist. And saw it start to *blacken*.

He remembered the drag marks on the floors, the dark, fibrous leftovers of whatever these things had done to the people who used to work here.

That wasn't happening to him.

Zane touched the metal floor, poured the Charge out through his fingers. He absorbed the metal, clean and rust free, drawing it in through his palm.

The pain in his wrist subsided. The X burned. The blackness on the skin of his hand *reversed* itself, healing.

The sounds in the room came back to life over the speakers. Static, hissing, voices. Angry and loud.

The creature pulled back, weakened by the Charge that was fighting back against it.

Key appeared out of nowhere, the glowing knives in her hands blurring the air.

The thing was solid, but the blades were plasma-charged, so they penetrated. Sparks and pieces of the thing flew everywhere.

The speakers flared as the blades struck downward, over and over.

The appendages loosened around Zane.

He pulled more energy out of the floor. But instead of pushing the thing off of him, he grabbed the tentacles on his wrist and pulled it right *to* him.

The thing had a mouth on that triangular body, jagged and pointed.

He grabbed its jaws, one sharp half in each hand, top and bottom, then pushed and pulled, channeling the Charge, all he had, fueling his muscles.

The sounds on the speakers roared at a fever pitch, filled the room.

The thing's jaws tore apart at the hinges . . . then kept going.

Zane strained until whatever the black thing was split in half. Thick, black, oily liquid sprayed across the room.

The creature went limp on top of him, and Zane tossed it away like garbage. It crashed through a table and lay still.

Key, holding the glowing knives, stared at him, stunned. It was a look Zane had gotten used to. He pushed to his feet as black liquid rained down from the ceiling.

"Jesus tap-dancing Christ," the girl said.

"He had nothing to do with it," Zane replied. He looked at his wrist, the one the creature had touched. The blackness was gone, the Charge had healed it.

Where the creature had fallen, the dark liquid was spreading outward now, like black mercury. Faster and faster, moving over the floors, spreading to the walls, up them, toward the ceiling.

Key stepped back from it, eyes wide, stunned.

Zane grabbed the data card he'd found earlier. Whatever answers were on it, he would have to look at them later.

Suddenly, the lights in the lab all flashed back on, filling the room with brightness. Alarms began to sound in the halls, loud and piercing.

Zane and Key looked at each other.

"I'll follow *you*," she said.

FORTY

MELTDOWN

Flynn felt like he was trapped in a coffin, his shoulders rubbing against the walls of the storage locker. Everything was stark black, even with the reactor powered up and the lights back on outside.

The static and the scratching from the speakers had been replaced by a blaring alarm tone—and something like a furious rushing of wind. The locker shook and vibrated.

Then, suddenly, it all calmed down, like some force had exploded through and out of the hot labs.

Flynn tried the door, but it was sealed shut. It didn't even rattle.

"Gable?" he yelled. No response.

He tried the door again, started to panic.

Flynn got his toes against the bottom of the door, pushed his back into the rear wall, started inching his feet up, adding more and more pressure.

The door burst open. Flynn spilled out onto the laboratory floor.

The room was covered in black now. A dense, oily, dark liquid. It dripped from everywhere: the walls, the ceilings, the equipment.

On the floor, he was quickly becoming covered in whatever it was. It was cold, too. Icy. The feel of it was unsettling, and he slipped back and forth, trying to stand.

He grabbed a table edge, managed to pull himself to his feet.

Everything smelled . . . chemical. Not organic. The swarming mass from the containment area was gone. Somehow, that didn't make Flynn feel any better

The alarms blared, loud and jarring. Flynn could see the screen of a nearby computer. It was bad.

FACILITY REACTOR WARNING
Meltdown Imminent. Evacuate All Personnel.

An X-Core meltdown was no place anyone wanted to be. He needed to get out of here. Fast.

But something occurred to him.

Evacuate All Personnel.

He'd worked in a lot of labs with quarantine lockdown protocols. There was only one thing that could override that.

A reactor meltdown.

He thought about Gable, about her insistence on turning the power back on.

Had she known? Had she done it intentionally, to override the quarantine and reopen the control center?

But she was gone. There was no way to know.

The floor rumbled under his feet. Sparks exploded in the hall outside.

The meltdown was under way. An *Xytrilium* meltdown.

Flynn moved for the exit as fast as he could, trying to keep his footing on the slick floor. The blue-boxed data drive hung by its cables in his hand. It was his way off this planet. And back to his old life. The thought filled him with hope and energy, spurred him.

He made it out the door, back the way he'd come. The black substance wasn't as prominent out here. He could run, which he did. Down the hall. Lights exploded above him, spraying glass. The floor vibrated under him.

He raced through the door back into the reverse engineering lab, moved through all the workbenches and the terminals . . . and froze in his tracks.

Sedona, the scientist who had been inside with Gable, lay on the floor inside the containment area. Next to her was a scalpel. Under her was a pool of blood, just visible in the flickering lights in the ceiling. Above her, on the polysteel wall, something was scrawled.

Sedona had written words there, in her own blood, it looked like. Her last gesture. Flynn's breath quickened as he read them.

"Kill her while u can"

The words could only mean one person.

Gable had seemingly saved his life earlier, but there was no question she was terrifying. Whatever the woman had done in this lab, to Sedona, to whoever else, it had made a mark. The words were a warning to Flynn. Not to let her leave a similar mark on *him*.

Flynn jumped as a strange wet, rattling sound came from the door he'd rushed in from.

Something stood there, revealed in the flashes of light from the ceiling. Not as tall or imposing as the creature from the hot labs, half that size, three-legged not four-, but it had the same glistening black, angular body.

It didn't move, stood rock solid. Even though it had no eyes that Flynn could see, it felt like it was staring at him.

Flynn's breath caught in his throat. He started to back away, turned toward the door out of the room . . . and froze again.

Another creature stood there. Just like the one behind him. Also totally still.

Flynn's muscles froze. The rattling sounds from the creatures echoed in the room, loud and sharp, threatening. Yet the horrible creatures made no move for him.

Gable's words played in his head. *They will let you pass.*

Flynn swallowed and clenched his fists, then, tentatively, took a step *toward* the creature in front of him.

It stayed where it was.

Flynn forced himself to take another step.

This time the creature moved, slowly and deliberately, but not toward him. It moved to the *side*, creating a small gap big enough for Flynn to pass by and through the door.

He felt his heart beat in his chest. He kept moving, one step after the other, until he'd walked right past the hideous black thing in the doorway. It didn't move, it did nothing at all. It was terrifying.

Flynn ran as fast as he could. The creature didn't pursue.

Had Gable arranged that as well? There wasn't time to wonder. A horrible metallic groaning filled the air as the walls began to crumple in on one another. Lights exploded in the ceiling. Flame shot from air intakes.

When an X-Core melted down, there was almost always a containment breach; even the reinforced enclosures couldn't withstand the gravity reversal. What was going on inside the core was essentially the same phenomena as a collapsing star, on a much smaller scale.

Flynn had seen the results on SMVs that had gone through a meltdown and hadn't managed to eject their X-Cores in time. The giant machines imploded, pulled into something probably a tenth the size of what they once were. That was going to happen to Site Eleven. And anyone inside was going to be compacted, along with everything else, into an incredibly dense mass of metal and plastic and polysteel.

Flynn ran harder.

He took the corner, toward the control center, which should be open now that the quarantine was lifted.

It *was* open, but not for long. He could see that the doors at the end of the hall were *closing*.

"Hey!" he yelled desperately. Someone was inside; he could see their feet. Two sets. "*Hey!*"

Flynn ran full speed into the doors, but it was too late. He bounced off them and hit the floor, right as they sealed shut, taking his chance of escape with him.

Flynn groaned in pain and rolled over, crawled to the now shut control center. He banged on the metal as hard as he could, but the doors didn't move. Inside, the ladder would have ascended, back to the surface. Back to the hot sun and to freedom, for whoever had been inside.

Everything rocked and shuddered around Flynn. The lights in the ceiling exploded, one by one, plunging everything back to darkness. Even the red emergency lights were gone now. The walls shook. Fire lanced through the air in the halls.

He wasn't going to make it. The meltdown was going to happen. And he was going to be crushed with all of it. A permanent fixture.

Flynn leaned his head back against the wall and looked at the blue data drive from the hot labs. He'd almost made it. Almost actually—

The thick metal doors behind him suddenly shuddered.

Flynn's eyes widened as they began to rise back up.

He rolled away and saw two giant hands underneath the doors, *lifting* them up.

Flynn's eyes widened in shock.

Sparks flew everywhere. The hallway filled with a loud screeching sound as the doors were forced back open, apparently by the owner of the hands. A feat that should have been humanly impossible.

Before Flynn could ponder it, two smaller hands grabbed him by the neck and yanked him under the doors and into the control center.

The doors slammed back down with a thunderous impact behind him.

Flynn looked up at the two people inside the small room, illuminated by the monitors and holo displays of the control center.

One was the biggest man Flynn had ever seen. His skin was ashen gray, his features nondescript, mainly because he had a muzzle on his face, but he radiated power and strength in a way Flynn had never, ever seen.

The other person . . . was *Key*.

Flynn's heart skipped a beat. A weight lifted. He said the first thing that came to his mind.

"Are you *okay*?"

Key blinked, staring down at him. A strange look crossed her face.

"Fucking peachy," she finally said. "Get your ass off the floor."

Flynn did, as fast as he could. Everything shook. Sparks flew as computer monitors exploded. A rending, screeching sound ripped the air. He could hear the walls outside buckling in on themselves.

"What is it?" Key yelled.

"The site's imploding," Flynn yelled back.

If they didn't climb out quick, they weren't ever leaving.

The big man grabbed Key like she weighed nothing and shoved her up into the shaft above. Then he followed after her, turned and reached back down.

The man's hand swallowed Flynn's, almost yanked his shoulder off as he pulled him up.

The control center shook and contorted. The walls started to tear apart, the room inside shrinking violently. Flynn climbed fast, following after Key and the Gray Man. Flynn could just see Key climb through the door up top, and felt relief. At least she was safe.

There was a rumbling below, a big one. Flynn stared back down. He couldn't help it. After all, he'd never been in a X-Core meltdown before.

The shaft below had completely closed in on itself; the control center was a mass of metal inside a tight pocket now, blended and crushed into everything else.

Everything shook hard. And a massive fireball erupted from below, rushed up at him.

Flynn's eyes widened.

A hand grabbed him by the neck and yanked him upward off the ladder and into the small room above.

"Hesitation gets you killed." The Gray Man studied Flynn in annoyance, and then threw him through the security door and out into the raging sunlight on the other side.

Flynn hit the sandy ground and rolled, came to a painful stop. From the ground he looked up in time to see the big man step outside, right as a mass of smoke and debris blew out the door as the facility underneath finally collapsed. The earth shook under them.

Then everything went quiet.

"Fuck me running," Flynn heard Key say, her face buried in the dirt next to him.

"Flynn?" a voice asked. A different voice. Masculine. And something about it was familiar.

Exhausted, hurting everywhere, Flynn rolled and looked behind him.

Two people sat in the shade cast by one of the rusted Crawlers: a man, in what used to be a white prisoner jumpsuit, and a woman, in doctor's scrubs. Pretty, with hair that seemed to waver between red and brown. Both were covered in the same black mess as everyone else. Both were as exhausted as everyone else.

Flynn's eyes widened. "Maddox?"

The man was dirty and tired, but it *was* Maddox. The prisoner he'd talked to on the train. The one he'd seen on the shuttle. The one who'd passed out at *Charon* intake.

Maddox wore a similarly shocked look. Everyone else noticed.

"Yeah," Maddox said eventually, "I got nothing . . ."

Flynn's head swam; he suddenly felt sick. His body was instantly coated in sweat. It took him a moment to realize why. It was *hot.* Inordinately hot. Probably 120 degrees. It didn't make sense. It hadn't been this hot earlier.

"Something's not fucking right," Key said, next to him on the ground. Sweat was pouring off her too.

Flynn looked west, up at the sun, which was visible just above the rim of the crater. It was bright and wavering, almost red now.

And there was something else, too.

It looked like storm clouds, stretching from one end of the horizon to the other, but Flynn knew what it really was.

Smoke.

The same smoke he'd seen earlier from the crater rim, only now it was much bigger.

Something was burning to the west, and Flynn had a dark realization of what it must be. *Not just something,* he corrected himself. *Everything.*

Whatever vegetation, sparse though it was. Whatever structures. Anything flammable. It was all on fire.

"What is it?" Key asked, staring west with him. Flynn felt her crawl closer.

An explanation occurred to him, the only one he had that accounted for all the data, impossible as it seemed.

Things have changed on the surface, Gable had told him.

"The Razor is shrinking." When Flynn said it out loud it sounded even more impossible. But he knew it wasn't. He knew he was right. And as it shrank, the Cindersphere expanded, burning everything in its path as it did.

Doing the math in his head, Flynn knew they only had days. And then they would either be burned to a crisp or asphyxiate from the lack of an atmosphere. Them and everyone else still left on the planet.

"You know," Key said next to him, on her back, staring up at the sky through the wrecks of rusting Crawlers, "I really should have killed you when I had the chance."

Flynn looked at her. In spite of everything, he smiled.

PART III

ARTIFACT A

FORTY-ONE

RABBIT HOLES

"Let me see if I have this right," the doctor said, her face crumpled, trying hard to make sense of it all. "The Razor . . . is *shrinking.*"

They all stood there, amid the Crawler wrecks—Flynn, Key, Maddox, Raelyn, and the big man—each leaning against the train cars, using them for shade from the scorching sun. The heat was getting intolerable.

"It's the only explanation." Flynn peeled the thick fabric of his white jumpsuit off his sweat-soaked chest.

Raelyn was working on a wound on Key's arm, disinfecting and bandaging it with supplies from her pack. To Flynn, it looked like a burn mark, a bad one, and he wondered how she'd gotten it. If the pain bothered her, she didn't show it, just tolerated Raelyn as she did her thing.

"Fuck that," Key said. "What's another answer?" She stared at him the same way as everyone else: confused . . . and worried.

"I wish there was one," he told them soberly. "But there isn't. The data doesn't lie."

"*How* is it shrinking?" Maddox asked. When Flynn had met the Ranger, on the train, he'd looked like he'd been taken apart and put back together. But he'd still been calm. And focused. Flynn had a feeling Maddox was always like that. Even hearing what Flynn was saying now, the implications of it, that every living thing on the Razor was going to be burned alive in a few days, he still seemed calm. But there was an edge in his voice, just perceptible.

"I don't know," Flynn said, rubbing his eyes—and regretting it. The sweat made them sting. "I'm not an environmental scientist."

"But you're really fucking smart," Key shot back.

Flynn sighed. "Look . . . the Razor exists because of a mathematical near-impossibility. The unlikely orbit of the planet creates its two main environmental zones. Their atmospheres push against each other, which creates the habitable zone in the middle. It's an unbelievably delicate phenomena. Any number of things could upset it."

"Like what?" It was a new voice. Deep and slow, easy. Zane sat on the edge of the doorway floor of one of the train cars, booted feet on the sandy ground. Since they'd been outside, the man, with his strange, grayish skin and the disconcerting muzzle over his mouth, hadn't looked up at any of them. He'd just stared at what looked like the thin, square lines of a single data card. He kept flipping it in his fingers, over and over, mulling it.

"It's just physics," Flynn answered, musing, feeling the familiar pull down the rabbit hole of a problem needing to be solved. "Somewhere, energy is either being added or taken away. The orbit of the planet could have shifted. Or . . . I don't know . . . the fusion in the star could have increased."

Another thought occurred to him. He went down its rabbit hole too. "Or . . ." Then stopped, his voice fell away.

"Or what?" Key asked.

He looked at her. "*Or* the atmosphere in the *Razor* is being depleted. If that were happening . . . the Cinder would rush in to fill it."

"Nature abhors a vacuum," Zane said quietly.

"Okay." Key rolled her eyes at the big man. "*And?*"

Flynn looked over her head, toward the dominant sight on the eastern horizon, visible above the crater rim.

The beacon.

The giant red beam of energy shooting into the sky a hundred miles away.

Everyone stared at it with him. The air seemed to thin around them all.

"Oh, shit," Key said.

"*That* thing?" Raelyn asked.

Flynn thought it through. "It makes sense. It showed up right before the evacuation order. I saw it outside on the *Charon*."

Raelyn finished wrapping Key's arm, taped it up, and cut off the rest of the tape. Then she turned and moved closer to Maddox. Flynn didn't know what she and the Ranger had been through to get this far, but it was clear that whatever it was had led her to trust him.

"You were *outside* the *Charon*?" Maddox asked in dismay.

Flynn shrugged, looked at Key. "It's a long story."

"How could it do what you're saying?" It was Zane again, but he still wasn't looking up. "How could the beam deplete the atmosphere?"

"I don't know," Flynn said, starting to get frustrated. "Some kind of plasma beam? It punctured the air envelope? I don't have *every* answer."

"But you think it's at the starport?" said Raelyn, but the question wasn't for Flynn.

Maddox nodded. "I think so, yeah. Direction and distance look right."

"What at the starport could do *that*?"

"Nothing I know of."

Flynn recalled something else. Something from the hot labs, before everything got genuinely chaotic. As he did, the tight feeling of dread in his chest began to build.

"She told me . . ." His voice was low. He couldn't take his gaze off the beacon now. It wavered in the distance. "She told me I had to get to the starport. She told me it was urgent."

"*Who* told you?" Maddox asked, confused.

"Gable," Flynn said. Key's head snapped around to stare at him.

"Who's Gable?" Raelyn asked.

"A . . . woman we met," Flynn explained. Key's look was dark.

"Prisoner?" Maddox asked.

"Fucking A," Key answered.

"She was loose?" asked Raelyn, confused.

"Not exactly," Flynn said. He skipped the part about being the one who had let her out.

"She said I had to get to the starport. She said there were . . . things going on there. She said the surface had *changed*."

"How the hell would she know *any* of that?" Key asked, confused.

"I don't know," Flynn admitted, though he had an idea. He remembered her touching the creature inside the containment area, remembered the way her body had frozen, how it had been like she was . . . talking to it.

"You said her name was Gable?" It was Zane again, and this time, when Flynn looked, the big man was staring at him over the rim of the muzzle. Flynn felt a familiar sense of fear, looking at Zane. As with Gable, there was a primal sense of power to him.

Flynn nodded.

"You're lucky to be alive," Zane said, punctuating each syllable. "Gable . . . is the name Dr. Gabliella Rosetta used."

Everyone froze. Flynn lost sensation in his body. The heat, the beacon, the growing red light on the western horizon, it was all forgotten.

Gabliella Rosetta. Dr. Rosetta. A brilliant geneticist and bio-augmentation scientist before she became a serial killer. That's what the UEG had labeled her, but it didn't really go far enough. Her victims had all been test subjects for her own experiments, to further her aims at changing herself into . . . something. But the state of the victims she left in her wake was horrific. Mutilated, altered at the genome level, implanted with different varieties of technology. And not all of them had died.

She spent more than ten years at the top of the JSCC most wanted list, and the stories of her spread through the galaxy. Much of them were embellished, Flynn had always imagined. But now, thinking back on the silver-haired woman—the metallic caps on her fingers, which she'd removed with pliers; how Sedona had killed herself, the warning on the polysteel—he wasn't so sure.

"Dr. Rosetta's dead," Raelyn announced, though it sounded like she was trying to convince herself as much as the rest of them.

That *was* the official story from the JSCC task force formed to bring her to justice. Killed resisting arrest on Voxx. Then cremated on a UEG battleship and the ashes flushed out an air lock. It had always seemed a little convenient, Flynn supposed, but like everyone else on Earth, he'd slept better after he'd heard that. That was four years ago.

"I don't know," Flynn said, the feeling starting to come back to his extremities. "I mean, she fit the description. And I don't just mean physically."

"I never heard anything about Dr. Rosetta being on the planet," Maddox said, "but we escorted plenty of high-profile prisoners to black sites like this one, and they were often unidentified."

"Supposedly she had done a lot of augmentation to herself, all kinds of dangerous enhancements," Zane thought out loud. "And you did find this woman in a *reverse engineering* lab."

"Yeah," Maddox said, nodding. "Why kill her when you can take her apart?"

"The task force to find her was extensive," Zane said. "A tremendous amount of resources went into it. *UEG* resources, not Corrections Council."

The implication was clear. The JSCC was just the branch of government that dealt with criminal incarceration and punishment. If the task force was UEG and not JSCC, it meant top level. It meant military.

"How do *you* know that?" Key asked suspiciously. "About the task force?"

The big man looked back to the data card. "Because I was part of it. Me . . . and someone else." At the last words, the data card seemed to spin faster in his fingers.

Flynn wondered who Zane was. For the moment he seemed cooperative, and having someone as formidable as him on their side should have given Flynn comfort, but it didn't. He couldn't help but wonder what would happen if the big man's goals, whatever they were, no longer aligned with theirs.

"Okay, fuck it," Key said, exasperated. "Whoever she was, she's gone. Happy trails. What do we do about *that*?" Key pointed at the beacon.

"We do what Gable said," Flynn answered, not liking it. The idea of taking the advice of someone like Dr. Rosetta was unsettling at best. "Get to the starport."

"And what *then*?" Key was beyond nonplussed. "Turn the thing off? Whatever it is? You think you can just pull a wire out of something like that?"

That wasn't his plan at all. "We have other reasons to be at the starport."

Everything stopped. Key's face dropped. Then her eyes slimmed in anger.

"What does *that* mean?" Raelyn asked.

Flynn realized what he'd let slip. He looked from to Raelyn to Key.

She glared back. "Don't."

His face contorted as he tried to resist. Shouldn't they know?

"Don't you fucking do it," Key told him pointedly.

Flynn couldn't help it. He took a step away from Key. "We have a way off the planet."

"God*damn* it!" she exclaimed, fists clenching.

Everyone, even Zane, looked at Flynn now.

"You have *what*?" Maddox asked, stunned.

Flynn told them, all of it. The Suit, the deal, why he had the data drive, and what the plan was. Get to the starport, exchange the data drive for a ticket off this world.

Oddly, though, the thought didn't fill Flynn with relief the way it had the first time he'd heard it. A ticket off the planet to . . . *where* exactly, he wondered. The headquarters of the company the Suit worked for? Then what? What would his life look like then?

But then again, what was the alternative? The Razor was *shrinking* . . .

"No one get excited," Key said with a hard edge. "The deal was for Flynn and me, not any of you."

Flynn sighed. "Key—"

"Bullshit!" She cut him off before he got going. As she looked at the others, her tone softened a little. But not much. "I get it, the planet's dying, that's tough, but we found this exit on our own. You'll have to find yours by yourself."

"Key . . ." Flynn said again. As selfish as her words came across, he thought he understood. When you came from the kind of world she did, any opportunity out of a bad situation, you grabbed hold of it. You defended it fiercely.

"What's going to happen when we show up and there's five of us?" she asked, looking at Flynn. "Not *two* like we negotiated? Guys like that suit don't respond well to renegotiating deals at the last minute."

"She's right," Maddox said, thinking it through. "It could jeopardize your arrangement."

"We have what he *wants*." Flynn held up the blue data drive from its batch of wires. "I have a feeling whatever is on this thing is worth transporting a hundred inmates off the Razor."

"But—" Key started.

"We're *not* leaving them," Flynn told her as firmly as he could. Key glared at him, clearly displeased, but didn't say anything further.

"It won't be an issue either way," Zane said now, matter-of-factly. They all looked at him. "I can be very convincing."

Flynn had no doubt.

"Okay, then," Maddox said, calm as usual, but the edge in his voice had been replaced with something else, something a little brighter. He touched Raelyn comfortingly next to him. "How much time do we have?"

Flynn looked through the gap between two of the train cars. The horizon above the rim of the crater was full of smoke and red, glowing light.

What little geology and thermal dynamics he knew told him it was more than just fire coming for them. It would be a wall of heat and radiation unlike anything any of them had ever seen. And it would be moving fast.

"Not enough," Flynn answered grimly.

"Not enough to *walk*, you mean," Raelyn said.

Flynn shook his head no.

"Then *what*, professor?" Key asked.

Flynn looked at something right in front of them all.

"Well," he said, feeling the tug of the rabbit hole again, "maybe we don't walk."

His eyes scanned down the length of the transport train, sitting on the tracks, the engine at its front, lifeless and dead.

Flynn smiled at Key. She didn't smile back.

FORTY-TWO

FLAGS AND CAKES

Flynn and Maddox walked the length of the train's exterior, the sun beating down on them, the temperature rising by the second, it felt like.

"Full circle, huh?" Maddox observed.

"Full circle would be on a shuttle off this world," Flynn told him.

Maddox nodded. "One step at a time."

It was strange, walking next to him. Flynn had never imagined he would see him again. He didn't know what all he and Raelyn had been through, but he seemed much more . . . alive than he had that first conversation.

"Will it get fired on?" Flynn asked. He meant the train. Maddox had told him where they were going: the Barrier. He, Raelyn, and Zane had seen it on their way here, a fight raging between two gangs. It sounded dangerous, but the tracks led to the train gate in the Barrier, so there wasn't any other choice.

"Only the guards have guns," Maddox said, touching the steel exteriors of the transport cars as they walked. "And hopefully the flag will stop them from firing on it."

Raelyn and Key were busy nearby, fashioning something from a bunch of new jumpsuits they'd found, still wrapped in plastic, in one of the train's supply cars. When it was tied together, it would be a pattern of white and blue, which, according to Maddox, was a color code for prison employees. It appeared on every employee's holofile in the computer system. They were gambling the guards up top would see the makeshift flag flying from the train, assume the thing was full of guards or other workers, and open up the gate, or at least the personnel door into the Barrier.

The first option would be best; it meant no fighting. The second meant they would have to take out the guards inside, or incapacitate them. If it came to that, Flynn reckoned, they had a good shot with Zane and Maddox on their side, but it wouldn't be pretty.

Of course, if neither worked, they would be stuck outside in the sun with the two warring gangs, on a working train engine, something that was incredibly valuable right now.

"How many prisoners?" Flynn asked.

"Two, three hundred a gang," Maddox guessed. "One was Scorpios; no idea about the other." Flynn didn't know who the Scorpios were, but the name wasn't exactly friendly. "It was a killing field last time I saw it."

"When was that?"

"Yesterday."

"Forever ago," Flynn replied.

Maddox turned and looked at him.

"You're different," he said. "Harder. Maybe sharper."

Flynn's eyes thinned at the last word. "Is that something I want to be?"

"On this world? Absolutely."

Maddox looked behind, to where the doctor was working on the flag. Key was there too, on her knees, tying fabric together. She hated it, Flynn could tell, mainly because she kept taking opportunities to glare at him over the distance.

Raelyn, though, seemed to be doing fine . . . except she kept stopping to rub her right arm, like it hurt.

She was pretty, of course, but it was something else that Flynn noticed. The meticulous way she worked, tying the fabric, sorting it, keeping everything equal lengths. It was habitual, Flynn knew, because he was the same way. They were both scientists. She wasn't like anyone else in the group; she reminded him of where he'd come from, the labs back at M-D. It was comforting.

"What happened on the *Charon* with you two?" Flynn asked.

"She helped me, I helped her," the Ranger said.

Flynn nodded. "I get it."

Maddox's gaze shifted to Key. "She's . . . a little harder-edged."

Key saw them looking at her, then frowned and flipped them the bird.

"Don't look at her too long," Flynn told him. "It activates her predator instinct."

Maddox laughed and looked back at him. When he did, his gaze sobered. "All that matters to me is that Raelyn gets off this world. If we get into a situation where you need to run and I'm not there, you leave. Do you understand?"

A hint of darkness returned to Maddox's voice. Again, Flynn wondered what the Ranger and the doctor had been through, but it wasn't his business. So he just nodded. "I understand."

Maddox studied him a second. "I'm glad you're not dead, by the way."

Flynn smiled back. "You and me both."

"I'm gonna help Zane," Maddox said. The big man was out in the yard, securing the "flagpole" from the junked SMVs.

"Right," Flynn said, and Maddox moved off.

"Fucking flag's done," a testy voice said behind him. "Should we bake cakes for the guards too?"

Key was standing behind him now. The look on her face was decidedly displeased. Flynn tried not to smile as he turned and headed for the train's engine at the front of the line. Key followed after him, what was left of the chain that used to connect them rattling from her wrist.

"You don't know how to bake," he said.

"I'm not in the mood," she shot back, voice dripping with acid. "Did you recognize the killjoy you had me working with back there? She's the doctor from the *Charon*. Fixed a shank wound on my leg once."

Flynn's eyes narrowed. "Your leg?"

"Femoral artery. Back of the thigh. Hit that, and . . ." Key shook her head, indicating how the rest would go.

"I guess they missed."

"Unfortunately for them."

As they walked, Flynn looked at the two plasma knives tucked where the hem of Key's rolled down jumpsuit met her lower back. The tank top she wore underneath was riding up a bit, and he could see the brown curve of her skin as it disappeared down inside the pants.

Flynn looked away quickly.

"She's got Slow Burn," Key observed.

Flynn looked at Key in surprise. "The doctor? Why do you think *that*?"

He couldn't see any signs of the glowing veins on Raelyn's skin, so if she did have it, it must be under her clothes. And it would be incredibly surprising, for a doctor. Slow Burn was the final side effect of too much synth use. Then again, this was the Razor. He supposed everyone came here for bad reasons.

"She keeps slapping her right arm," Key said.

"What does that have—"

"Slow Burn feels like someone's putting cigarettes out on your skin, but you don't want to scratch it, because it causes more pain, so people slap it instead. It helps."

"I didn't notice that," Flynn replied, thinking. "She hasn't taken that lab coat off yet either, even though it's boiling out here."

"Trust me, she's got it."

The two stepped up into the train engine. The interior was larger than Flynn had expected. Maas-Dorian designed all kinds of transport and cargo trains, most of them for use on colony worlds, where shuttle craft either weren't prevalent or, as on the Razor, couldn't fly at all.

Near the front and the polysteel windshield were four pilot seats and an array of instruments, holo screens, and controls, all dark and lifeless now.

"How do we get this thing going?" Key asked, staring skeptically at the controls.

Flynn walked to the back of the car, where the small X-Core rested in an enclosed container. Even though it was sealed, Flynn could hear it humming as the processed Xytrilium broke down and released staggering amounts of energy.

The problem, of course, was that the energy wasn't going anywhere.

Flynn studied the walls and saw what he wanted. The access hatch to the train engine's power router. He yanked it open, revealing the mass of wiring, compactors, and circuit boards inside.

He could see the HVDC cable coming in, right where it should be. Saw the AC out, the converter and the transformers. He pushed more wiring aside, found the DC-out route box, cables branching into the floor and the walls, headed for the controls and, more important, for the big turbines underneath their feet, which turned the train's wheels.

"The train's X-Core still works," Flynn told her, "but smaller devices like computers don't because they need the current coming out of this router to be converted to AC power."

"I'm fucking riveted," Key said, watching him stick his hands into the cabinet and push wires aside. "Don't kill yourself, please."

Flynn smiled, found the unit number for the turbines, and scanned the corresponding numbers on the router box. "Transformers do the power conversion to AC, but there's no way to turn them on and off anymore, because of the pulse."

"Oh, please. Tell me *more*."

Flynn found the cable he needed, started unscrewing its connections. "But anything that uses *DC* power, like the turbines on this train, doesn't *need* a transformer. Which means they can still be turned *on* if you can get power to them."

"Say you get it running," Key said. "Then what? Full steam ahead to the Barrier? I heard one of the gangs waiting for us is Scorpio. Scorpios don't like other people breathing that aren't Scorpios. And they're *bionics*."

"I trust Maddox," Flynn answered.

"Then you're an idiot."

"He used to be a Ranger."

"Used to be . . ." Key shook her head. "Everybody used to be something."

Flynn unscrewed the terminal and pulled the lead out, trying really hard not to touch anything metal. There was lethal voltage flowing through it, right from the X-Core. Slowly, he rested the live lead down then started unscrewing the other end of the cable from the opposite side of the router.

"I can't *believe* you told them about the shuttle," Key accused him. He'd been waiting for it. "It makes me so mad, I want to claw your eyeballs out."

"I'd prefer it if you didn't," Flynn replied as he pulled the opposite cable from the router.

"We don't need these losers, and you *still* told them. It's like you think you're fucking Saint Jerome. I mean, what *is* that?"

"Don't *need* them . . ." Flynn's voice turned sarcastic now. "How about we analyze that one? There's Zane, for starters, who can rip steel apart with his bare hands. The former Ranger, who probably has the surface of the planet memorized. And the doctor, who knows how to heal shank wounds. Yeah, I see what you're saying, they're really not bringing all that much to the table."

"I've already explained it, dickhead," Key shot back testily. "We're better off on our own. You don't ever seem to *listen*."

Flynn froze with his hands buried in the cables, as what she'd just said registered. He looked out of the cabinet at Key. "Oh, it's *us* now? *We're* better off?"

Key's look went dangerous. "Don't get a hard-on, professor. If you didn't have a shuttle coming, I'd be somewhere else."

Flynn smiled, held her look. "Don't think I didn't notice, by the way."

Her eyes slimmed. "Notice *what*?"

"You could have left. At the labs, when Gable cut us loose. You had a straight shot back to the control center, all you had to do was kick out the repressor and you were home free. But you *stayed*."

Key's tone became overly defensive. "That . . . thing knocked it loose!" she stuttered. "The door came down!"

"And where were you when that happened? *Inside* the control center? With the ladder right there?" Key glared at Flynn. It made his smile bigger. "You knew you would *miss* me."

Her hands slid toward the knives on her back. "I swear to Christ . . ."

"You *like* me."

"I will cut your balls off." Her tone was fiery, but it only made his smile bigger.

Flynn liked how volatile she was, how she said whatever the hell came to her head, how she wore every emotion right out front. Key wasn't like anyone he'd ever met before.

She stared at him warningly. "Lose the smirk."

Flynn held her look a second more, then turned back to the power cabinet, back to the cables inside. He pushed the two he'd removed earlier toward the metal inside the cabinet wall, where there was a bracket. It was thick enough to serve as a current throughput.

Sparks blew outward in a violent spray. Key jumped.

But Flynn heard the distinctive sound of the turbines rumbling to life under the floor. The train shook underneath him as the vibrations rattled up through the superstructure.

"It's okay," Flynn said, sitting up, looking at her again. "I like you too."

Key stared at him, hovering on the verge of a smile that never came.

FORTY-THREE

FIRST NAMES

Maddox sat in the first car behind the engine, a refrigerator car lined with shiny, climate-controlled steel compartments for transporting food. He'd checked them all before they'd gotten under way, but they were empty. Too bad. A steak would have been nice.

He watched the Razor flash by outside the car's huge hydraulic door. He had to admit, he was surprised. The train was moving. Fast, too. And the flag they'd made flew on the top, flared in the wind, a trailing mix of blue and white.

It wasn't a total long shot; those colors would be instantly familiar to anyone who used the prison computer system. But that didn't mean the guards at the Barrier would feel obligated to open the gates, especially given the warring gangs that were probably trying to scale the walls by now.

Raelyn sat down next to him and sighed. She took off her pack, the one Zane had found for her, and started removing the meds from it.

Maddox watched her. Her right arm was facing him, covered by the lab coat.

"Let me see," he said.

She let him slide up the sleeve. The Slow Burn glowed bright on her soft skin. It had moved up past the bend in her elbow now, and down almost to the top of the wrist.

Maddox winced. The pain must be bad, yet she didn't show it. Raelyn was tough, no doubt, but it still made him angry. She didn't deserve this.

"It's slowing," Raelyn said, somehow sensing his feelings. "I promise."

Maddox looked at her oddly. "You're reassuring *me*?"

"Well, you seem concerned," she said, setting up an autosyringe, loading it with a med vial.

He watched her hands work with the hypos. The right hand was shaking now. Just slightly. "It *will* stop spreading?"

"Yes." Raelyn cocked the autosyringe like a gun, slamming the med vial in place. "But if it doesn't . . . I'm going to need you to cut the arm off."

Maddox's eyes widened.

Raelyn laughed, looking up at him. Even though the joke was at his expense, Maddox didn't care. He liked her laugh. It had a freedom to it that he envied.

"Actually, why wouldn't that work?" he asked, thinking about it.

"I'm sorry?"

"Taking the arm."

"Oh, you *want* to cut it off?" she asked with fake animosity.

"I mean, if that's where the Burn is . . ."

She seemed to find the question adorable. "The part you actually see is the *end* stage, the nerve growths starting to metabolize. The growth itself is already layered through the nervous system. Cut it off or not, it will still spread." She looked at him harshly. "Sorry to *disappoint* you."

Maddox looked back thoughtfully. "What about just the head?"

She laughed again. "*What?*"

"If we cut your head off, and put it in a vat . . . would it still spread then?"

Raelyn kept her blue eyes on him. "Yes, James, it would."

In the harsh sun, her hair looked red. He wanted to touch it. "Too bad. That would be a good look for you."

"Headless? You think so?"

"No, *bodyless*. But, yeah. I think so." It was a flirt; it felt like something he would have said in the past, when the world was different and certain dire choices hadn't been made. Saying it here and now left him feeling unsettled. Flattering her, even honestly, felt like taking a step toward connection, and connection should be the last thing on his mind.

A blush formed on Raelyn's cheeks. She kept her blue eyes on his. The stare and the silence lasted another moment, then Maddox forced himself to look away.

He took her right arm, the one with the Slow Burn, and started massaging it. Raelyn winced a little as he did.

"That okay?" he asked.

"Helps the circulation," she said, nodding. The autosyringe hissed as she injected its contents into her leg. She winced once more.

Maddox felt the stirring of anger again, watching her in pain. He kept rubbing her skin. The desert flashed by outside the door, but there were starting to be signs of greenery. Small trees, shrubs, grass patches.

"You really think they'll let us on the shuttle?" Raelyn asked.

"Flynn said he would make sure you got on," Maddox answered.

"And you?"

Maddox said nothing. He got the dark look from her he'd expected. "James . . ."

"When did we graduate to first names?"

"I use first names when I scold," she told him.

"I told you I would get you out of here," he said.

"How magnanimous of you." Her tone was bordering on severe.

"Raelyn . . ."

"We're still *here*?" she asked. "You're still just . . . finished? Nothing's changed?"

He'd expected the look, but not the words. Not the bitter and hurt tone in her voice. Maddox stared at Raelyn in confusion. Of course nothing had changed. How *could* it?

Raelyn shook her head, pulled her arm free of his hands. "Forget it."

She looked out the big door of the cargo car. The train had turned, and now the view was west. The horizon was full of smoke there. And the sky was red and wavering, like nothing he had ever seen before.

Fire. Fire that would consume everything and leave nothing but ash. Beautiful and terrifying at the same time.

"You're a fucking asshole," Raelyn whispered.

Maddox was still at a loss. How did he make her understand? "You don't know the things I've done, Raelyn."

"That's not why you're an asshole," she said, turning her whole body now, keeping her back to him. She hugged her knees, kept staring at the horizon out the door, the landscape flashing by. "You're an asshole because all you care about is you."

Maddox stared at her back, covered in the dirty lab coat. He didn't know what to say.

The whine of the train's brakes filled the interior of the car and he could feel the machine starting to slow suddenly.

As the train came to a stop, Maddox immediately noticed that there were no sounds. Sounds of screams or battle. Sounds of gunfire from up high.

Nothing.

A huge figure appeared in the door outside.

It was Zane. He stared at Maddox.

Maddox stared back. "What is it?"

"See for yourself."

Maddox and Raelyn jumped to the ground and followed Zane. They were at the Barrier, in the valley they had looked out on from atop the bluff to the west. The giant wall towered over them, stretching in either direction, into the horizon, until it disappeared. He could see the train tracks, moving east, dead-ending into the sealed tunnel in the Barrier. Next to it hung the giant SMV gate, for letting Crawlers move in and out.

And everything around it was silent and empty.

No one was on top of the Barrier. No guns fired down. No armies of gangs slammed into each other in front. Only the two Crawlers from before were there. Burning, sending plumes of black smoke into the sky.

The valley was dead. And abandoned.

FORTY-FOUR

BLOOD AND FIRE

Key stared at the desert valley—red rocks, dried-out weeds in burning sand—stretching all the way to the Barrier in the distance, and she didn't like it. No sounds. No movement. Nothing here was as fucking advertised.

And the thing that pissed her off? The stupid flag Flynn had made her work on dangled limply on the rusted antennae right above her. There wasn't anyone home to see it. The Barrier and everything around it was deserted.

Zane appeared and leaned against the train engine next to her. Her wings itched a little, and she felt the reassuring pressure of the plasma blades on her lower back.

"Whatever happened here," Zane said, studying the valley, "it checked *all* the boxes."

Key nodded. "Fucking A."

The Barrier loomed in the distance, quiet, like everything else. The two Crawlers, or what was left of them, were smoking wrecks, billowing blackness into the air.

Everyone stared at everyone else, unsure, frozen. That pissed Key off more than anything.

"So now what, geniuses?" She pushed away from the train, raising her arms. The chain rattled on her wrist. "I don't know about you, but to me, a thousand-plus hostile people vanishing equals a red flag. And what about bodies? Shouldn't there be a few of those?"

The others looked to verify what she'd already noted. The sand in front of the Barrier and around the burning Crawlers was totally barren. No bodies. No *anything*.

Everyone just stared, unsure.

Key groaned. Fuck this planet. Just when you started thinking maybe you were making progress, it threw another smoke bomb in front of you. And behind the smoke was usually something really unpleasant.

"It doesn't change the situation," Zane said.

"Well, it doesn't *help* the situation either," Key replied.

"What are you suggesting we do?" Raelyn asked, a few feet away. "Or do you just want to complain?"

"I was gonna suggest we send *you* to scout it out," Key said, staring back at the woman.

Zane stepped away from the engine, started moving. "We'll have to open the train gate ourselves if there's no one inside."

"And what if there *is* someone inside?" Key asked as Zane moved toward the huge wall in the distance. Everyone else followed after the big man, ignoring her. Even Flynn. "I'm raising good points here," Key yelled after them. No one listend.

Key conceded, started following along too.

They reached the side of the Barrier in a few minutes, and Key looked straight up at the giant wall. The top was a dizzying height above, and it stretched like that in both directions, until it disappeared. She'd never seen it from the outside. It annoyed her to admit, but it was impressive.

The SMV gate and the sealed train tunnel sat about two hundred yards away. Flynn, Zane, and Maddox, though, were all looking at a much smaller entry door inset into the side of the metallic structure. There was no control panel next to it, no handles, no way at all to open it from the outside. Key figured that was by design.

Zane stepped forward, reached out, and ran a hand over the door.

"No hinges," he said. "Hybrid alloys. Steel and aluminum. Locking bolt . . . here."

His hand stopped on the right edge of the big door. Zane made that hand into a fist. A few seconds later, the spot under the fist began to glow.

Orange at first. Then red. Then almost *white*.

Key and Flynn stepped back, eyes wide.

She'd seen Zane do something like this back in the black site, but things had been happening fast—not to mention that a monster had been trying to kill her—so it hadn't really registered.

The spot on the door glowed hotter, then began to blacken and dissolve. A few seconds more . . . then Zane punched right *through* it. The metal blew apart in a shower of blackened fragments.

His muscles flexed, one arm buried in the thing. Zane pushed, groaning hard with the effort. The door flexed, bent . . . then moved, sliding on its railing.

Key and Flynn stepped back again, looked at each other.

When it was over, the steel security door was open about three feet, leaving it a crumpled wreck that looked more like deflated tinfoil. Not a big opening, but enough.

Zane pulled his arm out of the opening. As he did, he nicked it on the jagged metal. He rubbed the cut with his hand; it didn't seem to bother him.

"All right, then," Maddox said, nodding, impressed. Everyone else seemed more on the unsettled side of the spectrum.

Maddox pushed through the ruined door. Raelyn followed him, then Flynn, leaving just Key and Zane. The big man moved ahead. When he did, Key noticed the cut. It was bleeding, like you'd expect. What you wouldn't expect was the blood's color.

It was silver.

Key watched him disappear on the other side of the door, deciding if she'd really seen what she thought she had. Silver blood? Who the hell had silver blood?

She pushed after him into the interior of the giant structure. Inside was a round room, with another door, cameras in the ceiling, and two ports on the walls, which Key recognized immediately as embedded guns. The lights in the room all flickered and flashed eerily.

"The room's powered down," Maddox said.

"The guards shut it off?" Raelyn asked. "Why would they do that?"

"I don't know," Maddox said, looking at her darkly. "I don't really need to know, either. The garrison's up top. We get there, we can find the chain room for the train gate."

"There might be supplies, too," Zane said. "Weapons."

Key felt a slight jolt of electricity at the word. She even smiled. "Well, what are we fucking waiting for?"

They all moved through the open door, and Key followed at the end, behind Zane. A cramped metallic hallway was on the other side. No frills, no monitors or tech, but there were barriers. Short walls of metal, each about half the height of a person, spaced about every twenty feet. Key guessed they were meant to hold up any inmates that might break in, and to serve as cover positions for the guards, in case of a firefight.

But there were no guards here now, just red dust blending in with the metallic floor, and flashing, sparking lights in the ceiling.

Key looked at the wall of muscle that was Zane's back as they climbed over the barriers. She could see the straps of the muzzle, where they connected on the back of his head.

"When are you going take that stupid thing off?" she asked. "You look like a sex slave."

The big man's head turned slightly toward her as he moved. "Is that a bad thing?"

"Depends on the planet."

He didn't say anything else. Key watched him walk in front of her. "What's up with you?"

"How do you mean?"

"I mean you . . . what? Draw power from metal? What happens if you draw too much?"

"Best guess? My heart explodes."

"And what exactly's your heart pumping? *Mercury?*"

His head turned toward her again, but he said nothing.

"I saw your cut back there," she said. "I saw you bleed."

He rubbed the small wound on his arm. "It isn't blood."

"No fucking shit."

"It's Xytrilium."

Key blinked. Something else unexpected. It was becoming a trend.

"A liquid form," the Gray Man clarified. "It powers the nanotech running through me."

"You've got *Nano*tech inside you?"

"It gives me a . . . *sense* of metal," Zane said. "I can feel through it to where it touches other metal. I can tell you how weak it is, how strong, where it's rusted or cracked. I can sense people and things moving over it, can tell you how much they weigh, how fast they're running—even whether they're carrying anything metal with them. And I can absorb it, break it down. My body uses metal to heal if it needs to. If not, then my muscles take it on."

"What happens then?"

"Bad things," was all Zane said.

Key listened intently, finding the whole thing fascinating. Hell, she was envious. In a galaxy as metallic as this one, that particular skill set would give you a leg up anywhere you went. She supposed that was the idea.

"Who was it?" she asked. "UEG?"

"Yeah." Zane's voice was dismissive.

Key figured. Fucking government. Always the same. Zane was just another notch in an armory rack. Another weapon for them to use. But, somewhere along the way, the role hadn't fit him anymore. What happened after that, she had no idea, and the truth was it wasn't any of her business. It would be people like Zane, people fucked with and manipulated and made into things they didn't want to be, who would bring the whole goddamned system down. She hoped she was around to watch. She hoped she got to help.

"Why tell me this?" Key asked. "The others don't have a fucking clue how you tick."

The Gray Man's massive shoulders shrugged. "They didn't ask."

They reached the end of the hall. Like Maddox said, there was an elevator, and it was powered.

They all crammed inside and Maddox keyed the top floor.

The thing stuttered, jolted, started to move.

The doctor, Key noticed, kept glancing at Maddox, who kept glancing back. They were at opposite ends of the compartment, more distance between them than any time since she'd met them. Key guessed they'd had an argument back on the train and the Ranger had come out the worst. Like most men, he was probably clueless about what he'd actually done and just let it hang there like an idiot. Or he'd apologized, even though he had no idea what he was apologizing for, which was even worse. Either way, he was screwed now.

Her eyes shifted to Flynn, and she studied him in the elevator. He looked back warily, like he was worried about what was going on in her head. She forced herself not to smile. Much as she hated to admit it, he wasn't like any other man she'd ever met. But, then again, he wasn't from her world. She wasn't sure if that was a good thing or not, but she liked it.

The elevator rumbled to a stop. The doors opened. The group stepped out.

A searing hot wind blew around Key, and her body was instantly soaked with sweat. All over again. The light from the Razor's sun burned in the sky to the west, a giant, blazing red orb of heat.

But that was the least of it.

This high up, from the top of the Barrier, they could see the true reality of just how screwed they really were. The horizon to the west had vanished in a wall of flame that towered in the air, swirling fire and energy, filling everything Key could see.

And it was all barreling right toward them.

Key could almost sense it moving as the atmosphere in the Razor shrank and the Cindersphere replaced it.

Key had never seen anything as horrifying.

"Beautiful," Zane said next to her.

"How is it moving so fast?" Raelyn asked in a shaky voice.

Flynn, next to Key, stared west with a shocked look. And with something else too. Curiosity.

"The Cindersphere's consuming the oxygen in the Razor," he said. "The more it oxidizes, the faster it consumes the rest. It's going to spread exponentially faster every second."

"We need to get the train gate open then," Maddox said.

Key looked down to the ground. Far below sat the train, snaking toward the heat in the distance. More than two dozen cars.

"We're pulling too much weight," Flynn said, staring down at the train too. "We have to find a way to disconnect some of the cars." He looked at Maddox. "The Barrier's shielded; all the tech in it should work. Is there a tool room? Or maintenance closet?"

Maddox nodded. "Reactor level. Raelyn and I can check the garrison. The guns in the armory should be clean, no biometrics."

For Key, the possibility of weapons didn't produce the usual hit of dopamine this time. The giant wall of cinders bearing down on them probably had a lot to do with that.

"And the train gate?" Zane asked, his voice calm.

"Midlevel," Maddox said. "There's a shaft where the chains for the gate move up and down. It has a manual release, but it's heavy."

"Is it metal?" Zane asked.

Maddox nodded gravely.

"Then I'll get it open."

No one said anything else. They knew what they had to do. The wind howled around them, spreading more heat into the air.

Key sighed in exasperation. "What the hell are we waiting for? Someone to say 'Go'?"

FORTY-FIVE

CONDITIONS

The garrison control center was dark, for the most part, full of angular shadows cast by the computers and holo displays along the walls, the terminals designed to control the facility and the defenses outside. And there was no sign of anyone, guards or otherwise.

Some of the screens still showed camera feeds from the valley below, and Maddox could see the burning Crawlers and the curved line of the train. Another screen showed nothing but the horizon to the west and the encroaching flames there, as if a guard had zoomed in on it intentionally. Maddox looked and found the outside environment metrics on a holo display.

One hundred fifty-two degrees.

Maddox shook his head. The dry air outside would help, but the temperature was getting awfully close to the survival threshold for an unshielded human. And that wall of heat was still miles away.

He had to get Raelyn off the Razor.

"What do you think happened here?" Raelyn asked. She was near the other wall, where doors led to the garrison's sleeping quarters, looking for a switch to get the lights on.

"Nothing good," he said.

He moved toward a different door, across the room from Raelyn. It was big and fortified, and for good reason. The garrison armory was behind it. Its control panel was still working, glowing blue and orange.

He swiped across the control panel, and a holo display formed in the air, a geometric pattern of menus and buttons.

Maddox tapped the code field.

The display flashed and became a keypad.

He typed in the last Ranger override code he remembered, and hit Enter. The menu flashed. And the large security door in the wall slid open.

The code still worked, four months old.

Regulations stated that if a Ranger was arrested and committed to the Razor, all Ranger codes got changed immediately, but that was a regulation far down the priority list, and those usually got overlooked in a bureaucracy like the one that ran this world.

Lucky for him.

Past the door, there were two shelving units, one laden with combat rifles, the other, sidearms. Maybe eight of each, a mix of ballistics and pulse weapons. It wasn't a giant cache, but given the state of technology outside the garrison, it was still a treasure trove.

"I don't know how you can ask me that," Raelyn said from the other end of the room. Her voice still sounded tense.

The relief of getting the armory open faded. Maddox felt a twinge of regret, but he still didn't know what to tell her. "Raelyn . . ."

"How can you *ask* that? To just leave, knowing you're staying here, that . . ."

Maddox looked at her. Her eyes were on the terminals and the monitor showing the wall of fire headed toward them. She looked haunted, staring at it. She looked miserable.

Watching her, seeing the image on the monitor, he finally understood, and he felt ashamed. He wanted to save her, but at what cost? He could put her on Flynn's shuttle, watch her fly off, but he'd be left to burn to death, wouldn't he? Burn with everything else when the Razor collapsed. Raelyn would live, but she would live knowing she had left *him*.

Everything they'd been through together meant coming to know her. Meant her coming to know him. There were responsibilities that came with that.

All you care about is you.

Maddox left the control panel and closed the distance between them. He stopped at Raelyn's back, while she stared at the monitor.

"I'm sorry," he said. He meant it.

She didn't look at him. "You're an asshole."

"I know," he said.

"It's not fair."

"I know."

Finally, she turned to him, looked at him with pained eyes.

"I can make you get on the shuttle with me," she told him. "I can *make* you."

He stared into her eyes. A part of him realized something then. "I *know.*"

His hands found hers. Her fingers slid between his. Raelyn was close. Inches away. Her blue eyes were right in front of his.

Maddox felt the pull. It was magnetic, almost. It had been growing for days. Every time he touched her, every time she hissed through her teeth at the pain. Every time the sun glittered off her hair, lighting it up like the fire to the west.

He felt the pull. It was wrong. Yet . . .

There was a click as the lights suddenly activated in the ceiling. Everything flickered in the bright harshness of LED light. Maddox winced slightly. There was no explanation for why they'd come on, but Raelyn gasped at what the light revealed.

Something on the floor. Something they'd both seen before.

Drag marks. Black and fibrous.

About the size of human beings. Five or six of them, leading to the hallway outside, which went deeper into the Barrier. The same way Flynn, Key, and Zane had gone.

The marks were unmistakable. So was what they meant.

"We have to warn them," Raelyn said, her eyes wide.

She was right. Maddox moved for the armory, for the weapons inside.

Then the edge of a shank, rough but still sharp, pressed itself against his throat. He stopped where he was.

"How about you don't," a rough, Cartel-accented voice said. There was movement all around them now.

Five men. Shaved heads. Each with one or more appendages missing. Missing and replaced by dull metallic bionics. And they all had tattoos on their necks; and the tattoos were scorpions.

The one holding the shank turned Maddox around. The guy was bloody, cuts and scrapes all over him, a long, wicked scar running the length of his face. The others were in equally bad shape. Bleeding and bruised. They'd been through a ringer.

"Thanks for opening the armory," Scar said, his breath smelling of vomit. "We'd all but given up."

FORTY-SIX

SAFE

Flynn and Key stepped into the garrison's mechanical room, situated at the bottom of the Barrier, probably almost at ground level. Two large generators sat in the center of the room, humming loudly.

The room was full of machines, too. Welders. Drill presses. Composite saws. Lathes. Even a 3-D printer for fabricating bolts and circuitry.

On the far end of the room were storage shelves, full of parts and tools and electrical equipment. And along the far wall sat a heavy security door, the flickering lights reflecting off its metal. By the thickness, Flynn knew it wasn't designed to keep people out. It was designed to keep radiation *in*.

It was the door to the garrison's X-Core. Flynn could feel the vibrations from the reactor on the other side, in the floor under him. The control panel glowed blue and red next to the door.

"There's saws in here," Key said, behind him.

It was an odd statement. Flynn turned and looked at her.

She raised her arm, showed him the shackle and chain still attached to her wrist.

"Oh," Flynn said. "Yeah."

"*Yeah*," she said back.

The chain was no doubt uncomfortable for her. He figured they had time.

Flynn moved for a machine near the right side of the room, a diamond-filament-bladed saw. It had laser guides, which would make the process a lot easier. And safer.

Key still eyed the machine warily.

There was a foot pedal on the floor. Flynn tapped it experimentally. The saw whirred to life in a loud, high-pitched whine as the blade spun through its track.

Good. It still worked.

Flynn grabbed a pair of eye shields hanging from the controls of the saw, slipped them on his face.

"Put your wrist here," he said, indicating the cold metal of the saw's baseplate. The blade gleamed in the flickering light, a long shaft of jagged silver metal with hundreds of tiny teeth.

Key didn't move, just stared at it warily.

"It was your idea," Flynn told her. "We can wait until—"

"No," Key said, putting her arm on the saw. "Cut the damn thing off."

Flynn took her forearm in his hands, and her skin was smoother than he expected. He guided her arm toward the blade, trying not to think about it.

Key's breathing was audible over the humming of the X-Core. Her eyes shifted to his. She wanted the cuff off, but he could tell she was unnerved about the saw.

"Close your eyes," Flynn told her.

Key looked at him doubtfully. "Do you really know how to use this thing?"

"My father had one in his hangar. I made my first jet foil on one of these."

"Jesus, you were a loser," Key said.

Flynn smiled. "Most people would probably be put off by your personality."

"Not you?"

"I think you use attitude to cover up your insecurities. You're good at it, but you have a tell."

She stared at him less harshly than he expected. "And what's that, professor?"

"You tremble, just a little, when you're anxious."

At that, Key looked down at her arm in his hands. It was trembling, just slightly. Something about the fact that she didn't take it away from him, Flynn liked.

"Close your eyes," Flynn told her again. "I won't let it hurt you."

Key frowned, hesitated a moment more, then did what he said.

When her eyes were sealed tight, Flynn pressed the pedal. The saw whined. He pulled the metal of the wrist cuff forward, gently, let it hit the blade experimentally. Sparks flew. The sound of rending metal filled the air.

Flynn pushed it back, studied the mark the blade had made. It was barely visible. The cuff was a composite alloy; it would take effort to get through it, even with a diamond blade.

"Was that it?" Key asked, opening up one eye.

Flynn tried not to smirk. "Afraid not. Hold as still as you can, and keep your arm *loose*."

Key swallowed, nodded, but without much enthusiasm. She shut her eyes again.

"You can trust me, okay?" he promised.

"Trust isn't in my wheelhouse."

Flynn nodded. He knew that much.

He could feel her hands shaking, so he slipped his fingers through hers. She gripped them tightly.

The saw whined again. Sparks flew as he pulled the cuff into the blade. Key, miraculously, kept her arm loose, let him guide her.

"You really fuck with my head sometimes," she said, when Flynn let off the pedal to check the progress.

"How do I do *that*?"

"You asked me . . ." Key trailed off before she finished. That, in itself, was unusual. She didn't exactly have a hard time saying what was on her mind.

"What?" Flynn prompted.

"So fucking pathetic . . ." She sounded pissed off now, didn't say anything further.

Flynn looked back to the saw. It whined again, more sparks flew. He stopped and rechecked the cut. It was deepening, and it was straight. He just had to keep going. He gripped her hand and arm tighter. She gripped him back.

"If I was okay," she said, a strange quietness to her voice. "You asked me . . . if I was okay."

Flynn looked at her, confused now. She kept her eyes closed.

"Back at the black site," she clarified.

Flynn remembered now. When he'd found her again. He'd been relieved she was alive. Not to mention she hadn't left. She'd *stayed*.

"No one's ever asked me that before," she said testily with her eyes glued closed.

It took a moment for the concept to filter through Flynn's mind. When it did, the weight of it hit him.

"No one's ever asked you if—" he started, but Key cut him off harshly.

"Cut the stupid cuff!"

Flynn did as he was told. The blade cut into metal again. As it did, Key seemed to alternate between varying shades of anger and frustration. Possibly embarrassment. The saw's whine died again.

"You know what the most goddamn pathetic thing is?" she continued when it did. "When I saw you, with that drive in your hands and all the wiring coming out of it, and it was obvious you'd spent your time tinkering with stupid mechanical shit . . . I didn't feel scared anymore."

Flynn checked the cuff again. It was totally cut through this time. The thing would snap right off now.

Key kept her eyes shut, still expecting her hand to be severed at any moment. "All the chaos in that place, and you still knew what you were doing. Like fucking always. Do you know how that makes me feel?"

Flynn stared at her in an entirely new way. She was expressing genuine emotion. Not her usual blood and fire. It made him uneasy, but also . . . something else. He didn't need to anymore, but he kept his hand in hers.

"How?" he asked.

"It makes me feel safe, you fucking dickhead," she announced.

Flynn studied her, unsure what to say. "You can open your eyes now."

Key's lids blinked cautiously open. When they did, Flynn snapped the cuff in half and let the chain fall to the floor.

Key didn't move to take her arm back or rub the skin where the cuff had cut into her wrist. Instead, she kept her hand in Flynn's. It seemed like her fingers fit perfectly.

Flynn was suddenly aware of how close they were. He could feel her breath on his neck.

And then Flynn and Key jumped as the lights in the machine room suddenly exploded in sparks.

Flame shot out of the heat ports on the composite saw next to them. A few computer monitors flashed and flared and burned out at the other end of the machine room.

"What the hell?" Key breathed.

Flynn craned his neck to look at what he instinctively knew must be the source. The radiation door to the X-Core.

Bright white light streamed from where the door was inset into the wall, a blue-illuminated rectangular outline, and it was glowing brighter and brighter.

Flynn moved to the door quick, swiped across the control hologram spinning next to it.

The door slid open.

Heat and noise and sound burst out.

Flynn saw the X-Core, a metallic column, wrapped in its polysteel cone, glowing and flashing. Lightning-like energy flashed, arcing over the glass.

And then he saw the bodies.

Blackened and blended together on the ceiling. Far more than at Site Eleven, *hundreds* of them. Mouths frozen in screams, faces frozen in pain, arms and legs and chest and throats all morphed and contorted into one shape that was slathered along the interior.

Flynn swiped the hologram again. The door closed, sealing off the horror and the light.

He looked at Key. "We might have a problem."

Sounds filled the room, coming through whatever audio speakers were there.

Static. Hissing. *Voices.*

The lights flickered once, twice, then died, plunging everything to blackness. The holo displays and computers in the room went dark.

Key glared back at him, pissed, the emotion from before gone. "Can we not go *anywhere* without—"

Flynn stuttered forward as the door behind him rocked hard. Something slammed into it from the other side, trying to break through . . .

FORTY-SEVEN

CHAINS

Zane stepped from the harsh light of the hallway into almost pitch-blackness.

The room was metallic, so he could sense its size and shape even without seeing it. Cramped, nothing more than a shaft, but it felt like it stretched the entire height of the Barrier, and he was standing on a ledge in the middle of it. The drop-off below him felt like four hundred feet, at least.

He sensed a metallic case on the wall next to the door. Zane opened it and pulled out the flashlight stored inside, flipped it on.

A thick blue beam of light lit up the chains, five or six strands of them, hanging in the dark. They were huge, each link about the size of his head.

There was a crank handle on the wall next to him. It had four spokes, and each one was slotted with a ratchet-like hole. The ratchets meant the crank was designed to be turned by some sort of mechanical apparatus. The train gate below must be heavy. Maybe even too heavy for him.

Zane shined the light back onto the chains, watching them swing back and forth slightly in the dark. It was funny, how so many things reminded him of her.

Astoria loved clocks. Old ones, with the gears and the weights—and the chains. You wound them by pulling the chains and hoisting the weights up to the top, where the tension kept the gears gradually and slowly ticking in time.

After Zane and Astoria ran, they never stayed in one place too long. He would get clocks like that for her whenever he saw them, to keep her occupied. Being occupied was good, for everyone and everything around her. If Astoria got bored, there was more chance of an incident.

She would sit in whatever cargo hold or abandoned factory they happened to be in that week and work on them for hours, taking them apart, tiny screw by tiny screw, until they were just pieces on the ground. Then she would turn around and put them all back together again. Just as fast as she took them apart. She did it all from memory.

"Why do you do that?" Zane had asked her.

"It makes me feel better," she said.

"Why?"

"It reminds me that no matter how taken apart something is, it can always be put back together."

Zane understood the allure of thinking that way, for Astoria especially. The UEG had done a number on her, made her into something that could never be put back together. But there was no harm in letting her dream.

In the end, it hadn't mattered. He'd fucked up, bought into the UEG's ruse. He'd managed to get himself out of the trap, but Astoria . . .

He would find her, he told himself. He would find her, and, in finding *her*, he would find the ones who took her. And then he would make them pay. Long and hard.

The key to finding her was somewhere on the Razor, and the knowledge of that filled him with urgency. The Razor was dying, being burned alive, and he was running out of time.

Zane sensed something through the metal under his boots that brought him back to the present. Movement.

Slight vibrations on the walls of the shaft, starting high up and filtering down. It was like a chain reaction. Motion at the top of the structure triggered motion just below it, again and again.

Zane's eyes thinned. He raised the flashlight. It was so diffuse it didn't penetrate very far, so he tightened the beam, made it stronger.

Then he saw them.

About thirty feet above him. Lining the walls of the chain shaft.

Black, bulging, gelatinous deposits, splattered and sprayed up and down all four walls as far as the light could show him. They looked like eggs. Or nests. Hundreds of them. Maybe thousands.

"Strange times," Zane said.

FORTY-EIGHT

SCAR

Maddox didn't move, the knife at his throat, the computer terminals and holo displays glowing around the small room.

The servos in the bionic arm of the Scorpio whirred in Maddox's ear, pressing the knife closer. The others had bionics too, basic appendages— legs, arms, hands. But one or two of the Scorpios were missing appendages entirely. Most likely because those appendages used to have weapons or emitters in them.

More Scorpios moved for Raelyn and grabbed her, pulled her away from him. Maddox struggled instinctively, but the grip on his neck tightened, the knife pressing closer.

They shoved her against the far wall. She shook, her eyes slimming, and she froze in place. There wasn't anything Maddox could do; he and Raelyn were too far apart.

"Seven, maybe eight hundred people outside when it started," Scar hissed into Maddox's ear, "Scorpios and Ferals dancing in the sand. Guards up here shooting everybody." Scar looked down to the drag marks on the floor. His look was pure hatred. "Then *it* showed up. Comes out of the sky to the west like it was following the rail line. Same rail line *you* came in on."

The creature, Maddox guessed. Whatever had been in Site Eleven. It must have escaped, just like they had. But . . . in the sky?

"Came down on us, pulled everyone away, yelling and screaming. Didn't care who was who, didn't care about colors, just dragged them in here. All seven or eight hundred. Never seen anything like it. Far as I know, no one left but us. And *you*."

Maddox swallowed, looked the man in his eyes over his shoulder. They jumped all over the place, trying to focus. Dilated pupils, red-streaked whites. He was high. Synth maybe, or something easier to get on a Crawler. It might give Maddox an edge.

"How'd you get that train running?" Scar asked, leaning in close. "How'd you get the gun locker open?"

The arm holding the shank was mechanical. Maddox could hear the servos whirring, could feel the sharp edges of the steel exoskeleton press into his back.

"You blind? Look at the neck," one of the other Scorpios said. "Guy's a fucking Fink."

"Well, look at that," Scar said behind him, seeing the brand. "What'd you used to do here?"

"Maintenance," Maddox lied. "Barrier detail."

"How's a piece-of-shit janitor know the gun codes?"

"Everyone gets the armory code," he answered, casually shifting his look over to Raelyn. She stared back, frightened. "In case of emergencies."

Scar pulled him even closer. "That mean you can program the metrics?"

Maddox kept holding Raelyn's gaze. The two Scorpios were close to her. One was running metallic fingers down her arm.

Maddox nodded once.

"Holy shit!" one of the Scorpios exclaimed suddenly.

Maddox looked and saw that the guy had found Raelyn's pack, the one Zane had gotten just a day ago. The one with all her Slow Burn medication. The one he'd killed *Scorpios* to get.

"It's Guido's," the Scorpio said darkly.

"Fucking kidding me," said another.

Servos whirred. Maddox grimaced as Scar's metallic grip clamped down on him.

"How you explain that, janitor?"

Maddox said nothing, just tried to think. He had to deescalate this quickly.

"We found Guido by the rise," Scar kept going. "He and Jace had their skulls crushed. And now that I'm looking at *your* pack, it looks a lot like Jace's."

"Just relax . . ." Maddox said, trying to stall.

The Scorpio with Raelyn's pack ripped it open and dumped the contents onto the floor. Raelyn moaned at the other end of the room, watching.

Water. Food.

Syringes and vials.

"Fuck me," the Scorpio said, his tone darkening. "Look at the meds."

"For this." The one near Raelyn yanked her lab coat sleeve up. The Slow Burn on her arm stood out. It had spread more than halfway up her bicep now, the glowing tendrils creeping toward her slender shoulder.

Scar laughed a single short note. "Fucking synth-addict doctor."

"*Relax*," Maddox said again.

He groaned in pain as the servos clamped down and the shank cut into his neck. "You don't get to tell anyone what to do, walking around with those packs," Scar hissed. He nodded to the armory, lined with the pulse rifles and ballistics. "You get in there. Reset us seven rifles. Pulse, not bullets. And you do it *now*."

Maddox didn't move, just stayed where he was. He knew the moment he handed over working weapons to the Scorpios was the moment they killed them both.

Scar smiled, guessed at the thoughts in Maddox's head. He nodded to the Scorpios by Raelyn.

One of them raised a foot up, then stepped down hard.

Two vials of Raelyn's meds shattered.

"No!" she screamed, pushing forward. She took the back of a fist to the face, got shoved against the wall. Still she squirmed, trying to get loose.

"Wait!" Maddox yelled.

More vials burst apart under a boot heel.

Raelyn screamed. A mechanical hand clamped on her throat.

"Okay! *Okay!*" Maddox shouted, trying to look Scar in the eye. "Pulse rifles. Just stop."

The Scorpio near Raelyn put his foot back down, sparing what was left of the vials. Maddox breathed.

"Get at it then," Scar said, shoving him forward.

Maddox checked Raelyn as he stumbled into the armory. Still pinned against the wall, her eyes were on the broken vials on the floor. She looked tortured. The Slow Burn blazed on her arm.

Maddox moved for the pulse rifles hanging in their racks. He could grab one, easy, but tuning it to his biometrics wasn't a fast process. Twenty seconds at minimum. They could slit Raelyn's throat three times by then.

But with a gun he would be the real threat. Maybe they would come for him, ignore her. Maybe she could escape. Maybe—

"*Now*, janitor," Scar said with venom. "Or we start making your doctor squeal. In all kinds of ways."

Maddox swallowed. He reached for a rifle. He didn't see any other option. It wasn't going to work but he'd try anyway. He wouldn't do nothing.

A new voice echoed in the room.

"Seven of you, one of her," the voice said. Older. Feminine. Icy and calm, with a thinly veiled note of condescension. "You must feel so powerful."

It was a woman, Maddox saw in shock. Standing at the end of the control room, lit by the glowing holo displays. She wore an immaculate white jumpsuit, and silver hair trailed down her back in a tight braid. An inmate, clearly, but she wore her jumpsuit like it was a silk dress. In fact, even just standing in place, everything about her presence was incredibly deliberate and meticulous.

Maddox would have guessed her age at late fifties or early sixties, but she didn't hold herself like that. She somehow radiated a level of vitality that seemed unnatural. Combined with her calmness . . . it was intimidating.

"But power, like most things, is relative," she said, and her eyes shifted to Maddox. As they did, over the distance, he thought he might have seen what looked like a sliver of golden light move from one eye to the next.

Maddox had a good idea who the woman was. And, if it was possible, he felt even more worried now.

FORTY-NINE

WASH AND REPEAT

Key watched the door to the X-Core pound in its frame behind Flynn. It occurred to her that he was bravely, if not stupidly, trying to keep it shut with his back.

"The same goddamned thing from—"

"Yes!" Flynn yelled back.

The frightening sounds filled the room from its speakers. Scratches and hisses and voices.

"*How?*"

"*Gable,*" Flynn said, as the door shook behind him.

Key's eyes thinned. Gable, now better identified as Dr. Fucking *Rosetta*, one of the scariest ghost stories in the galaxy. She hadn't asked Flynn what had happened to the bitch, and Flynn hadn't said anything either. All Key knew was that when they saw each other again the scary woman wasn't there.

But none of that explained what the creature was doing *here*, like it had fucking followed them.

"So what do we do now?" she asked.

"Do you know what an impact driver is?" Flynn asked back.

"How the hell would I know what a—"

"It looks like a drill, a really big one," he shouted. "You do know what a *drill* is, right?" The door kept shaking behind him.

"Don't push it, Doc!" she yelled, already running for the supply shelves at the other end of the room. This impact driver was probably the reason they'd come down here, though she didn't know why. Then again, she didn't really get much of what was going on in Flynn's head.

"We need a *cordless* one!" Flynn left the door, ran for the shelves. The door behind him kept rocking in its frame. Whatever was on the other side wanted in. Bad. And it would no doubt get through. "That means no wires!"

"I know what cordless means!"

Key and Flynn reached the storage wall, which was divided into metallic bins. Dozens of them, on four shelves, running the length of the wall, about thirty feet, full of all kinds of tech and equipment.

"Hurry!" Flynn yelled.

The door rocked. Lights exploded in sparks all around them. The reality of the situation hit her then. That thing was in the *reactor* room. It had tapped into this X-Core just like it had the one in the black site. Which meant . . .

"The Barrier's going to fucking implode isn't it?" Key looked at Flynn with wild eyes.

"Well, not all of it," he said, rifling through the bins in front of him. "Just this part of it."

"The part *we're* in!" How did this keep fucking happening to her? "Where do I look for this thing?"

"Pick a bin!"

Key ripped open the bins in front of her, searching through them. "Why do we need it?"

"Because we're dragging about two dozen more train cars than we need."

The lights in the ceiling all exploded in sparks, and the room went pitch-black, except for the light streaming in around the doorframe to the X-Core. It was enough to see by, but barely.

Key found a drill with a big-ass crankcase. She pulled it out.

It had a cord.

"God damn it . . ." she cursed.

"We need one without—"

"I know!" she yelled, yanking open another bin. Then another and another. Saws. Regular drills. Grinders. Arc welders. But no motherfucking cordless impact drivers. "We're not going to find this . . ."

"It's *here*," Flynn told her.

The door to the X-Core rocked hard; she could hear it ripping loose from its frame.

"It's here," he told her. "We'll *make* it."

Other men had promised her similar things. The difference, for whatever reason, was that she believed Flynn. She had no real idea why. Maybe it was because every time they'd hit a wall he'd found a way over it. Whatever it was, he'd managed to elicit in her something very few people had.

Trust. As much as he pissed her off, he made her wings stop itching. No one had done that before.

Key rifled through the bins, one after the other. She finally saw what looked like a drill with a big crankcase.

Key's heart skipped. She grabbed it, pulled it loose.

There was no cord . . .

She smiled, felt energy fill her, held it up.

Flynn ripped his gaze to the big device in her hands. He smiled too.

Then the door to the X-Core exploded inward in a spray of metal. Light flooded the room. And within it, horrible writhing black shapes stirred.

"Go!" Flynn yelled.

They ran. Hard. Carrying the impact driver.

The sounds in the room flared loudly, drowning out everything. Something burst through the reactor door. Key turned and looked, eyes wide. Angular shapes, three legs, fibrous, glistening metallic skin.

Just like before. The horror all over again. Wash and repeat.

And through the door, she saw the bodies. Blackened. Morphed together. Mouths open and screaming. Hundreds and hundreds, lining the walls and the ceiling of the reactor core.

Dripping down and out of them, solidifying on the floor, were more creatures. Forming over and over again, and rising up.

"*Flynn!*" Key yelled in terror, running as fast as she could through the tightly packed equipment.

Flynn burst through the door ahead of her, turned as he did, held out his hand. Key could hear the creatures' rattling sounds bearing down on her.

Flynn yanked her through the door, into the hallway beyond, just in time.

He hit the control panel on the wall. The door slammed shut, locking the creatures away.

Then it rocked, just like the one before, the creatures pounding on it. And just like before, Flynn put his back against it. Futilely. *Protectively.*

The fucking moron.

"You called me Flynn," he said, staring at her.

He was right, she realized. She had.

"First time for everything," she said, then yanked him forward by the collar of his jumpsuit. She kissed him. Hard. Tasted his tongue, felt his lips twist around hers. Flynn wrapped his hands around her waist and pulled her against him, while the lights sparked in the ceiling.

Key let it last a moment more, then she shoved Flynn back against the door and stared into his dazed eyes.

"I would like to leave now," she informed him.

Flynn nodded, gathered himself. They both started running again.

FIFTY

STAY AWAKE

Zane studied the eggs—he wasn't sure what else to call them—under the harsh blue beam from his light. Round globs on the walls, stretching up and down in all directions.

Running between them were thick, gelatinous tubes that looked like . . . what? Veins? They connected each egg to every other egg, up and down the shaft, disappearing into the darkness below, where his light couldn't penetrate.

He hadn't seen anything like this in Site Eleven, but the substance these things appeared to be made of looked identical to the creatures he'd encountered there. Black. Fibrous. Glistening and soft in appearance, but hard as metal.

Could it be from the same creature? If so, what did that mean? It had escaped the facility? And come . . . here? The same place they were heading?

The abandoning of the planet. The beacon in the sky to the east. The creature from Site Eleven. The shrinking of the Razor.

The smart play, anyone could see, was to leave. Take Flynn's shuttle when it came.

But that wasn't an option. Zane hadn't found what he needed yet. And he wasn't leaving until he did. Countless things had tried to kill him over the years and they'd all failed. He didn't see why a planet should be any different.

Zane sensed something new.

The eggs were throbbing. Or, more specifically, whatever was *inside* them was throbbing.

It wasn't visible, the movement, but Zane could feel it through the metal. And the movement was increasing.

Zane moved for the crank handle he'd seen earlier, grabbed one of its arms. The steel was solid, very pure, no rust at all.

It was meant to be turned by some kind of device or machine, but Zane didn't have that. He only had his muscles. And the Charge.

That had always been enough.

He grabbed a second arm on the crank handle, one in each hand, clamping down on them tightly.

Then he let the Charge trickle out through his hands.

Zane felt the crank arms begin to heat up. Carefully, he pulled the Charge back. He wanted to absorb power from the arms, but only enough to give him the strength to turn the crank, not to melt it in half.

Pain formed in his head as the X burned—dull, not sharp, not yet.

Zane pushed and pulled, turning the handles counterclockwise, groaning, feeling the Charge feed his muscles.

The big chains rattled in the shaft, started to shift in alternating lines, some moving up, others down.

Just like a clock.

A grating sound shot up from below. Something heavy and metallic starting to move. Zane could feel the vibrations of it through the floor under his feet. It was the train gate. It was lifting.

Just slowly.

He felt something else then, too. The vibration in the eggs on the walls was much greater. It was growing fast.

Zane kept turning, one slow crank after another.

The chains moved. The gate below kept raising. As it did, sunlight began to shine into the shaft.

He could see the eggs in the new light. Could see them throbbing and bulging. And it wasn't just one thing inside each egg. It felt like many, many things.

Zane knew the truth. He wasn't going to get the gate open in time. At least, not this way.

He remembered Astoria, with her clocks, working with the chains. And he remembered what happened to the counterweights when one of those chains *broke*.

Zane let go of the crank, moved to the edge of the landing. The chains hung right in front of him. There was no way to know which chain was the right one. With the pulley system above, he had a fifty-fifty shot.

"Fuck it," he said, and grabbed one of the huge links at random. It took both his hands to hold it. He could tell immediately just how thick it was. Thicker than anything he had ever tried this with before.

The eggs throbbed and shook, coming to life up and down the shaft. They were about to burst.

Zane poured every bit of the Charge into the huge chain link in his hands.

Immediately, it started to glow. Zane kept funneling his power into the steel.

He felt the X burn as it disassembled and stored the energy from the metal. The pain in his head started to grow. The chain link kept heating, glowing hotter and hotter.

A rattling sound, thick and wet, filled the chain shaft suddenly. It was coming from the eggs all around him. He was almost out of time.

Zane's veins burned, his muscles screamed. The pain in his head flared suddenly, like someone had sunk a knife into his temple. His body felt like it was on fire, Slow Burn times a hundred.

Zane roared, the sound drowning out the wet rattling and everything else. And still he kept drawing more energy from the link, kept absorbing it into himself.

The link glowed white hot now, searing the flesh on his hands. The Charge had fully penetrated it.

But it wasn't going to be enough. He couldn't take it all in. He wasn't going to be able to—

Zane flinched as the chain link burst apart in his hands in a shower of molten metallic shards, ripping into his chest and face.

The chain dropped off heavily into the darkness at his feet. A screeching sound filled the shaft as the other chains started to pour through the pulleys, the tension on them gone.

More light filled the shaft below as the counterweights keeping the gate shut lost their grip on it and it was yanked violently upward. Zane had guessed right.

But he could barely concentrate enough to register his victory.

His body was on fire. His brain was worse.

He'd absorbed too much. He had to release it.

With another roar, Zane grabbed the crank handle from the wall and yanked it off like it wasn't even attached, spraying metal and mortar.

He swung the handle like an axe, buried it into the opposite wall.

He kicked the door behind him off its hinges and into the hallway outside.

He punched a hole in the wall twice the size of his fist. Then another one. Then another.

He struggled to keep his balance as the dizziness and pain swept over him.

Zane collapsed to the floor. Blood pounded in his ears. His vision started to go dark. He was passing out.

Stay awake, he ordered himself.

He crawled forward on the floor, that was all he had the energy for, dragged himself through what was left of the doorframe he'd just obliterated.

Stay awake . . .

And behind him, the rattling sound reached a fever pitch.

The nests exploded, busting apart in showers of putrid blackness that drowned out all the light coming from below.

The swarm surged down the length of the chain shaft, toward Zane.

Everything was going dark in his mind.

Stay awake!

Zane pushed to his feet, found the strength to run. The black swarm was everywhere behind him, the wet rattling of it filling the air.

FIFTY-ONE

LIONS

"Who the *fuck* . . ." Scar hissed between his teeth.

He and the other Scorpios all stared at the silver-haired woman standing casually in front of them. Maddox looked to Raelyn, and judging by the look on the doctor's face, she'd also guessed who the woman was.

"Where you come from, bitch?" one of the Scorpios near Raelyn asked. "The retirement ward?" The Scorpios all laughed.

As they did, Maddox inched toward the pulse rifles. He preferred ballistics, but a pulse wouldn't need an ammo clip; he could get it firing quicker.

The woman ignored the laughter, studied each of the Scorpios in turn as she spoke. "Two hundred years ago, on Earth, there was a creature called a lion. Beautiful beasts, huge and fast, predators. Man killed them, of course, just as he kills everything he secretly envies or covets."

"A fucking talker," Scar said. "Sozo, kill this bitch before she gets going."

One of the Scorpios, the biggest of the five, moved toward the older woman. He didn't seem happy with the idea, like the act was beneath him, but he moved toward the woman regardless. The others turned back to Maddox and Raelyn, as if it was already done. It wasn't.

The woman was faster than anyone Maddox had ever seen, young or old.

She sidestepped left, away from Sozo. Her arm flashed upward. And the big Scorpio shuddered and froze where he stood. His eyes went wide. A gurgling sound came from his throat.

Everyone's attention snapped back to the woman again.

Her index finger was at Sozo's throat, dead center, tapping the eye of the scorpion tattoo on his skin there. It looked like he was frozen in place by the woman's touch.

Blood began to drip down the big man's chest. Maddox noticed a little pinprick of silver gleaming from a puncture wound in the back of his neck.

"Lions were pack hunters," she continued, in the same calm, disinterested tone. "What distinguished them was that a lion pride consisted mainly of *females*. Sometimes ten lionesses to one male."

As she spoke, she stared curiously down at the top of her finger, to where Sozo shuddered at the end of it, his eyes bulging. She seemed to be studying him.

The Scorpios looked back and forth, stunned, trying to make sense of it. Maddox had a feeling things were not going to go in their favor.

He saw the gun he wanted, slowly reached toward it. Raelyn, eyes wide, watched him from across the room, but none of the other gang members seemed to notice.

"The females were the hunters," the woman explained, eyes still on the gurgling Sozo. "They stalked and killed creatures sometimes three times as large as themselves, and do you know what would happen when they dispatched their prey?"

The woman turned her wrist. Sozo spasmed, something unseen twisting inside his throat, something connected to her finger. Blood sprayed from his mouth and nose.

"The male," she continued, her voice taking on a tone of bitterness, "the lion, would claim what *they* had achieved. *He* would eat first. *He* would grow fat off their sweat."

More blood. Sozo contorted. The others, the looks on their faces showed, were moving beyond simple shock now. They were approaching fear.

"It is the way of the world. Women do not realize their power, because it is in man's interest to hide it from them." Her voice was intense and dark now. "Have you ever wondered what a world would look like where the lioness *killed* the lion? Where she ate him alive?" She twisted her finger. Sozo's eyes rolled into the back of his head. He spasmed again. "I have. Shall I show you?"

The woman yanked back her finger. And Sozo, spewing blood, fell to the metallic floor in a heap.

A blood-coated shaft of perfectly shaped metal extended from the tip of her finger.

The Scorpios all stared at one another, Maddox and Raelyn forgotten. Their expressions were pure horror.

"What . . . what the *fuck* are you?" Scar said, his voice shaking.

The woman's eyes looked up from Sozo's body and peered into Scar's.

While everyone watched, she raised her hands and turned them so the palms faced each other. The skin at the tip of every finger sliced open as blades, just like the first, pushed slowly out into the open air. Ten of them, gleaming like prisms in the colored light from the holo displays.

"Isn't it obvious?" The silver-haired woman sounded almost perplexed. "I am your end."

The woman closed the distance with a speed that seemed physically impossible.

The nearest Scorpio twisted and fell in a shower of blood as the blades in her fingers passed through flesh and ligament like it wasn't even there.

Maddox watched in stunned silence, unable to move, as the woman's blades sliced open a second man's stomach. He fell as fast as the first.

Raelyn screamed. The sound spurred him to action. Maddox yanked the rifle off the wall.

The remaining four Scorpios charged the woman. She was faster, beyond faster, dodging, striking down with both hands.

Scar yelled as his mechanical arm was severed from his body. The blades, whatever the hell they were, sliced through metal as easily as skin.

Scar fell to the floor as the other two rammed into the woman.

Maddox flipped the power switch on the rifle. It beeped twice. A holographic keypad projected in the air above it.

Another Scorpio fell in a shower of blood. The last turned to run, but the woman leaped on him.

Scar, however, was back on his feet, even with only one arm. He moved for the woman as her blades drove down into the Scorpio underneath her, ending him.

Maddox keyed in the four-digit code.

The handle under the muzzle flashed red. He gripped it with his palm.

The handle flashed green.

Maddox raised the rifle, aimed.

It flashed three times. Three pulses flared from the barrel.

All three sizzled as they hit Scar in the back, blowing him against the wall before he could reach the silver-haired woman.

The woman didn't seem to notice. She stood up from the Scorpio underneath her, quivering on the floor, blood draining out of him, and stared down at him with a disappointed look.

"As I said, it's just the way of the world." Her blades sank through both his eyes. He shuddered once, then went still.

Raelyn gasped, pushed into a corner of the room, staring fearfully at the woman in the center of it.

Maddox sighted down the barrel, locked on to the woman, finger on the trigger.

She turned gracefully, taking in the room, studying the devastation and the blood.

Then her eyes found Maddox. If she was bothered by the rifle aimed at her, she didn't show it. Her once pristine white jumpsuit was covered in blood now. She didn't seem bothered by that, either.

The blades withdrew back into her fingers, blood dripping from the tips. It occurred to Maddox it wasn't just the Scorpios' blood. It was also her own. The blades slit her own skin whenever they were used.

"Marcus Flynn," she said simply. With her gaze on him, Maddox felt a chill. "Where might I find him?"

FIFTY-TWO

TERRIBLE THINGS

Flynn and Key burst into the raging sunlight outside the Barrier, running full force, their boots digging deep into the red sand.

"It's open!" Key shouted behind him, looking over her shoulder.

Flynn looked and saw what she meant. The train tunnel was open, a black outline that now let the train tracks through.

Zane had done it. But where was he?

Where was *anyone*?

"Move!" Key yelled, as she ran past him.

Flynn pushed it—and felt the heat. On a scale he'd never experienced before, one he didn't even know was possible. The heat and pressure were like being in a giant mass spectrometer.

The reason why was in front of him.

The wall of fire loomed over everything to the west now. Flynn could almost see it pushing forward, stretching from one end of the horizon to the other, just like the Barrier. Soon the Barrier itself was going to be consumed.

And then the Razor.

Key reached the train engine first, leaped inside the cockpit door. Flynn followed after her, as quickly as he could, climbing inside.

"Get the engine online!" He grabbed the impact driver out of her hands as he ran by.

"If the others aren't here, we have—"

"They'll make it!" he yelled, running past the electrical cabinet he'd hot-wired earlier, wires and cables spilling out of it. He'd shown Key how to do the same thing, before, and he hoped she remembered.

Flynn yanked open the door at the rear of the engine.

Just outside was the first transport car. Flynn stepped across its connection, reached for the door handle, and shoved the big, heavy door open.

He rushed inside the refrigeration car, lined with its climate-controlled storage bins. He raced past them, reached the next door, yanked it open.

More light flooded in. Another connection between the cars. Flynn jumped over it, moved for the next door, and stopped.

Another figure was running for the train. A big one.

"Zane!" Flynn yelled, twisting the circular handle and shoving the door open. "I need you!"

He ran through the darkness of the second train car. Chains rattled in the ceiling, where prisoners were secured, and Flynn remembered his first ride in one of these. He shuddered and kept moving, found the handles for the big double side doors on the car, yanked them down, started to push the doors open.

Light streaked in through the crack between them as they widened, slowly. They were heavy. He groaned with the effort.

Two massive hands reached in from outside.

The doors slid open easily, slamming into opposite sides. Light and heat flared in.

Zane stood framed in the train car door, staring up at Flynn. And he didn't look good.

His skin seemed even more ashen than usual, his eyes were shut. He grabbed hold of the open door for support, and it looked to Flynn like there was a trickle of liquid under his nose. Something . . . silver.

"You okay?" Flynn asked.

The big man's eyes opened to slits. "What do you need?"

Man of few words. Fine by Flynn. "We have to get the rest of the train disconnected." Flynn showed him the impact driver. "Fast."

Zane pulled himself up into the train, and the two moved for the other end of the car. They yanked open the door, revealing the next storage car and its connections.

These train engines ran at incredibly high torque, for pulling massive weight. If they were going to run the thing full speed and it didn't have enough weight behind it, it would flame out. Two cars should be enough; the rest they could lose.

Flynn wiped sweat from his face. Jesus, it hurt to breathe. They weren't going to last long in this atmosphere.

Flynn studied the connections, saw the bolts that held their car to the superstructure. They couldn't just disconnect the cars in the usual way;

they were secured together by electric means, and nothing much electric worked anymore on the Razor.

Flynn pulled the trigger on the impact driver. It stuttered and whined, coming to life. He nodded. He could do this.

"It's here," Zane said from above.

"What's here?"

The walls of the Barrier shuddered.

Pieces of it exploded outward, hurtling into the air up and down the length of the giant structure as something exploded through to the outside.

Flynn watched, eyes wide, as a surge of pure blackness burst into the air from the Barrier, turning the sky dark.

It was the same swarm he'd seen at Site Eleven, inside the containment area—the same one that had dissolved polysteel. Only now it was a hundred times larger. It filled the air, churning and writhing, completely blocking the view of the top of the Barrier.

"Holy shit . . ." Flynn felt his body go cold, in spite of the insane heat.

The car rocked underneath them as the train began to move. Key had gotten it powered.

"*Quickly,*" Zane reminded him in his deep, honeyed voice. It sounded strained, though. He'd been through something in the Barrier, something that challenged even him.

"When I get the bolts off," Flynn said, lying on his stomach and leaning over the edge of the car, "the connections are going to be stuck from the pressure. Can you push the cars apart?"

"I can." Zane stepped over him to the railing of the other train car.

Flynn got the impact driver over the first bolt, held it in place. He squeezed the trigger. The drill rocked hard, hammering with lots of torque, just like it was supposed to.

Rust sprayed as the first bolt came loose. The tension eased. The bolt was ripped off.

Flynn yanked it out, repositioned the drill on the second bolt. It whirred. The second bolt came off just as easily.

The ground was starting to move past under him, a few feet from his head, faster and faster. He could feel the train picking up momentum.

Flynn tried to put the bit of the driver on the third bolt, but the platform rocked. He had to hold on with one hand, which made positioning the drill a lot tougher.

"Maddox," Zane said above him. Flynn looked up.

People were running toward the moving train. Maddox. Raelyn. And . . . *someone else.* Flynn couldn't make out details, but whoever it was, was *fast.*

Zane's hand grabbed the driver, helped Flynn position the bit on the third bolt.

The blackness was still pushing out of the huge structure and into the air, filling everything above with darkness, and seemingly ripping the structure apart as it did. The entire thing was shaking, debris falling off it in showers of dirt and metal.

It was more than just the swarm, though, Flynn knew. Just like at Site Eleven, the creature had somehow tapped into the garrison's X-Core. It was melting down. The gravity implosion would collapse this part of the Barrier—and seal off their way to the starport, if they didn't hurry.

Flynn pulled the trigger on the driver.

It whirred, grabbed the bolt, started hammering it loose. The train rocked as it picked up speed. The drill slipped off. Zane shoved it back on, and they tried again, Flynn holding down the trigger.

The drill stayed on. It ripped the bolt off the supports.

The car groaned loudly as the metal connections began to tear.

Everything went pitch-black as the train roared into the train tunnel.

Flynn couldn't see the bolts anymore. Couldn't see *anything.*

The train rocked. *Everything* seemed to rock—the rails, the ground, the tunnel itself.

The Barrier was going to implode around them, and even if the train engine made it out, with the rest of the cars connected it would be like stomping on a snake's tail while it slithered away.

"Flynn!" Zane shouted, his hands on the impact driver, holding it in place.

Flynn felt for the last bolt, guided the drill toward it, holding on for dear life as the platform shook under him.

Zane helped hold it steady. Flynn found the bolt with the bit.

It slipped off. He tried again. Got it, pulled the trigger.

The drill whined. The bolt began to turn.

The train rocked hard . . . and the drill fell from his hands.

It clanked as it hit the connections, disappeared into the dark. Lost.

"No!" Flynn shouted, felt his heart sink.

"Move," Zane said, pushing Flynn up and away.

He put one leg on Flynn's car and the other leg on his own car.

Then he pushed. With his feet and his hands. Hard. Groaning. Then yelling. In pain.

Flynn's eyes widened. The tunnel shook. He could see the light from the other end, the other train gate, coming.

Zane pushed one last, hard time . . .

And the cars burst apart in a spray of rust and metal shards, seperating.

Zane collapsed in a heap, spent, almost fell into the breach, his legs dangling.

Flynn grabbed his shoulders, pulled with everything he had, helped Zane crawl back on.

The light from the far tunnel suddenly went black. There was a roar around them now, louder even than the train engine. It sounded like the world was tearing to pieces.

The Barrier was collapsing. The X-Core had melted down.

Everything went bright white as the engine roared out of the tunnel and into the heat and the sunlight beyond, leaving the rest of its cars behind.

Flynn saw the Barrier again, this time from the opposite side, huge and looming—and then Flynn saw it start to *fall*.

It was surreal, something that gigantic crumpling in on itself in a massive, plummeting cascade of steel and concrete and burned-out technology. It didn't look real.

The cars they'd just disconnected shuddered as the tunnel collapsed around them. They ripped loose from the rails, disintegrated into the hot sand outside the tunnel, blowing apart everywhere.

It would have been their fate, too, if he and Zane hadn't gotten the cars loose.

A shadow passed over everything.

Flynn looked up from Zane, who was passed out cold. The sky was full of a swirling, writhing black swarm of thousands and thousands of pieces of darkness that, unlike before, were now focused and moving as one entity through the air.

The swarm accelerated, rolling around itself, outpacing even the train, but heading in the same direction.

East.

The beacon stood out there in the sky, the train tracks leading straight toward it. It was larger than he had ever seen it, looking like it was shooting into orbit. For the first time, the beacon seemed ominous.

And the black swarm was headed right *toward* it.

Flynn studied it all with a feeling of dread. "What have we done?"

"You seem surprised, Marcus," a lush, feminine voice said behind him.

Flynn felt his veins turn to ice. He knew that voice. It was burned in his memory.

She stood right behind him, leaning against the doorway into the prisoner car, silver hair trailing down her back. She was covered in blood. On her jumpsuit. On her fingers and hands.

If he could, Flynn would have backed away . . . but there was nowhere to go.

Her eyes were not on him, though. She was watching the swarm in the air, rolling over itself as it surged eastward, but she didn't do so with horror or even trepidation. She seemed fascinated.

"I told you, didn't I?" Gable asked, a note of anticipation in her voice. "We would do terrible things together."

FIFTY-THREE

NAMES AND TITLES

Raelyn was right behind him as Maddox burst into the prisoner car, the rifle in his hands. It was an M32B assault rifle, the kind he used to use back in Colonial, and it shot 10×24mm steel-jacketed ammunition, each embedded within a rectangular propellant block of nitramine 50. In other words, it did a lot of damage, very quickly.

"Don't move. Stay where you are," Maddox said, aiming the rifle at the back of Gable's head. She was across the car, at the very end, next to Flynn, who seemed frozen in shock.

The silver-haired woman kept peering through the car's open door, watching the Barrier crumble in on itself and fall to the ground in the distance as the train pulled away.

"Zane!" Raelyn pushed past Maddox before he could stop her, moving for the big man, who was laying half in and half out of the train car. It looked like he was passed out.

"Flynn, help her pull him back," Maddox said, keeping the gun on the woman. After what he'd seen in the armory, he had very little doubt who she really was. He'd never seen anyone move like that.

Flynn grabbed one of Zane's arms, with Raelyn, and together they were just able to pull Zane into the center of the car, away from the door and away from *her*.

The woman still hadn't moved, just kept staring out the door.

"Hello?" Maddox said.

"You said not to move," the woman replied evenly. "This is me. Not moving."

Maddox gripped the gun tighter. He'd escorted dozens of the worst, most sadistic criminals the galaxy could produce to various black sites or hypermax installations all across the Razor. And they all had one thing in common. That icy calm. No matter what they'd done, no matter where they were going. They always thought it was them who was really in control.

The woman at the other end of the car had that same calm.

"We know who you are," Maddox announced.

Gable breathed deeply in the doorway. "It is what we do that defines us, James. Not names. Not titles. And I am the woman who saved your life."

On the floor next to him, Raelyn's hands were moving over Zane. The Slow Burn stood out on her arm, but she didn't seem to notice. She was in her element, helping someone who was hurt.

"I didn't get the impression saving us factored in all that much," Maddox said. "I think you just liked the blood."

"Do you think?"

"I've seen enough of your kind to know."

Finally, slowly, she turned. Maddox tensed, finger on the trigger. He didn't have the laser sight on. She was too fast. If she came for him, accuracy wasn't going to count for much. He'd have to fire full spread, shoot at angles. And pray.

But she just locked onto him with her eyes. "You're a former Ranger," Gable said. It occurred to him suddenly that she not only knew he'd been a Ranger but also knew his first name. "If anyone understands the necessity of killing men like that, it would be you."

"There's a difference between necessity and enjoying it."

Gable smiled. It was altogether unpleasant. "You've never enjoyed it?"

Maddox hesitated, words not coming as easily as he hoped.

Key suddenly burst into the train car, then ground to a halt as she saw what was happening.

"Fuck me running!" Key exclaimed behind him, eyes wide, staring at Gable.

Flynn looked up at Key from the floor, where Zane was comatose. Her presence seemed to wake Flynn up, somehow.

Gable's gaze shifted to Key, the smile staying in place. "I'm so pleased you survived, Key. The last I saw you, things looked desperate indeed."

"Where did . . . Where did she . . ." Key stammered, obviously shocked.

"It doesn't matter right now," Maddox said.

"I think it does," Flynn responded.

The engineer stood up next to Maddox. Key stayed behind them. Maddox wished Raelyn would do the same, but she was working on Zane.

"How did you get here ahead of us?" Flynn asked Gable.

Gable's gaze shifted to him. "I had hoped you would be happier to see me, Marcus." There was a strange note of fondness in her voice, Maddox thought.

"*How?*" Flynn insisted.

"Bargains were made at Site Eleven." Gable shrugged. "You saw that yourself."

At that, Maddox looked at Flynn, confused. So did everyone else.

"Oh," Gable said with concern. "They didn't know? You . . . didn't tell them?"

Flynn seemed suddenly apprehensive, and it didn't sit well with Maddox. "Tell us what, Flynn?"

He looked at Maddox nervously. "The hot labs, at the black site, had one of those . . . *things* in it."

"We all saw those," Key said behind him, her voice just as suspicious.

"This one was different," Flynn said. "Nothing's ever scared me as much as that thing. And it . . . it talked to her."

"Talked?" Key asked "It spoke fucking English?"

"No, I mean . . . I don't know, telepathically, or—"

"What did it *want*?" Maddox cut off the scientific musing.

"I don't know, but she let it loose," Flynn said. "She reconnected the reactor, which gave it the power it needed to escape."

"Technically, Marcus," Gable said pointedly, "*you* reconnected the reactor. At my urging."

Maddox's stare hardened even more. He saw Key glare at Flynn in exasperation.

"Jesus fuck, Flynn," she said.

"It was the only way to get out of there!" Flynn answered. "You don't know what it was like!"

"A reactor meltdown *would* override a quarantine lockdown." It was Raelyn, on the floor with Zane, the one person on this whole train who might actually be able to go toe to toe with Gable, and who was barely breathing.

"Raelyn is correct," Gable stated. "There was no other choice. The actions Marcus and I took allowed all of you to escape." Her gaze locked on to Maddox again. "You might say that I have saved some of you more than once, now."

Key drew one of her plasma knives from her jumpsuit. The blade glowed hot orange.

"I say we put a knife in her skull right now," she said. Gable seemed unintimidated.

"I don't know the feasibility of that." Maddox forced his eyes back down the barrel of the M32B. The silver-haired woman just stood there, casually, calmly. Like she was in control. "You didn't see her back there."

"I've seen plenty," Key said. "I've seen enough."

Maddox thought about it. One particular solution stood out, but somehow he doubted Gable would go for it.

"I think the best thing," he said, "would be for you to . . . jump. Out the door. Onto the ground."

The smile returned to Gable's face. "Best thing for whom, James? Certainly not for me. This train is going where I wish, with *whom* I wish."

Her eyes moved to Flynn.

Maddox didn't like that look very much at all. When this was done, he and Flynn were going to have a long talk. "Then we do it the hard way."

He gripped the rifle. Gable's eyes narrowed. Key tensed.

"*Or . . .*" Flynn's voice cut through everything. "She could lock herself in the chains."

It took a moment for what he was suggesting to run through Maddox's mind. He meant the prisoner chains hanging from the ceiling of the car.

"Could I?" Gable said with distaste.

Maddox thought about it, studying the chains and the cuffs hanging from the ceiling. Maddox had watched Gable's blades slice right through a Scorpio's bionic implant, but these chains were composite steel, a lot stronger, and she would be cuffed at the wrist.

"Why are you so fucking eager to keep her around?" Key's voice was incredulous. "You know who she is!"

"I'm just looking for an alternative to everyone dying in this car," Flynn said with forced patience. "Gable, is that something you would do?"

Maddox watched the woman's face as she thought it through. She gave no indication of what was playing in her mind. Maddox had a feeling she didn't display any outward emotion unless it was intended.

"Being imprisoned here was a price I paid willingly," Gable said slowly, "but I swore I would never be imprisoned again."

"Let's just do this," Key said tightly.

"*Gable . . .*" Flynn said.

"These restraints are electrically unlocked," the woman noted. "Without the train's controls working properly, how will you unlock them?"

If it was up to Maddox, he wouldn't, but he didn't say that. "They have an override."

Gable looked from Flynn to Maddox, held his stare a moment, considering.

"As you wish, Marcus," Gable finally said. The tension dropped out of Key, but she held on to her knives nonetheless. "On one condition. I want to speak to you. Alone."

Maddox and Key both looked at Flynn suspiciously.

"Sure," Flynn told her. "Fine. Just, you know . . ." He nodded to the chains above her head.

Slowly, without looking up, she reached up and took one of the cuffs and locked it into place on her wrist. Then she did the same with the second one. When she was done, Gable hung from the chains, bound to the ceiling.

Key breathed a sigh of relief. Maddox didn't join her. He was still alert, and he'd stay that way while this woman was anywhere near Raelyn.

The doctor's hands moved over Zane. She was using what was left of her lab coat to rub something away from the big man's face. It wasn't blood. It was *silver*.

"What happened to him?" Maddox asked.

"I don't know," Flynn answered. "He looked out of it when he showed up. He looked weak."

Maddox's eyes thinned at the last word. Weakness wasn't anything he would ever associate with Zane.

"He told me before that if he drew too much power, it could kill him," Key said as she slipped the knives back into her jumpsuit.

"We should take him to the refrigerator car," Raelyn said.

"Why?" Maddox asked, already moving to grab one of Zane's arms. Key and Flynn moved to the man's legs.

"My guess is that when he draws power from metal, it heats him. He's burning to the touch. Dropping his temperature might help."

Together, they started pulling Zane into the next car. Maddox looked up at Flynn as they did. "Is there anything else you haven't told us?"

"No," Flynn said, hard, holding his gaze.

Maddox frowned, looked back down the line of chains on the ceiling until he found Gable. *Gabliella Rosetta.*

Her eyes were closed now. She seemed relaxed, she could have been sleeping from the look of it, hung by wrist cuffs in the rocking train car.

Maddox felt a chill all over again.

FIFTY-FOUR

COME WITH ME

Maddox stepped into the train engine cockpit, dragging the last of the equipment bags he'd taken from the armory.

He had no idea how he and Raelyn had gotten them all the way back to the train, much less how they had run while doing it, but they had. He'd learned long ago not to question what you could do on adrenaline.

Maddox found Raelyn curled up in one of the cockpit's big, cracked leather seats, the ground of the Razor, racing toward her, visible through the windscreen.

They'd only been moving for an hour, but the landscape was already changing drastically. The Razor included complete ecological zones, going from tundra on the Shadowsphere side to desert on the other, with everything in between. And it shifted quick.

The red sands were gone, but the land was still barren. Fields of yellowish-orange reeds stretched in both directions. By the time they reached the starport, everything would be green.

At the thought, Maddox's eyes followed the line of tracks that now stretched due east. Almost dead center rose the beacon.

They were maybe a hundred miles from it, and its sheer size was staggering. Maddox could see the clouds spinning, slowly and powerfully, around it.

Looking at it now was so different from the first time he'd seen it. Dragging Raelyn through the burning sand of the Cindersphere, both of them melting inside their rad-suits. Then, it had been a savior, guiding him east out of the heat. He wouldn't have made it without it. Neither would Raelyn. Now, though, it looked more and more like what it was. Something that didn't belong. And possibly something dangerous.

Next to him he heard a sound that, despite everything he'd been through, he'd never heard before. It was the sound of Raelyn crying.

She was curled up into a tight ball in the cockpit seat, and when Maddox looked down at her he winced. Her lab coat was gone, he could see all of her right arm. The glowing, vein-like lines had spread all the way to her shoulder.

She shuddered in the seat, head tucked into her arm.

Next to her, on the floor, was one of the autohypos, full of the brownish liquid. The only one left. The Scorpios had smashed the rest.

"I was the last to infect myself." Her voice was full of bitterness and pain. "I said we needed a control, needed to parse out the trials. The truth was, I was just scared. I didn't believe we really had it in us. I guess I was right."

"Stop it," Maddox said, bending down to pick up the hypo. "Use this."

"Why? It's not enough, not anymore."

"We're going to the starport. We're almost there."

"And how long will it take for the shuttle? How long will it take to reach an outpost or a command ship with a med bay?" More bitterness crept into her voice. "Days? Weeks? Do you know how far it will spread by then?"

Maddox didn't know what to say.

"I should just let Zane do what he offered." Her voice had a scary note to it now.

"*Stop it!*" Maddox made her look at him. "Don't go where you're going. I've been there."

"How would I know?" Her tone was harsh and sad. "You never tell me anything. You just stay shut down. You make me feel alone."

Maddox stared at her, torn. He knew what she wanted to hear.

"If I told you," he said, eyes still on her, trying to find the words, "you wouldn't—"

"Maybe I'd surprise you," she said. Then she moaned, curled up again, shuddered. "God, it hurts . . ."

Watching her there, shaking in the seat, rubbing her burning arm, the source of his hesitation became clear. If he told her, he might lose her. She might want nothing to do with him. She might never again look at him the way she sometimes had.

He was surprised. Not just that losing her would be painful, but that he could feel pain at all after everything he'd done. She had changed that. In this short amount of time. Made him care. Even more to his surprise, Maddox found he wanted to tell her.

"There was someone," he said, his voice wavering. "Someone I was supposed to save. I didn't."

Maddox told her everything. Whistler. Marcias. Canek.

As he did, Raelyn slowly uncurled in her seat. She turned and looked and listened. She didn't look judgmental, she didn't recoil. She just sat there and took it in.

When he was done, she raised her glowing right arm. Her fingers touched his face.

"I'm so sorry, James," she said. Maddox cupped her hand with his own. Her eyes, pain-free for the moment, bore into his. "Come *with* me."

Maddox looked back. It had been so long since he'd felt anything.

"If you come with me," she said, her voice almost a whisper. "I think I could make it."

Maddox stared into her blue eyes a moment more, then he just nodded.

Raelyn smiled, and the smile reached her eyes. The world raced past outside the windscreen, and the beacon loomed even larger.

FIFTY-FIVE

WINGS

When Zane woke, he was strangling someone.

A woman, squirming above him, trying to rip his fist off her throat with both hands.

The glaze in Zane's eyes bled away and he focused. It was the one with the wings and the bad attitude, the one more scared than she looked.

Zane let go and Key fell off him, to the floor, coughing raggedly.

"Fucking . . . hell," she gasped.

Zane blinked, didn't move. His head throbbed with intense pain. It felt like his skull was going to explode.

He remembered the chain room, how much metal he'd pulled into the Charge. Way too much. Zane remembered other things, too. The eggs lining the shaft, the black swarm that exploded out of them. The giant wall of fire bearing down on them from the west.

Key rolled onto her back next to him, still breathing hard.

"I'm sorry," Zane said, staring at the ceiling. "I was dreaming."

"Must have been a bad one."

Actually, it had been a dream of Astoria. A week they'd spent in a cabin on Rangoon, after they'd gone dark. It was a winter world, no real seasons, just snow and ice all orbit long. Astoria had never seen snow. She loved it. She caught snowflakes on her tongue and laughed all day.

Like that world, it was cold now, he noticed. He realized he was in the refrigerator car and the climate control bins were open, apparently in an effort to cool him off.

Everything rattled around Zane, the floor vibrating under him. He could feel the metal of the train car stretching forward, felt where it connected to the second car behind and into the engine ahead. He could feel the big metallic wheels sliding over the tracks, could feel the tracks stretching east into the distance.

"What happened?" he asked.

"The creature," Key said, her voice dark, "it was at the Barrier. Only a lot fucking *more* of it. It melted down an X-Core, same as last time. We barely made it through the tunnel before the wall came down."

"I saw it too," Zane said. "Where the chains were."

Key turned her head to him. "What do you think it is?"

Zane thought about it. "Just something trying to stay alive, like everything else. Something scared."

"It didn't look scared to me."

Zane tilted his head to look at her. "Different things show it in different ways."

Key stayed silent a moment. When she spoke next, Zane could barely hear her.

"One time, when I was a kid," she said, "my mom left me a week by myself, out scoring synth or some other bullshit. We were on Pantheon then. Closest thing to Earth I ever saw; nice terraforming. And I remember this storm came while I was alone. Lots of wind. Almost flipped over the old storage container we were living in. They have birds on Pantheon, did you know that? Big ones, huge wings. When the storm hit, I watched out the window, all fucking pathetic and crying because I was scared, and I saw one of those birds. It had its wings stretched out, and it just circled, rocked by the winds, just flying out there like it was any other day, back and forth. I watched that bird until the storm died, wishing I had its wings. Wishing I could fly and not be scared. If you have wings, storm winds don't matter."

Zane listened to it all. His eyes moved down her back. He could just see the faint beginning of the tattoos there.

"The first memory I have is waking up on a lab table and looking into purple eyes," he said.

"Purple?"

"She was strapped to the table next to me. Her name was Astoria. She became . . . important to me. From that moment on, we were never apart. Until recently. I always wondered who I would have been, if I hadn't woken up with *her*. Better or worse? I think worse."

He looked away from Key's tattoos, back up to her eyes.

"You can't be the bird," he told her. "Humans aren't built like that. Your problem is you think depending on someone else makes you weak. It doesn't. The reason you're scared is *because* you're alone. The wings you want aren't on the inside, or tattooed on your back. They're other people."

Key blew air out her nose sarcastically. "Pretty words from a man who doesn't need anybody."

"Do I look particularly self-reliant right now?" he asked without bitterness. He imagined that if he tried to stand, he'd fall over. The Charge was rebuilding itself, and him along with it. It would take time.

Key smiled thinly. "No, you look like shit, actually. More than usual." She was candid. Zane liked it.

"You're looking for the girl, aren't you?" Key asked. "The one with the purple eyes."

Zane nodded.

"She's your wings?"

Zane nodded again.

A strange look crossed Key's face. She looked past him, to the sealed door at the other end of the car.

"There's someone else here now," she told him. "The same bitch Flynn and I ran into at the black site."

Zane pushed his senses through the floor of the train car, feeling for the people inside it. He found her quickly, sensing her weight, the litheness in the way she stood. She was one car over, with Flynn. And she was bound with chains.

"Rosetta," he said. That complicated things in a way he didn't need. "How did she get here?"

"Fuck if I know." There was a note of fear in Key's voice. "Sounds like she saved Maddox and the doctor from some Scorpios, but I don't give a shit. If she's who you think she is, then she's as dangerous as anything on this fucking planet."

"I'll watch her."

Key frowned. "You can't even sit your ass up."

"I'll get better," he said pointedly.

Key glanced at the muzzle over his mouth. "Might get better a lot quicker if you took that stupid thing off your face."

At the mention, he felt it biting into the skin of his neck. He'd actually forgotten about it.

The door opened from the engine and Maddox stepped into their car. His eyes found Key quickly.

"You should see this," he said. "Get Flynn, too. If he isn't too busy with the witch."

FIFTY-SIX

DARKNESS

Gable studied Flynn, at the opposite end of the prisoner transport car, with her hands in the chains. He made no move to come closer, just watched her warily. He hadn't spoken since the others left. It disappointed her. He still had a long way to go.

"You seem on edge, Marcus," Gable observed. "Am I not chained? I did it for you—no small gesture. I did it so that you might feel *comfortable*. I know how important that is to you. The Razor, though . . . has become quite an uncomfortable place, hasn't it?"

"Why are you here?" Flynn asked, his voice shaky.

"Because we have much to do."

"There's nothing you want that I want, Gable."

"No?" Gable asked back. "It strikes me, Marcus, that you are much like a dog."

Flynn blinked, taken aback.

"With the others, I mean," Gable went on. "You are vital to their survival, but still you do as you're told, don't you? You put their needs first."

Flynn blinked again. "That's not—"

"Dogs are accommodating and obedient," she cut him off. "Willing to share their food or give up their bed when it is cold. They suffer for those who feed them, because they don't feed themselves. But what do you think happens to a dog, Marcus, when the wolves come? It is killed. It is *eaten*." As he listened, Flynn's gaze became heated. "Which would you rather be? A dog? Or a wolf? I can tell you which one you must be to survive this world, but I don't think I need to."

"I'm . . ." Flynn started, staring back at her, "I'm not—"

"I agree with you, Marcus. You aren't a dog, not really, but you *believe* you are, and that is the same thing. There is a darkness inside you. You ran from it. A long time ago. Didn't you?" Flynn stared back. She could hear the blood beginning to pulse in his veins. "But there are things we

| 315 |

cannot run from, parts of ourselves we cannot hide, and I can tell by the way your heart is beating right now that you know what I mean."

Flynn said nothing, just stared back at her with intensity.

"If you want to survive here, you will have to let your darkness out. And it is imperative that you survive."

"Why?"

Gable smiled again. The mere suggestion of being important always elicited a response from him. Gable noted it. "You are still planning to leave? To escape?"

He looked at her like she was crazy. "The world's burning."

"What if it wasn't?" she asked.

"It's a *prison* planet."

"And you won't be in prison if you leave? The ones whose bargain you've accepted, they won't lock you away just the same?"

Flynn faltered. "I don't . . . There's no other option."

"Answer the question. What *if* you could stay?"

He stared at her a moment. She could hear his breathing pick up in pace. Thoughts were swimming in his head, ones he didn't like, ones he probably entertained only briefly before pushing them away, because they frightened him, made him question who he really was.

That was all very good.

"There is no one else here, Marcus," she said, soft and slow. "No one is close enough to listen. If they were, I would hear them." Gable added a note of warmth to her voice. "I am the last person who will ever judge you. I don't believe in it."

Flynn stared at her another moment, thinking it through.

"Before . . . it was . . ." he began.

"What?" Gable prompted gently.

"All I wanted," Flynn said. "To get my life back. How it used to be. I had so many plans before, but they were taken away."

Gable smiled. "And now, Marcus?"

The words started to form, but he shook his head. "It doesn't make any *rational* sense."

"Say it anyway."

"Before I came here, everything I did was for someone else. It's why I wanted my own company, why I wanted to leave M-D. But . . . since I've been on the Razor . . . everything I've done has . . ."

"Mattered," Gable finished for him.

Flynn nodded. "It's been life or death. It's . . . *mattered*." He looked up at her with a look that suggested he was coming to conclusions. "You're right. Even if we get out of here and I go back, nothing would really change. It would be just another cell—nicer maybe, but still a cell. They'd never let me go. They'd use me until they couldn't anymore. And everything I did there, it would be for them, not *me*. It wouldn't feel like *this*; it wouldn't feel like it does here."

Gable felt warm. They were more alike than he would be comfortable knowing.

"There are ways . . ." she told him.

"How? The UEG will come back. The Razor's too important."

"More important than you imagine. But there are *ways*. It will require difficult choices. Choices that will no doubt haunt you, but nothing worth having ever comes without cost, Marcus. I know of what I speak."

Flynn's look and mood darkened. He studied her differently. "*Are* you Dr. Rosetta?"

Gable clucked her tongue in disappointment. "Oh, Marcus. We were getting along so well."

"I answered *you*," he said pointedly.

"My given name is Gabliella Rosetta," she said, and watched as he took the expected step backward. "But I have grown in many ways since. I continue to grow. As do we all."

"What did that thing tell you in the labs?" Flynn asked directly.

"It conveyed what it wished, and I understood."

His stare hardened. "*What* did it tell you?"

"All it knew," Gable answered. "But only half."

Flynn stared back, unsatisfied. He wanted to know. It was his strength, that trait. Insatiable curiosity. It was also his weakness. For a moment, she considered telling him. All of it. Everything she knew. It would be a risk, revealing it. It would take a special mind to hear these particular truths and not take the off-world shuttle they were being offered, even if it meant just another cell. But Flynn . . . he might very well be that mind. In fact, she was counting on it.

But she had to be certain first.

Gable sensed a new presence coming from the train engine, could hear feet on the floor. "We must continue this later, I'm afraid."

The door from the refrigerator car opened.

The woman with the wings. Key. She stood there, and her eyes went to

Flynn. She refused to look at Gable. But the glance she gave Flynn was suspicious at best.

"Maddox wants us up front," Key said tightly, forcing her eyes up to Gable's, making herself hold them. "When you're *done*."

Then she disappeared back through the door.

Flynn looked back to Gable with an uncertain stare, before he followed after Key.

Complications were ensuing, as they inevitably would. Gable hung in her chains once more, waiting patiently. Like always.

FIFTY-SEVEN

FULL THROTTLE

Flynn stepped into the engine room, with Key right behind him. He'd felt her eyes on him the whole walk from the prisoner car to the cockpit, but she hadn't said anything. She was clearly suspicious about the talk he'd had with Gable, and probably mad that he hadn't told her everything.

There just hadn't been time. They'd been going full throttle since the black site's X-Core meltdown.

You had time to listen to her bare her feelings, though, didn't you? Time to kiss her.

Though, admittedly, it was really more like *she'd* kissed *him*. Jesus, he could still feel her against him.

But, judging by her glare, she wasn't in the mood to repeat that anytime soon.

At the front of the engine car, the landscape flared by outside the windshield. Green now. Rolling hills, some mountains in the distance, spots of trees. Keep going east, Flynn knew, and it would be even lusher. Forests, swamps, jungles, before it all began to thin out again and grow cold and dark.

Where they were headed was right in front of them, Flynn saw. And his eyes widened in amazement.

"My God," he breathed, stepping up to the front of the cockpit.

The starport stood in the distance, illuminated by the faint, brownish light of the sun, buried and frozen on the horizon. Flynn could see the buildings from here, the warehouses and dormitories, the giant pyramid terminal building, made of clear polysteel, glittering in the permanent dusk. The highest of them was the control tower, in the center, a needle-like structure, part control center and part deep space transmission relay. And it was all surrounded by the giant fortified wall of concrete that wrapped around the facility in a kind of figure eight pattern.

But most all of it was obscured by plumes of rising smoke. Lights flashed from the top of the wall, bolts of energy flaring downward and then billowing up in flame and shrapnel from the ground.

It was an automated defense system—gun turrets, Flynn guessed, magnetically shielded—and it was working overtime right now.

Even from this distance, ten miles maybe, the crowd of people outside was clearly visible. It looked like a swarm of ants attempting to overrun a toy fort.

Inmates. A thousand or more, lining the length of the starport's wall, trying to breach it, but then being repelled by the autoturrets on the walls. Flynn wondered how high the bodies were stacked at the base of the fortifications.

"Fucking Razor," Key said. "When do we catch a break?"

"What did you expect?" Maddox asked. He was standing at the train's controls, watching the action they were quickly coming up on. "That beam is like a giant X on a map. Every prisoner who escaped on this side of the Barrier would make a beeline for it."

"There's only maybe a thousand inmates outside," Key stated, staring into the distance.

"There'll be more soon," Maddox said grimly. "A lot more, coming from all over the Razor; all the different installations, all the different Crawlers. This place will be overrun, and those turrets won't be enough."

Flynn stared past Maddox and Key.

Even through the thick haze of smoke in the air, the beacon flared, its powerful light diffracting into glittering starbursts.

It was unbelievably massive now, streaking straight upward and through the strange glowing, circling clouds above it.

Flynn's mind struggled to make sense of what he was seeing. No technology he knew of would produce an effect like this. And it seemed to be shooting straight up through the *middle* of the starport.

Flynn felt his heart start to pound. There was a mystery here, something to solve, and as dire as the situation was, it drew him.

"Can we get through?" a weaker voice asked, next to Maddox.

It was Raelyn's voice, and there was a notable edge to it now. Flynn looked down and saw her crumpled in one of the cockpit seats. There was an empty autohypo on the control bank, and Flynn looked at her arm.

When he did, he winced.

The entire appendage was lined with the glowing, vein-like growths. He couldn't imagine the pain.

Flynn noticed she was holding Maddox's hand as she sat there. Tightly.

"The gate *will* open, right?" Maddox asked, looking at Flynn.

Flynn thought about it, nodded. "The wall looks powered, otherwise the turrets wouldn't be firing, so the train gates probably are, too."

"It doesn't need a transponder on the train?"

Flynn shook his head. "It's all pneumatic, just a pressure switch on the rail."

"Bigger issue is all the fuckheads outside," Key said, staring through the windscreen at the mass of prisoners outside the wall. "They'll see us for miles. To them, this train is their ticket inside the starport."

"She's right," Maddox agreed. He moved for the rear of the engine car. Sitting there were the gear bags he'd managed to drag back from the armory before the Barrier imploded. He started zipping them open. "They'll try and board us."

"What do we do?" Flynn asked warily, though he was already getting the gist.

"Run the gauntlet." Maddox grabbed two big guns out of one bag and a dozen or so ammo clips from a second. The weapons looked brand-new, modular most likely, ballistic, not pulse, with black polycarbon bodies and long barrels. Assault rifles.

"Fucking A." Key moved eagerly toward Maddox. The Ranger kicked one of the weapons toward her and she grabbed it off the floor.

"Code is all eights," he told her. "You know what to do after that?"

Key flicked a switch near the trigger and a holo display glowed to life in the air. She keyed in four eights on the virtual keypad, and the handle near the barrel glowed green. She gripped it, waited until it flashed again. "Damn straight."

She slammed an ammo clip into the carrier, then yanked back the firing pin.

Key seemed more at ease now than anytime Flynn had ever seen her. Something about her holding the rifle like that, the glint in her eyes, made him wish they were alone . . .

"Feel better?" he asked her.

She smiled broader. "Keep it in your pants, tough guy."

Flynn barely caught the handgun that Maddox threw him. He eyed it hesitantly.

"We can't let them in here," Maddox said pointedly.

Flynn nodded, looking at the weapon. *If you draw, you pull.*

"If we go full speed, it'll make it harder for them to board," Key said.

"Can we stop, once we pass through the gate?" Maddox asked.

It was a good question. The yard was meant for trains coming in at minimum speed, not full throttle. It would be packed with all kinds of flammable objects.

"I'll do my best," Flynn said.

"Guys . . ." Raelyn said.

Everyone looked back out the windscreen. They were in the smoke now, and the starport rose ahead of them. Flynn could see a mass of prisoners up ahead, running full force to intercept them. A hundred. Maybe two. All different colored jumpsuits.

Ahead, the tracks stretched forward another mile and then dead-ended at the train gate set into the fortified wall.

Flynn swallowed. This was it.

Maddox kissed Raelyn's forehead. "Strap in." She nodded, started following his advice.

Flynn looked at Key. She looked back. "Don't kill us," she said, then crawled outside the door of the engine car, scampering onto the roof with Maddox as the train darted forward.

Flynn moved to the controls. His hand rested on the throttle.

"Shit," Raelyn said in a shaky voice, buckling into the seat.

"Yeah," Flynn agreed.

The giant column of energy towered over everything, shooting into the sky. They were here. They had made it. But things were far from resolved.

Flynn swallowed nervously . . . then pushed the throttle forward to full.

FIFTY-EIGHT

GAUNTLET

Key slipped hard as she tried to pull herself onto the roof of the rocking train car, and Maddox grabbed her by the shoulders and yanked her the rest of the way.

She glared up at the Ranger. "I had that."

"Clearly." He moved off, somehow balancing on top of the slick, metallic roof like he'd done it a hundred times. Maybe he had. It didn't mean she had to be fucking impressed.

Key grabbed the rifle from her back and rolled over onto her belly. Much better. She felt more stable, less likely to go spilling over the side at eighty miles an hour.

"How's your distance shot?" Maddox asked, flipping a switch on his rifle. The barrel and stock extended, a scope snapped up, the reticle inside lighting green. Sniper configuration.

Key rolled her eyes, raised her own rifle just like it was.

About five hundred yards out was the first mass of inmates, hauling ass. Blue, red, green, all different colors. Key tapped the trigger six times.

Six people fell in the distance, got trampled by the others.

Key looked at Maddox. He looked back, impressed. "Don't need much of a fucking distance shot with them clumped up like that."

"Fair enough," Maddox replied. "Hit 'em."

Maddox and Key opened fire as one, bullets streaking outward as the train roared forward.

The inmates fell in batches, going down hard, run over by the ones around them. Every time, the survivors hesitated for a second, then picked up the pace toward the train. Maybe they'd already been desensitized by the autoturrets. Maybe they understood that the train was their last chance to find a ship off this world. Either way, they kept coming.

Key studied the prisoners as they got closer.

Every color of jumpsuit you could think of, working together. Key grudgingly admitted that there was something cool about it, even if they were trying to board the train and kill them all.

Maddox and Key kept firing, bursts of muzzle flashes ripping the air.

Goddamn, it felt good to fire a gun again. Rifles, knives, and sex had always been the three things that quelled her fear. But she'd never had a taste of a life where fear wasn't lurking somewhere in the background. Not until she'd met the idiot downstairs, driving the train. Somehow, he made it feel like she was going to be okay. Even now.

Key remembered kissing Flynn in the Barrier. The electricity of it. He was a skinny little brainiac, and yet he'd heated her up more than anyone had in a long time. What the fuck did she do with that?

"The gate!" Maddox yelled.

Key looked, saw what he meant.

A gate in the wall blocking the tracks was sliding open. On the other side she saw plenty of bad news. Other trains, dozens of them. Buildings and warehouses. Gas tanks. Cranes for on-loading and off-loading. Auto-loaders. All things they were going to slam into if Flynn didn't stop this hunk of junk.

Key could tell that wasn't going to happen.

"We're not gonna be able to—"

"No!" Maddox yelled. His gun flared in full-auto mode now. The inmates had reached the train. Of the ones dumb enough to try and leap on, the vast majority got thrown backward when they hit the train, spinning wildly into the grass. The rest, she and Maddox blew away before they managed to get a second handhold.

"We gotta jump!" Maddox yelled.

Key spun to him, eyes wide. "Are you fucking kidd—"

Maddox jumped. He disappeared over the side.

"Shit," she yelled, and then she was jumping too.

FIFTY-NINE

STARPORT

Flynn woke to Raelyn tapping him lightly on the face.

She was disheveled, hair in her eyes, a gash on her cheek, but she seemed okay.

"Flynn," she said, snapping her fingers in front of his face.

His brain started working again. He remembered wiring the train's brakes into the reactor power as the train burst through the gate into the starport. Everything had thundered around him as the machine slammed into whatever was in front of it. The world went orange-white through the windshield and shook itself apart as the train tore loose and slammed into the ground on the outside.

"*Hey.*" Raelyn tapped him on the face again. "Flynn. Come back to me. Come back."

"What . . ." He started, his head still full of static.

"Follow my finger," she said, holding up a single digit. With his eyes, he tracked it back and forth a few times.

"Good. Move your legs and arms, one at a time, and *slow*," she told him. Flynn did. They hurt, all four of them, but they moved. "You're in one piece," she declared.

He felt a slight breeze on his face, realized he was outside the train now.

"That was the worst fucking braking I've ever seen," Key said, appearing above him. Flynn felt relief when he saw her. She was covered in dust, had some cuts, but she looked okay, too. Maddox was next to her and looked about the same.

Flynn sat up. Smoke and dust were everywhere. He looked back along the rail line to where the gate was closed again. None of the inmates had made it in, and the autoturrets were flashing and raining down death on the wall at the edge of the yard.

"What about Zane?" Raelyn asked, still catching her breath. "And . . . *her.*"

Flynn remembered. Zane was in the refrigerator car, Gable chained in another part of the train.

It looked like the engine had come loose when it hit the rear of another train and sent both of them flying, ripping trenches into the ground. What was left of a gas tank sat burning nearby.

Their two cars, though, were still on the tracks. They were buckled and leaning opposite directions, but they were in one piece.

"If anyone could survive that impact, it's those two," Maddox said. "We've got bigger problems."

Flynn followed his gaze straight upward. The beacon hung over everything. It was enormous, maybe two hundred yards in diameter, a pure, throbbing, solid beam of red energy that shot into the sky.

As Flynn had guessed, it was right in the middle of the starport. In fact, it was shooting straight up out of the main terminal building. It was a giant structure, shaped like a pyramid, its exterior made almost entirely out of polysteel, and there was a hole in the top, where the beam hadn't just punched through it but had *melted* it.

Flynn had never seen anything like it. He didn't even know if the melting point of polysteel was a published statistic, but there it was. The entire top of the clear structure had bubbled and cascaded down its sides as the beam pushed through.

"Fucking hell," Key moaned, looking past the terminal, following the beam with her eyes.

Flynn saw what she did. They weren't the only ones who had made it past the perimeter wall.

The huge swarm of blackness from Site Eleven surged and writhed in the air, circling the beam, back and forth, in a massive cloud of darkness. The comparison between the two, dark and light, was staggering.

"It's *here*?" Raelyn asked, with a note of fear. "Why is it here?"

"Drawn here like everything else?" Maddox wondered.

Flynn didn't think so. Whatever the thing was, it wasn't just working on instinct. Gable had communicated with it. According to her, it had expressed desires. Motivations. It was *intelligent*.

As he stared at the swarm, his eyes followed the beam higher and higher, to where it passed through the churning clouds. Something occurred to him then. Something critical and staggering.

"The beam is blocking the EM tunnel," Flynn stated.

Everyone looked away from the swarm back to him.

"How the hell do you know that?" Key asked.

The starport's main terminal building, shaped like a pyramid, had been designed to point straight up through the Razor's EM tunnel, the only clear access point through the planet's charged ionosphere. And the beacon was shooting straight through the pyramid's apex.

"It's shooting right through the tunnel," Flynn said. "If it's enough to melt polysteel, then it's enough to . . ."

"Seal off the planet," Maddox said.

Key looked around the starport. Visible here and there were the various landing pads for different ships. All deep space freighters, all magnetically shielded. "Any one of these things would fly . . ."

"But you'd never make it off the surface," Flynn finished for her. And if you couldn't take off, you couldn't land, either. Which meant their shuttle wasn't showing up anytime soon.

"That's why we haven't seen any Ranger squads or guards redeployed to the planet," Maddox said, staring at the beam. "They can't get here."

This was certainly the problem the Suit wanted Flynn to solve. If he could open the EM tunnel, then the shuttle could land, they could be rescued. But how?

"What do we do?" Raelyn asked.

Everyone looked at Flynn. He looked back. He had no clue where to even start.

A buzzing filled the air suddenly. The smoke from the gas fire swirled as something tiny, with flashing blue and red lights, appeared through the haze, hovering in the air.

Key raised her rifle, but Maddox stopped her. "Wait."

Flynn saw why. It wasn't one of the swarm; it was a drone. A tiny one, with four props, carrying a small camera under its belly. The camera whirred as it focused and shifted, and the machine didn't stop until it hovered directly in front of Flynn.

Everyone just stared at the hovering device in confusion.

"I hate this planet," Key said.

An idea occurred to Flynn. He took a step toward the drone. It moved backward with him. He took a step back. The drone didn't move, just hovered in place.

Flynn took another step forward and the drone moved backward again. Flynn took more steps and the drone turned and flew ahead, weaving through the wreckage from the train engine crash.

"It wants us to follow," he said, and quickly walked forward.

"Flynn, wait!" Raelyn yelled, but he was already moving, picking a path through the trains and the autoloaders and storage units in the train yard, following after the drone as it whizzed through the air.

A minute later they were at the opposite end of the yard, where a strange set of nondescript concrete stairs descended into the ground. The drone buzzed downward toward the door at the bottom, and Flynn followed.

It was almost dark at the bottom, with the dim light outside, but he still could see a massive fortified composite-steel door inset there. A camera and security scanner were embedded above the door. Whatever was on the other side, it didn't seem like something just anyone got to see.

Flynn's heart beat a little quicker.

The tiny drone hovered next to a glowing control panel, which, similar to the ones at Site Eleven, showed a red outline of a hand.

"More security doors," Key moaned.

The others had all followed Flynn down, and they stood behind him now, watching. Maddox reached forward, toward the control panel.

"Hey . . ." Raelyn said, but Maddox ignored her, placed his hand on the screen.

It beeped and then flashed red. Nothing happened.

"Great. Locked. Let's go," Key said, grabbing Flynn's arm.

"Wait," he said. Why would the drone lead him here if it was just a dead end? Slowly he reached over and placed his own hand on the panel.

It beeped, and then flashed green.

The door groaned as it slid open, slowly and powerfully, revealing a large room beyond. The drone hovered through the door and disappeared.

"It opened for you," Key told him, stating the obvious. Flynn looked at her. "That's not a good sign."

No question she was right. Someone wanted him right here, right now, in this spot. But Flynn didn't care. The answers were inside. He knew it. This was the only way forward he could see.

Flynn and the rest stepped cautiously through the door.

The room was a semicircle, its only wall a rounded, clear surface of polysteel. Computers hummed everywhere. Terminals flashed, holo displays glowed in the air. It was a control center. A huge one.

And outside the windows was a giant cavern.

It plummeted down into the distance and stretched maybe two miles in every direction, its rocky walls visible in the distance. Hundreds of lighting rigs had been installed throughout, but right now they weren't needed.

In the center, on an island of rock surrounded by a drop-off, sat a massive machine, filling most of the huge cave with its metallic presence. Oblong and weirdly shaped, its surface was pure silver, and the cavern's lights reflected off it brightly.

It looked like a huge sculpture, elegant and beautiful, and Flynn had never seen a design like it. What stood out, though, more than anything else, was the giant red beam shooting from the top of the silver machine and through the ceiling above. It was the source of the beacon.

As Flynn looked closer, he saw something else. Objects circled the beam in the cavern, round and round it in the air.

Computers. Desks. Rad-suits. Workbenches. Electronics and tools. All circling the energy column like electrons around a nucleus.

It was mesmerizing to look at.

The monitors in the control center suddenly all flashed as one. The image of a person appeared on them, staring through the screens.

But it was not the Suit. It was the last person Flynn ever expected to see.

A woman. In her seventies, but vibrant, eyes still sharp. She wore glasses, and Flynn could just see the hem of a lab coat on her shoulders.

"Marcus," she said, a slight smile in her voice.

Flynn knew her well. He'd worked for her. Her name was Evelyn Maas, half the power at the most powerful corporation in the galaxy, Maas-Dorian.

And, not all that long ago, she had framed him for murder.

"It's so good to see you."

SIXTY

BETTER DEALS

Flynn stared at the woman's features on the monitors in front of him, while random objects floated in circles around the giant beam in the cavern on the other side of the glass.

"Dr. Maas." Flynn didn't even attempt to hide the animosity he felt. This woman had taken everything from him. He wanted to smash the monitors that held her image.

"You may be skeptical to hear it," Maas said, "but I am very glad to see you alive. You've arrived almost too late."

Flynn recognized the background behind Maas. The metal bookshelves that ran the entire length of the wall behind her desk, full of tech journals and glowing holo frames, all in the same position as the last time he'd seen them. Something about the fact that she was communicating with him in the comfort of her own office, like they were having a project status meeting, made him even angrier.

"Skeptical doesn't begin to describe what I'm feeling," he retorted. Key looked at him in a different way. She'd never heard him speak in that tone before.

"You should know that it was Francis's idea to fabricate the charges against you," Maas said.

Francis Dorian, her partner and cofounder.

"And you . . . what?" Flynn asked. "Knew nothing? Disagreed? Is that what you're going to say?"

"I cannot say that, no," she said evenly, removing her glasses and placing them gently onto her desk. "I signed off on the idea. It seemed logical at the time."

Flynn's fists clenched at his side. "Logical . . ."

"You were an incredibly valuable resource, but we would have lost you either way. Your patent was brilliant, and it was a threat. It would have made you a rival overnight."

Flynn felt a grudging sense of appeasement. Evelyn's voice was calm, like it always was, but Flynn could see the lines under her eyes. She was tired; what was happening on the Razor was becoming a strain.

"I don't expect you to understand," she continued. "You've never built something from the ground up, seen it flourish and grow. It becomes your whole self, it becomes you—and you wouldn't allow someone to harm you, would you, Dr. Flynn?"

He said nothing. Could hear himself breathing heavily.

"But in hindsight . . . it was a mistake." Maas looked uncomfortable for a moment. "You are five times the mind Francis and I thought."

"How flattering," Flynn said.

"You've made a deal with someone else, our intelligence tells us. A deal to extricate you from this planet, with the data drive you're carrying."

He pulled the wires of the drive tighter to him. He could sense her trepidation. Whatever was on this drive, losing it would hurt. Good. He *wanted* to hurt her.

"Site Eleven is gone, destroyed by the Cindersphere's expansion," Dr. Maas said. "That drive is the only record of the research we were conducting. It is incredibly valuable."

"Come and get it," Flynn said.

"That is exactly what I would like to do, Marcus. I would like to make you a . . . more *substantial* offer than our competition. Free passage off the Razor, of course, but instead of an existence hiding for the rest of your life, in a role where your talents would never be recognized or acknowledged, I would offer you . . . your life *back*. As it was. Intact."

"What a load of horseshit," Key said behind him. Flynn was inclined to agree.

"Look outside," Maas continued, "through the containment shield."

Flynn did, his eyes finding the beam that shot from the strange, gleaming machine below.

"I was standing where you are two weeks ago," Maas said. "I've spent a great deal of time on the Razor because of this machine."

"How did you build this?" Flynn asked, still amazed by the sight of it.

"We did not build this, Marcus. No human built it."

It took a moment for the weight of her words to filter through his brain. He looked back at Maas on the monitor, his eyes wide.

"Precisely," she said, reading his expression. "Our anthropologists have dated the machine as something in the order of eleven thousand years old."

Flynn heard the reactions from the people in the room with him. They were as stunned as he was.

"We labeled the device Artifact A. It was found at the groundbreaking for the starport fifty-two years ago, buried by eons of dirt and tectonic shifting. Its placement, we came to understand, was not by coincidence. The beam has two purposes. To seal off the EM tunnel with a super-powerful, high-throughput magnetic beam—"

"And to deplete the atmosphere of the Razor," Flynn finished for her. Part of it was what he had guessed earlier, back at Site Eleven. Part of it was new, and he was starting to understand the reasons.

Maas seemed impressed. "Correct. The other sites we have found have given our anthropologists clues, but no true definitive theories, as to this planet's previous occupiers' culture or motivations, though they clearly relied on Xytrilium as a power source."

Flynn only heard a small part of what Maas had said; the rest faded into the background. "Other sites?" His pulse began to quicken.

"Oh yes, Marcus." Maas began typing on a keyboard, offscreen in front of her. "Currently, there are nine active dig sites on the planet, within all three of its zones."

A giant holographic image of the planet appeared, rotating in front of them in the room. One side was red, representing the Cindersphere. The other side was blue, representing the Shadowsphere. Running in between them was a thin, long strip of green.

Markers flared to life on the holographic planet, with designation information and coordinates. Each one was labeled.

Artifact B . . . Artifact C . . . Artifact D . . .

Most of the markers were up and down the length of the Razor, but several of them were much farther away, in the blue and red zones. Some of them very, very deep into those zones.

Flynn stared in fascination, his mind racing. Eight more sites like this one. *Eight . . .*

Not just *evidence* of alien life—something that, in all its expansion, humanity had never encountered—but actual, physical, working technology. Flynn couldn't help it. He smiled. The possibilities for research and knowledge were staggering.

"The creature you encountered at the black site was found at Artifact F, a site deep in the Cindersphere," Maas said, and the map flashed. The other markers vanished, leaving only one of them, deep in the red zone.

"It took a sizable amount of research and investment to access the site, given the extreme radiation. You would have found the work fascinating, I think, Marcus. When we breached it, it initially seemed far less interesting than we hoped. A single room, sealed, but channeling the radiation above. Flooding the room with it, in fact."

"And that fucking thing was inside it," Key said, and Flynn almost jumped. In the excitement of what Maas was saying, he'd forgotten the others were there.

"A solidified, inactive version, yes," Maas continued, "compacted in an incredibly dense spherical mass. We didn't even recognize it as a life form until we removed it from the site. But on its way back to the hot labs, it began to . . . desolidify."

"Because the heat was removed," Raelyn stated, figuring it out.

"Yes," Maas said. "The only thing that seems to contain it, though only to an extent. The team transporting it encountered a great deal of difficulty en route to Site Eleven."

"I bet they did," Maddox said darkly.

"With a source of organic material," Maas continued, "it can alter its organism into any form it wants. But it needs one other component to do so."

"Power," Key said.

"Xytrilium, to be specific. The creature's molecular structure is, in many ways, incredibly similar to that of raw Xytrilium. Observe."

Maas hit more keys. The hologram shifted into two series of complicated and jumbled hexagons and lines that Flynn recognized as polymorphic molecular structure maps. Maddox and Key looked at them like they were Greek. Flynn and Raelyn, though, studied them intently. The structures, as Maas said, were very similar.

"It can feed off raw Xytrilium at an unsettling rate. With processed X, it is orders of magnitude higher in efficiency. It can drain the power from a standard-bandwidth X-Core in a matter of hours."

Flynn kept staring at the molecular maps, mystified.

"It is an amazing organism. If it could be made docile," Maas mused, almost to herself, "perhaps by stunting its brain activity, there are a host of applications that—"

"You gotta be fucking kidding me," Key spat, staring at the woman on the monitor. "Your people aren't just dead back at the lab, lady, they're goddamned fused together. And you wanna make a pet out of it?"

"Science always comes with risks," Maas said with severity.

"Tell that to your lab team," Key said hotly. "You people are all the same. Making everyone else do all the shit you're too scared to do. If you were here, I'd slit your throat, end to end."

"Can we get back to the giant energy beam, please?" Raelyn interjected, before Key could unleash more venom.

"What does it have to do with the thing outside?" Maddox clarified.

"Artifact A became active at almost exactly the same moment that Site Eleven initiated its quarantine lockdown," Maas said.

Flynn got it then. It all made sense. He had no idea if that black, swarming mass above was an indigenous creature or something else, but someone had been very worried it might break out of its prison one day. "It's a fail safe," he said. A powerful one. If the creature ever reconstituted itself, the beacon would activate and do two things: first, drain the Razor of its atmosphere, letting the heat of the Cindersphere rush in and hopefully contain the thing before it got going. And second, seal off the EM Tunnel, so no one else could land on the surface and make the same mistake they had.

Maas nodded. "The creature, in its inactive form, is virtually indestructible. We believe it was imprisoned at Artifact F."

"And you fucking woke it up . . ." Key said icily.

"A mistake, without question. One of several. But all mistakes can be rectified."

"By *us*, you mean." Key stated flatly.

"You mentioned something before about a deal," Maddox said. "A *better* deal."

"If the beam is allowed to deplete the Razor," Dr. Maas said, "the planet will no longer be accessible. That means we would lose all the work we have done here. As well as our source of Xytrilium. The corporation finds that scenario unacceptable."

Flynn could see where this was going, where the negotiations would lead. He was right there, on the cusp of getting exactly what he'd wanted since his sentencing. Maas was desperate. So why wasn't he elated?

The holographic map reappeared in the center of the room, floating in bright, prismatic color, the markers of all the different sites standing out.

"Look at the map again, Marcus," Maas said. "I know it holds the same allure for you that it does for me. You can't even imagine what the other sites contain. The creature, this device below, they are just the *beginning*.

Stop the Razor from shrinking, return our data, and you can lead the research on any dig site you want. Think of it, Marcus."

Flynn's eyes moved to Key, then Maddox, and finally Raelyn. She was holding her right arm, the glowing veins of the Slow Burn all over it, peeking through the gaps in her fingers.

Unless he took this deal, she wouldn't last long.

Then again, if he didn't take the deal, none of them would. Saying no meant being burned to cinders.

"My friends," Flynn said. "I want them freed too. *Really* freed, not hunted. Records closed, all of it."

Maas smiled on the monitor. "Anything can be arranged. But *you* must deliver."

Flynn thought about it. "You said it was a magnetic beam?"

"An incredibly tightly focused one," Maas replied.

Flynn suddenly understood. "It's puncturing the magnetosphere."

Maddox looked at him, confused. "What does that—"

"It's drilling a hole in it," Flynn explained. "And that hole is letting the solar wind from the star strip out the Razor's atmosphere. Any other planet, it would take a decade, maybe two, to drain away the atmosphere, but the Razor's so small compared to the rest, and the Cindersphere is such a powerful opposing force, it's happening in days."

"Days until the process *completes*," Maas said, with a troubling tone, "but, by our calculations, less than an hour until the process can no longer be *reversed*. At that point, even with the beam turned off, too much of the Razor will have vanished to push back the Cindersphere's heat."

Everyone looked at the monitor with supremely grim looks.

"As I said," Maas continued, "you arrived almost too late."

"How do we shut it down?" Raelyn asked.

"There is a control center at the base of the device. However, our linguists have been unable to decipher the controls. Our only hope, Dr. Flynn, is that you can succeed where they have failed."

Flynn swallowed. *No pressure.*

"And the environment inside?" Maddox said, looking past the monitors and into the cavern, at the hundreds of objects circling around the magnetic beam. "You got stuff flying around that beam like its attracting it."

"It is, in fact," Maas agreed. "Magnetically *and* gravitationally. The field, however, extends only a few feet from the beam. Stay out of its perimeter and it won't affect you."

Maas's eyes bored into Flynn's then. He stared back just as intense.

"Would you like to come home, Dr. Flynn?" she asked pointedly. "This does *not* have to be your life."

The words hit hard. It was what he'd held out hope for, all this time. But, for some reason, he had no idea what to say.

So he simply nodded.

SIXTY-ONE

THREES

They made it to the base of the device in less than a minute, running down a circular railing that descended from the control center. They passed through a work area that had been set up near the edge of the drop-off. It was full of computers, workbenches, and other equipment, all of it still humming and brightly lit, surrounded by a gridwork of scaffolding that held wires and cables and larger sensory equipment.

A railing traversed the giant pit around the machine, and Key looked down as they crossed it. She couldn't see the bottom, which made her very uncomfortable.

But that was nothing compared to what she felt when they reached the base of the machine. She stared up at the giant silver device, along with everyone else, stunned. Goddamn, it was beyond massive. And fucking horrifying.

Eleven *thousand* years old? And it was still polished to a mirror finish. Angular in some places, rounded in others, it was clearly anything but human made. The worst part was that it didn't make a damn sound. The beam, sure. There was a strange rhythmic humming coming from it as it ripped the air above them, but from the giant, silver, smooth-skinned device, there was no sound at all.

Something about that made Key's wings itch badly, made her feel small.

"She said there were controls," Maddox said, the look on his face suggesting he felt similar to Key. "But I don't see any terminals, or even any buttons."

Flynn stepped closer, eyes moving all over the thing. He look enraptured, and it pissed Key off. "Maybe it's—"

The air in front of them suddenly lit up in beautiful, mesmerizing color. The air filled with shapes. Icons, Key thought. All of them angular and three-sided. Some by themselves, some connected by anchor points to the others.

They spun and hovered all around the viewers in glowing red and orange light, the color reflecting brightly on the machine in front of them.

"Dear Lord . . ." Raelyn breathed next to Key, staring at it all like it was beautiful. Key didn't share the sentiment. To her, none of it made sense; the lights were frightening.

"Okay," Flynn said, reaching forward to touch one of the icons, like a little kid with a new toy.

"Flynn!" Key admonished, too late.

He touched one of the symbols. There was a sudden flash from the others. They all turned and morphed into different symbols, and the one he'd touched went pure white in the air.

On the machine, new symbols appeared, also angular and three-sided, glowing in color, standing out against the metallic background.

"What in hell . . ." Raelyn said.

"It's the controls," Flynn said. "Touching the ones in the air reveals them on the machine."

"Why?"

"I . . ." Flynn started, thinking, "have no clue."

"Well, we better get a fucking clue, really fast," Key told him.

Flynn stared at the symbols in both locations. In the air in front of them, and on the machine itself. "There's something about this . . ."

"No shit," Maddox said, perplexed. He gripped the rifle in his hands tighter.

Flynn touched more of the floating symbols. Again, they shifted. More controls appeared on the machine.

"Flynn . . ." Key said, watching him, "do you have any idea what you're doing?"

"I think . . ."

He touched another—and then all the color faded away. The controls on the machine went dark. The icons in the air flashed off.

A few seconds later the symbols flashed back to life, but in their original configuration, just like they had been at first. The whole process, whatever the hell it was, had started over.

"Huh," Flynn said. "I think . . . They're not icons. They're not even alphabetic symbols."

"Numbers?" Raelyn asked, just as fascinated.

"Yeah," Flynn said, looking at the doctor. "Numbers. And I think they're in groups of three."

"Threes?" Maddox asked.

Flynn thought about it a second. "We think in groups, number-wise. Batches. For us, it's batches of ten."

"Ten tens is a hundred," Raelyn said, following his train of thought. "Ten hundreds a thousand. Maybe whoever *they* are, they think in threes. Or they used to . . ."

Key looked closer at the symbols. She recognized the shapes now. Triangles. All the symbols in the air were variations of triangles.

"So what the fuck is it?" she asked. "Math class?"

"Actually . . ." Flynn said, looking at her. "I think it is. I think it's a codex."

Key stared at him, feeling very out of place.

"The key to a cryptogram," Flynn clarified. "The *source* code to something. I think maybe it's designed to teach their number system."

"Why do that?" Maddox asked.

"Maybe they expected others to find this," Raelyn said. "Maybe they want to show us how to use the machine."

"Which means we can turn it off," Maddox said, looking at Raelyn.

Above them came a giant crashing sound. Flames and sparks sprayed everywhere, debris rained downward, crashing onto the floor of the cavern.

And then came the surging swarm of blackness, pouring inside the cavern, from the air up and outside. Somehow, it had broken through the floor of the main terminal building into the cavern where the device sat.

"Oh shit . . ." Key said, watching it swirl downward. As it did, it circled the beam of energy, drowning out its color and light, kept going, until it was writhing around the machine itself, right above them, the black shapes reflected in its polished exterior.

Lightning crackled around the exterior of the device. The beam shooting into the air flickered for a moment, then readjusted, brightened.

"The swarm's going after the machine," Flynn said.

"I'm guessing that would be bad," Maddox said.

"You saw what happened when the X-Cores melted down," Raelyn replied.

Key got the picture. Another big implosion. And with the size and power of this thing, it was probably going to take out the entire starport.

"Maas said the machine was tough," Maddox remembered. "Maybe these things can't hurt it."

More lightning crackled. A strange pulse of sound ripped outward from the machine, echoing up and down the cavern loudly.

"You want to take that chance?" Flynn asked.

"Not particularly."

Flynn looked back down at the spinning triangles in the air. "If we can keep it off the device long enough, maybe I could find a way to power it down."

"Heat," Key said immediately. Everyone looked at her. "Basically, that bitch said it hated heat. She said it was the one thing that could contain it."

"Lines up with what we saw in the black site." Raelyn looked at Maddox. "Remember, it didn't like the Slow Burn."

Maddox nodded. His eyes scanned the cavern quickly, looking for something specific. Key could guess what it was. All up and down the length of the giant cavern walls, next to the lighting rigs, were large, golden squares of polished, fragmented metal. Key knew what they were.

"The heat sinks," Maddox said. "They're retentive cellular; they *store* heat to convert it to energy. With this beam active, I guarantee they're red hot inside right now."

"We pop a couple of those," Key said, finishing his thought, "the swarm bugs out . . ."

Maddox looked at her. "Maybe more than a couple. We gotta get it really hot in here."

Key looked at Flynn, hefted her rifle. "So, okay then. Smart people here, tough people out there."

Out of nowhere, Raelyn grabbed Maddox and pulled him to her and kissed him deeply. The Ranger didn't seem opposed; he kissed her back. Key raised an eyebrow, watching. *Well, how about that . . .*

Flynn, she noticed, was looking at her oddly. She frowned. "Not a chance." She turned and headed back toward the work area of the cavern.

"Key," Flynn said behind her. She didn't look back. What was the point? "Be safe."

She couldn't help it. "You too. Idiot."

Then she and Maddox were running.

SIXTY-TWO

HEAT SINKS

Maddox ground to a halt and stared up at the heat sinks all around them, attached to the walls near the lights, glowing bright gold.

The swarm circled everywhere in the room.

"How many do you think there are?" Key asked, running up next to him.

"A lot," Maddox said, staring at the mass of blackness in the air. He aimed his rifle, pulled the trigger. The muzzle flashed.

At the top of the cavern, one of the heat sinks exploded in a burst of sparks and shattered glass. What was left of it glowed bright red as the heat inside let loose—probably four hundred degrees—but it didn't have much of an effect.

Key fired next. Another heat sink blew apart.

But the swarm didn't even seem to notice, just kept circling and flooding the cavern.

"We're going to have to hit a lot more," Maddox said. "Maybe all of them."

"Then why are you talking to me?" Key's rifle started firing rapidly. More heat sinks exploded.

Maddox joined her, sending slugs into the air, watching fire spray out from the walls, watching more and more heat sinks turn bright red.

Even so, Maddox couldn't feel any heat. The cave was just too big. And he was only shooting the ones at the top; the rest of them were blocked by the scaffolding that circled the work area.

He looked around while Key kept firing. The main floor was full of desks and workstations, everything that had been on them scattered all over the place, probably from when the science teams ran in a panic after the Lost Prophet order came down.

The scaffolding was on the edge of it. If Maddox got on top of it, he could hit *all* the heat sinks.

"Stay here," he told Key. "Keep shooting."

"What are you going to do?"

"Climb," he answered. He hit the scaffolding running, started scaling it, felt the adrenaline flow. He'd put his body through more than he thought possible in the last few days, but he still felt energized. The energy came from Raelyn. He was going to get her out of here, get her safe.

And he would go with her, impossible as the idea seemed.

The top of the grid system shook and swayed underneath him. He was probably thirty feet off the cavern floor now, and he had an unobstructed view of the cavern walls. A hundred heat sinks glowed golden all over them.

Maddox aimed and fired again. With Key shooting on the floor below, the heat sinks were exploding left and right.

And finally, blessedly, Maddox started to feel heat in the air. They were doing it. They were raising the temperature.

The swarm felt it too.

A new sound ripped the air. A wet, metallic rattling that violently bounced off the walls.

As Maddox watched, the swarm writhed and banked hard—right toward him.

"Holy shit!" he heard Key yell down below.

Eyes wide, Maddox dropped as the swarm roared over him and the scaffolding. From under his arms he caught glimpses of the tiny creatures as they blew past. Wings. Nothing else. No legs. No feet. No mouths or eyes, nothing that even looked like a head. Just sharp, angular bodies made of the same strange black material.

He twisted as best as he could and looked down toward the cavern floor.

The swarm dove and slammed into it, exploding in masses of putrid, black ooze that sprayed outward . . . and then almost immediately started to pull back *together*.

More and more of the swarm hit, until the floor was covered with the glistening ooze, and it kept slamming down, piling higher and higher, the small creatures blending and fusing together into a mass fifteen feet tall.

The mass shuddered, shaping itself into something else.

Something more than just a body with wings. Pieces of it divided, spread, broke apart, until it stood on three triple-jointed black legs that held up a triangular body with three razor-sharp spiked appendages.

The thing rattled, just like the swarm in the air, but when it did, the horrible sound filled the cavern completely.

Maddox stared at it, stunned. Then the scaffolding under him buckled and tore itself apart and Maddox was falling in a shower of metal toward the ground.

SIXTY-THREE

CUBE

Flynn stared at the swirling, glowing shapes in the air around him. There was gunfire from Maddox and Key, but it barely registered, so intensely was he fixated on the puzzle in front of him.

He'd completed eight series so far. Eight correct choices on the codex progression of triangular numbers. It wasn't a linear progression. At any point in the series, there was more than one choice that would advance you to the next, and Flynn had been down all the paths so far. With every progression, more and more controls lit up on the surface of the machine.

He was starting to see it now. The shapes were becoming less abstract, more concrete. It was like when he was younger and had finally seen equations as ideas and meanings, not just ones and Xs, when he could look at a whiteboard full of them and read it like a book.

But he wasn't there yet with these numbers. He couldn't get past this series, and it didn't make sense.

"Which one did I hit last time?" Flynn asked. He was starting to get worried. He didn't know if he could do this.

"This one," Raelyn told him, pointing to a specific shape. Three triangles, connected at their apexes.

Flynn studied the symbols one last time, made his choice. It fit the pattern. It had to be this one.

He tapped it.

The symbols went dark. The controls on the device died.

"Damn it!" he yelled in frustration.

The symbols reappeared in the air, back at the first series once again. Flynn exhaled, started tapping them again.

"Maybe we're thinking wrong," Raelyn said, moving closer, studying the floating shapes.

"How?"

"We're assuming it's a progressive order of numbers. One, two, three, four."

"Right," Flynn said, tapping another symbol. The controls on the machine's exterior glowed again. "Except they're groups of threes, and the sequence resets at the fourth."

"What if it doesn't reset?" Raelyn said, squinting up at the symbols. The Slow Burn glowed on her arm, covering it completely, but she didn't seem to notice right then. "What if it *triples*?"

Flynn froze, hand reaching for one of the symbols of the eight series. "Cubed . . ." he mused.

"Cubed," Raelyn echoed.

The series eight symbols appeared again. He studied them in a new way.

If it was a cubic progression . . .

Flynn chose a new symbol, tapped it. The entire grid flashed one more time, then seemed to explode in a shower of holographic color. The full grid of controls flared to life on the wall of the machine.

Elated, Flynn stared at Raelyn. "You're brilliant."

She shrugged. "I do what I can."

A massive crashing sound rolled in from the main floor.

The scaffolding that Maddox had climbed buckled and collapsed, falling over in a shower of metal and wood. The Ranger was just visible on top of it, and he disappeared within the cascade.

"Maddox!" Raelyn yelled. She didn't hesitate, dashed back toward the work area.

"Raelyn, don't!" Flynn yelled, but it was too late. She was gone.

The swarm slammed into the ground on the other side of the drop-off, over and over, blending and fusing itself together into something new and horrible that was rising.

And Raelyn ran right toward it.

SIXTY-FOUR

DANGEROUS

Zane dreamed deliriously, one image after another, and she was in all of them. Then again, she always was.

Astoria stood over him, staring down with her purple eyes, wearing the same half-smile she always wore, like she found him amusing to no end.

"Wake up, Zane," she said.

Zane stared at her, mystified. In all the dreams he'd ever had of her, she'd never once spoken. He'd forgotten the sound of her voice, he realized with a pang of guilt. He loved the sound of it.

"I miss you," he said.

"Then you have to wake up," she responded. "You're so close."

Zane sighed. "But I like this dream."

Astoria smiled, her nose crinkled. "Who says it's a dream?"

Zane blinked, looking up at her, unsure . . .

"*Wake up!*" The power of her voice blew him backward in his mind.

Zane's eyes snapped open.

Pain flared in his head, his vision blurred. The X pumping in his veins still felt thick and hot. He wasn't healed, a long way from it, but he forced himself to focus.

He was still in the refrigerator car, but it was different now.

Everything was tilted at a steep angle, and the big exterior double doors were split open, allowing dim sunlight to filter in. Most of the refrigerator doors had ripped loose from their compartments and were scattered around the interior.

The world spun as Zane sat up. He closed his eyes, let it pass, then slowly dragged himself to the broken doors of the car and looked out.

He saw the first place he'd ever seen on this planet, where his shuttle had made Razorfall. The same place every new inmate saw.

The starport.

The pointed control tower, the pyramid-shaped terminal building, the rail yard and cranes and warehouses. Everything was covered in smoke and dust, and he could hear the sound of autoturret fire close by.

Above all of it hung the beam.

It was massive, shooting into the sky, right through the center of the terminal. And circling around it was the *creature*.

As Zane watched, the swarm descended, lower and lower, until it reached the apex of the polysteel pyramid terminal building. Then it burst through in an explosion of glass.

Zane's eyes thinned. This was not good.

He felt through the metal of the train car, could sense how torn apart it all was. They weren't here. Maddox or Raelyn. Flynn. Key. They were gone, had most likely headed to the beam.

He thought of the dream he'd just had, Astoria's words.

Who says this is a dream?

If it wasn't a dream, it could only mean one thing. She'd been in his head. And if she was in his head, then she was close. On the *Razor*.

If these people died, then he would die. And if he died, so did she.

Zane forced himself up, fighting the dizziness and the pain. He moved to the rear of the car and passed through the door there, into the prisoner car at the end of the line.

Dr. Gabliella Rosetta hung in chains from the ceiling. One of them had snapped loose from the impact of the train but the other was still secured around a wrist. It seemed to Zane that her eyes were on him before he even entered the car.

"I wondered when you would come." She spoke slowly and meticulously. "Hopefully it isn't too late."

"They're in trouble," was all he said. Zane used the doorframe to keep his balance. His strength was returning, but slowly.

"So are we." Her eyes moved over him, piece by piece. "You're Zane. Aren't you?"

Zane nodded.

"You hunted my children." There was a tinge of darkness in her voice.

"I did."

"Tell me . . ." Her eyes thinned, genuinely curious. "How did you find them?"

Zane thought about it. He'd fought plenty of Augments on the task force. Maybe more than anyone else. His encounters with them had always been short and violent, and they'd always ended the same way.

"Strong," he said. "Deadly. But, like most, they just didn't have it in them."

"Have what?"

"The will to survive."

Gable smiled slightly, nodded. She seemed to like the answer. "Ultimately, that is all that matters, isn't it?" She settled against the wall behind her, still patient. "I have many plans on this world I must see to."

"I only have one."

"What shall we do, then, Zane?"

"I know you're dangerous," he said, pushing away from the doorframe, testing his balance. "But dangerous is what I need right now."

The smile returned to her lips. "And once we reach the denouement? What then? You will not find me the same as my children. I very *much* wish to survive."

Zane moved through the car. When he reached her, he raised his hand and touched a finger to the joint on her wrist cuff. He pushed the Charge out—and it felt like razor blades going through him.

Pain flared in his head. He gritted his teeth, let the pain make him angry. Anger was something he could use.

"Someday, I get the feeling, you and I are going to have a moment," Zane said, looking into the woman's eyes. "But not today."

Gable held his gaze easily.

The joint on the cuff began to glow, hotter and hotter.

SIXTY-FIVE

PROGRESSIVE COMPLICATIONS

Key picked herself up off the floor in time to see the giant, black, hideous creature take its first steps. Her wings itched furiously.

What the fuck *was* this thing?

It was probably twelve feet tall. Three legs, triangular body, with three deadly looking spiked appendages.

It made the same rattling sound the others had made in Site Eleven, but so loud it made Key flinch.

The good news was that they'd managed to piss off and distract it by blowing the heat sinks. That was also the bad news.

"Maddox!" she heard Raelyn yell from across the railing, where Flynn was working on the machine controls.

Key snapped her head toward the sound, saw the doctor running to the crashed scaffolding. To Key's relief, Flynn wasn't following. He stared after Raelyn a second more, obviously torn, then moved back to the machine.

Good. This was no time for heroics. He needed to get that thing off-line.

The creature suddenly moved for her, stomping on its giant legs, spiked arms raising.

"Balls," Key said. She rolled out of the way as the thing struck down and tried to impale her. She lunged forward again, barely missed another strike.

She twisted, got the rifle up, switched to full auto, and fired.

The gun kicked hard, the muzzle flashed. Bullets sparked all over the surface of the thing, spraying debris everywhere.

Key groaned. The sparks meant the gun wasn't penetrating, which meant she was screwed.

The creature rattled and turned. Key did the only thing that seemed appropriate. She got to her feet and ran. The thing stomped behind, after her.

Key decided that if she couldn't hurt the thing, she could at least piss it off a little more. Oddly, she didn't feel a lot of fear. She guessed she was just too fucking busy.

Key aimed the rifle up as she ran, found more heat sinks. Fired.

The contraptions burst apart, what was left of them glowing red, adding more heat to the air.

The creature rattled in anger, moved quicker in pursuit.

She was running for the edge of the drop-off in the cavern floor, firing and blowing open as many heat sinks as she could hit, when the mass of blackness in the air—what was left of it—rattled and banked hard, swarming straight down toward the silver machine.

Key's eyes widened.

The swarm slammed into the device, exploding in sprays of black liquid that quickly reformed into other shapes, all over the exterior.

The silver vanished, replaced by the black, fibrous material, which itself began forming into clumps. Clumps that were starting to look a lot like *eggs*.

Key's eyes widened, watching lines form between them, like giant veins, stretching all over the machine. None of that could be good.

There was a crash behind her. The three-legged thing used one of its spikes to send a workbench and all of its equipment flying toward Key.

A computer monitor slammed into her back, sent her reeling. The rifle fell out of her hands and skidded away.

The workbench contents that didn't hit her got pulled into the gravity around the beam, started circling with all the rest in the air.

In pain, she tried to lunge out of the way of a strike by the creature. This one, she didn't dodge entirely.

Key groaned as it sliced a lovely little gash across her back.

She rolled quickly, trying to get away. It wasn't enough.

Another spike went right through her leg, pinning her to the ground. Blood sprayed. Key screamed, loud and hard.

The creature stood over her. Faceless. Eyeless. Rattling.

"Progressive complications," that's what Mace had always called it. One thing went bad, lots of other shit tended to go bad right after. He said if you bought into that model, lived understanding it, you rarely got surprised.

Looking at the thing above her, Key was of the mind to agree. It just hovered there, its angular, triangular body looming over her. If it had a mouth, it would probably be licking its fucking chops. At least she wasn't gonna get eaten alive.

"Go fuck yourself," she told it, tasting blood.

In her pained haze, Key thought of something odd.

Triangular body. Three legs. Three spiked arms.

Threes. Just like the symbols Flynn was dealing with.

Weird shit . . .

Then she yelled again as the creature yanked its spike out of her leg and raised it to strike down again and end her.

SIXTY-SIX

DROP-OFF

Maddox groaned, buried in the metallic debris that used to be the scaffolding. He could hear more gunfire from Key, the rattling of the giant creature, and the now disjointed humming from the beam in the air.

He didn't need to see any of it to know things were going badly.

The refuse on top of him shifted. Dust and grime fell into his face as pieces of the scaffolding were lifted off.

Raelyn appeared, staring down in fear, the Slow Burn covering her entire arm and spreading along the line of her neck.

"Raelyn, what are you—"

"Shut up," she told him sternly, started shoving the debris off him. "Don't move."

Pain lanced through his shoulder. Clearly, he was more hurt than he thought. But it didn't change anything.

"What are you *doing*?" he yelled. "Get out of here! That thing—"

"It's busy." She pulled more debris off. "With Key."

Maddox twisted, ignored the pain, stared through the metal pipes as best he could. He saw Key running and firing at more heat sinks as the strange, angular monstrosity chased after her.

"I have to help," he said.

"And how are you going to do that if I don't get you out of there?" Raelyn asked testily.

Good point. Maddox tested his other arm, which moved without pain, for the most part. He used it to help Raelyn shove the scaffolding off.

"It would be nice to go somewhere where we aren't on the verge of dying in some horrible way," Raelyn pointed out, getting her hands under a piece of tubing.

"It's definitely become a trend," Maddox said, getting his own hand under it. "What are you thinking?"

"Always heard the Donovan Nebula cruises were nice."

Together, they pushed and lifted the metal pipe up and off, taking more of the debris with it. Maddox could feel circulation coming back to his legs.

"I hate cruises," he said. "Trapped on a ship. All the people. No clear escape routes."

"Yeah, but there's a casino. And they fold your hand towels into these little animal shapes, leave them on your bed."

"You gamble?" Maddox asked, genuinely curious. They started moving another piece of scaffolding. It was heavy, not cooperating.

"Dice, mainly," Raelyn said through her teeth. "I'm really good."

"Can you teach me?" Maddox said, groaning. The piece fell off and away. He was almost free.

"Military guy," Raelyn said, breathing hard, "and you never learned to play dice?"

Maddox shook his head. "I was always at the rifle range."

The scaffolding shook all around him suddenly and Maddox felt himself being dragged across the floor. Raelyn tripped and fell as the scaffolding swept her off her feet.

Maddox saw what was happening. The crumpled scaffolding had fallen off the edge of the deep drop-off that circled the silver machine. It was all bolted together, and as each piece fell into the breach, it pulled the rest with it.

In about a minute, the whole thing was going over, Maddox included.

Raelyn and Maddox looked at each other, eyes wide.

"Cruise sounds great," Maddox said.

"It's a date."

Frantically, they again started trying to lift the scaffolding pieces off. As they did, Maddox felt himself slowly being pulled toward the yawning edge of the pit.

They got another piece off. Another.

But Maddox could tell it wasn't going to be enough. He was about five feet from the edge now, and the whole thing was moving faster, bending and groaning as the weight caught up with it.

"Raelyn," he told her. "You need to get clear."

She ignored him, kept shoving the pipes, trying to rearrange and move them off him.

"Raelyn!" he yelled, as the metal debris shook badly, pulled forward.

"I'm not leaving."

"You have to!"

"You didn't leave *me!*" she shouted back at him, angry now. Her eyes were red.

Maddox swallowed, held her look.

The scaffolding shuddered badly, slid another foot. They were almost at the edge.

"Raelyn, please," he said, desperate. "Please just go."

The scaffolding around him pulled closer to the edge. It was about to fall.

Raelyn just shook her head, stared at him. "What would be the point, then?"

Maddox sighed. He took her hand, pulled her close.

The scaffolding shuddered one more time . . . then fell over the edge, dragging Maddox and Raelyn with it into the dark chasm. Maddox shut his eyes, felt the pull of the void.

Then everything stopped in a violent jerk.

Maddox opened his eyes, stared upward.

Two hands held the last piece of the scaffolding, holding the entire weight from falling.

"*Zane!*" Raelyn yelled in shock.

The big man stood there, feet planted, exertion on his face, preventing the scaffolding from going over.

"Any time now . . ." Zane said, strained.

Maddox saw what he meant. The big man had lifted the scaffolding up off the ground. Maddox wasn't pinned anymore.

He and Raelyn slid out from under the gridwork as fast as they could. When they were clear, Zane let go.

The scaffolding yanked forward and into the pit, disappeared over the edge.

Breathing heavily, Maddox looked up at Zane.

The big man was breathing heavily himself. There was silver liquid coming out of his nose. Clearly, he was nowhere near close to a hundred percent.

"You two are a lot of trouble," Zane said.

"We were just discussing that," Maddox replied.

A yell came from behind them. The creature had impaled Key's leg with one of its spikes and was about to finish her.

Zane turned to face the thing, studying it.

"Zane . . ." Raelyn said, her voice emotional. She could tell, just like Maddox, that the man wasn't in any shape to fight something like that.

"Strange times," was all he said, then he charged toward the black tripod in the distance.

SIXTY-SEVEN

SENSE OF METAL

Zane watched Key roll into a ball as the triangular creature reared up to strike again.

His vision was blurry and he couldn't focus. His head still throbbed. His legs were shaky. He clenched his hands, but the fists they made didn't feel strong.

He was in a bad way, but it didn't matter. These were the cards he'd been dealt. And you always played your cards.

Zane ran as fast as his legs would carry him. He thought of Astoria as he did. The sound of her voice from the dream, which may not have been a dream at all.

It had been so good to hear her he hadn't wanted to wake up. It pissed him off. Complacency. Giving in. That wasn't who he was.

He let the anger build, let it give him what the Charge didn't seem able to.

Zane slammed into the rock-hard body of the creature. It staggered backward off Key and slammed through a workbench and into a whole other set of scaffolding, bringing the whole thing raining down on top of it.

Key stared at him with wide eyes. "Took you long enough."

The creature pushed itself out of the debris, sending plumes of dust everywhere. Zane stared at it. Key started to rise, then winced, hobbled back to the ground.

"Get clear," he told her.

"This thing . . ." she said. "No fucking offense, but the shape you're in right now—"

"Get *clear,*" Zane cut her off, keeping his unfocused eyes on the creature as best he could.

Key pushed to her feet, using a workbench to balance herself, moving out of the way as the monstrosity pushed free of the scaffolding, rattling with its macabre, wet sound.

Zane managed to dodge a strike from one of its pike-like appendages, stepped left, and wrapped his arms around one of the thing's legs. He lifted with everything he had.

The thing rattled again, losing leverage, then tipped over completely. It crashed to the ground, hard.

Zane moved toward its body, looking for weak points.

Its legs suddenly lashed out, catching Zane squarely in the chest.

He'd never felt an impact like it.

Zane flew backward, crashing through a row of storage shelves, knocking them over, spraying electrical components everywhere.

Pain arced through his back and his shoulder. He'd probably snapped something.

He tried to stand, but the creature was too fast. It lashed out again, sent him crashing to the ground, rolling wildly.

Zane felt a rib go, this time.

"Zane!" Key yelled nearby.

Zane shook his head, pushed to his feet.

Angry rattling filled the air. He took a blow to his other shoulder, and the impact drove him to his knees. Another hit sent him crashing into a bank of computer servers. They sparked violently, shorting out.

He'd been an idiot to try this, but there really wasn't any choice.

If you die, he thought, *she dies too.*

Zane rolled over, watched with blurred vision as the creature moved slowly toward him. It didn't seem eager. In fact, it seemed like it was dragging this out. What did that say about it? That it had thoughts swirling around somewhere in that steel-like exterior?

Zane eyes thinned. Steel . . .

Its body *did* feel like metal. Not like any metal he'd ever absorbed, but . . .

It stomped toward him, almost in slow motion now, raising one of its sharpened arms, ready to strike down and finish it.

Do or die . . .

Zane grabbed the arm as it descended, and used all the strength he had left to stop the razor-sharp edge, inches from his heart. The appendage sliced into his hands, spraying silver.

It hurt, bad. The pain gave him the anger he needed.

Zane poured the Charge into the thing, out of his hands and up through its arm.

The creature rattled horribly, the sound echoing everywhere.

For one intense second, pain shot through Zane as the Charge tried to pull energy and power from the metallic skin of the black creature.

Then his eyes snapped open wide.

Static and noise ripped into his mind, hissing and screeching, and underneath it all rose what sounded like . . . voices.

Thousands. More. Many more.

All pouring into his head, filling his stomach with a nauseating, oily sickness.

But power arced through him, too, in a way he'd never felt, almost instantly giving his muscles energy, wiping away any sense of pain, snapping his vision into focus.

He felt his ribs join back together and fill in. Felt his shoulder snap back into place.

The feeling of power rose, and at the same time the insane sounds of the voices and the static did, too.

Zane drew as much energy as he could with the Charge, storing it, building it, until he just couldn't stomach it anymore.

Then, still grabbing the thing's razor-like arm, he pulled and slammed the huge creature to the ground in a thunderous crash.

The voices and static vanished from his head. His vision cleared. His eyes focused.

The thing rattled, shook, flipped to its feet angrily.

Somehow, Zane sensed it. He couldn't explain it. But he knew the creature was about to strike with its center arm, right toward his chest.

He moved, dodged it easily, then drove his fist right into the thing's triangular body. The hand left a deep crater in the thing's shell.

The creature stumbled back, rattling furiously.

Zane sensed its next move too. He blocked another strike and drove his elbow into the joint of the arm, snapping it in a spray of black, oily liquid.

The creature rattled even louder.

Zane realized drawing power from this thing must have tapped him into its head, but he didn't waste time questioning how. All that mattered was the power flowing through him, and that this thing was going to die.

Zane ran full force and drove the creature to the ground all over again.

SIXTY-EIGHT

EQUATIONS

Flynn dove out of the way as the swarm surged in the air and slammed into the silver machine, covering it with blackness.

He watched the blackness re-form itself and then merge together into masses that looked like the eggs he'd seen in Site Eleven, the kind that produced this exact swarm. And they were forming all over the machine.

As they did, more purple lightning arced. The machine vibrated. A pulse of sound echoed from it, bouncing all around the cavern.

The creature was trying to destroy the device, draining its power like it had done to the X-Cores before. Maas had said they'd determined that the alien machine ran on Xytrilium, so Flynn had no doubt that these things could do the job if they were given the time.

But why? Were they just attracted to the energy, the equivalent of a food source? Or was it more than that?

"They are no different from you or me," a voice said from behind him. Flynn forced his gaze upward. Gable stood there, free of chains, watching the swarm as it re-formed and reshaped itself on the machine above. "They have an interest in survival too." She looked down at him, offered her hand to help him up.

"How did you get free?" he asked, studying her warily.

She frowned impatiently. Flynn supposed it wasn't the time. He let her pull him to his feet.

They moved for the glowing controls reflected in the machine's silver surface. They were made up of the same kind of shapes as the ones that had floated in the air as part of the codex, but the triangles here were arranged in strings now, in line with each other, or sometimes diagonally above and below.

It was an entirely new puzzle, and Flynn felt desperate all over again.

"What do we have?" Gable asked.

"Numbers. I learned the system from a visual codex earlier."

"The triangle combinations represent numerals."

"Yes, they're grouped in—"

"Threes," she finished for him, studying it all. "Instead of tens."

Flynn nodded. Gabliella Rosetta was a biologist and genetic engineer, a brilliant one. Number patterns would be as apparent to her as to him.

"But this . . ." he said, looking at the controls themselves. "I don't know."

Gable looked closer. "These appear to be setting controls—up, down— and these look like dials." She motioned to arrows and spherical shapes that, in fact, did look similar to directional controls and dials.

"I think you're right," Flynn agreed. "One series of numbers for each."

There was a string of the triangular shapes above each set of controls.

"It would follow that they are descriptors."

"They're numbers, not alphabetic characters," Flynn said. "They went through a great deal of effort to teach their *number* system."

"Math is universal," Gable said. "Alphabet systems and iconography are not. If you were forced to teach someone how to use a set of controls with only numbers, what would you do?"

Flynn thought for a moment. The answer actually seemed obvious. "I would use equations." Gable raised an eyebrow. "Like you said, math is universal. So are equations. The laws that govern our math govern theirs as well. The only difference would be nomenclature."

"Do you recognize the equations, then?"

Flynn looked at the strings. There were no variables here, only numbers, so if they were equations, they were completed. Theoretically, he *might* be able to fill in the values, which should reveal the equation.

Lightning flashed on the machine again. Another deep, metallic pulse of sound echoed through the cavern. The sounds of gunfire bounced everywhere.

"We're running out of time," Gable said.

"This one," he said, pointing to one of the number strings. Something about it was familiar. "It's . . ."

"Let the idea form," Gable instructed.

Flynn did. He *recognized* the string. Part of it anyway. "It's *almost* Newton's second law of motion!" he exclaimed, excited. "But it's been added to."

It wasn't uncommon. Newton's laws got added to and modified all the time, especially by thermal dynamics and waveform engineers.

Waveforms . . .

"It's . . . a phase shift equation," he blurted. "Harmonic motion evolves over time!" He felt a burst of energy and enthusiasm, the same kind he always felt when solving problems.

"And what control would that correlate to?" Gable asked, keeping him focused.

"Frequency," Flynn said immediately. It had to be.

"And this one?" Gable pointed to a longer string above a virtual dial in the middle of all the glowing controls

Flynn recognized it now, too. "Gravitational potential energy. It's the controls for the beam's gravity effect."

Flynn scanned the other controls, and the equations glowing above them. He was starting to see them as more than three-sided symbols.

"Electrical conduction equation," he said, pointing to one. "So, amplitude controls." He pointed to each one now, going in turn, deciphering them on the fly, becoming more and more excited. "Heat conduction equation. Focus controls. Stefan–Boltzmann law, beam intensity. Reed's theorem, so . . . I don't know, beam purity, maybe? Resonance? Probably resonance." He looked at Gable, eyes wide. He felt amazing. "I can do it. I can shut it off!"

"Can you?" she asked, her demeanor much less engaged.

Flynn nodded, pointed to the last equation of the last control on the virtual board. "Power equation. The rate at which energy is transferred from one place to another. It's the power switch. Off and on."

"And then, with the beam gone, the EM tunnel will reopen," Gable said pointedly, holding his gaze. "And Maas-Dorian whisks you away, back to exactly how everything used to be. Everything you've wanted."

Flynn's euphoria vanished, and he had no idea why. Because, like she said, it *was* everything he'd wanted, since he'd been sent to this godforsaken place. He'd wanted his old life back. He'd wanted off this world.

"There's no other choice," he said.

"Are you certain of that, Marcus?"

In fact, he wasn't, he realized. Flynn looked back at the controls and the alien equations that identified them. There was another choice, now that he knew the equations. A much harder one.

"The wavelength."

"What of it?"

"I can *shift* it," he said. "It won't be easy, there's no actual control set for it, but I think I can phase shift the beam so it's not strong enough to puncture the magnetosphere anymore but still strong enough to seal the EM tunnel."

There it was. The answer. The way to save the planet and yet not give it up.

"The Razor would still be barricaded," Gable said, a note of satisfaction in her voice. "And it would be saved."

"Yes . . ." Flynn said, but it didn't really matter. It wasn't an option. He looked up at the silver machine towering over him, to the black, fibrous material of the creature that had formed in hundreds of egg-like masses all over it. He watched as the purple lightning flared and the machine rocked and vibrated dangerously. "But the creature's going to overload the machine, either way. If we don't turn it off—"

"If what you say about the wavelength is correct, it will leave," Gable said firmly, cutting him off.

He looked at her, confused. "Why would—"

"Because it's here for the same reason you are." As she spoke, her words became more intense. "This beam is a threat to it. Once the Razor stops shrinking, once there is no more threat, the creature will leave, regardless of whether the machine is still active. I feel it has many other ambitions to attend to, much lost time to atone for, and in that regard, it and *myself* are very similar."

"But . . ." Flynn started, but he couldn't finish. Ideas swirled in his head. Emotions too, desires. He was trying to make sense of it all, while the chaos continued all around him.

"Don't you see?" Gable pressed, moving closer. "This planet, all the mysteries it contains, can be ours. The most important planet in the galaxy."

Flynn looked back at her, eyes wide. "You're crazy." But the words were not voiced with much conviction.

"No," Gable told him decisively. "I am many things, but not that. You will come to learn as much, Marcus. But we must *survive*."

It took a fraction of a second for Flynn to weigh the options. Shutting down the beam meant giving up everything. It meant going back to a life he now realized he didn't even want. What he wanted was here. This world. On the Razor . . . things mattered. Here, *he* mattered. And Gable was right, there was a chance to preserve it . . .

Flynn made his choice. He ran for the controls on the machine, glowing on its silver-plated skin, triangular shapes put together in strings.

I can do this, he told himself. But he had to hurry; things were spiraling out of control, fast.

The problem was, there was no control for the beam's wavelength. But there were controls for its amplitude and frequency. Theoretically, he could adjust those to alter the—

"Marcus," Gable's voice cut through his thoughts. She'd moved close in behind him; her voice was in his ear. "You must act."

Flynn nodded, focused. His hands moved for the amplitude controls, adjusted the glowing virtual dial there, and as he did, he stared up at the giant beam above. He watched as its color began to shift, just like he'd expected. It was working . . .

His hands moved toward what he assumed were the frequency settings. It was another virtual dial, but this one had additional number symbols arranged around it. It must be numerical settings, but Flynn wasn't completely sure what they were. He would have to—

The purple lightning suddenly arced wildly over the machine and there was a bright flash.

Another vibrating, pulsing tone of sound blared, and it filled Flynn's mind with pain, blackened his vision.

Then everything around the cavern was ripped into the air.

Computers. Monitors. Tools. Spare parts. Water bottles. Papers. Tablets. Everything the M-D scientists had left went straight upward.

Except for him and Gable. For some reason, they stayed perfectly in place, watching as everything inside the cavern catapulted toward the beam in the ceiling.

It was a gravity pulse, Flynn guessed, from the malfunctioning machine, and it was probably about to melt down completely. They had run out of time.

SIXTY-NINE

GRAVITY

Key watched Zane fight the creature. A fight he'd been losing in a major way about two minutes ago and had now turned into something almost completely one-sided.

She didn't know how he was doing it, but he was dodging every one of the thing's strikes, predicting every one of its moves. Then ramming it hard, punching and kicking, grabbing and slamming it to the floor, leaving dents all over its surface. Black ooze dripped from wounds in its steel-hard exterior.

Still, the thing could take a punch. As roughly as Zane manhandled the thing, it just seemed to get back up for more, rattling out that horrible sound.

Whatever mojo Zane had tapped into, it wasn't going to be enough.

Key sighed. *Do I have to do everything?*

She drew the two plasma knives from behind her back, flicked the switches on their handles. The blades burned to life, glowing bright orange.

She balanced on her punctured leg. It hurt, but she could still run.

Yet she felt the usual grip of fear on her spine, freezing her in place. Try as she might, she couldn't make herself move.

Key looked down at the wound on her leg, oozing blood. The plasma knives glowed hot in her hands.

Pain focuses you. Pain blocks everything else out. The gray-skinned man going toe to toe with that black monstrosity had told her that.

"Fuck it," Key said. She touched the glowing blade of the plasma knife to the wound on her leg and instantly seared it with intense heat.

Key screamed, held the blade on her leg as long as she could, the pain flashing through her, then yanked it away. The wound smoked. It was blackened and red, but it wasn't bleeding anymore.

And it stung like a bitch.

Whatever fear she'd been feeling was gone. All there was now was the pain and what she had to do. Key gripped the knives and dashed forward.

The creature was distracted by Zane, didn't even see her coming.

She jumped as high as she could, and slammed into it, hit the top, flailed, started to slide on its slick surface. She struck down with the knives. They punctured its fibrous hide, the plasma digging the blades in, burying them almost dead center at the top of its torso.

The rattling echoed again, horrible and violent. So this bastard could feel pain then.

Good.

The creature shook wildly, trying to yank her off. Key slid down its body, dragging the blades with her, ripping gashes in the thing as she went. Black, putrid liquid sprayed everywhere.

The plasma knives cut all the way through the torso of the thing—and then Key fell.

She hit the ground, hard. The air blew out of her lungs.

The creature rattled, spun, raised another spiked leg as it bled.

Zane slammed into it and drove it to the ground before it could strike, pushing it forward, black fluid gushing out of it.

Then, from across the cavern, a bright flash came from the machine.

A vibrating, electronic pulsing tone of sound blared everywhere, and filled Key's head with pain, blackened her vision.

She fell back to her knees, felt sick suddenly, like she was going to puke.

Everything around her suddenly rose into the air. And so did Key.

"Holy shit!" she yelled, as she was pulled off the ground and yanked toward the beam in the distance.

She just barely grabbed one of the workbenches, considered herself lucky the thing was bolted down. The workbenches and the scaffolding along the rim of the research area were the only things holding on.

Even the creature was yanked off the cavern floor. One of its append-ages lashed out, punctured the same workbench Key was holding on to, anchoring the monstrosity in place.

The supports groaned, threatening to tear loose.

Zane rammed into the creature from underneath, grappled and pinned its arms.

It rattled furiously.

It was a weird sight—or as weird as anything else happening right now—watching Zane wrestle the monstrosity in mid-air, pinned in place.

The workbench's supports were ripping loose. It was about to go.

Zane grabbed the thing's pole-like arm, the one stuck in the workbench, his face a mask of concentration.

The creature rattled horribly, spasming wildly.

Key didn't know what was going on until she saw the appendage start to glow, where Zane held it.

She got it then. Zane was pulling power from the creature *itself.* It felt like metal, after all. But, shit . . . what would that do to him?

The arm kept glowing, hotter and whiter, becoming thin and brittle. And then the big man kicked down and snapped it apart.

The thing rattled again as it jolted into the air, trying to drag Zane with it, but he pushed it off. It hurtled toward the ceiling, spinning wildly, then disappeared into the fluctuating beam with a giant flash of light.

Key's strength gave out. She lost her grip on the workbench and was yanked upward into space, after the creature.

Zane grabbed her forearm as she sailed by. Her hand clamped down on his. With his other hand he grabbed what was left of the black appendage impaled in the workbench.

"Hold on," he yelled at her.

"Great advice! Thanks!"

They both did just that, as everything was pulled upward, blowing wildly, sucked up and through the ceiling far above in a blast of gravity.

SEVENTY

FAULT

"Raelyn!" Maddox screamed, as she was ripped upward, just like every-thing else around them, flying into the air and disappearing through the ceiling.

Maddox grabbed the scaffolding near him, locked his arm around it, tried to hold on. Raelyn's hand clamped down desperately on his.

Pain shot through his body as he tried to hold her.

"James!" Raelyn yelled. Her second hand reached down and grabbed his, too.

But he could feel her starting to slip. He wasn't going to be able to hold on.

"Flynn!" Maddox yelled, as loudly as he could, looking back toward the machine. For some reason, the lack of gravity wasn't affecting him and Gable.

Gable.

Maddox felt dread. The idea of her having Flynn's ear, right this second . . .

"*Flynn!* Shut it down! Shut it *down!*" he yelled desperately.

"James . . ." Raelyn struggled. He could see the Slow Burn glowing on her arm. Could feel her hands slipping. He looked into her eyes, terrified.

Please. Don't let this happen. Please don't make this my fault too . . .

"James, it's okay . . ."

"No!"

"You can let go."

"Shut up!" he yelled, terrified. He could see it in her eyes. She was through, she'd run out of road. He gripped her hands with everything he had. "You shut up and hold on!"

"I . . . don't want to." Everything was blowing crazily around them. The workbenches were ripping loose, the scaffolding was tearing apart. All of it being sucked straight upward with the beam. "I was never going to last much longer. You know it's true. The pain . . ."

"Flynn! Shut it down!"

"This isn't your fault, James," Raelyn said. Maddox looked back up at her, eyes wide. "And I would have loved that cruise."

Raelyn let go. Maddox screamed.

SEVENTY-ONE

CHOICES

Flynn stood in the gravity pocket produced by the machine, unaffected by the surge ripping through the cavern. No one else was as lucky.

"*Flynn!* Shut it down! Shut it *down!*" Maddox yelled in the distance, trying to hold on to Raelyn as she flailed in the air.

Flynn stared in pure desperation at the controls for the beam's frequency. He'd already tried adjusting the glowing virtual dial, but it wouldn't move like the others had, wouldn't do anything at all when he touched it.

What was he doing *wrong*?

Flynn looked behind him, saw Raelyn grab on to Maddox with both hands, saw hundreds of pieces of equipment and debris being ripped straight upward into the air around them.

"Marcus . . ." Gable was insistent.

"I'm trying!" he yelled, turning back to the controls. The glowing circular dial had the alien numbers all around it, as if the dial could be turned to them as settings. Flynn's first thought was that they were the alien symbol equivalents of hertz settings, but that didn't totally line up with the numbers that were being shown. None of the other controls had settings marks like these. What did it mean?

Maybe, the idea occurred to him, it wasn't a dial at all. Maybe he was thinking two-dimensionally.

Experimentally, instead of touching the dial, he touched one of the setting markers that circled it.

The symbol flashed. The dial was illuminated in white. Flynn, eyes wide, kept his finger on the one setting mark and now tried to turn the dial.

This time the glowing circle turned in his hand. He'd cracked it.

"The numbers aren't settings," Flynn exclaimed, "they're the base constant for setting the frequency! It makes sense. It lets you adjust along various frequency ranges."

He looked at Gable. She smiled, knowingly.

Raelyn's scream echoed in the distance, over all the chaos flying around them.

Flynn's attention snapped back to her and Maddox, and the smile was ripped from his face. He saw Raelyn yanked wildly into the air, saw her tumble and fly upward toward the ceiling and the blazing beam, along with everything else, to where it punctured the starport and burst out into the sky above. The beam flashed brightly as she hit it.

And then she was gone.

Flynn shut his eyes tight. The world burned around him with piercing sound and he didn't even notice. He couldn't feel anything. Everything was frozen.

"Flynn," a calm, detached voice said from somewhere far away. "Look at me."

Flynn ignored it, kept his eyes shut. Raelyn's scream was embedded in his mind, echoing back and forth, over and over. It wouldn't go away. Neither would the sight of her in his head, spinning and twisting and flying away. He hadn't been fast enough. He hadn't—

"*Look* at me, Marcus." Fingers grabbed Flynn's chin tightly, lifted it up forcefully.

Flynn made his eyes open. Gable's eyes were inches from his. As he watched, a sliver of golden light moved from one eye to the next.

"She's gone," Gable said simply. "But *Key* is not."

Flynn blinked. The idea flowed through his mind, giving him focus again, pushing him back to the surface. Gable was right. If he didn't do something, he'd lose all of them. He'd lose Key.

Flynn turned back to the glowing controls, found the frequency dial, scanned the numbers there until he saw the one he wanted. If he was right, it would set the baseline where he needed it.

He touched the symbol. It flashed. The dial went white. Flynn turned it, and as he did, the machine vibrated above him. The beam flashed brightly. It was working . . .

Flynn turned the controls slowly, watching the beam as its color shifted again, fading slowly from a dark orange to yellow.

He pulled away. The dial and the settings froze in place. That should be it. That should be the right wavelength.

But nothing changed.

The creature was still all over the machine, showing no sign of leaving.

The gravity was still going crazy, sucking everything up into the cavern ceiling.

Flynn stared up at the giant, pulsing yellow beam of energy. "Nothing's happening!" he yelled.

"Patience," Gable said next to him, watching intently.

The lightning kept flashing over the machine. Nothing was changing. The creature wasn't leaving. The gravity was still haywire, pulling everything upwards.

Flynn had made an educated guess, but it was a guess all the same. He was dealing with an alien number system; he could easily have miscalculated. And a miscalculation here meant that the beam was still shredding the Razor's magnetosphere, high above them. For all he really knew, he could have even accelerated the process.

Flynn looked back toward the work area and saw Key and Zane struggling to hold on while the gravitational maelstrom sucked up everything around them. They weren't going to last much longer. He was going to lose her too.

Panicking, Flynn moved for the controls again, for the power equation. He had to shut the thing down completely. It was the only way to make sure. He'd been a fool to try to—

Gable yanked him back in place, hard. "*Patience.* You must learn to trust me."

"Trust you?" Flynn struggled. "She'll die!"

Gable's eyes bored into him while everything spun and flew through the room.

"Die? *Die?*" Her hand moved in a blur from his hand to his throat, so fast he didn't even see it move. "What is her life to *me*? What is yours? You claim to know who I am, but it does not seem so. You have *heard* the stories, yes? They are not hyperbole, I assure you. Your life . . ."

Her grip tightened on his throat. Flynn choked, struggled. He had to get loose, he had to save Key.

"You are only alive because you are useful to me. The moment you become useless is the moment I slit your throat and watch as the life drains out of you. And do you know what I would feel while you squirmed on the floor in your own blood, Marcus?"

She held her free hand up to his face, leveled a single finger at him. Something pushed out from it, slowly, breaking the skin, causing blood to run from the tip.

A long, wickedly sharp silver blade.

Flynn's eyes widened. He tried to pull back, but she held him in place, let the blade extend until it was inches from his eye.

"I would feel *nothing*," she told him casually, eyes burning into his. "*That* is what your life is to me."

She held his eyes a second more, and then the blade withdrew, back into her finger. It bled freely. "Look at the machine, Marcus. Look at the creature."

Flynn did, shifting his eyes. The egg-like things vibrated and throbbed on the device's exterior.

"You. Must. *Learn*," Gable said, accenting each word.

The eggs exploded into thousands and thousands of black, swarming pieces that burst into the air and writhed upward in a streaming, curling mass of darkness. Flynn watched the swarm get caught by the gravity, too, get pulled straight up toward the ceiling and the now yellow beam.

And then he watched it funnel out, the giant spinning mass, into the open air on the other side of the ceiling. He watched until the swarm was gone. And without it on the machine, draining or damaging it, the lightning faded away. The fragmented humming from the device died.

The gravity in the room suddenly went back to normal.

Everything that was in the air fell in a shower of pieces and parts, thundering down everywhere.

Gable's grip on his throat loosened. Flynn stumbled backward, fell to the ground in front of the machine, the symbols still glowing on its surface. He glared up at the woman, rubbing his throat, furious.

Gable studied him. Her look was calm and cold once more. "Do we have an understanding now, Marcus?"

"You stay away from me," Flynn said, his voice shaking. "You stay away from me, you stay away from *her*."

Gable smiled. "I take that as a yes."

All around, the sounds of chaos were dying, everything was returning to quiet again.

Breathing hard, Flynn looked to Maddox, across the room. The man lay there, unmoving, staring darkly at Flynn.

SEVENTY-TWO

DEAD PEOPLE

Key climbed the ladder that would take her to the top of the starport's fortified wall.

The automated gun turrets had gone silent. She could hear the yells and cheers from the inmates on the other side, who'd been trying to find a way around those guns.

They thought the coast was clear. They were wrong.

Key reached the top and slipped through the gap between two of the big guns. She could feel the heat coming off them.

The green hills of the Razor stretched out before her, lit up by the brownish light from the sun, frozen in the sky—in the same place it would be hours from now, due to the planet's unlikely orbit.

There was smoke on the horizon, from the foliage that was still burning, but the glow was receding. Flynn had done it. The Razor's atmosphere was normalizing, pushing back the Cindersphere.

She looked down to the crowd of sweaty, dirty men and women forming below, a wash of color from different jumpsuits. Hackers. Smugglers. Pirates. Thieves. Killers. Her favorite kinds of people.

They stopped and stared up at her, but she knew that wouldn't last long. Hesitate in front of this group and they would scale the wall before she had a chance to tell them what was what.

"You are some delicate-looking assholes, you know that?" Key shouted down at them.

Stunned murmurs spread through the crowd.

"The fuck are you doing up there?" someone shouted.

"I'm not up here, dickface," Key yelled back. "I'm dead. Just like you."

Laughter came from the crowd now, some of the weariness and blood forgotten. These were her people, for better or worse. She knew how to talk to them. She just hoped talking was enough.

"Far as *they're* concerned, anyway. If the UEG could come back for this place right now, you think they'd lock you up again? Nah. They'd turn these turrets back on and let them finish. We're *dead* to them. And I say that suits me just fine. The only question we should be asking is who are we gonna be now?"

"Start making sense, bitch," another prisoner yelled—a Scorpio, judging by his mechanical legs.

"You see the beam back there?" Key asked, pacing on top of the wall. "A minute ago, it was stripping away the atmosphere of the Razor. Now it's not. But it's still on, and as long as it is, the Maas-Dorian assholes can't land here."

"How do you know all this?" a Grimm yelled back up at her.

"'Cause I'm with the man who did it. His name is Flynn. He figured that thing out, knows how to control it. Which means the most important fucking world in the galaxy is ours. We own the Razor now."

"Don't know what this 'we' is," the same Grimm said. "What's stopping me from taking it right out of your hands?"

He was big—lots of muscle, an eye patch. He looked like trouble. So Key spun the M32B around from her back and pulled the trigger.

The Grimm was blown backward into the crowd. He didn't get up.

The laughter and smiles vanished.

"Me. For one. Flynn, for another."

"He sounds like a lot of brain, not much brawn," a big man with dreads and voodoo tats said. Bloodclan.

"Exactly," Key said. "Anyone fucks with him, that beam gets shut *off*. That happens, the UEG floods back down here with gunships and Ranger squads and we're all dead. Again. But that isn't even really the selling point."

"What is?" the Bloodclan asked.

"The purest X in the galaxy. Run by a planet full of people who know how to mine it."

More murmurs passed through the crowd below; different gangs, different people, all standing in one bunch without trying to strangle each other. It was already a milestone.

"There's a thousand of us here," a girl said, bandanna wrapped around her scalp. Her gray jumpsuit was covered in blood. "If that."

Key understood her concern. By themselves, they weren't enough to hold the starport, even from other gangs. The Razor had Crawlers and supply depots and sorting facilities all up and down its entire length, something like two hundred thousand prisoners total. Key had no way to know how many of those inmates were left alive, but even half that number meant there were a lot of people on this world that would challenge them.

"All our lives, people in high places have squashed us down, never gave us a second look," Key said. "Well *fuck* them. Now those people get to come beg for what this planet has. And that's going to be a pretty attractive setup to every other survivor on the Razor. Word'll spread. Our numbers will grow. But we have to be ready."

They all stared up at her with fire burning in their eyes. Key liked it. They could start something with this.

"I'm going to open these gates," she said, "because I have a feeling we have an understanding. Anyone comes through those gates, whatever color you're wearing, your ass belongs to the Razor now. No more bitching. No more backstabbing. That shit's over, or I kill you myself. You come through those gates, that means you want to build something. Something the galaxy's never seen before. And if you don't give a shit about any of that, if you just wanna raise hell, well . . . I got a feeling there's gonna be plenty of opportunity for that, too." She studied them hard, looked as many as she could in the eye. "What do you assholes say?"

It took a moment, but the crowd below cheered. The waves of sound washing over Key felt good. She could get used to it.

Key gave the inmates one final look and one final warning. "Behave."

Then the gates in the fortified wall slowly started to crank open.

SEVENTY-THREE

RED BOOK

Zane entered the code Maddox had given him into the door's control panel. It had worked at the armory, it might work here too. Sure enough, the door slid open, revealing the small, totally colorless room beyond, brimming with technology.

It was the White Room, the place the computer system back at Site Eleven had told him about. Magnetically shielded, deep underneath one of the starport's power plants. It recorded and stored every bit of data that moved on and off the planet. It also had access to the Razor's computer network, all linked, even the black sites. If it was on a data drive connected to the network, it could be accessed here.

Zane stepped into the room.

It had white walls and ceilings, and the harsh lights above made it seem like he was inside a petri dish. Two leather chairs sat in front of a bank of controls and half a dozen monitors on the walls.

The room sensed his presence. The screens all lit up as he entered. On them scrolled all kinds of metrics for the planet. Some were tapped into the satellite system in orbit, displaying distance imagery, topography, weather tracking, images of different sites on the surface. The Razor stretched almost twelve thousand miles around the circumference of the planet, and everything on it—the rail network, hundreds of supply depots, repair facilities, sorting docks, Crawlers—could all be monitored from this room.

Looking at the imagery, Zane saw the state of the planet. Fires burned everywhere, both from the expansion of the Cinder and from the rioting and looting by inmates. Whoever wanted to control the planet now, they had a lot of—

Zane heard something.

A hissing. Like static almost. Faint, but audible. Behind him.

He turned quickly.

There was nothing in the hallway beyond the door to the White Room, nothing anywhere that he could see. He was alone.

The static sound vanished. Like it had never been there at all.

Zane shook his head to clear it. Since the fight with that creature, he hadn't had any pain, no dizziness either. He felt better than he ever had, actually. But then the static had started.

He heard it only occasionally, a slight hissing in the back of his mind, and only when it was very quiet, like in this room.

If he listened carefully, it sounded like there were . . . voices underneath the hiss.

Zane wasn't an idiot. There wasn't a mystery to what it was. He'd absorbed a part of that thing with the Charge. It had blended into him, maybe permanently. And it had changed him. What effect, exactly, he didn't know. But he had a feeling he would, sooner rather than later.

It only made finishing what he had to do all the more pressing.

"Query," Zane spoke out loud. When he did, the computers hummed to life. "Project Gray Book."

The air lit up in a holographic data grid in the center of the room, different pieces of data arranged in the air. Documents. Spreadsheets. E-mail and v-mail. Lab results. A huge spread of information.

"Project summary," Zane said to the room.

The grid vanished. Information scrolled in front of him.

UEG Defense Initiative Research Project
CLASSIFIED. SEALED. OFF-BOOK.
Weapons development. Human physical augmentation trials.
Project status: COMPLETE
Project result: SUCCESS

This was his project, Zane knew. The project to create him. He had no memories of anything before it, not even any memories of the project itself. Just waking up on that UEG destroyer, far from the Razor, and likely long after this file was marked the way it was.

Zane stared at the final word. *Success.*

According to whom?

The Book project was an ambitious UEG endeavor, Jovenheimer had told him, before Zane threw him off a building. *Gray Book—you—was one. But there were many more.*

"List parallel research projects to Gray Book conducted on the Razor," Zane said.

The holo display flashed and twisted. It displayed a string of icons, labeled, in turn,

Blue Book . . . Black Book . . . Red Book . . . Green Book . . .
White Book . . . Brown Book

"Query. Of these, which have a status of 'Complete'?"

Red Book. Green Book. White Book.

"Query. Of these, which have a result of 'Success'?"

Red Book.

Zane's eyes thinned. "Project summary of Red Book."

UEG Defense Initiative Research Project
CLASSIFIED. SEALED. OFF-BOOK.
Weapons development. Human psionic augmentation trials.
Project status: COMPLETE
Project result: SUCCESS

Psionics. It was her. It had to be.

"Project details."

The air flashed, displayed an information grid similar to the one Zane had seen for Gray Book. Documents. Videos. Communications. Project reports.

Zane ignored all of it, tapped on an image file in the air.

The icon expanded, blossomed into an image of a girl with short dark hair, maybe ten or eleven years old, sitting on a bed in a nondescript room and taking apart a large antique clock, the mechanical guts of it strewn everywhere. She was staring up into the camera with purple eyes.

Zane forgot to breathe.

She was a few years younger here than when he'd met her, but it was Astoria. The sight of her brought emotions to the surface.

Loneliness. But also anger. Deep anger. That she had been taken from him.

"Query," Zane said, his voice dark now. "Location of project Red Book research."

A map flashed to life in front of him, showing a location with a marker. The marker read "Site Seven."

Comparing the map in the air to the satellite imagery on the monitors, Zane saw that the location was almost across the globe, on the other side of the Razor, but it was on *this* side of the Barrier. Which meant it was possible that the Cindersphere hadn't completely torched it.

Getting there was going to be tough, a slog through a lawless wasteland. Zane could see on the map the kinds of things he would have to pass through. The Sea Gap. The Spire Lands. Moriarty's Fissure. More than that, gangs would be reuniting now, dangerous social structures forming. What Key and Flynn were trying here had a leg up on those, because they had the starport, which let them control access to the planet for now, but there were still plenty of threats on the surface, and none of them was inconsequential. This planet held the worst of the galaxy's criminals, and the Cindersphere expansion had guaranteed that only the strongest of them had survived.

But those were the cards he was dealt. And you always played your cards.

Zane remembered one last thing.

He looked to the wall near the monitors, saw input slots for a variety of media. One of them was for data cards, like the one he'd recovered at Site Eleven. The one that contained, presumably, the information about who he used to be. Before Gray Book.

He pulled the small card out, held it between his thumb and finger. It was fragile. He could snap it in half if he wanted. Or he could put in the computer and find out who he really was.

Zane stared at the data card for a long time, flipping it in his hand.

Then he drew from his belt the new knife he'd gotten—a long, sharp, serrated one—and cut a small incision in the leather of one of the chairs.

Zane stuffed the data card inside, hiding it.

Someday, he thought. *But not now.*

He turned and started to leave the room, when he felt something under his nose. Warm and wet.

He wiped it away with his hand. It was his blood, but it wasn't just silver this time. Now it was laced with black.

SEVENTY-FOUR

NOW

Flynn stood in the center of the control room for the dig site, surrounded by symbols he was just coming to understand.

The air was full of holograms of the alien number system he'd encountered on the machine below. They were glowing and spinning as he moved them around the small room, ordering them into groups and strings that were making more and more sense.

It was almost like starting all over with mathematics, learning it in a new way, and it was invigorating. The groups of threes made their system less robust, more elegant, but also more adaptive somehow. It was like music written in a different clef, and he'd been staring at it all for hours. No food, nothing to drink, no rest, and no intention of stopping.

"Hello, Dr. Flynn," a familiar voice said over the room's speakers. A voice he hadn't heard since he'd been in another control room. A voice he'd been expecting.

"Am I ever going to know your name?" Flynn asked, without looking at the monitors. He knew the image of the Suit was there.

"No," the man answered.

"What do you want, then?" Flynn kept moving the symbols around. He was trying to construct an equation with them—and not just any equation, either.

"Once more, I have underestimated you," the Suit continued. There was a note of bitterness in his voice. "It will not happen again."

"That sounds vaguely like a threat."

"The data drive you have belongs to us. We made a deal for it."

"Maas-Dorian likely disagrees with you."

"You control the starport," the Suit said. "For the time being, you control the Razor. And whoever controls the Razor controls the galaxy. But I don't think you will control it for long. Betraying Evelyn Maas is one thing, Dr. Flynn. Betraying *Francis Dorian* is quite another. He will come for you, and he will do so with all the power Maas-Dorian has."

Flynn sighed, turned away from the triangular symbols reluctantly. "I've been thinking about that."

"Oh?"

As Flynn expected, the visage of the Suit filled the screen of one of the room's monitors, as if he were staring through the glass. He looked tired, Flynn thought. Much more tired than last time they'd spoken.

Join the club, Flynn thought.

"I'm looking at the contents on this data drive."

The Suit's eyes thinned. "I don't see the data on this port."

"I localized it. Your people are too good at hacking live systems," Flynn said, sitting down in one of the room's chairs. "Frankly, I don't think the info here is as valuable to you as something else."

"And what would that be?"

"Maas-Dorian tech is, for the most part, dependent on the purity levels of the Razor's Xytrilium. Other, lower-quality X won't power the systems in the same way. They're going to start forfeiting contracts soon."

"Yes," the Suit said. "Hence why you will be paid a visit from them."

Flynn leaned back in the chair. "If I can control who *can't* get onto the Razor, then I can control who *can*. You could have access to the purest X in the galaxy, mining rights or no mining rights."

The Suit studied him thoughtfully. "If . . . what? The ones I represent provide you aid?"

"Well, it's my current thinking," Flynn said, folding his hands behind his head. "I'm a fast thinker, though. New ideas occur to me all the time. Better ideas, sometimes."

The Suit looked back at him through the monitor. The implication was clear. "As I said, I will not underestimate you again."

The two men considered each other in silence.

"What would you have done?" Flynn asked. "If you were me?"

"Why ask me that, Dr. Flynn?"

It was a good question. Why had he asked? And of this person, specifically?

"Maybe because you're the only person I know who wasn't there."

The Suit removed his glasses and rubbed his eyes. Without them, he seemed less intense, less dangerous. "I think that, in a gambit, you give up a pawn in exchange for a lost game. I think you found a unique way out of an impossible problem. And I think it benefited you tremendously. I'm not sure if I would have thought to do the same . . . but I'd like to think that I would. Does that answer your question?"

"I guess so," Flynn said.

"I will make your proposal." The man slipped his glasses back on. "I will be in touch before long."

"Not too long," Flynn told him. "I have a feeling there's going to be a lot of calls on this monitor soon."

The Suit nodded sourly, then his image flashed off.

Flynn exhaled slowly. He wanted to close his eyes. But if he did that, he would see it all over again . . .

"Still in your jumpsuit," Key's voice said from the security doorway. Flynn hadn't heard it slide open.

He spun in the chair and looked at her through the glowing holograms. She wasn't in her jumpsuit anymore; she was wearing tight, pocketed pants and a blue padded vest over a black tank top. She leaned against the doorframe, arms crossed, a displeased look on her face, the kind that didn't bother him anymore.

Seeing Key, some of his weariness lessened.

"There's all kinds of clothes up top," she informed him. "We're stripping down the supply trains. It's a treasure trove, you should see it. Electrical shit, components, machine parts. We're pulling it out of trains that were in the warehouses."

The starport warehouses, Flynn had confirmed, were magnetically shielded. Anything sitting inside them would be protected, too. Those parts were going to be essential to getting things back up and running.

"I don't know," Flynn remarked, looking down at the tattered and torn white jumpsuit he'd worn since his first day here. "Kind of gotten used to this thing."

"It smells really fucking bad."

Flynn smiled. "I'll go get something."

Key looked from him to the symbols dancing in the air, glowing orange and yellow. In the middle of it all was the equation Flynn was trying to build, a long string of symbols.

"What is it?" Key asked with a tone that implied she didn't care much for the symbols. To her they represented nothing but trouble, things better left alone.

Flynn looked at the spinning triangles and his weariness vanished.

"An equation I'm trying to make with the alien numbers," he said. "My favorite equation."

"Should have known you had a favorite equation," she said, and pushed off from the doorway, walking toward him slowly. "Tell me. Get it over with."

"It's called Euler's identity. Basically, it . . . links all the major parts of mathematics together, and it does so using just the three most basic operations: addition, multiplication, and exponentiation."

"Fascinating . . ."

"But the most interesting thing is that, at the end, all the major parts of mathematics, they equal zero. They equal nothingness."

"Why is that important?" Key asked, stepping into the spinning holograms now, eyes glued to him. They fractured in colored starbursts as she passed through them, then snapped back together.

"Because nothingness is something too. If I can figure out this equation using the alien numbers, then I can really understand all the rest of—"

Key leaned down, grabbed the back of his neck, and pulled his mouth to hers.

All the thoughts of numbers vanished as her mouth moved over his. When she was done, it took a moment for his mind to work again. Jesus, no one had ever made him feel like she did . . .

"Maddox is leaving," Key told him.

The words sobered him. The taste of her was forgotten. "Leaving?"

"Zane found where he wants to go. Another black site, pretty far from here. Maddox is gonna guide him."

"Why?"

"As opposed to staying here?"

She was right. Why would he stay here, where Raelyn had—

The feelings washed over him again, the same ones that washed over him every time he took a break from the numbers for too long.

"I should talk to him," Flynn said in a low voice.

"And tell him what?" Key asked sharply. "I don't get the sense your head is very clear on this."

Flynn looked into her eyes. "I could have saved her. If I had been faster, if I hadn't—"

Key kissed him again, and he went silent. The scent of her washed over him. She pulled back again, just a few inches. Her breath was sweet. "If, if, if," she said. "Ifs are useless. All we have is *now*. And if you couldn't save her, no one could."

Flynn shook his head. "If I had just shut down the beam . . ."

Her hand moved through his hair, grabbed hold of it firmly. "And what if you had? They've known about this thing for fifty-plus goddamn years, and they haven't told anyone." She pointed past them, to where the polysteel windows of the control room looked out on Artifact A, the huge, silver alien device, the yellow beam of energy streaking upward.

"You know why? Because they don't fucking *want* to. Because it's the tip of the iceberg. They framed you for murder over a *patent*; you think they'll let us live knowing about *this*? That is not how the fucking galaxy works," Key continued with fire. "Three hours after we make a starbase, you, me, Maddox, Raelyn—we're dead. Holes in our heads, flushed out an air lock. Because our leverage is gone." She pointed at the device again. "*That* is our leverage. *That* is how we fuck them. We lost her. It sucks. But you could have lost everyone. All I care about is you and me. And the fact that, when I'm with you . . . my wings don't itch."

She straddled him in the chair, pushing hard against him. It took Flynn's breath away.

"Do you get it?" she asked.

Flynn nodded, stared into her eyes, ablaze with emotion.

"If you draw," Flynn said, "you pull."

Key smiled. "Fucking A."

She kissed him again, ground herself against him as he pulled the vest and the tank top away and let her skin free. The whole time, the holographic symbols filled the air, glowing in shades of orange and yellow that showered them with pulsing light.

SEVENTY-FIVE

FOUNDERS

Maddox moved through the huge rail yard warehouse, pushing past the throngs of inmates as they jumped on and off the train cars, unloading them of the storage bins and crates inside, going through the contents.

Maddox had already exchanged his jumpsuit for real clothes, most of it Kevlar and monofiber. It would last longer, be more protective.

He watched the inmates at the trains as he moved through them, and they parted for him as he did. He could tell they recognized him, knew he was one of the "Founders"—what the prisoners called him, Flynn, Key, Zane, and Gable, the ones who had deactivated the beam.

Some of them were going about their business better than others, probably because they'd had warehouse duty when they were prisoners. He looked at all of it with skepticism.

The EM tunnel was sealed, but there were still ways to get onto the surface.

Drop pods didn't have any engines to short out; they were designed for one-way trips. The UEG would lose some coming through the ionosphere—life support failures, things like that—but they could get boots on the ground if they were motivated enough. Once they showed up with ships, they could deposit special forces, at a minimum—a battalion-strength division, at worst—and take back the starport.

But Maddox didn't particularly care.

Zane had asked Maddox to go with him, to look for another black site. It was a long trek, through hostile territory, but that was something he was used to. And he needed the distraction.

He didn't want anything to do with this place or that thing underneath it or Flynn and Key's plans.

Now that Raelyn was gone, he didn't know what his purpose was. It was the first time in forever that there was nothing pushing or pulling him.

He wasn't Flynn, who had found something.

He wasn't Zane, looking for something

And he wasn't Key, running from something

So who was he, then? Did he even want to know? Did it matter?

All he knew was that the emptiness he'd once felt had been replaced. First by warmth and light. Now by sadness. Sadness was all he seemed capable of. And her blue eyes and her hair, sometimes red, sometimes brown, was all he was capable of seeing.

Maddox pushed her away, scanned the lines of cargo cars until he saw the one he wanted.

It sat at the very back of a line, in a corner of the warehouse, where the tracks ended. A big silver train car with the label "AWT" painted on its side. It meant active weaponry transport. The trains were coded because the JSCC didn't want prisoners clueing in on what these particular cars carried, though Maddox always guessed that the electrical locks and the fact that they were never allowed close to them probably tipped them off all the same. The inmates might be criminals, but they weren't idiots. Not all of them, anyway.

Maddox reached the door to the train car and keyed in the Ranger override code.

The door unlocked, just like the armory door back at the Barrier, and he slid it open, revealing the dark interior beyond. He hopped up into the car, pulled the big door shut behind him until it was just cracked.

He flipped on a flashlight, shined the beam around the room.

Crates and boxes, all sealed, all full of weapons and ammunition. Ranger gear, a storehouse of it, and this was just one car. There were likely a few more scattered around the rail yard, ready to be deployed to garrisons in the Barrier or to one of the stockades on the other side of it.

If those train cars were sitting inside a magnetically shielded warehouse like this one, then everything in them would work just fine.

Maddox rummaged through the crates, grabbing what he needed. Ammo clips for the M32B, field armor and optics, a framed backpack, camping gear, a new knife, two months of MREs, a digital first aid kit.

He found the final item after a few more minutes looking. A red, square, aluminum case.

Maddox opened it. Inside, nestled in foam, was an air drone, about two by two feet, six props, and all kinds of technology brimming on its exterior. A wilderness survival model. All Rangers deployed on solo operations in the field had one, and these had saved his life more than once.

From outside, filtering in through the cracked door, came voices.

"That chick's serious," a voice said, rough and gravelly, a man's voice.

"There's only one of her," a low voice replied, female, so low it was hard to make out.

"Five, technically," another said, male, high and sarcastic. "Five Founders. And one of them . . . they say he's *Zane*."

"Zane's a ghost story," the first voice responded.

"He look like a ghost to you, man?" A different male, smoother voice.

"I don't care if he's the tooth fairy, word is he's leaving, he and the Ranger Fink, and you know what that means?"

Maddox froze. Whoever they were, they'd chosen a spot at the back of the warehouse for their little discussion, thinking it would be empty.

"Means just the girl, the one with the wings," the female voice said.

"And the others, the two scientists," the high-pitched voice chimed in.

"They look like threats to you?"

"I don't know. The old woman . . . something about her . . ."

"They're making friends, making deals," the smooth voice pointed out.

"Exactly. Another few days, this Key will have muscle, she'll have control locked down. So we hit her *now*. All of them. Her and the pencil pushers."

"Then what?"

"Then *we* run things. Then we make shit happen for us."

Maddox moved for the door and shoved it open.

The four of them—three men, one woman, all tattooed, all wearing green jumpsuits—stared up at him, shocked. Their eyes went wide. They recognized him.

"Generally," Maddox said, "it's best not to have conspiracy meetings where the subjects might hear you."

They all stared up, dumbfounded. He didn't have the rifle, but he did have a new 10mm in a shoulder holster.

"Look, man," one of them started, fumbling his words, "we—"

"It's okay . . ." Maddox told him, sincerely.

He drew the gun in a blur, aimed just as fast. Four muzzle flashes, four bodies hit the ground. The sound echoed everywhere in the warehouse.

"I'll make it quick," he finished, sliding the ten back into his holster.

Maddox jumped down to the ground. Everything had stopped in the warehouse, all the inmates were staring at him warily.

Maddox frowned. "You were *told*. No conspiracies. No power grabs. No plots. *This* is what happens." He let the message sink in for a moment. "Get back to work."

Everyone did, unloading the train cars even faster now.

"What's this?" a voice asked behind him.

Maddox spun, drawing the 10mm again, raising it in a flash.

Flynn stood there, eyes almost as wide as those of the guys Maddox had just killed, staring at the gun pointed right at him.

At the sight of him, an angry heat rushed through Maddox's body. His nails dug into his free hand.

This isn't your fault, Raelyn had told him. Right before she'd been yanked away.

Maddox kept the gun leveled, could feel the warmth of the trigger under his finger. It felt good.

"That's a good way to get yourself killed, Flynn," he said, and he could hear the edge in his own voice.

Then he shoved the gun back into its holster. He grabbed the red case of the drone out of the car and shut the door, locked it using the control panel.

"What happened?" Flynn asked again.

"Consider it my second-to-last favor," Maddox said, turning back to Flynn. "The last favor is ZTH24862." Flynn just looked at him, confused. "Ranger override code. It still works. It'll get you into most places locked with a security panel. Like this train." He pointed to the AWT logo. "Anywhere you see that, it's got weapons inside. I'd keep them under watch. Lot easier for guys like that to have an insurrection when they're armed."

Maddox grabbed the drone case and started walking through the inmates busy unloading the train cars. He heard Flynn start walking after him.

"You're leaving," Flynn said.

"I am."

"We could use you."

Maddox almost laughed. "You *definitely* could."

"Maddox, I . . ." Flynn trailed off.

Maddox slowly came to a stop, let the inmates move around him as they worked. He could tell where Flynn wanted to go, what he wanted to say.

"Saw a guy once," Maddox said, keeping his back to Flynn, "back during the Outlier War. Just a kid, worked the landing pad on a hover carrier. One of the old T-88s, the big intersystem transports, one of them came down right on top of him. Craziest thing I ever saw. This guy's top half sticking out, flailing around, the rest of him just disappearing underneath the landing strut. Guy survived it, didn't even seem to be in pain. Clean sever of the spine, they said. Of course, once they lifted the gear off him, everything inside him was just going to . . ." Maddox didn't finish, figured it was pretty clear. "Whole time he kept talking about how he had twins. How he had to get home for their second birthday, because he'd missed the first. Kept talking about it while they figured out how to prop the ship up and manually raise the gear. Talked about it until he just fell asleep." His eyes held Flynn's. "Life is always now or never, Flynn."

"I *tried*," Flynn said.

"Did you?" Maddox turned around and stared at Flynn, tried and failed to keep the anger out of his voice. "You could have shut that beam off. Instead you chose something that took longer. You chose it because you wanted *this* . . ." Maddox looked around at all the former prisoners, unloading trains, stockpiling . . . building.

"It's not that simple, Maddox."

"Who are you trying to convince? Me or you? You could have saved her and you didn't. You did nothing. Doing nothing . . . you'll have to figure out how to live with. Just like I did."

The two men stared at each other. After a moment, Flynn nodded, like he accepted it, like it was something he couldn't change. That was good, Maddox thought. Because he couldn't.

Maddox considered him a moment more. "Watch Gable. Watch her *close*. You understand?"

Flynn's eyes thinned, but he nodded.

Maddox turned and headed out of the warehouse, into the permanent dusk that sat over this part of the Razor. It all felt cold.

SEVENTY-SIX

SHADOW AND FIRE

Gable stared at the silver machine that towered over her, projecting the yellow beam up and through the ceiling, its light reflected in the device underneath it.

The machine was smooth and rounded, seemed to have no lines whatsoever, and stood out in sharp contrast to the remnants of the creature that still clung to its flawless exterior.

Where the egg sacs had been, there now were rippled masses of dried blackness that looked wet and soft but were hard as steel. To Gable, the creature, with its sharp edges and seemingly chaotic behavior, was a far more amazing creation than this machine.

Machines were instruments. They came to fruition through ingenuity and blueprints, their creation almost a foregone conclusion, but a biological entity, something complex like the one that had left these pieces, was very much the opposite. It was alive, it was beautiful. Honed by evolution into the thing it had become. Honed by its own will.

It was a miracle.

Gable's eyes moved to the machine's controls, glowing bright orange. She reached up with her hand—

The controls went dark. Gable frowned. The machine seemed tuned to only work for Flynn now. That was appropriate in its own way, she knew. Anticipated, even. In fact . . .

"I know you know I'm here," Flynn said from behind her.

It was true. She'd heard him coming long before he got close, descending from the control room.

"And I know what you're holding," Gable said.

There was a click as the gun's firing hammer was pulled back. Even so, Flynn's heart rate was beating slowly, normally. He had come far.

"You pointed a gun at me once before," Gable stated, slowly turning around to face him. He wasn't wearing his jumpsuit anymore. He had a white button-down shirt, sleeves rolled up to his elbows, tucked into a pair of green cargo pants.

Flynn didn't waver. "I think the result might be different now."

"I think so too." And she meant it. He had finally accepted the reality of his situation, that he was either to succeed here, against overwhelming odds, or die. He was fascinating. Brilliant, certainly, but also malleable. Adaptable. She still didn't know where he had come from, what past had shaped him into such a unique individual, but she would.

"You are exploring your darkness," Gable said, a smile slowly forming on her face. "Whether you want to or not. It is a very good thing. You won't survive otherwise."

"We're talking about *your* survival right now."

"Surviving is an art form I have mastered. Do you really believe that gun threatens me?"

Flynn held the gun up another moment, then lowered it. "No. And I think if you really wanted me dead, I would be."

"You are learning. But you must learn *quicker.*"

Flynn's eyes went past her, to the dark controls on the machine. "It doesn't like you."

"Well, I don't understand it. Not in the way you do. Machines are your world, not mine."

"Before, you said the creature had only told you half."

"That's right," Gable said.

"Is *this* the other half?" Flynn nodded toward the glowing triangular shapes, toward the machine. "The part I'm learning?"

Her stare hardened. "Light and dark. Shadow and fire. All worlds need both."

Flynn thought about it. "How did you know it would leave, once the beam was shut down?" he asked. "Are you still talking to it?"

"No," Gable said, firmly and immediately. "We . . . spoke only once, but I discerned enough about it to understand its baser motivations. It's something I've always been good at. Reading other beings, knowing who they really are, underneath the layers they build for themselves."

"And what does it want?"

Gable shrugged. "The same as everything. To avoid suffering. To quell its fears."

Flynn looked at her skeptically. "It doesn't look like it has all that much fear to me."

"Everything fears something."

He studied her intently. "Why are you still here, Gable?"

"Because I need you, Marcus. And though you don't know it yet, you need me."

Flynn sighed. Shook his head and rubbed his eyes, frustrated.

"If I am obtuse," she told him, "it is because I know nothing for certain. I only have theories. But I believe this world's true value has yet to be revealed. Change has already come to the Razor; more change is coming. We must be ready for it."

"We . . ."

"*We*," she said. "You will need my help to hold what you have gained."

Flynn stared at her a long time, considering. He did not trust her, that much was clear. Then again, if he did, she would have been disappointed.

"Light and dark, huh?" Flynn asked.

Gable smiled. "Shadow and fire."

SEVENTY-SEVEN

BLUE

Key stood in the middle of the mass of former inmates, moving around outside in the starport's main grounds, right in front of the giant, crystal-clear terminal building. The beam still shot straight up through the top, a bright, wavering yellow.

The grounds had been nice once, she could tell. Trees and grass, flower gardens, a big-ass fountain that stretched the length.

Now it was torn to shit, used as a staging area for all the spoils they were bringing off the supply trains. It was the first thing Key had thought to do. Anyone who worked supply detail on an SMV knew how much it took to keep just one Crawler outfitted. The supplies for every single Crawler on the planet, all one hundred and seventeen of them, came through the starport's loading docks, and she'd bet the trains were loaded down.

She'd been right.

It had been a good idea for other reasons, too. Kept the inmates focused, sure, kept them working—but the fact that, this time, everything they pulled off those trains was for them, and not some asshole guard or Crawler captain, kept them *motivated*.

She'd already started talking to leaders of some of the more prominent gangs. She'd gotten lucky, because the ones who had the most numbers here weren't exactly the ones with the most numbers planetwide. Blood-clan, for instance, wasn't very represented, but Grimm was.

That meant leverage, meant she could offer them something. Help her now, and that meant power for them down the road, no matter how big their gang was altogether.

It was working. She'd assigned team leaders to different tasks and established a reporting structure. But security was still an issue. She needed muscle.

Her attempts at leadership on the *Charon* had been a disaster. She'd doubted herself back then. But after everything she'd been through since then, she felt . . . confident. And it felt fucking good.

"Not bad," a deep, honeyed voice said behind her.

Key turned and watched Zane as he walked past her.

He was wearing a pack stuffed full of supplies and equipment. He had a scattergun, too, biometrically tuned. The Founders were the only ones allowed to have guns right now. But that would change, once groups earned Key's trust.

She stepped in pace next to Zane, walking through the grounds, past all the supplies being sorted. As they did, the crowds of inmates parted for them, eagerly, clearly intimidated by the big man's presence.

"You see the way everyone moves the fuck out of your way?" Key asked. "Like a walking Scythe Hawk?"

"I'm used to it," Zane said dismissively.

"I know. That's why you need to stay."

Zane looked at her briefly. "I'm confused. *Why* do I need to stay?"

"Because it would help me out a whole hell of a lot."

"Ah . . ."

"Look, I get it, it's not convenient, it's a little annoying, but shit, you should *see* some of the stuff we got coming off the trains. This place is gonna be Sodom and Gomorrah when we get it running."

"Both?"

"You know what I mean," Key said.

She followed Zane through the supplies in front of the terminal building. They were being sorted by type and function, into large piles. Clothing. Food. Electronics. Liquor. Power cells. Medical supplies. Books. Everything that came in on the big freighters to keep the Razor running. When she'd sorted it all, Key would decide how to organize and parse it out.

But she needed time. Time she didn't have right now, always watching her back. She needed Zane.

"Chocolate," she said, tempting him. Who knew what vices a guy like him had. "Real pillows. *Whiskey.*"

Zane hesitated a second, almost looked back at her . . . but kept moving.

"*Cigars,*" she said with emphasis, drawing a long stogie out of her vest pocket. She'd saved it just for him.

Zane looked at it. "Corealis," he said, impressed, then looked away again, found what he wanted. The sorting pile for all the tools coming off the trains. Hand tools, powered ones, spare parts, batteries, everything. Zane started digging through it.

Key sighed. He just never stopped, always going forward. He only had one throttle setting, it seemed. It was going to kill him someday.

"You need to rest, for once," she told him, as he dug through the tools. "You haven't even figured out what the hell the effect is going to be from Charging on that thing. I'm worried about you."

"Worried . . ."

"Yes. I *mean* it." She knelt down next to him. "Take a week, frighten the natives for me, rattle their cages, while I build my own muscle. *Then* you can take off."

"Such a tempting offer, Key," he said.

"You need it. It'll be the easiest week you've spent in years. No one's going to fuck with you here."

Zane grabbed something specific from the stash. A pair of bolt cutters. He held them in his hands, looked at her again. For such a big, dangerous force, his eyes were very soft now.

"You're right," he said. "I don't know what the effect of absorbing that thing is going to be, which is why I need to get moving. If things are going to get problematic, I need to finish what I'm doing before it happens. Besides . . . I thought you wanted to be alone."

Key blew air out her nose. It was a good fucking point. She had wanted that, for as long as she could remember. But things had changed. Even if there wasn't necessarily safety in numbers, there was comfort. Her mind went to earlier, with Flynn, in the control room.

She could tell there was no convincing Zane; his mind was set. Key studied him seriously. "You know where you're going?"

"Loaded question."

"Nah, I don't ask those."

"Another black site. Far from here. Maddox has been there, though."

At the name, Key looked away. "How is he?"

"Changed," Zane replied. "Like all of us."

He reached up with the bolt cutters and slipped the blades in between the straps holding the muzzle on his face. They snapped in half and the muzzle fell off. Zane rubbed his skin where the thing had been rubbing into it for days now, and then dropped the hand away.

Key smiled. He wasn't ugly at all—had the cut chin you'd expect from a guy with his testosterone, nice lips, a formerly broken nose that had healed pretty well.

Still, she liked to fuck with him. "Oh, man. I was wrong. Put that thing back on."

Zane smiled, or at least that's what it looked like. It was more of a sneer, really, like a shark trying to grin. Disconcerting, at best.

"Okay, now you're freaking me out," Key said.

Zane's eyes looked down to the cigar, still in Key's hand.

Key sighed, then handed it to him. "You earned it."

Zane stuffed it in his vest, kept the smile on his face.

He was an enigma, Key thought. Someone Key felt the most kinship with but also the one she was most estranged from. She didn't know where he was going, or who he was really looking for, but she admired the hell out of his drive. She would miss him. And she didn't miss anyone.

"Strange times," Key said.

"Fucking A," Zane replied.

Key smiled with him, as the crowd moved around them and through the starport, walking freely in the dim sunlight. None of them wore jumpsuits. None of them wore colors. They weren't prisoners anymore. They weren't gang members, either.

They belonged to the Razor now.

SEVENTY-EIGHT

EPILOGUE

Darkness was everywhere around her, swirling and writhing, but it was not everything.

There was light, too. A slight flickering, like the last embers of a dying fire, traveling in lines up her arm. And with it came pain. Intense and bright.

She didn't know how she'd gotten here. She didn't know where "here" even was. All she knew was that the dark was cold, and that the cold was comfort beyond measure.

You are special.

It wasn't voices, not exactly, and she didn't really truly hear them either. It was in her mind, some sense of a meaning conveyed all at once, that repeated and echoed inside her head, wrapped in what sounded like static.

She didn't know how she understood, but she did.

We can take . . . We can use . . .

The pain, she somehow knew they meant. The voices would take the pain away. But it was more than that. They meant the *light*, too. The last of the light. And when it was gone, there would be only the dark, the thing that scared her more than anything.

But . . . the pain. It was so much now. It burned so hot.

You will be more . . . We can use . . .

"Yes," she said. The sound of her voice echoed back at her sharply. Wherever she was, she was cocooned in shadows and metal. "Yes. Please."

Things moved. Things rattled. Tall, horrible things with three legs reached for her. Chilled appendages wrapped around her tightly.

Fear gripped her. She regretted it then, the decision. But it was too late, far too late.

The light on her arm flared brightly, and pain like she had never known lanced through her body.

Raelyn screamed.

Then the cold blew over and chilled her, every part of her. It took her breath away. It felt wonderful. It felt blissful. No more heat, no more light.

You are special . . . You will be more . . .

The darkness was everywhere around her, swirling and writhing . . . and it became everything.

Acknowledgments

This book was written, almost in its entirety, at my favorite saloon, the Alley Cantina in Taos, New Mexico, the only place I've ever carved my initials. Where the bartenders are Harvard educated and critique your grammar. Where the waitresses have wings and the owners let you drink on the roof if they like you. The ghosts and vagabond spirit of that place informed the characters of this story in a myriad of ways, and I am eternally thankful.